Advance Praise for
Broken Fortune

"*Broken Fortune* by Aly Mennuti is a poignant portrait of one woman's grief as she struggles to keep her family together in the aftermath of her step-mother's death. Elizabeth is the eldest of five very different children, whose lives are forever intertwined when their parents remarry. From the beginning, it is clear that this is no ordinary family, and despite its glamour and dazzling wealth, it is 'unhappy in its own way.' Tolstoy is clearly an inspiration for this tender, perceptive tale exploring the circle of life and the family bonds that bind us. With all the drama and wit of *Succession* and set in exclusive Caribbean islands and lavish Manhattan penthouses, you'll be swept up by this gorgeous tale. Mennuti's characters are as real as your siblings. There's a plot full of gasp-out-loud twists and turns. And you'll be rooting for Elizabeth to embrace her new role as matriarch and get the happily-ever-after family she deserves."

> – CHLOE ESPOSITO, Bestselling Author of the *Mad, Bad and Dangerous to Know* trilogy

"When secrets bubbling away under the surface come back to threaten the present and undermine the future, *Broken Fortune* explodes into a smart, compelling page-turner that makes the reader question whether it is better to be inside a family looking out or outside looking in."

> – SAM BLAKE, Bestselling Author of *Three Little Birds* and *Mystery of Four*

"Epic, topical and painfully honest. One woman battles for love and basic human connection amidst a toxic blended family with extreme wealth. Ms Mennuti's deeply flawed characters sprinkled with reality-based comedy form the perfect recipe for a page turner. Broken Fortune simultaneously twisted my stomach and hooked me in. More please."

> – JENNY WOODWARD, Author of *Ninety Days without You*

BROKEN FORTUNE

A Novel

Aly Mennuti

A REGALO PRESS BOOK
ISBN: 979-8-88845-218-9
ISBN (eBook): 979-8-88845-219-6

Broken Fortune
© 2024 by Aly Mennuti
All Rights Reserved

Cover Design by Jim Villaflores

Publishing Team:
Founder and Publisher – Gretchen Young
Acquiring Editor – Adriana Senior
Editorial Assistant – Caitlyn Limbaugh
Managing Editor – Aleigha Koss
Production Manager – Alana Mills
Production Editor – Rachel Hoge
Associate Production Manager – Kate Harris

As part of the mission of Regalo Press, a donation is being made to Change The Ref as chosen by the author. Go to http://changetheref.org to find out more about this organization.

Regalo Press
New York • Nashville
regalopress.com

Published in the United States of America
1 2 3 4 5 6 7 8 9 10

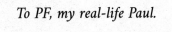

To PF, my real-life Paul.

"*Every person in the house felt that there was no sense in their living together, and that the stray people brought together by chance in any inn had more in common with one another than they, the members of the family...*"

—TOLSTOY

PROLOGUE

June 1988

BEFORE THE DAYS OF CONSCIOUS uncoupling, "thoughtful" co-parenting, and supporting your partner's individual choice to remove you from their life, people just got *divorced*.

It was frequently ugly, rarely on equal terms, and whatever vestiges of affection remaining between the couple were quickly dissolved in the quest for *half*.

Half the house, half the money, half the car—every object in their formerly shared life was subject to a symbolic slicing. The problem is that no matter how hard you try, no matter how many lawyers get involved, you can't exactly halve children.

My family, the Bernard-Sunderlands, didn't *halve* anything; they aggressively expanded. They were pioneers. While everyone else in the 1980s were splitting apart, they undertook the seemingly impossible—constructing a blended family, the combined result of two divorces, producing five children who ranged in age from four to ten.

Except Benjamin Sunderland and Kate Bernard didn't want to truly be a *blended family*; they wanted something far more bloodless and idiosyncratic. They wanted to apply the distinctive business management philosophies of the 1980s—massive abstract sums without a margin call in sight—to their *lives*. Their marriage was to be a merger of two distinct corporate entities, fusing together for invigorated growth, a collective wiping clean of the books, and as with any change in management, the "old guard employees" either had to adapt to the new regime, or take early retirement.

In this case, the "old guard employees" happened to be their five children, and they couldn't simply *fire us*, so our organic memories of the past—either personal or collective—would have to be shoved aside for the overall good of the venture.

Their plan was, of course, pure daft fantasy.

Did they somehow believe five children could suddenly cancel out their personal histories so they wouldn't be an incumbrance on their future?

Yes.

That was precisely what they expected on June 29, 1988—the day of their wedding. The day that not only did Benjamin and Kate become bound for eternity, but *all of us* did...except it worked out far better for the parents than the children.

To absolutely no one's surprise—except *theirs*—the fissures in Benjamin and Kate's shared delusion became apparent immediately.

Four-year-old Caroline, Benjamin's youngest daughter, immediately staked a claim to her preferred role—the perpetual baby of the family—when she walked down the aisle with her basket of rose petals and threw them on the guests, instead of lining Kate's path to the altar. After emptying her charge, she ascended the steps, turned to the guests, and bowed, basking in her performance. Benjamin clapped at Caroline's blatant flouting of etiquette, likely to play off his embarrassment.

Julian, Kate's youngest who was two years older than Caroline, had been missing for several hours. Benjamin and Kate's reaction toward Julian's absence was a preview in microcosm of their parenting style. Instead of jumping into action, frantically scouring every inch of space up and down Fifth Avenue, they sent their kids and the Plaza hotel staff on the hunt. Meanwhile, they sipped champagne, laughed with their wedding party, and posed for photos. When our conjoined search for Julian proved fruitless, they said he'd eventually get hungry and make his presence known, and they decided to begin the ceremony without him.

Tessa, Benjamin's middle child—and now the middle child of this new motley arrangement—had attempted to gain favor with Benjamin and Kate by taking the opposite approach of the other kids. She *overcommitted* to the wedding, appointing herself the wrangler of Caroline and Julian so our new parents wouldn't have a care in the world on their *sacred* day. She imagined they would thank her profusely and look forever upon her as the child they could always count on, the irreplaceable one, the *favorite*.

Following Caroline's curious interpretation of a flower girl and Julian's disappearing act, Tessa had to admit she had utterly failed, and her only recourse was breathing heavily into a paper bag in the Plaza kitchen—surrounded by equally stressed out employees overtaxed by management—while watching her dreams of favorite-child status fade.

Holding the paper bag to her lips and rubbing her back was *me*, Elizabeth Sunderland, the oldest of Benjamin's daughters. I kept whispering to Tessa—because even a normal tone in speech seemed to set her nerves further on edge—that she couldn't control how everyone reacted to the wedding, and how it meant something different to each of the children. She didn't need to be perfect for Benjamin and Kate to love her. I calmed her down enough that she was able to breathe normally again and leave the kitchen.

A few minutes later, when Kate found us, she was visibly annoyed we weren't ready to walk down the aisle. Tessa, looking to preserve her image as the responsible child, said *I* was the one who had an anxiety attack, and that she needed to take care of *me*.

I walked down the aisle, contemplating Tessa's betrayal—the first, but not the last, time she would sell me out to gain favor with Kate. I looked ahead and saw my new stepbrother Paul waiting alone and wearing a similar expression to mine, as if it had finally dawned on him as well: this wasn't only a wedding. It was the road to an alternate reality.

Paul was Kate's oldest child, two years and three months younger than me, and looked as uncomfortable in his tuxedo as I did in my lilac chiffon dress. When I got closer to him, I noticed his fists were balled so tight that his knuckles had turned white, and his nails were digging into his palms and leaving marks. He hadn't said a word all day, but his face kept getting increasingly more flushed.

That changed at dinner, when all the guests were laughing and dancing, and he sat down next to me.

"Do you know why I'm mad?"

I looked into his eyes—ringed with potential tears—and shook my head.

"Because you're not," he said.

"Why would I be mad?" I asked, not following his train of thought.

"Because," he said, sighing at my lack of foresight and throwing his head back, "we're the ones who are going to have to make this plan of theirs work. And they're not even going to love us for it."

"There's five of us," I said. "We can all love each other."

"Wrong," he said. "What we saw today is all we're capable of."

He was correct.

Thirty-three years later, an Upper West Side penthouse, private schools, the building of Kate and Benjamin's financial euphoria, and Caroline has matured into throwing metaphorical objects at everyone, Julian is still mostly unaccounted for, Tessa remains undaunted in her quest to be the favorite child, Paul has sublimated his rage into a successful career, and I'm still waiting to prove Paul wrong...to prove we're capable of more.

The odds aren't in my favor. We never graduated past that day in 1988. We never blended. The merger turned out to be a hostile takeover.

We never became people outside of the *people* Benjamin and Kate needed us to be.

We are all still children waiting for someone to make us a family.

And now one of us is dead.

CHAPTER ONE

May Present Day
Day One

OPEN YOUR EYES, I SAY to my daughter Winnie, as she's sprawled across her bed, sleeping sideways on her stomach, arms outstretched, like she's surfing in a dream.

Spring sun streams through the gaps in the curtains, throwing shadows across the floor and tinting her dirty-blonde hair a shade lighter.

Looking at Winnie is like looking in my own mirror circa 1993, with a Nirvana sweatshirt, the oversized boxers around her hips, and the neon-green socks—slightly sagging in the feet—that she tried to take off during the night, before deciding it wasn't worth the effort. It is disconcerting, jarring even, when your *daughter* becomes your own reflection, when you realize that the styles of the parents will one day be passed down to the children.

"Winnie," I say softly, trying a different approach.

As I inch toward her bed, I'm deafened by one of the dozen songs Taylor Swift has written about a break-up with some narcissistic actor—she deserves better—pouring from Winnie's phone and acting as a futile alarm.

She shows her first sign of life, and to encourage this promising development, I put my hand to the side of her face, ready to rub her cheek. Winnie swats away my hand, reaches over to the nightstand, turns off the alarm, and goes back to sleep.

"*Winnie*," I say. "I can't do this with you this morning. I need you to get up."

Her head inches off the pillow. She scans the room and then collapses back onto the bed.

Losing my already limited patience, I pull the orange and cream Urban Outfitters duvet off her body. I'm preparing to move on to the sheet when her eyes snap open, and she glares at me.

"I'm *up*, Elizabeth."

I refuse to engage with Winnie on her terms, and slam the door shut to ensure that she stays *up*. The second I hit the hallway, I hear the strains of my son Theo's alarm, programmed to Beethoven's Seventh.

As I get closer to his door, the symphony celebrating Napoleon's triumph over the failed French Revolution reaches its crescendo, and the dog starts barking, as if he's providing an ironic counterpoint. I allow myself to hope that Theo is awake, and that I don't have to repeat my grueling Winnie experience.

Yet there he is, snoring away, as if he's lying in a pastoral field surrounded by babbling brooks and deer nibbling on rose petals. From his mop of luxurious brown hair that he refuses to style, to a glass-sharp jawline that he forgets to shave—but is built for a CNN anchor chair—to his long, gangly limbs, which like a puppy, he still trips over daily, as if he's confused and betrayed by their existence, Theo is one of those teenagers who has all the incubating hallmark signs of an attractive adult that haven't quite coalesced yet.

"Theo," I say, kissing his forehead. "You need to get ready."

The only one listening is the dog, who intuits my presence as the sign for a potential walk and bounds off the bed, carelessly stepping on Theo's head.

"Jesus, Barry," Theo says, annoyed. "What are you doing?"

Considering that crisis over, he turns and covers his face with the blanket.

I begin nudging his arm, like he's a piece of dough that refuses to form.

"I'm not kidding," I say. "*Get up.*"

He rolls over, and just like his sister, looks into my eyes.

"Are you tired?" he asks.

For a moment, I wonder—did I raise a seventeen-year-old boy who cares, who can read the strain around my eyes and knows I was up all night?

"That means you're going to be cranky," he says, disabusing me of his love, his kindness, and my years of ceaseless trying. "This gives me pause about sitting next to you on the plane."

Pause about sitting next to *me*? He's the one who practically demands an emergency landing if he can't begin charging his laptop the second we hit cruising altitude.

"You need to be ready in forty-five minutes," I say, ignoring his sarcasm.

"Forty-five minutes!" he repeats, perturbed, in disbelief that I've burdened him. "What are you waking me up now for? I got this."

"Do you have this?" I ask. "Because I've got seventeen years to back up my concern about you *not* having this."

And before I slam the door on my way out, I'm assaulted by the merciless sonic barrage of my husband Nathan's alarm.

Unlike our children's personalized selections, Nathan has remained faithful to the annoying pre-programmed factory default setting of a monotone pulse that just gets progressively *louder* out of convenience, not preference, and only because I haven't had time to change it for him.

I step into our bedroom and can't help but be shocked by how peacefully he's sleeping, even with the throbbing noise coming from under his pillow. I'm equally struck by how much he still resembles his twenty-three-year-old self—the age we met—save for a few extra pounds, a little more salt than pepper in his curly hair, and the first signs of fine lines around his deep green eyes. Those eyes that won me over, that saw me, really *saw* me, in a way no one had before.

And just like when we met, once he passes out, nothing can make him stir, including his own wife, who spent last night six inches away from him, unable to sleep, tossing and turning, occasionally coughing to get his attention, while binge-watching BBC repeats of *Brideshead Revisited* and *A Handful of Dust* in a desperate attempt to calm down enough to close my eyes.

"Nathan," I say, beginning to reel off instructions. "I packed everyone last night. Our suitcase is by the foot of the bed. Theo's and Winnie's are in their rooms, close to the closets."

I'm getting incredibly specific, which means I'm more frustrated than I thought...*which* was already pretty frustrated.

"I need you to have both children, yourself, and all the luggage downstairs in forty-five minutes." I glance down at my phone. "Actually, forty-two."

Nathan murmurs, not completely conscious. "Are they up?"

"I woke them, but they probably went back to sleep. And you need to make sure they're out of bed."

He raises his head, looks at me with his still half-closed lids. "Where are you going?"

"To take Barry to *fucking* City Dogs," I shout, louder than intended.

Nathan starts to slowly rise. "I'll take Barry."

I shake my head, possessing neither the time nor inclination to indulge his half-hearted attempts to help. "You're not dressed. You're half-asleep. That's ridiculous."

He drops one foot on the floor. "I got it." He starts looking on the nightstand for his keys without opening his eyes. "Where's the dog?"

I snap my fingers, point to Barry sitting next to me. "Just get the kids ready. They're in their *rooms*."

I call Barry and we start walking down the stairs.

"I'm not kidding, Nathan. Forty minutes. A real forty."

After dragging Barry, seventy pounds of pure, limp golden-doodle across the parking garage—with his nails digging into the pavement with every single step, followed by the seven-minute car ride to City Dogs, where he sat next to me, heavily breathing like an obscene phone caller, since like me, he has deep-rooted generational trauma—I drop him off, get back in the car, finally alone, and prepare to enjoy the fleeting minutes of peace before I have to return home.

I turn the ignition, drive one glorious block, and at the first red light, it begins:

Nathan: "*Where did you say the luggage was?*"

Theo: "*Did you pack my chargers?*"

Winnie: "*Where are all my sweatshirts?*"

Nathan: "*Found the luggage. No worries.*"

Theo: "*Mom. Mother. Mom. Elizabeth. I need my charger. Why are you ignoring me?*"

Winnie: "*Can I just borrow Dad's NYU sweatshirt?*"

Theo: "*The one you wear all the time and insist on calling Dad's?*"

Winnie: "*I hate your face.*"

Theo: "*God I hope I get into a better school.*"

Nathan: "*Okay. That's just needless.*"

Theo: "*Why do you need a sweatshirt? We're going to an island.*"

Winnie: "*It's cold on the plane you idiot.*"

Nathan: *"Liz. Will you please answer the kids?*
They are literally driving me insane."

Winnie: *"Theo's so annoying."*

Theo: *"Dad's so annoying."*

Winnie: *"Agreed. And you are too."*

Theo: *"Why are we bringing my sister?"*

Next, I receive a call from work to tell me a delivery is late, and of course, it's perishable. After that, a minimum of thirty more missives are sent in the group chat.

I resist the urge to answer one to make the barrage stop.

I do have a life outside of all of you—my *family*, my loves—as much as you seem not to notice, or actually you *do* notice, and make an informed decision to ignore it.

We relocated from Manhattan to Washington, DC, ten years ago for my position with a Fortune 100 company that I loathed even before they promoted me, required me to move, and loaded me with extra work and responsibility. I even hated my title: *Executive Vice President of Public Affairs*. I didn't feel like an *executive* or someone in charge of *public affairs*. It was as if the CEO decided other corporations had someone occupying that title and they needed one too, kind of like how nuclear stockpiles get started.

But I didn't complain. It was for *you*—Nathan, Theo, and Winnie—so everyone could continue to enjoy the lifestyle you'd grown accustomed to, which was splendor, before it could be short-circuited. Admittedly, the potential schism in our income was my decision, but even if you knew *why*, you still wouldn't have noticed.

Two years later, when your father sold his first script to Hollywood, his dream for almost fifteen years—a dream he chased while I was the sole earner—you certainly did notice and couldn't have been more impressed or invested in his success, down to the point where you guard his time and yell at me for disturbing him while he wrestles with the throes of his genius.

But with *me*, my dear children, neither of you have the slightest hesitation to call in the middle of a meeting because you forgot your lunch, have a permission slip that needs to be signed, or need an asthma inhaler before a tennis match that I can't possibly bring to you while I'm in Amsterdam. Meanwhile, your father is home, and—contrary to popular opinion—he is not upstairs baring the darkness of his soul onto a blank page. He's adapting a video game about alien invasions. Fucking Hemingway he is not.

But with the benefit of Nathan's significant extra income, I was finally able to leave my dreaded public affairs position and pursue my own dream of opening a bakery, Madeleine, located in Georgetown.

And even then, I had to chase my dream within an acceptable walking distance to our home just in case anyone needed me.

And you have never ceased to need me.

And—I have never ceased indulging all of you, likely stemming from having never been indulged my entire life and knowing the pain that comes with not being a priority. But even granting that, today's performance is a bit much even by *your* standards.

I've arrived at the inescapable conclusion that without me and my constant attention, all of you would live in absolute filth, wear the same clothes for days, eat take-out for every meal, the dog would die—the dog you all desperately wanted—and the worst part is, I'm the only one who would care that you're living like this. You'd probably even be upset when I interrupted your slide into complete devolution.

Why can't you care about yourselves for five seconds? I'd appreciate it. It might free up those five seconds for me to actually care about *myself*.

I pull up to the Watergate, which in addition to housing our home, acts as a convenient reminder that apparently wherever I live, secrets are constantly being stolen, privacy violated, and trust betrayed—individually, nationally, and generationally.

On my way to the parking garage, I spot the driver of a black Suburban—our ride to the airport—talking to the doorman, probably telling him to call my family downstairs.

I pull in, throw the car into park, slam the door, lock the Volvo XC90, and make a half-hearted sprint to the elevator. I tap my foot obsessively until I reach the penthouse floor where we live.

I open our door and notice the foyer is empty, and every single feeling I've been mercilessly squashing all morning rushes to the surface:

"All. Of. You. Need. To get the *fuck* downstairs *right fucking now*."

I barely finish my sentence before I hear the put-upon trudge of three different sets of frustrated footsteps making their way down the staircase, clanging their luggage on each individual wooden slat.

"God, Elizabeth," Winnie says. "We can hear you."

But do you? If you did, you would have been downstairs already, loaded in the Suburban, and I'd be joining you, after dropping off *your* dog.

"We're here," Nathan says, giving himself credit for doing the bare minimum and achieving it *late*, a chronological certainty in my family.

I've almost forgotten the person I was before I met Nathan and had children: a person who was *early* for everything, a person whose fastidious punctuality was not only remarked upon, but a defining aspect of her identity.

I feel my heart break, the concrete wall I'd encased it in to survive today crack under pressure. I lose control, unable to dam up my emotions for another minute. I can't prevent the inevitable flood streaming from my eyes.

"What's wrong?" Nathan says.

What's wrong is that any other day I could handle this. Any other day I could go along with this being my life. Any other day I would happily do everything for everyone and expect nothing in return. But not *today*.

Not the day I have to get on a plane to St. John's and join my entire family to spread Kate's ashes across the bottomless froth and flux of the ocean.

CHAPTER TWO

Four Months Ago

THE LAST TIME I SAW St. John's was on New Year's Eve, a day traditionally marking change, the beginning of a fresh start, a tabula rasa waiting to be filled with bold, redemptive plans and new possibilities. But over the course of three decades, the Bernard-Sunderlands, both parents and children, have studiously avoided uncapping the pen.

The evening began as a typical Benjamin and Kate production, an annual august *event*—people like my parents didn't simply throw a party—that unfolded on the white-light strung terrace of their private villa at the exclusive Eleusinian Resort.

The carefully curated menu for the celebration featured endless locally sourced and organic hors d'oeuvres, multicolored caviar in crystal bowls, Wagyu beef flown in from Japan that morning, several types of seafood begging to be dipped in butter, and a fully stocked and freely flowing bar.

"Does this seem even more gluttonous than usual to you?" Paul asked, standing beside me, the two of us separated from the unfolding spectacle—our preferred point of view within the family. He dug his hand into the overflowing ice, picked out another oyster, and buried his cynicism in the bite of raw shellfish. "Even by their standards."

"No," I said, blasé, used to Paul always probing the most infinitesimal details at collective events for buried clues. "It seems about right."

He shook his head back and forth, then dipped back into the ice for another oyster. "I'm not sure."

"Can't you just enjoy having everyone together?" I asked. "It's been a while…. Julian wasn't here for Christmas. Caroline came at the end of Thanksgiving."

Paul mischievously raised an eyebrow. "Don't I look like I'm enjoying myself?" He motioned his arm across the expanse of the terrace. "I'm making a New Year's resolution. Less of *this*. Treating myself to a little self-care."

Paul and I have differing views on the Bernard-Sunderland level of solvency. In his frequently expressed opinion, money is the sole bond tying our blended family together, and it's an exercise in futility to pretend otherwise, to imagine there are hidden depths, untapped resources, or the potential of a functional unit buried under years of indulged, almost tacitly encouraged, dysfunction. In his opinion, if you removed Benjamin and Kate's fortune, our lives would resemble Pompeii the day *after*, with miles of skeletons eternally preserved in pitted ash, staring out from impromptu graves, and wondering just when *time* started over again.

"No, you won't," I said, smiling. "You'll come if I call you."

He sighed, knowing I was right. Even though Paul has what I'd call a charitably caustic view of the family, he doesn't have the same feelings about *our* relationship.

"I've been following you around for thirty-three years," he said. "The Sancho to your Don Quixote. And Lizzie, they're all our windmills. It's a fool's errand." He took a sip of champagne. "Actually, it was a fool's errand *ten years ago*. Now we're starting to be the ones who look pathetic."

According to my stepbrother, I am dangerously optimistic, blindly reckless in my belief that, although Benjamin and Kate's money arrests maturity and allows my siblings to not face consequence or growth, if you stripped away those factors, the family might actually blend, become *actual* people. Functional adults.

Occasionally, Paul will accept aspects of my premise, but with the caveat that even *if* that were true, Benjamin and Kate would never allow it to happen, because it would rob them of the control they wield if the siblings had each other to rely on. Their entire time parenting has been spent putting down a potential mutiny on every corner, and they are the avowed masters.

"Remember our pact," I said, pulling out my trump card—over three decades' worth of being best friends. "We *promised*..."

He ran his fingers through his hair and groaned. "I know what you're doing. And it's not going to work."

"No matter how insane *they* get, we are untouchable. All we're doing is biding time until we get the chance to salvage everything our parents have proven they *cannot*."

"Yeah," Paul said, his defenses melting, but still trying to resist. "But it's taking a *really* long time. And I don't know if I can hang in with the rest of them until you get what you want."

"What *we* want," I said, reminding him of the last part of the pact.

"Come *on*," he said, in an indulgently annoyed tone. "Can't we just miss *one* holiday. I mean...look at them."

I turned my head and saw Caroline standing by the bar, the island light cascading off her long wavy brown hair spotted with specks of honey, and facing her "date" for the evening, a member of a rotating and recently dwindling troupe of men dusted off for family occasions.

He was obviously enchanted by her silver-moon eyes, her puckish bow lips, and a smile shuffling between mirth and malice, unaware that her appearance was an almost metaphysical metaphor, part of her subterfuge, the way smaller animals are graced with camouflage coloring. Caroline hypnotizes men with her beauty before they realize that at thirty-six, she still possesses the temperament and emotional range of a high school sophomore.

But I'm not sure if that night's contestant cared. I've watched the wheat noticeably dissolve into more and more chaff the older

Caroline becomes, watched how many of her companions have stopped even bothering to hide their wedding rings. Granted, her "dates" were never more than props, haute-couture missiles aimed at Benjamin, flailing attempts to make him take notice that she was *not* a baby anymore, that he needed to allow her some form of agency. At this point, though, both have started to show signs of terminal exhaustion.

I averted my eyes from Caroline's weary rebellion, almost embarrassed for my sister, and spotted Julian sitting alone on a lounge chair strategically located by the *exit*. This is his preferred position since he escaped Benjamin and Kate's wedding years ago, and his opinion hasn't changed since.

He wore a white linen shirt rolled up to his elbows, maritime blue shorts, and the same Birkenstocks he's had since he was a teenager, resembling an NGO worker out for a relaxing Caribbean night after a long day of distributing aid and attempting peace. The sight was fitting since *that* was his job, yet ironic since he couldn't find an ounce of serenity in sight.

I watched him stare longingly around the space, an atomized speck against the night, while crunching ice with his back teeth and finishing off his sixth Diet Coke since the party started—anything to keep the anxiety at bay about the foregone conclusion that he was never more alone than when with his family. His eyes finally settled on Paul, who as usual, wasn't paying attention or had no desire to meet his younger brother's gaze.

"Paul," I said. "Why don't you sit with Julian?"

"I don't know, Liz," he said. "Why doesn't he sit with me?"

Paul and Julian have a complicated relationship that actually isn't all that complicated; rather, it's the end result of years of childhood resentment carried over into their adult years, an adopted pose that has become so ingrained that neither of them could probably tell you how or why it started, but both are firmly convinced that they are correct.

Before he could answer, Tessa's voice—thin, reedy, and amplified by drunkenness—blotted out all the sound around us:

"*So, I just booked the tickets to Bali.*"

"That'll help her life," Paul whispered to me. "Anyone as happy as Tessa obviously needs to plan their next vacation, while on vacation."

It was typical Tessa, seizing center stage to announce, to remind everyone once again—just in case they *forgot*—how rich and happily married she was, a stance that played into Tessa's biggest flaw: she could never read a room, especially one filled with our family. Everyone here was rich; it wasn't an exotic attribute. But no one was *happy*, so flaunting that fact wasn't doing her any favors. Oddly the tactics she used to try and make us all jealous just had the ring of desperation, but it never stopped her from trying, regardless of how ill-timed.

I took my eyes off Tessa, mostly for relief, and spotted Miles—her eternally besieged husband, who I imagined viewed going to work in the pressure-cooker of Kate's firm as an opportunity to decompress—looming off to the side, looking as exhausted by my sister as the rest of us.

"I told you not to book it for that time," he said, caught somewhere between whining and scolding. "I'm only free for half those days."

"It's fine," Tessa said, nonplussed. "I'm bringing the nanny."

There are some people whose entire aura is effortless, who seem to rise in the morning calm, refreshed, and ready for anything. Then there are the *constructed* people, where you can feel the time spent getting prepared reverberating off their body. But Tessa goes far beyond construction; that trait defines her, and in the case of our family, frustrates her being. She can wage draconian control over every inch of her life at home, but she cannot control her brothers and sisters, cannot make us conform like children, cannot make us believe what she fervently needs to *believe*. That we all grew up idyllically, in a fairy tale, in a lifestyle it is our solemn duty to pass down from generation to generation.

I heard the clink of a fork on the side of a wine glass, followed the crystal bellow, and saw Kate standing before the immoveable feast, gesturing for all of us to listen:

"Benjamin and I wanted to share some news with everyone. And since you're all here in one place, we decided now would be the best time."

Paul gently nudged my elbow. "Do you think they bought another house they have no intention of ever living in?"

"No," I said, slightly hushing him, but not intending to dismiss Paul's point—which was entirely accurate. Our parents *do* collect empty homes like others collect aspirational books, or any project that stands in as a synecdoche for a larger longing. But there was a quake in Kate's voice and a quiver in her lower lip, telltale signs of losing control from a woman who *defined* control with never a wasted motion, mental or physical.

"Nine months ago," Kate continued, "I had some tests, and the doctor explained to me that I have ovarian cancer."

What the fuck? Three words I remember echoing in my head, bouncing around my brain, followed by outright rage. Did Kate just say she had cancer? And she found out *nine fucking months ago?* They waited the length of a pregnancy to tell us Kate was sick.

"We didn't want to tell any of you until we knew for sure what the prognosis would be. But after second opinions, third opinions, an experimental treatment in Zurich that just made things worse, the outcome is…"

She searched for a way to finish, and settled on:

"They say I have six months at best."

Benjamin, intuiting the incoming emotional outpouring, rushed over like a frantic director desperate to control an actor going off-script.

"This isn't about *us*," he said. "So I'm going to need everyone to keep it together. Right now, it's all about Kate. Don't be selfish. We owe her the best six months possible."

Don't be selfish. Due to both of their combined inabilities to face reality—the brute fact that money isn't impervious to cancer, and that a generation that grew up in the last halcyon time in America would actually *die*—they stole almost a year of time from me.

When someone is dying, when they're on the opposite end of the hourglass, it's the last chance to preserve stories, shared history, regrets, undisclosed memories and secrets, the painful and loving words left unsaid. And they *stole that*, because controlling information, controlling history, controlling *us*, is what has kept the family afloat in their image all these years. They wanted to keep that intact *more* than they wanted to give us Kate's last year, reducing fleeting precious hours into an afterthought that could no longer be avoided.

I couldn't help myself, couldn't hold back any longer. I exploded in a mess of hot tears that instantly scalded my sunburned face.

"Jesus Christ, Elizabeth," Benjamin said. "What did I just ask everyone to do? You're supposed to put Kate first."

"I *am!*" I shouted back. "That's why I'm crying, you asshole."

Desperately searching for moral support, I turned to my siblings. The next few minutes unfolded in a blur.

Paul grabbed my arm, hard, and before I could react, pulled out his phone and began busily texting. When I regained the ability to think, I looked over his shoulder and saw he was writing to Luc, his biological father and a chronic failure, a man whose role in my stepbrother's life ended in theory with his sperm and in *reality* when he and Kate divorced.

Slightly disappointed with Paul's reaction—if Luc was fine with leaving Kate *as a wife*, I couldn't imagine this was going to move the needle—I shifted my gaze to Miles, who was trying to comfort

Tessa, to hold her, but she broke free before his hands touched her and started shouting at Kate that there were *still more options*, that they should go back to Zurich, that she would go with her, each word increasing in hysteria, to the point one would think *Tessa* only had months to live.

"This isn't a fucking field trip, Tess!" Caroline shouted, diverting my already highly *diverted* attention. I wasn't surprised; shutting down a room is one of Caroline's preferred methods to avoid living in the moment, and if she gets to insult Tessa at the same time, she's really winning. Next, she turned to her "date," demanded he take her clubbing on the island and let her stay at his hotel to avoid this disaster, which was, not coincidentally, Caroline's other method of avoiding the fray of family tragedy.

Suddenly, a long shadow cut across my view, bisecting Paul's face, and I noticed the sure-footed scampering of Julian making his way to the exit. His plan was quickly foiled when he realized the gate was locked. He weighed his options: he could stay here, with the family, or plunge sixteen wooden stairs to the beach below.

He lifted his leg over the gate, and I didn't see him for the rest of the trip.

I cried harder, realizing the profound depth of isolation and alienation around me.

The only person who seemed more forlorn was Kate, who—after taking in the maelstrom surrounding her—shifted her focus to me, locking eyes with her oldest, the only child trying to *feel* the gravity of the announcement, the only child not hiding from the pain and the fear. I was riveted to my spot, imagining a world without her.

A shift in her face took me by surprise, steely, yet terrified and heartbroken, assured in the unwanted knowledge that *nothing was okay*, least of all her.

CHAPTER THREE

May Present Day
Day One

AS I LISTEN TO THE rumble of the Eleusinian Resort ferry engine, to the floor spasmodically shivering and shaking in response, I realize *this is happening*, that the helm of this seafaring craft is beginning its tortured path from St. Thomas to St. John, delivering me to the inevitable.

If I had a mirror, I would likely be staring back at Kate's exact face on New Year's Eve, the last time any of us felt moored, especially *me*.

"*Dry bones can harm no one,*" I hear Theo say, reading aloud. "*I sat upon the shore, fishing, with the arid plane behind me. Shall I set my lands in order?*"

I stare around me at the lovesick vacationing couples holding hands, at the families huddled together like frozen stone and recording the boat's journey on their iPhone cameras, as if the trip wasn't already real, as if the event can't happen until other eyes experience the image. I secretly hate them, hate that they have the audacity to *live*, hate that the world moves on for everyone else while I am locked, static, stationary in my grief.

"*These fragments I have shored against my ruins.*"

I stare off the side of the ferry, at the undulating azure water, at the side of the boat bobbing like a cork among the calm waves, at the sailboats and yachts streaming past, filled with scantily clad revelers, spinning like thoughtless tops, reduced to fingerprints against the enormity of the vessels on which they travel.

The last time I was on this ferry, I was one of them.

"Then spoke the thunder. DA. Datta. Dayadhvam. Damyata. Shanti. Shanti. Shanti."

Theo slams a collection of T.S. Eliot's poetry, including his most famous poem, "The Waste Land" closed in frustration and yells at Nathan, who is standing by the side with Winnie. "I hate this poem. It's not even in English. And you're writing this paper."

Theo, like any boy his age, is a tinderbox of choked feelings that only have two possible expressions: anger or laughter. That is the entire scale of his emotional register, and instead of admitting he is crushed by the loss of Kate, the grandmother he loved and adored—far different from the *stepmother* that I knew—he has decided to take out his frustrations on his homework.

"I didn't get it the first time I read it either," Nathan says, indulging our son's aversion toward high culture, allowing him to feel normal for a moment. "It's one of those poems that comes to you when you're ready, when you need it."

"And *that*," Theo says, interrupting Nathan's lecture, "is why you're fit to write this paper. Which is incidentally due on Wednesday."

"That's *two days* from now!" Nathan says, shocked by Theo's irresponsibility.

"It's not my fault," he says, attempting to curry favor. "Mom should have reminded you."

I haven't been the type of mother they're used to since learning that my own stepmother was dying. Gone were the days of me reminding everyone about tests, scheduling tutors, driving to school dances, attending orthodontist and dermatologist appointments, *enduring* Barry's vet visits and grooming needs, regularly washing sports uniforms and socks reeking of stale teenage sweat, and making sure the refrigerator was filled with local, organic, preferably farm-to-table snacks and meals. I haven't regularly listened to the kids drone on interminably about friends lost and gained, relationships torn asunder, teachers' expectations, and how Winnie's grades are just *temporary*.

"It's not your mother's fault," Nathan says, baffled by Theo's audacity. "I told you to write *all* due dates on the big calendar in the kitchen." He looks to Winnie for support. "That's why everyone got their own marker color."

"Yeah," Theo says, not giving an inch and looking to Winnie, "she wrote down she was having her period on the day the assignment was due."

"I wanted you all to share in my suffering," Winnie says. "You know, especially since men have taken such an interest in female *healthcare* as of late."

"I know," Nathan says, standing his ground. "I've *marched* with you."

Nathan *did*. He's tried to fill in for me in the only way he can, which is simultaneously sweet and completely chaotic, like if a dutiful understudy had watched me for years and delivered his own unique interpretation of my performance, one that—on the surface—looked surprisingly similar, but underneath marched to his own decidedly off-key rhythm.

He didn't only apply his unique methods to the kids, but he made sure I remembered to eat and sleep; he booked my train tickets to Manhattan; he suffered silently through countless hours of mind-numbing television to help me find equilibrium, while always making sure the freezer was full of a guaranteed cure: mint chocolate chip ice cream.

"Tell your teacher your grandmother died and we're at her funeral," Nathan says. "That should give you an extension."

"I grant you, in *theory* that sounds plausible," Theo says, ceding Nathan's point. "Unfortunately, Grandma has already tragically passed away three times this semester. In biology, Mandarin, and comparative literature." He laughs and looks at me, drawing me into his routine. "Mom signed the notes."

"Liz," Nathan asks, confused. "Did you let him do that?"

I probably did. The air was sucked out of my body, my brain, when we learned Kate was sick, and everything else has been a blind spot, apparently bigger than I'd imagined. I was singularly focused on spending time with her, to carve out any moment that could shed some light on the enigma that was Kate Bernard, the woman who—for better or for worse—had been my mother. When I was seven, my *actual* mother had bailed on me and my sisters to go find happiness without us on a commune in the Colorado mountains, which was apparently devoid of any way to communicate except a yearly note exclaiming how fulfilled she felt.

"I did *not*," I say, doubling down, not wanting to feel guilty that I've been an absentee mother when I pride myself on never missing a thing.

I wish I could say the same for Kate in her final days. She was the maternal figure in my life who managed to depart without saying she loved me, without bequeathing me a single intimate or personal memory I didn't already have, and ultimately leaving me behind with far more questions than answers, including *why* she brought us all to St. John to spread her ashes.

She owed me *that much*. I was the only child who put their life on hold to be with her, to bear witness, to fucking accept the reality that we didn't have much time.

Tessa didn't; she took two more vacations to far-flung locales and came home from one with malaria, bought herself a new Range Rover, plus the apartment *upstairs*—because everyone needs a third floor in Manhattan to house four people.

Caroline didn't; she fucked half of Manhattan, and when she ran out of eligible prospects, would come and crash on my couch to fuck half of Congress. She visited Kate maybe a grand total of three times, mocking my attempts to see her more, to realize this was *final*, not like the rest of her life, which she treated as a dress rehearsal. She responded to my advice by telling me if I didn't shut up, she'd fuck a Republican.

Julian didn't; after New Year's Eve, he hopped on a plane to Tibet, and has been climbing mountains across Central Asia ever since. He occasionally sends me an email whenever he descends the snowy peaks long enough to find an internet café, in which he tells me he's getting closer to finding nirvana and that I should join him.

Paul, being *Paul*, differentiated himself from the siblings. He did visit Kate, but he never tried to scratch the surface, reminding me constantly that I was in search of the one thing she was incapable of giving *anyone*. We both knew I was setting myself up to be crushed, and that I'd end up worse off pursuing this path. Then he went and purchased land to build an entire French import food and retail *marketplace* on the Wharf, reminding me that he is *truly* his mother's son, leaving me with nothing but open mysteries and ambiguity when they both know I don't relish shades of gray, preferring pointillist black and white boxes.

"I hope everyone shows up," I say to Nathan, only to realize that while I've been lost in my thoughts, they've all walked away, taken seats, and begun scrolling on their phones. "Did everyone just *leave* me here?"

Nathan looks up from his phone. "You seemed like you were really going through something."

Winnie follows her father's motions. "We wanted to give you your space."

"I don't need *space*," I say. "I need to know when we get off this boat that Caroline and Julian are going to be there."

"Of course they will," Nathan says, more sure of his opinion than anything I've seen since our wedding day. "There's money at stake."

"I'm not sure I follow," I say, unsure of whether it's because I'm starting to feel seasick from the boat rocking, or if Nathan is about to enter into one of his esoteric explanations for human behavior that comes with the territory of marrying a writer.

"Simple. If any of your siblings don't show up, your father is just going to fucking disinherit them."

"*Oh*," I say. "And what makes you say that?"

"Liz. Your family, like the former Yugoslavia, like Iraq under Saddam, only operates when there's a dictator in charge. There's too many competing interests, petty concerns that could open up pure terror. Kate was able to hold everyone together through emotional manipulation and casual, tossed-off cruelty. But your father lacks that kind of sophistication. He's stuck with brute force and *money* to do it with. Sure. Money was always the unspoken thing with Kate, but with your father it's going to be the *only* thing."

For once, with a complete lack of hesitation, I have to admit Nathan is right. I think back to just a few days ago, to how Benjamin handled Kate's eventual passing, the days of watching her waste away, dragged further from the woman he married, by acting as if they were both still going to work and meeting for dinner afterwards. There was no urgency in his actions, no crack in his facade, not even the slightest lilt or choke in his voice. Kate wasn't *dying*; the doctors were wrong. Anything to avoid their life plan being interrupted. She was going on a business trip; she was just running a few minutes late; she was...she was...

And then she *wasn't*, which he handled in a similar fashion, calling me three days ago to tell me Kate had died.

Actually, he didn't *call*. He texted me to call him. One of the many manipulative games he plays to act out the power imbalance in our relationship. He won't give you the choice *not* to call him, while simultaneously refusing to be the one who does.

"*Hi, sweetheart. Thanks for calling.*"

"Well, I got your text."

"Are you busy?"

"No, Dad," I said. "Just walking to work."

"This will only take a second," he said, clearing his throat. "I need you to check your email."

I stopped at the corner, opened the email app on my phone, and sitting at the top of my inbox was a message from him. I tapped it, and inside were four e-tickets to St. John, leaving in a few days.

"We're taking a trip?" I said, stunned.

"Yeah," he said, as if it was self-explanatory. "Kate died."

"Wait," I said, starting to cry, speaking through expectant sobs, lacking even a rudimentary understanding of what happened. "Wait. Kate's dead?"

"I just said that."

"When?"

"Last night," he said.

"And you're just calling me? Wait. Who was with her?"

"It was just me."

"But...but I didn't get to say goodbye."

"She knew you loved her," he said. "You barely left her side."

"I think...I think I need a minute to process this."

"You take all the time you need, Elizabeth," he said. "I've got to go. See you in St. John."

"No, no," I said, raising my voice. "Why are we going to St. John?"

But he had already hung up, presumably moving on to the next child.

And four days later, as I'm forced to return to the place where my life changed forever, I am *still* unsure of why we're here.

Why are we going to the *fucking beach*? Why aren't we having a funeral in Manhattan? Why aren't we having a service filled with extended family and lifelong friends? Why are we erasing Kate in a matter of seconds, leaving nothing to remind everyone of how much she meant to all of us and denying everyone a chance to collectively grieve? Are we *really* just going to share a few anecdotes, then throw her ashes into the ocean, call it a day, and go *swimming*?

How am I even going to *see her again*? I can't visit her; there will be nothing left to remember her by. No grave, not a small urn—we're not even planting a fucking tree. It's just *nothing*, endless nothing, like the sea she's about to call home.

"*And if you look straight ahead,*" the ferry captain says, sealing my destiny. "*You'll see we're almost to the Eleusinian.*"

I hear the ship's skipper rush to the front, readying to tie the boat to the dock.

Suddenly I feel flushed, dizzy, light-headed, *sweaty*, as if my stomach is falling to the bottom of my feet. I try to find a spot to focus, to try and rectify the spinning world around me, but it's for naught. I can't hold back.

I shoot up and start running, almost trip over some seats, and reach the side of the boat in the nick of time to throw up what seems like several days of food into the ocean, as if my body is trying to extravagantly empty itself before docking.

"Dad," I hear Theo shouting across the stern of the ferry. "Mom's puking in the ocean..."

CHAPTER FOUR

"JESUS, SWEETHEART YOU LOOK FUCKING terrible." I take my first tentative steps off the boat onto terra firma, hear Benjamin's clarion call of immediate concern for appearances around complete strangers—which I have clearly violated—and spot him on the dock.

It isn't hard.

While everyone else is wearing swimsuits or carrying equipment for oceanic exploration, he's dressed like it's casual Friday at the office, with his perfectly pressed Tom Ford trousers, navy and white striped Thomas Pink oxford shirt, and Gucci loafers. These are curious fashion choices under a blazing island sun bent on searing all available surfaces, bleaching the world, and leaving unguarded secrets out to burn and bake.

I move in to give him a hug and feel his hands on my back, reluctantly drawing me in like an icy boss at a perfunctory retirement party. Affection is anathema in Benjamin's eyes, tantamount to admitting *need*. It's the same reason we couldn't have any pets growing up.

"Did you gain weight?" he asks, starting to disconnect from our hug. "It must be spending all day around those pastries."

I pull back and meet his gaze. I've been marinating in three days of dread, three days of imagining this precise scenario, three days of wondering what it would be like to interact with my father minus Kate as a buffer. Although it beguiles belief, Kate managed to *soften* him around the edges, to turn him into a reluctant and semi-disengaged—as opposed to completely absent—father. And without her by his side, he has defaulted to his original factory setting: scorching irony with a side of aggression waiting to over-flow. I would know. I'm the child who spent the longest time with Benjamin *unfiltered*.

"Nope. I'm still the same size as the last time we saw each other. Two weeks ago."

"Yeah," he says, slowly contemplating, mesmerized by the shimmering heat. "I don't think so, Elizabeth."

"I apologize for not *looking good*. But maybe...just maybe, you should take some responsibility for my current state."

"I think that's a lot to lay at my feet."

"You called me seventy-two hours ago to tell me Kate was dead. Then sprang an impromptu trip to St. John on all of us. Then didn't return any of my calls for three days...."

"I was busy," he says, getting defensive. "My *wife* just died."

"So did my *stepmother*," I say, finding the voice I buried while Kate was sick. I want to remind him that Kate was a mother and not just his wife, that her illness took a toll on all of us—different than the one bestowed upon him, but not any less epochal. But even in her death, he still can't grant she was our parent, nor become one himself.

"It's not the same," he says, refusing to budge.

"Regardless...where, exactly, in that constantly expanding circle of stress, would you like me to have made room for self-care? Tell me that, Dad."

"Elizabeth," he says, in a tone reducing me to a teenager refusing to accept reality. "I think you need to calm down."

"And I think you need to be more upset," I say, refusing to concede, refusing to accept his historic approach of deflecting grief by antagonizing and belittling his child. I'm so tired of my father—and maybe *all* men of a certain age, worldwide—telling women they're overly emotional while we're forced to protect everyone else's mental health and safety from their existential unraveling.

"Let's just start over," he says, stepping back. He opens his arms to hug me again, likely to try and tamper down the scene I'm about to unleash.

"I'll pass on your interpretation of a hug," I say, putting up my wall of protection, an over twenty-year project that Nathan unceremoniously stripped away, feeling I was too "unaffectionate" in the beginning of our relationship.

The sensitive soul I married desired a partner who wanted to hug, to hold hands, who had a reaction beyond "Thanks" or "I know" when he told me he loved me. But when you grow up with Benjamin and Kate, that's a natural response. How was I supposed to trust anyone else's sentiment when the people who are supposed to love you—who are *made* to love you—are callously indifferent to your very existence. You aren't equipped or prepared for a person in your life who simply wants a *hug*, no ulterior motives included.

My love for Nathan was so sudden it shocked me, but my ability to embody that sensation with a hug didn't follow the same timeline, arriving in staggered stages. At first, I tried it out randomly and without reason, grappling with him like a loosed alligator, surprising him from behind when he was making coffee in the morning or heading to the shower. He suffered through my growing pains, aware I was flailing, trying to find a comfort zone until I finally succumbed, realizing the troubles of the day vanished in his arms and momentous moments could be improved and immortalized with a spontaneous show of love. Once I found my footing, I outpaced him in hugs, downright smothering him, to the point I often wonder whether he regrets pushing me in that direction.

When Theo and Winnie were born, I went after them with a vengeance, hugging and kissing them without respite, covering their tiny hands in mine even while walking up our stairs. I promised them I'd never let them feel like me, never let them grow up with a gaping black hole in the center of their heart that took years to close. But now, looking at Benjamin across from me, I hate Nathan—hate that I've basked in his love, hate that I've grown accustomed to his amorous enthusiasm and been left totally vulnerable to Benjamin's glacial take on paternity.

"Since you don't want my hug," Benjamin says, sliding down a pair of Dior sunglasses from the peak of his hair over his eyes. "Let's go. Your brothers and sisters are waiting for us."

"All of them?" I ask tentatively.

"Yes, Elizabeth," he says, as if he can read my mind. "*All of them.*"

His answer catches me off guard. If everyone is in attendance, *on time*, arriving before me, that doesn't seem *good*, doesn't seem in keeping with the family I've known for over three decades. They all studiously avoided Kate's *dying*, but are showing up for her death, which means Nathan is right—money *is* all that matters. I turn back to look at Nathan, gauging his response. All he does is nod his head knowingly, his body language doing all the verbal heavy lifting: *I told you so.*

"And don't get any ideas," Benjamin says, raising his sunglasses. He looks either ready to wink or have his eye twitch from stress, a condition I've been known to force upon him. "Just because Kate isn't here, doesn't mean *you're* going to become everyone's surrogate mother. I'm still in charge."

"Jesus, Dad," I say, feigning shock even though I'm certain we're on each other's wavelength, and have the other's number. "I'm here to say goodbye to Kate. Not try to usurp your rule. Everyone knows *you're* the king."

"Trust me," he says, lowering his sunglasses to the bridge of his nose again. "If they had any doubts, I plan to dispel them over the next few days."

He turns and saunters off the dock. People fan out, scattering from his path, probably sensing this is not a man who *waits*. Even the benches and deck chairs seem to shoot up at crisp attention as the expanse of his shadow spreads across their shiny finish.

Suddenly, he pulls a pair of keys from his pocket and motions to a brand-new golf cart with the "Eleusinian" crest on the hood.

"Grandpa," Winnie says, overjoyed. "Did you buy this? Can I drive it?"

"No, Winnifred," he says, dampening her enthusiasm for vehicular oddities. Back home, she's desperate to get her license and force us to buy her a vintage VW Bug. "My bad knee is killing me. I couldn't make the walk from the hotel to the dock, so they let me borrow it."

"But can I drive it?" she continues, pleading.

"My knee really hurts, in case you plan on caring," he says, sliding into the driver's seat.

"How did you hurt your knee in the first place, Dad?" I ask, still patiently waiting for an explanation about his "injury" nearly thirty-four years later. It was first brought to my attention when I asked him to coach my soccer team. Some children might have interpreted his sudden ligament ailment as an *excuse*, one that he has doubled down on for three decades, refusing to admit the lie and fully committing to the role. But not in the case of Benjamin Sunderland. His evasion is part of a larger unfinished puzzle encompassing the entirety of his past *before I was born*. Do I have uncles? Aunts? Grandparents? Cousins? Did he have summer jobs? What was he like as a teenager? As a toddler? Who knows? *I don't.*

Most parents are eager to share their history with their children, to leave something larger behind—whether it's a narrative legacy or silly stories that still garner laughs sixty years later. Not my father. His past is best summed up by his personal mantra: *if you look back, they'll devour you.* To this day, I'm still unsure who *they* are and why they are committed to devouring my father, but he seems dead certain *they* are always swimming around the isolated boat of his formative years, those halcyon American days before the world went to hell. Maybe Benjamin was just ahead of the curve. Maybe we all should be this scared.

"Shotgun!" Theo calls out, jumping into the passenger's seat. He puts his arm around my father, happy to be by his side—the little Judas. Nathan, Winnie, and I are forced into the cramped backseat, which faces the opposite direction. This means that, after throwing up, I'm about to be driven *backwards*, which is sure to perform wonders for my stomach.

Benjamin careens out of the spot, unconcerned with any peripheral action, and speeds across the paved path lining the circumference of the resort. I'm instantly rocketed back, terrified of the next few minutes, of driving with Benjamin absent a two-ton chassis enclosing me from his auto Armageddon. I quickly tuck in any exposed limbs, and before I get a chance to grab Nathan's hand, he has already grabbed mine.

"How can a golf cart go this fast?" Nathan asks with awed sincerity.

"I don't think it wants to," I say, pointing out the sobbing engine, the choking exhaust, and the transmission about to self-eject, all hallmarks of what Benjamin does to machines and to people. The golf cart is merely the latest addition in his roster of destruction. Every move he makes is calculated; every object in his path is a potential victim pushed aside in the name of progress. His urgent rush reduces any deviations to his grand plan to a flickering, fluorescent blur in the rearview mirror.

Benjamin is one of those quintessentially American boot-strapping success stories, a man whose business prowess screams out for an autobiography gifted with a title that combines extreme grit, masochism, and something about rugged individualism. The little I do know about his past—because it's shoved in our faces as an example of our family's deranged decadence—is that he grew up in a duplex in Queens, gained a scholarship to Columbia, then gained *another* to Wharton for his MBA. He graduated broke, destitute, barely able to buy a suit for his first job interview, a position for which he was hired *on the spot*, because they smelled the intensity that would allow him to demolish anything standing in his way. He wanted to become the next Rockefeller, an unruly quest that climaxed in his current incarnation as one of the most successful and notorious venture capitalists on the planet.

And "venture capitalist" is a rather lofty title for what Benjamin's job actually entails—*gambling*. He may study statistics, scrutinize growth patterns and possibilities, and strenuously interview the entrepreneurs, but really, he's gambling, guessing, playing heightened Russian roulette with a lot of people's money—including his own. Charitably, he's among the best in the field, occupying rarefied air, worth an ungodly sultanic sum of money. But what *really* gets him up in the morning is the chance to make millions off his natural inclinations: unalloyed extremism, a permanent avoidance of the middle ground, and the opportunity to dine on the failures of others, which he does like a modern-day Titus Andronicus.

"Get the hell out of the road!" Benjamin bellows, banging on the almost apologetic golf cart horn and pointing at a family of chickens holding up his left turn.

"Grandpa," Winnie chastises. "This is their home too."

"But *is* it?" he barks back. "Do they pay fifty thousand dollars a week for the pleasure of this property?" He raises his sunglasses. "*Do they?*"

Winnie rolls her eyes. "Why can't you just learn to share?"

Benjamin turns around, stops castigating the chickens, and speaks to the back of my head. "This is your fault, Elizabeth."

"It always is, Dad," I say, keenly aware that our ideologies on life and success will forever keep us at arm's length, because when it comes to clinging tight to personal belief systems, to living authentically, I can out-stubborn even Benjamin.

"*Finally*," Benjamin says, watching the chickens end their silent protest and scamper off. My father slams down on the gas, relieved he can make the turn into the Eleusinian villas.

"Dad," I say, tapping him on the shoulder. "I wanted to ask you something while we're still alone."

"What?" he answers, already annoyed before the question passes my lips.

"Did Kate give you any kind of…*reason* why she wanted us to come here?"

"Elizabeth," he says. "I told you. She wanted her ashes spread."

"But I mean…*why*? Why would she even want to do that? Why wouldn't she want an actual *funeral*? Why wouldn't she want everyone to be there to say goodbye."

"I can't answer that for her," he says. "But maybe she can."

"*How?*" I say, more lost than before. "Can you for one second stop being cryptic?"

"She left us all a video to watch together." He takes his eyes off the path for a second, looks back to see my reaction. "That's where we're headed now."

CHAPTER FIVE

"IF YOU'RE ALL WATCHING THIS, *it means I am no longer with you,*" Kate says, a spectral image haunting the sixty-five-inch flat screen festooned on the wall of Benjamin's villa, where I sit on the couch with my family watching her, bordered on all sides by my siblings spread out in diverse defensive pockets, and my father is in the corner, looming over the room, arms crossed, foot tapping, like a nervous director screening a rough cut that he can't control anymore.

Kate stares directly into the camera, the lens preserving a vision of her before illness had enacted its true toll, but the cracks in the facade were already present: her tailored clothes dangling off her frail body; her mouth a rictus of purpose; her eyes wearing the same fixed, yet far away, stare I saw the night she announced her illness to us. The night when our house built on sand was flooded and swept away.

"*You're likely wondering why I brought you back to St. John instead of having a funeral in Manhattan,*" Kate continues. "*At least, I'm sure Elizabeth is. The incessant questioner.*"

If Kate was expecting a little levity—a gruff acknowledgement from all present as to my role in the family—it didn't work. No one cares. Everyone stays silent, motionless, *emotionless.* Winnie, sensing how uncomfortable it just became to be *me*, comes over and sits on the floor in front of me and wraps her arms around my legs, like she did when she was little.

While we all wait for Kate to begin again, I look across to Paul, seated alone, slouched in a large leather chair that seems to be devouring him. He winks at me, and it's a sign I know all too well. It's a deliberate decision *not* to smile. He only smiles when he knows things will be okay—which is why it's so rare. Clearly, he hasn't decided on Kate's video yet.

I avert my eyes from him and gauge the state of the rest of my siblings.

Caroline is seated on the floor, legs crisscrossed, scrolling through Instagram and texting with friends. I nudge her with my knee to get her off the phone, and she death glares at me in response, a petulant child annoyed at being yanked toward consequence.

Julian is next to her, simultaneously shell-shocked and sobbing, a curious reaction from my baby brother, who had fled the continent the minute Kate confessed her illness. I can't help but wonder *who* he's crying for.

Tessa, seemingly uncomfortable with Julian's outward show of sadness, audibly clears her throat to have another sound filling the cavernous room. She looks to Benjamin for moral support, for approval, seeing as he's the only one in the room she really cares about. But he doesn't respond, just stares vacantly at Kate on the television. I notice he never removed his sunglasses.

"*I brought you all here to save you from yourselves. You have each handled my illness in your own idiosyncratic ways. And I know you will all handle my death in a similar fashion. However, there is one area in which I am certain all my children would be in lockstep. Denial. And I refuse to allow you to have it. You must let the finality of my absence wash over you. And you must do it with each other. Alone. Other people surrounding you would give you an excuse...the salve you're all desperately seeking, the chance to avoid mourning yourselves and transfer it onto others. There will be no more hiding. Starting now.*"

I hear Paul emit a gruff laugh, like he just finished gargling acid, and put my finger to my lips to shush him.

"I can't blame all of you for the way you process the world. For the people you have become. I helped cause it. Denying my own hand in your fate would be an act of cowardice, one I've been guilty of throughout your lives. But I have finally found the strength to force you to undo it, to see—and maybe embrace—a different way of living."

I hear Benjamin making his way to the bar, then the clinking of ice in a glass and the breaking seal of a bottle of Scotch. "How much longer is left in this thing?" he says to no one in particular and pauses the video to check the counter.

I stare at my father—stopping Kate's last testament to her family with an Apple TV remote he's holding upside down—then back to Kate's frozen visage, then *back* to Benjamin, and wonder why the fuck Kate waited thirty-three years to summon the inner strength to kamikaze our static lunacy, and also, *why the actual fuck* did she wait until she was dead to do it, leaving us with Benjamin as the only possible guide?

He brings the drink to his lips with shaking hands, drops the remote to the floor, and as it hits the tile, the video plays, and Kate's voice fills the room again.

"This family has been built on a series of escalating lies, secrets, and omissions, all papered over with dollar bills. Money has come to dominate all our encounters, our discussions, and our relationships, because it was the only topic anyone in our home was allowed to talk about openly. Every problem could be solved with it. Every second of discomfort or challenge to the status quo could disappear with the swipe of a card. No one in this family has had to feel in decades, because we are all numbed into submission and acceptance by money. But our continued silence costs more than we have in the bank."

"It's a lot of money, *Mom*," I hear Tessa mumble under her breath.

"Dying itself is meaningful, but it doesn't necessarily impart meaning. I refuse to have my death mean nothing more than an ending. As Julian has told me: From death, comes life. From pain, comes wisdom.

You will all leave this island changed people. You will all learn things about one another. You will learn things about me. And what you finally choose to do with this opportunity is in your hands. You can ignore it, experience life-in-death, a feeling which you're all intimately familiar with. Until you wake up one morning and realize it's too late. Like me. Or you can look it in the face; you can rise. You can take this chance I'm giving you, this parting gift, to become the family we always could have been. We are better than we have shown. We are worth saving. All of us. Collectively. Individually. And without me, maybe you finally can be."

I watch the video fade as Kate dissolves into isolated pixels. The television switches to a screensaver, a floating shot of arid desert dotted by weather-beaten rocks. I can *feel* the eternity in these blasted mineral ruins populated by ancient lizards, a stretch of land ripped from time's embrace. Apparently, so can my family.

Everyone is staring at the screen, searching the void. Everyone is *silent*, a rare feat Kate has finally managed after thirty-three years of motherhood and marriage. She has shocked the unshockable, achieved the unthinkable. We haven't begun recruiting tenuous allies to a lost cause, haven't flipped any furniture, haven't brought to the fore who has suffered more. We are simply meditating on our mother's dying wish for us to be better.

Her words, *my words* since I was ten years old, reverberate in my head. An endless loop. There is a daunting chance before us, a solar eclipse event within the Bernard-Sunderland family. We can stop measuring love in bank balances, to fuse together instead of splitting apart, to stop wasting precious hours and blend for *real*. And judging from the pin-drop quiet in the room, Kate's parting words may have had the requisite force to make them all wake up.

"*Fuck this shit,*" Caroline says, using my knee to launch herself off the floor. "I'm not becoming a star in Kate's fucking beyond-the-grave reality show." She picks up her bag and shoves her phone inside. "I played that role when she was *alive*, and it sucked. It should never have made it out of fucking pilot season." She looks around the room for anyone to share her sentiments. "I'm out of here."

I grab Caroline by the wrist, stopping her from storming off. I'm desperate to keep her from spoiling this opportunity, just as she has *every* opportunity handed to her in life. "You're being selfish."

"*Me?*" she says, trying to remove my fingers. "Kate uses her death to tell us we're all failures, that she helped make us that way, and that we need to change to give her life meaning. Why didn't she try to give our lives meaning when she was still here?"

"Let her go, Lizzie," I hear Julian say, as he stands up next to Caroline. "I'm going with her."

"You were just *crying*," I say, trying to hold onto my last bit of composure in the face of a spreading revolution. "Kate's words didn't mean anything to you?"

"I was crying," Julian says, checking his pockets, "because seeing her like that reminded me of a time that *was*. And that is gone. This is just a desperate attempt to pump some oxygen into something even more dead than my mother, and I'm not going to be a party to it." He breathes in. "It nearly killed me once. I'm not letting it happen again." He smiles sadly, flashing his usual lopsided grin I've seen a hundred times—the one where his face moves but his lips stay shut, the one telepathically confessing that he's needed this family to function as much as I have...but he's drained of the strength to keep caring.

"Survival of the fittest, Lizzie. We learned it from the best."

I watch Benjamin place his drink on the counter, sighing. "I assume that was directed toward me, Julian."

Tessa waits to see if Julian plans to respond, and upon realizing he's content letting that comment be what it is, starts to walk to the center of the room, her steps filled with hesitation, searching for her sea legs. Then she straightens up, fixes the group with an intense glare, and says: "I'm going with Julian and Caroline. The

Kate on that video is *not* the woman who raised us, and I'm not going to participate in honoring the wishes of some woman I can't even recognize anymore."

Her words silence the room. Julian and Caroline share a knowing look. The dissenters now number three, and the odds are no longer in my favor. And I'm mad. I'm past the point of delicate persuasion and ready to just start calling *bullshit*.

"What the actual fuck, Tess," I say, jumping to my feet, holding my hand out as if I'm directing invisible traffic. "You wanted to be Kate your entire life, to the point you stabbed us all in the back to get closer to her. You bad-mouthed and blamed us to make yourself look perfect. And now...*now* all of a sudden you're what... the *rebel*?" I stop to catch my breath. "I excused your conspicuous absence when she was dying, trying to cover for you, figuring it was just too much for you to handle. You know, like *everything else*. But I will not excuse you leaving. You owe it to her. You owe it to us, and you owe it to me. You kept me from getting close to her our entire lives, so you could be her favorite. You started blaming me from the day our parents got married and you *never* stopped. You've made all our lives a nightmare by endorsing every mistake Dad and Kate ever made, so they'd love you more. Well, I'm pulling the brakes. You're staying." I point at each of my siblings individually. "You're *all* staying."

"Liz," Paul says, interrupting my putting down of the peasants' revolt. "Stop, okay? It's not going to happen. I *know* how bad you want this. I know you think my mother just gave it to you. But it's too late. I'm going with them. Our little thirty-year experiment is over."

I fall back and sink into the couch, deflating. Paul's words take the air out of my lungs in a gut punch I never thought I'd receive from him.

He looks down at his shoes, unable to break my heart the way he just broke our pact. "Believe it or not, I'm doing this for you. I don't want to watch you be crushed. You'll never survive it. The rest of us would."

All four of my siblings, for once in their life united, *against me*, walk to the door, ready to close the chapter on our family and never look back.

"*Do not touch that fucking door,*" I hear Benjamin say, his voice booming off every piece of animate matter and using the same primal force he deploys in full hostile takeover territory. "Lizzie's *right*. We are not going anywhere."

He takes his sunglasses off, his piercing blue eyes an ocean of anger.

"Anyone in the mood to test me?"

CHAPTER SIX

NATHAN, THE KIDS, AND I leave Benjamin's villa under the wrathful stare of eight eyes all holding me responsible for being trapped on St. John. Yet I feel triumphant. I cross the road to my family's villa, and the triumph begins to slowly fade out of focus. My victory becomes blurry. Once we arrive, I swipe the key across the lock, the door pops, and my face turns instantly sour. Nathan and the kids ask me: *What's wrong?* I don't answer, just begin ascending the staircase to the bedroom.

Nathan follows me, a few steps behind, tentative but determined. He lets me enter the bedroom first, pauses, then shuts the door on Theo and Winnie. Our kids are trying to peek in, anxious to take the temperature on my mood, which silently reminds me I am once again failing them as a mother.

"*Hey*," Nathan says, arms outstretched, questioning, confused how my mood went south on the walk to our villa and the front door. "You thought Kate wasn't going to leave you a way that pointed to a future. She gave you what you always wanted."

I don't respond, not prepared to grant his point when I have my own questions that need answering.

"So why do you look like you're about to vomit again?"

"Why did my father agree with me?" I say, a question as existential as it is interrogative.

"Who cares why?"

"I care," I say. "I've known that man for forty-three years, and he never agrees with *anyone*, especially me, unless there's some ulterior motive. Some gain in it for him. It's not like Kate died and he suddenly became some bastion of altruism. For fuck's sake...the first thing he told me when I got off the boat, *after* my stepmother died, was that I looked fat. And *what*? Kate leaves behind a video, and he's fucking father of the year?" I throw my hands up. "Do you not know *him*? He's the same Benjamin Sunderland who left a check tucked under your door for two hundred fifty thousand dollars on our wedding day to not show up. But, right...he *cares*."

"Yeah, but his kids are all he has now," he says. "He's lost his wife. Maybe he can't take *losing* anything else."

I bite my lower lip, cogitate, consider Nathan's alternate history.

"I think I want to go," I say, surveying the bedroom. "Good thing I didn't unpack."

I'm dead certain my father has embroiled me in a nefarious trap, a play-within-a-play, and I don't want to stick around and watch my good intentions get twisted around in his little game. Kate, on that video, wasn't playing a *game*. She was honest, heart-felt, and truthful. Three adjectives that could never be applied to Benjamin, who probably just agreed with me so he could sabotage the plan from within and consolidate control after losing his contrite partner-in-crime.

"We're not *leaving*," Nathan says.

"You don't have to," I say, refusing to negotiate on those terms, refusing to accept that in three words Nathan stripped me of my ability to imagine a world in which I was leaving, a fantasy I allow myself to entertain when things get grueling even by my family's standards. "If you think my father has miraculously turned over a new leaf, I don't want you to come home with me."

"That's not what I'm saying...."

"That's what *I'm* saying, Nathan."

"Okay," he says, realizing he overshot and is now forced to play along with my Byzantine thought process, the very thing he hoped to avoid. "What is his reason for taking the one thing you wanted in life and cheapening it...to fit his own design..."

Before Nathan can finish, there's a blushing, almost sorrowful knock on the door.

"That can't be our kids," I say, confused and disappointed it isn't them. I'm unprepared to deal with *whichever* member of my family is lurking. I walk over to the door and click it locked, just to get the message across to the unwelcome visitor.

"Liz," I hear, then another almost plaintive knuckle rap. "Come on. Let me in."

"Paul?" I say to the last person I want to see right now. I'd rather have fucking Caroline throwing a fit or Tessa's passive-aggressiveness than the person who is capable of hurting me, who *did* just crush me. "We are *not* friends right now. I don't have anything to say."

"Yes, you do," he says. "I've been standing out here for three minutes deciding whether to knock, and you haven't *stopped* talking."

"Well, none of it is directed towards *you*," I say.

"Elizabeth!" Paul says, now banging on the door and turning the knob. "Open. The. Goddamn. Door."

"No," I say. "Why don't you go see all your new friends."

"*Enough*," Nathan says, storming over to the door and unlocking it. "You two need to make up right now." He leaves and exposes Paul, looking pale and drained, and holding a bowl of mint chocolate chip ice cream that he clearly just had delivered from room service.

I focus on the glass ice cream dish in Paul's hand, canceling out all the noise and focusing on the signal. It's impossible for me to remain mad at Paul when he arrives bearing languorously melting green goodness studded with decadent chocolate chips. That bowl means more than ice cream—*although not to be overlooked*—it also contains our past, countless nights at the kitchen tables of our lives, dating back to when we were children. I take the dish from his hands, still not hinting at any hopes for forgiveness, bring the spoon to my lips, and like a madeleine dipped in tea, return to Paul's and my own personal Combray.

The night is seared in the memory chain Paul and I share. Less than twenty-four hours after Benjamin and Kate's wedding, they departed for their honeymoon to the Maldives—a locale none of the children could pronounce nor find on a map—and left us in the care of a rotating live-in-staff we hadn't met before but were assured came *very highly recommended.*

Within forty-eight hours, the housekeeper had exposed Bogey, Tessa's favorite stuffed bear—an already critical case, sutured together like a cross between FAO Schwarz and Frankenstein's lab—to a spin cycle, under which he pretty much dissolved. Upon Bogey's untimely passage, Tessa swore off sleeping and eating and dedicated herself to hyperventilating, breaking out in hives and turning mute, save for endless sobbing. Bogey, a parting gift from our absent mother, was Tessa's only cure for her anxiety—but he had dematerialized, leaving her rudderless, orphaned in her new life.

Caroline hadn't suffered the destruction of anything crucial to her well-being, but she was making great strides in *destroying* the penthouse. She had fractured a Faberge egg, modeled one of Kate's vintage Chanel dresses while dining on spaghetti, short-circuited Benjamin's exercise bike in a cluster of sparks, and crafted a cape out of the blue velvet living room drapes while flying around the kitchen, crashing into the chef just as he was transporting a pot of boiling water. My baby sister was too young to understand our lives had irrevocably changed, that we had a new mother—replacing the woman who left her behind before she could walk—and a semi-distant father about to become a vaporous substance in a suit. No one ever sat her down and explained, tried to make her comfortable, considered it might strain her four-year-old consciousness that *this*, almost out of the blue, was her new family. And she was lashing out the only way children understand: the desperate drive for negative attention.

Julian hadn't lost a treasured furry keepsake or committed triple-digit damage to our new home. Point of fact, he'd spent very little time there, excusing himself from the blended family experiment on three different occasions. Twice, I found him in Central Park, attempting to strike up conversation with hot dog stand owners and petting the beleaguered horses standing in line, waiting on tourists. The third time he was attempting to flee in Benjamin's Porsche, having stolen the keys, turned the car on, and suffered the indignity of realizing his feet couldn't come close to the pedals. I found him in the garage, mimicking driving, radio blasting, convertible roof open, eyes alive with an imagined highway he was racing down.

Paul hadn't inflicted mass carnage against innocent household objects or attempted to take a stationary joyride. He simply hadn't left his room since Benjamin and Kate *left us*. He hadn't tried to interact with anyone, outside of ordering the staff to deliver his meals at specified times and leaving them outside his door.

Late on the third night of dysfunction in action, I was sitting at the kitchen table, eating mint chocolate chip ice cream and watching *My Two Dads*, pondering what it would be like having *two* fathers care about you, let alone one attentive patriarch.

Without notice, or seemingly any *sound*, Paul appeared in the kitchen. He didn't speak—just sat down at the head of the table. After absorbing a few minutes of my preferred sitcom, he turned to me and said, "This show sucks."

I rolled my eyes at my new brother, a veritable stranger I had met barely six months ago and was now sharing the same house as me. "I didn't ask you to watch it with me."

"Good," he said. "I wouldn't have come down if I knew you were going to."

I dipped my spoon back into my bowl. "Do you need something?"

He picked up the carton of ice cream. "Mint chocolate chip? Horrible choice."

"Once again," I said, unfamiliar with the unique challenges of dealing with a brother. My sisters had a veritable panoply of moods, ranging from silent despair to fits of rage. Meanwhile, Paul seemingly had two settings that frequently overlapped: anger and sarcasm. Apparently, he would be treating me to both. "Didn't ask."

"I prefer cookies and cream."

"You would," I said. "It's perfect for people who can't make up their mind about anything. Do you want cookies? Or do you want cream? Make a decision."

Paul put the container down on the table. "You'll be happy to know I've been abandoned."

I nod, trying to match his newfound theatricality with a little sarcasm of my own. "I can't imagine why."

"I called Benjamin and my mother's room, and they weren't there. I called the hotel, and they didn't know where they were either. And they haven't called me *back*. Then I tried my father to see if he'd rescue me from you people, but he was on a date and couldn't be bothered." He watched me thoughtlessly spooning out more ice cream. "Have you heard from them?"

"No," I said.

"*No*," he said, mocking me. "Aren't you mad?"

"No. Why would I be mad?"

"We've been abandoned," he said. "And nobody cares."

"So you've said," I responded. "Except for the fact there's like twenty-two people in the house."

"You're either incredibly stupid or can't see what's going on here." He searched my face. "Which one is it?"

"*You're* stupid," I said, not entirely sure why either of us was stupid, but standing my ground.

"What do you think? That this is just going to get better?" he asked, raising his hands in frustration. "Benjamin and my mother are just going to be around less and less. My father is probably going to marry whatever teenager he's dating and have more kids. And things are already falling apart." He raised his voice. "And you're here eating ice cream." He grew louder. "And who's going to take me to soccer practice?"

"I'll go with you," I said, responding to his vulnerability—something I'd never imagined I'd see from Paul.

"Do you even know how to ride the subway?"

I grabbed my backpack from the floor, stuck my hand inside, and pulled out an MTA subway map that I picked up when I first moved to the city. "I can learn." I opened it and began inspecting the colored intersecting lines.

"It doesn't even matter," he said. "We have a driver."

I began folding the map back up, defeated.

"Fine," he said, folding his arms. "We can ride the subway together."

I looked at him, at how lost his gaze was, and realized when I looked in the mirror, I saw the same reflection. It's a common symptom of the oldest—those who knew the life before, and weren't entirely sure what was scarier: going ahead with the new one, or returning to the old. It's something the other siblings could never and would never grasp about Paul and me. Time had banished us from their palace of innocence.

I *knew* Benjamin before Kate. Paul *knew* Kate before Benjamin. We had seen them at their lowest, their most broken, which—without fail—leaves something broken in *you*. It's crushing when your parents cease being superhuman, infallible, when you still have a right to cling to hallowed illusions.

He took a long look at me spooning the last of my ice cream. "You're not going to just give up on this?"

I couldn't answer—my mouth was still full—but he didn't need me to.

"You're going to force this *thing* into a family."

"Why not?" I said, shrugging. "No one else is going to."

He shrugged back. "You can't do it alone."

"I don't plan to," I said, fixing my eyes on him. "You're doing it with me. You want the same thing, you just don't know it yet."

"I'm not sure I'm ever going to know it," he said.

"Paul," I said, trying to speak in terms he might understand. "Remember how you told me once your soccer coach said 'fake it till you make it'? That's all we need to do. If we stay together, if we act like we're *actually* siblings, everyone else will get the idea...and before Benjamin and Kate realize it, we're a family."

Paul leaned in closer, looking to swipe an errant scoop of my ice cream, which I pulled away on principle. "Say you'll do it. Or no ice cream."

"I'm not saying I *will*," he said. "But I won't *stop you* either. And I will be your brother."

Looking at Paul now, standing across from me—thirty-three years and one less parent later—it's become clear that he does intend to *stop me*, to put an end to our partnership and dissolve the project I've committed most of my life to bringing to fruition. Of course, there's little to show for all my efforts, except ever-increasing levels of alienation from everyone involved, including *him*.

"I'm sorry," Paul says, risking conversation and moving further into the room. "But if you'd just listen to me, let me explain..."

"I don't want to hear it," I answer flippantly. I'm hurt, exhausted, and lacking the inner resources to handle losing Kate *and* having to convince Paul for what feels like—and what may actually be—the four hundredth time that this family is worth more than he ever allows himself to believe. "I heard everything you said at Benjamin's."

"Liz," he says, equally exhausted and not in the mood to run up against my legendary obstinacy on this topic. "It's not just *us* having a private debate over the feasibility of this viper's nest. When the continued survival was put to a democratic vote, we just learned: everyone wants out. *No one* agrees with you."

"They're wrong," I say simply, not indulging his debate.

His eyes grow wide. He places the ice cream atop a dresser so he can use his hands again to vent his inordinate frustration with me. "Why do you fucking *care* so much? In all this time, there has been *no* movement that would in any way indicate you are right. In fact, there has been nothing but *counter* movement in the completely opposite direction. The longer we're together, the worse it gets every year. Get with the program and let it go. I mean, what the *hell?*"

I play my trump card, which fills me with tremendous schadenfreude toward Paul and lets me flee from having to answer that question. I don't know what makes me want to keep us all together, any more than they know why they all want to run. I just know I'm right. And I am *rarely* wrong. "Benjamin agrees with me."

Paul opens his mouth, but can't seem to find words, choking out strangled syllables.

Before he recovers the easy use of his tongue, the phone rings. I don't answer it; I just keep staring, locked in a battle of wills, waiting patiently for a pithy comeback currently escaping him.

"Mom!" Theo says, at an alarming volume usually reserved for when he's playing video games with his best friend, Abdul, and the fate of the planet rests in their uniquely unqualified hands. "Grandpa is on the phone for you."

The second consecutive shock is too much for Paul. "My new friends? Look at you. Look at you, Elizabeth. We have one disagreement, and you replace me with…with *him*. Your mortal enemy. The whole reason we bonded in the first place…"

I know that tone. Jealousy creeps in when Paul thinks someone else in our family is potentially taking his place, occupying my attention that should solely be focused on him. He *can't* stand that.

I walk over to the nightstand, pick up the phone, and before I say hello, Benjamin is already shouting in my ear.

"Kate is missing..."

CHAPTER SEVEN

I HOLD THE PHONE AWAY from my burning, sweating ear, as if Benjamin's panic and rage has assumed electric form, buzzed through fiberoptic cable, and is trying to embed itself in my cochlea.

"What is he saying?" Paul asks, glowering, wondering what news his presumed successor could need such *volume* to express. But this time I'm not keeping a secret to force him to stew—I'm actually too fucking shocked to put the revelation into proper speech:

Benjamin lost Kate.

To be honest, he didn't just *lose* Kate; she is outright missing, not to be found. I know this because Benjamin has recited the litany of his efforts, punctuated by copious expletives. He called his household staff in Manhattan, who couldn't locate the urn *anywhere*, then he ransacked his villa to diminishing returns, and finally he decided to retrace his steps across varied modes of transportation. He yelled at any airline representative he was transferred to, all of whom seemed eager to pass him along. Then the equally oblivious charter boat captain, who—while sympathetic to Benjamin's loss, himself a widower who devoted himself to a life at sea after losing the love of his life—hadn't seen the container holding my stepmother. Finally, he interrogated the entire Eleusinian staff, who thoroughly searched all recently arrived luggage and came up empty. Feeling so horrible they couldn't help him, the staff gave him several complimentary spa treatments to work out some of the *justifiable* tension.

Having collected this batch of unhelpful clues, Benjamin is *now* convinced that one of my siblings must hold the answer he's looking for. Unfortunately, he's so flummoxed by playing detective for a few hours that he needs *me* to be the messenger.

And now, my foreboding feeling has transformed into outright dread. This is an unmitigated disaster, likely the one Paul glimpsed coming. A second wave of dread immediately hits me. My father losing Kate was the only reason he agreed with me to follow my late stepmother's plan in the first place. He didn't take my side out of solidarity. Not to fix our family and walk hand-in-hand to a bright new future. No. He didn't want to tell anyone Kate was missing. He was trying to buy himself enough time to relocate her before having to tell anyone he was going to have to postpone spreading her ashes, because there aren't any ashes to *spread*. I lock eyes with Paul, calculating, cogitating how best to maneuver a silent showdown I know I'm going to lose, because I don't have a choice except to recruit him on this errand. A task, much like Benjamin, I am in no emotional shape to handle solo either.

"I forgive you," I say to Paul.

He folds his arms, refusing to react, playing the game. "Isn't that wonderful news. Care to explain *why?*"

"I love you," I say, smiling.

He cracks. "Out with it. What happened?"

"So," I say, drawing out the inevitable, "Kate is missing."

Paul cranes his neck to the right side, trying to make heads or tails of what's happening. "*What?*" He doesn't give me time to answer. "You know what…I don't want to know." He pauses, then starts again, revving up his rage like the engine of a sports car. "But this is exactly what I was talking about…."

"So, you'll help me?" I say, ending his sputtering.

"I know Julian went back to Manhattan before coming here. He said he wanted to say goodbye to Mom on his own before the St. John spectacle took it out of him."

Paul and I walk single file out of the bedroom and down the stairs, passing Nathan in the kitchen and telling him we'll be back soon and to see if the kids want to go to the beach. He acknowledges the request with a distracted grunt while angrily reading aloud and typing an email—that I assume—is about how *he* knows better than all of Hollywood how his latest screenplay should be written. He may also be scouring his inbox and the internet at large for examples to bolster his argument, eternally hunting for his "gotcha" moment, which I think at this point fuels his writing career more than any actual desire to write.

Seven minutes and a tenuous peace negotiation with Paul later—one in which he mused philosophically on how, in the grand totality of our parents' forced errors, this latest could be granted a spot in the top ten but didn't present a real challenge for the *top five*—we arrive at the door of Julian's suite and knock.

Julian cracks the door warily; his long hair wet and limp and hanging to his shoulders; his face clean-shaven, minus the stubble that dotted his cheeks when I first saw him in Benjamin's room. Apparently, Julian's newest method of surviving family trauma is to shower.

Paul clears his throat. "Can we come in? We're looking for Mom."

I notice a well-thumbed and highlighted copy of *Siddhartha* by Hermann Hesse. It's the book I gave him years ago—before he left on his first journey to Tibet—to help him realize having no answers was still a state of transcendental nirvana, just inverted, like everything else in our lives. Hence why everyone in our family is a dedicated reader—a habit Benjamin and Kate demanded while never actually reading anything themselves. Like many of their mandated decisions, it blew back on them, allowing us to create a kind of morse code of suffering between ourselves that can't be spoken aloud, only transmitted through sacred texts, almost how science was kept alive during the Dark Ages.

Julian walks toward us, steps outside the villa into the sun, and conspicuously closes his door, subtly denying us access.

"Mom was only *missing* during life," Julian says. "She's home now. Part of every speck of the cosmos, the earth, the blades of grass. Whether you realize it or not, we are all made of stars. Sometimes I feel like I can feel them explode in my stomach."

Paul ignores Julian's mystical soliloquy, rolling right into the tangible facts unfolding before us, sighing at me that he's forced to endure this. "Let me try and be clearer. Mom is missing. As in, her ashes are gone. Can't be found. And we can't let her return to where *all life* reverts upon death, until we can spread the fucking ashes, Julian."

He pauses, as if finally noticing something horribly off in the mise-en-scène of our visit. "Why are we talking outside?"

"Are we?" Julian says, looking around. He feigns surprise, as if it never dawned on him until Paul brought up the obvious fact that we're standing in the blazing sun.

"Don't you think that's odd, Liz?" Paul says, addressing me but not taking his eyes off Julian.

It dawns on me why Paul refuses to stop questioning our location, and with that realization a pit forms in my stomach. I join my brother in looking into Julian's eyes, searching for the tell-tale signs: the pupils that have devoured the iris, the red-rimmed lids, the glazed over expression, the fractured speech missing varieties of nouns and verbs—yet still overly packed with information.

"Jules," I say tentatively, like I'm negotiating someone off the ledge—either him or me and Paul at this point. "Are you using again? Are you high? Is that why you won't let us in?"

"I wasn't getting high," he says, in an affronted tone usually reserved for when he *has* been doing exactly that and just got caught.

"We just got worried for a second," I respond, imploring, always living on edge of being the one who puts Julian on edge, which leads to all our conversations having *an edge*. "Kate dying is so new…. We're all still trying to find our way in a world without her."

"*Not me*," he says, shutting me down. "That's you, Elizabeth. I may be an addict, but it takes one to know one. You're just addicted to whatever fantasy you have of this family. And apparently you convinced my mother to share in your addiction while she was dying."

Julian's words vivisect me, straight from his lived experience, straight from months of rehab, where he learned family is the ultimate addiction that you're never able to outrun. I know it better than anyone, including him.

But my addiction is different.

Julian's first few awkward steps with budding addiction started his freshman year of high school at Dalton, and like any habit that becomes a lifestyle, it crept in quietly, beginning with Friday and Saturday night parties at friends' parentless penthouses, where great attention was taken to the interior design, but no one noticed their kids were spending whole weekends in a foggy weed-haze. And obeying the ineluctable calculus of addiction, soon Julian and his new friends were smoking joints on the way to school or cutting class to get high in the boys' bathroom.

Julian had finally found his true métier in substance oblivion, altering his consciousness enough to find a home where he felt comfortable. And to fend off any inevitable return of the *real*, he graduated to faster modes of delivery, tossing Benjamin's two-thousand-dollars-a-bottle Scotch and Kate's prescription pain killers into the mix. Both our parents remained blissfully ignorant that their own methods of coping were being replaced with Jim Beam and Motrin, despite my constant entreaties for them to *pay attention*—that something was wrong with Julian, that he'd been replaced with an alien version of himself hatched straight from a pharmaceutical pod.

But it was when Julian finished high school that he also finished treating alcohol and drugs as a hobby. He decided it was time to develop a habit to match his college status, his maturing into a Harvard man, and he chose cocaine. He'd met his soulmate, the one he'd never get over, the only one who actually cared, the one who made certain he'd never get back up.

True love does that sometimes.

After taking Benjamin and Kate's place during parents' weekend, I noticed he was further gone than I'd feared, sacrificing everything for his new relationship—grades, long-lasting friendships. He was reducing his life to a set of transitory transactions, except the actual *transaction*, cocaine, the center of his being. By the time his four years were finished and he graduated with the fashionably termed "Gentlemen's B-minus," I sat my parents down again and expressed my fears that Julian was about to be unleashed into a world that expected some demonstrable skills, even from a Bernard-Sunderland child. They placated my concerns by sending him to graduate school.

After he came out of graduate school uneducated *and* addicted, it was decided Julian should pursue his doctoral studies, allowing my family another four years at least to avert their eyes from the obvious. But I couldn't; I feared he wouldn't survive to receive his diploma. When I expressed those concerns, he lectured *me*, explaining in stuttering, scrupulous detail that *I* had the problem, that I'd become a new mother and consequently decided any fun was verboten, that *everyone* around him partied from time to time and I needed to stop worrying. Soon enough, he'd buckle down and throw away all his frivolous habits when he graduated.

But the tree that he'd mistaken for a deer—whose life he had valiantly spared—wasn't *frivolous*. It nearly stopped his life just shy of twenty-eight.

I was the one the police called. Kate and Benjamin were away on business—London and San Francisco, respectively—and weren't picking up their phones, leaving me as the one who had to go to the hospital, the one who had to sort out the mess, the one who had to call our lawyer, and the one who had to break it to Paul. All because Julian had made me his back-up emergency contact after Benjamin and Kate, not his own brother or biological father.

I couldn't face the hospital room. I spent hours staring at him through pebbled glass, unable to face the damage. His body had been bruised and broken, reforged in the glass and steel he soared through. I met with his doctors who gave me the diagnosis without frills: he'd recover from the crash. But his addiction would kill him.

The doctor's brutal advice has never left me. I feel Julian's soul hurting in the marrow of my bones, the marrow of my own soul. I let his criticisms wash over me, unanswered, knowing he needs to take out his confusion on someone *safe*, and Paul doesn't fit that description. More than anything, Julian's reaction makes me want to grip Kate's advice with both hands until my knuckles are raw from trying to save this family. To find nirvana for my little brother. And maybe for myself.

"Jules," I say. "We don't want to fight. We just want to know if you have Mom."

"Why would you think I have her in the first place?" Julian asks, moving his eyes between Paul and me—his dueling inquisitors.

"I thought you might," Paul says, trying to focus Julian's attention away from arguing with me and on to the task at hand. "I know you stopped at the apartment before your flight to say good-bye to Mom."

"I *did* and I *was*," Julian says, turning back toward the closed door, overly eager for us both to go. "But I didn't take Mom."

Before he gets his hand around the doorknob, it opens from inside, and a little boy, maybe five years old at the most—who bears a striking resemblance to Julian at that exact age—looks at me and Paul with curiosity. The longer I stare at this unexpected visitor, it dawns on me just *how* striking the resemblance is: the same dirty-blond hair, the same big gray eyes, the same tiny little rabbit legs. Then he stares past Julian, who is quickly trying to move him inside, and fixes me and Paul in his line of sight.

"*Daddy.* Who are these people?"

"Yeah, *Daddy*," Paul says. "Who is this?"

The child rushes between Julian's legs and makes his presence further known, much to my little brother's chagrin.

"I'm Oliver," he says, beaming.

Julian bends down, picks up a resistant Oliver, and starts bringing him back into the villa against his will. He deposits him safely inside, then slams the door behind Oliver. He turns his attention back to me and Paul.

"Don't you fucking say a thing to anyone about this," he says, pointing at the two of us. "I swear.... Just stay quiet."

CHAPTER EIGHT

PAUL WAITS AWHILE, STARES AT the shuttered door, curious if it's going to open again, and when he's certain it's going to say closed, says "What the *fuck*," to me, knocks on the hard wood a few times, calls out Julian's name, calls out Oliver's name, as if our newly discovered nephew might want to emerge and finish our chat, and when he's greeted with continuous silence, turns around to me and says: "I don't think he has Kate."

I push Paul out of the way. "You're probably scaring poor Oliver. He's going to be traumatized soon enough by the whole family.... There's no need to have him start off hating us." I begin knocking, hoping Julian will respond better to me—the *nicer* one, the one who has always tried to be there for him—and come outside to tell us what in the actual fuck is going on. I raise my hand to knock again when Paul intercepts it.

"Let it go, Liz," he says. "They've walled themselves in."

We both stand in silence, unsure of what to say. We see Julian inside, quickly closing all the curtains and shutting out all the light cascading from the wrap-around windows.

I turn to Paul. "Why do you think he wouldn't tell us?"

"That's not really what concerns me right now," he says. "Instead, I'd like you to consider a provocative question. What the *fuck* is Oliver doing here in the first place? Because if Julian hid him for years and is currently reenacting *Rio Bravo* inside our villa, I think we can be pretty sure it wasn't his idea to bring him here."

Instinctively, I put my hand to my mouth, shocked. "Do you mean...the video...*Kate*?"

"I do mean that," he says, none too pleased. "It appears we're in her game now, Liz. She wasn't kidding. *All* the secrets are coming out." He shrugs. "Still happy we stayed?"

Before I can answer, Julian rips open the window, pokes his head out, and says: "I'm not talking to you.… You're wasting your time. Instead of standing here, you should go find Tessa." He rolls his eyes, as if it's the most obvious thing in the world. "She's their fucking neighbor."

After Julian slams the window shut again, Paul puts his hand on my shoulder. "He's not wrong. And god, I wish he was."

Julian is *right*. Paul and I should have started our absurdist treasure hunt with Tessa and spared ourselves from knowing something that is going to make this hellish trip even worse. Tessa has been Benjamin and Kate's stalwart Upper West Side neighbor since she graduated from college with a degree in art therapy. At her first job, she quickly proved uniquely unqualified for any career path involving *therapy*, managed to terrify several classes of children in the process, and then settled into an elaborately forged simulation of Benjamin and Kate's life drained of any substance.

As we round the corner to leave the villas and set foot on the Eleusinian property proper, I grab Paul by the arm, slowing him down. "Can't we just text her and *ask* if she has them?"

"I tried that already," Paul says, showing me several messages to Tessa that haven't gone through and are trapped in undelivered purgatory.

"Maybe we'll get more bars the closer we get to the pools," I say, taking his iPhone and holding it above my head, hoping to conjure some subterranean signal to avoid the inevitable. "The fucking service here is nonexistent."

Paul grabs his phone back from me. "Or it could just be Kate."

"Because you're supposed to come here to relax," I say, realizing the cruel irony that only my family would bring death to such a place.

Paul stops short. "I usually vacation *after* our family's vacations to relax. And Tessa is a huge reason why." His glare intensifies. "I caught her going through my phone when we were all in the South of France. When I called her out on it, she acted like it was fine, and said, 'Who cares? We're all family. We don't have any *secrets.*'"

"Paul," I say, suddenly panicked by his memory of Tessa's inability to respect any human boundaries. "You cannot even so much as *hint* at Oliver's existence in front of Tessa. Nothing. Not until we figure out what the fuck is going on."

"Okay, *Benjamin*," he says. "Have you decided to close ranks and sort this out internally? Do I need to write a check to someone?"

I feign a laugh. "Aren't you droll?" Then I turn serious again. "For real. Even though you act all innocent, you *love* to start shit. And telling Tessa, which could be admittedly funny on another occasion, is going to burn this thing down faster than either of us can imagine."

"That's where you're wrong," he says, pausing, daring to dream. "I *can* imagine it. It's glorious."

Tessa finding out about Oliver would be many things, but "glorious" is not quite how I'd phrase it. It is a much-lamented fact of Bernard-Sunderland lore that Tessa is our family's "narc," the permanent snitch, her presence denoted by the shadow of two tiny shoes under doorsteps. She obviously eavesdrops on everyone's conversations to store up secrets like a squirrel builds a rainy-day fund of downed chestnuts. But Tessa doesn't merely use her maliciously acquired gossip for blackmail and control; she uses it to start conflict that only *she* can solve, thus making her appear the indispensable hero to Benjamin and Kate. Honestly, I wouldn't be surprised if she took Kate's ashes just to make a point, to be able to blame us all for thoughtlessly forgetting our stepmother—*totally* overlooking the fact that someone might have remembered her, even sheltered her remains for safe keeping, had she not beat us all to the punch looking to score points.

"I need a drink," Paul says, shielding his eyes from the sun. "Like now." He swings his head, scans his eyes across the immediate horizon, and spots a submerged bar in the corner of the packed infinity pool. He makes a daring dash to the line, leaving me behind and cutting off several clusters of honeymooning couples and families waving to the kids they left in the shallow end. It's as if he's been stranded in Serengeti for days and needs to quench a dire thirst. He begins waving to get my attention and says: "What do you want?"

"Just get me whatever you're getting," I say, calling across from the other side of the pool.

"I'm getting *two* Aperol Spritzes," he says, approaching the front of the line.

"I'll just take one," I say, then cup my hand over my eyes and spot Tessa just a few feet from where Paul's standing. I don't have the heart to tell him before he's had a few sips from his cocktail to steel his nerves.

I watch him stagger over, drinking from a straw and holding my drink in the crook where his forearm meets his elbow. He hands me my drink and takes another sip of his, at which point, I tell him to look just a *slight* bit to the right of where he was just standing, and he says:

"Ah, fuck me."

One drink down and a brief straw transfer later, we approach Tessa reclined in a navy-striped lounge chair. She's wearing a floppy straw hat and dark Jackie O glasses—as if she just stepped off some Greek tycoon's yacht—while thumbing through *Swann's Way* by Marcel Proust. She instructs the nanny to reapply sunscreen to my niece and nephew, Meredith and Mason, without looking up from the book.

"Who the fuck reads Proust by a pool?" I ask, then quickly answer my own question, remembering Julian was just reading

Siddhartha. Although, he was likely searching for a clue to what awaited his mother in life after death. Tessa, on the other hand, is searching for an instruction manual on how to manage the collapse of the aristocracy, and to seamlessly navigate the smoldering ruins while maintaining your title and privileges—*after* your beloved mother leaves a videotape behind calling it all into question.

"Do you think she's *reading* it, though?" Paul asks, as we inch closer. "Or is it just another vacation status symbol? Like when she brought Dante to Florence and was reading it upside down because she didn't know it was in Italian."

I laugh at his truth—the first time I've smiled for the past three days—and we sit down on the empty lounge chair next to Tessa, who pretends not to see us. In the interest of not wasting any more time, I decide to sledgehammer through whatever ennui-drenched theme Tessa is going for, and rip off the Band-Aid:

"So, Dad lost Kate's ashes," I say. "Have you got them by any chance?"

Tessa lowers her sunglasses to the bridge of her nose. "*Lost* Kate?"

"Is there an echo?" Paul asks, getting drunker and more eager to move on. "That's what Liz said. *Lost. Kate.* You have my mother or not?" He looks around the pool like he's taking attendance. "You know what...where's Miles? He can answer questions without all this studied *ambience*." He starts losing it further, indulging in one of his favorite past times: mocking Tessa's pretensions. This is unlike Caroline, who mocks Tessa out of her own insecurities. "Proust?"

"Unfortunately," Tessa says, moving into lecture mode, "Miles can't be here until tomorrow. He's in the middle of managing a massive merger and couldn't get away." She takes a breath, waiting for the importance of her husband to register. "He's not like Nathan, you know. Miles can't just take a day off whenever he feels like it."

"Right," I say, shrugging off the Nathan insult for more fertile ground—like how strange it is that Miles would skip a second of saying goodbye to his mentor who just died, and who seemed to prize him above any of her own children. "If Miles missed a day, the firm would declare bankruptcy, and the dollar would lose all value."

"Fuck you, *Elizabeth*," Tessa says, flying off the handle in a way her supremely controlled facade will not allow. "Shut the fuck up."

"Jesus...I'm sorry," I say, feeling a little guilty that I pushed too hard on Miles's absence. I arrived on the island with a built-in support network of Nathan and the kids, and *usually* Paul. But Tessa is facing this alone, with no shoulder to lean on except for the nanny...who looks like she may throw Tessa in the pool at any second. "I didn't realize Miles not being here shook you so hard."

"I don't fucking care Miles isn't here," Tessa says, rising up in the lounge chair. "He's gone half the goddamn year, and it doesn't affect me. I'm pissed because Kate screwed me." She fully removes her sunglasses to stare me down. "She picked *you* to deliver her eulogy. *You.*"

Tessa's news takes me off guard, pulling the ground out beneath my feet. The mere thought of having to eulogize Kate renders my mind blank. But one nagging thought stays—why does Tessa know this before me? I wanted something from Kate all those days spent with her at the end. Anything that would make me feel like I mattered in her life. And the one thing she left me, Tessa got to know before me. Why didn't Kate ask while we sat in her quiet room? Why didn't she tell me she chose me? Why did she give this to Tessa? Before I can ask Tessa any of these questions, she gives voice to the words I can't find.

"*You*," Tessa repeats. Her tone is laced with venom. "I mean, that's *preposterous*. Insane. You have lived your whole fucking life in opposition to *everything* they wanted for you. I didn't. I did everything they wanted. Everything they asked. Including marrying *Miles*. And what do I get, Elizabeth? *What?* They owed me that. I worked my whole life to be able to be the one they picked when it *mattered.*" She gets up and starts to walk away from us, likely about to cry—something she refuses to do around people who try to love her.

I know Tessa has followed every one of Benjamin and Kate's orders; she's been their regime's loyal foot solider, ready to execute any task. But she forgot the golden rule. They know the one thing you want from them, and they will never give it to you. If they *did*, they would lose control—including the ability to play divide and conquer, to keep all the kids so busy fighting that we forget our parents are the ones who started it in the first place.

She turns back. "And *no*. I don't have Kate's ashes. I have no clue where they are. And right about now, I don't fucking *care.*" She stops, breathes in, and summons the oxygen to continue her tantrum. "I wish you luck with your eulogy, Elizabeth. But don't come crawling to me when you realize *I'm* the one who knew her better than anyone."

CHAPTER NINE

"HOW THE FUCK DO YOU sum up Kate in a simple eulogy?" I ask Paul, considering it took me countless years of therapy to gain a basic, microcosmic illumination into her, and even then, I barely breached the submerged iceberg before retreating from the process with the full support of my analyst, who seemed equally terrified to delve any deeper into my stepmother, as if he'd finally met his match, a person who can't be talked *through*.

"Better you than me," Paul says, smirking while we stand in line at yet *another* bar, this time next to the beach. After leaving Tessa, Paul and I had only one sibling left who might possibly have Kate's ashes—Caroline. We have been searching the resort property for the past forty-five minutes with no luck.

But behind the smirk, he's serious. He and Kate had a charitably complex relationship on their best day. Paul never got over, never recovered from, never made peace with his biological father leaving and *consciously* blamed Kate for the divorce, to the point he refused to bond with Benjamin out of spite toward his mother.

My eulogy-inflicted breakdown is interrupted by a ping on my iPhone. I check it to see what fresh hell is going to be delivered fiber-optically, and see a text from my father:

Have you found Kate yet?

I show the phone to Paul, desperate to recruit someone to share the stress of Benjamin's missive. "What do I say?"

Paul holds the screen close to his face, mulling it over for a minute. "Tell him *no*. We haven't found my mother. But we did find

Julian's kid. Tell him he's a grandfather again." He smiles, knowing how absolutely *fucked* we are. "Float it. Let's see how it plays."

In all fairness, I'm not sure it's playing any better with *me* than it would with Benjamin. And depending on his level of ignorance regarding Oliver, I'm willing to bet we likely have the same questions too. Like why would Julian deliberately hide him from all of us? I know better than anyone about the galactic push-pull of bringing children deep into the Bernard-Sunderland family. I even considered—and half the time still do *consider*—whether or not to pull Winnie and Theo out when I can feel their grandparents rubbing off on them, or when I hear things that could only have come from Benjamin and Kate shoot out of my children's mouths. But I still didn't, because as much as they drive me crazy, Benjamin and Kate have a right to know their grandchildren, and their grandchildren have a right to know them, to have the chance to make their own relationship—for better or worse—independent of my own feelings. And I'm forced to admit that my children gave me a chance to glimpse a side of my parents I would have never expected. And that canted angle, that possibly presumptuous prism through which I view Benjamin and Kate, is why I have held on to the fervent belief that there is something *more* for this family, a better future.

Personally, I would have loved to have known Oliver—my missing nephew—all these years. I would've loved to have babysat or bought birthday presents or been invited to parties. It's not in a family's nature to deny them parts of their own *families*. Even ours. And Julian hiding Oliver is the same pattern, the same selfish facet, the same self-destructive will for everyone to feel as miserable and betrayed as he does daily, imposed upon all of us, and most especially *his son*. Julian will never understand, and doesn't even seem to *care*, that there's as much pain in this world to equal and exceed his own. He seems compelled to hurt us all, as if we *still* don't know how much he hurts.

"Let's just concentrate on finding Caroline," I say. I point to his now refilled Aperol Spritz. "I think you have enough to continue on."

He takes a long sip and faces the beach before him. "You know what. This is bullshit." He stares straight ahead at the ribbon of blue without a termination point in any direction. "Julian's playing house. Tessa's laying out by the pool like she's on vacation. Benjamin's probably watching Satellite TV and drinking *alone*. And who knows where Caroline is?" He points to me. "And what are *we* doing? What we're *always* doing. Cleaning it up. The garbage people of this family who get treated like *garbage*." He holds his drink in one hand and rips off his flip-flops with the other. "Think about it. Benjamin's going to find out about Oliver. We know it. Kate definitely *knew it*. And Julian's still going to get less shit for hiding a kid than we do on any given Sunday." He sinks his toes into the pillowy grains. "I'm calling this for a hot second. We're going to put our feet in the ocean."

But before my toes have a chance to join Paul's in our mutual rebellion against our positions in the family, I hear a voice shout my name:

"*Lizzie!*"

I follow the sound and see Caroline standing under a burnt-orange straw umbrella, waving her arms and flagging me down. She's wearing a bikini that is stopping traffic and turning heads. Her exuberant method of grabbing my attention makes it extraordinarily difficult to pretend I don't see her, because even though she is our last stop on this morbid treasure hunt, I didn't imagine she'd be in such good spirits...particularly after trying to storm out of Benjamin's villa seconds after our dead stepmother's heartfelt plea that we all band together to save ourselves.

"*Lizzie!*" she continues. "*I know you see me.*"

Feeling caught, I raise my right hand, wave affirmatively, and begin walking to her. I notice a curious absence on my other side.

"Hey," Paul says, standing a few feet behind me and punching the screen on his phone like it personally wronged him. "I've got service, and I need to handle something that came up at work." He looks down again. "You've got this, right?"

I lift my Oliver Peoples and squint. "You know I have a business too."

"That's not a *business*," he says disparagingly, frustrated by whatever commercial carnage is befalling him back in DC. "It's a *store*."

A year after I opened Madeleine in Georgetown, Paul set out on his own venture a few blocks away called La Maison de Francois, an ornate, tony experience promising an immersion in the fineries of French cuisine. He worked like a man possessed, sleepless with purpose, spending months in France curating a menu, interviewing hundreds to select *just* the right chef, shipping all the ingredients back to DC, buying the furniture and décor from Parisian stores—including the linens, the dishes, the cutlery, the pots and pans—and even having a local designer make matchbooks rendering the Champs-Élysées in black and white with "La Maison de Francois" printed under the historic district. If I wanted Madeleine to feel like a cozy home, Paul wanted his restaurant to feel like you stepped off the streets of DC and into a slice of Paris, minus the rude waiters and the pervasive anti-American sentiment among the customers. But that was only the beginning of his seemingly unending stream of culinary triumphs, all of which made poor Madeleine appear like a small seafaring craft in the midst of a Bermuda Triangle sinkhole of millions of dollars I wasn't making.

"*Lizzie!*" I hear again, even louder. "*Are you coming?*"

The die is cast. I begin my slow journey to my sister, who is still windmilling her arms—as if to mockingly remind me that I'm trapped and about to be a captive audience to whatever salacious shenanigans she wants to parade before me, instead of actually *experiencing* how she feels about losing Kate. And unfortunately, from the looks of her current counterfeit happiness, it must be going very badly for Caroline.

"Lizzie," she says when I arrive, and points to a man in his early forties sitting next to her. "This is Sean." The man does not resemble one of Caroline's typical playmates. He looks sophisticated, classic, like he recently emerged from a Ralph Lauren store window slightly crossed with the ruggedness of Jon Hamm or Dermot Mulroney.

Sean rises from the cushioned lounge chair and offers me his hand, which I decline.

"*Really*, Caroline," I say, regretting that I didn't adopt Paul's method and skip the encounter altogether. "What? You see Kate's video and you pick up the first guy on the beach you see? When are you—"

"I didn't meet him on the *beach*," Caroline says, interrupting me and probably intuiting how I'm about to lecture her like I do Winnie and Theo. She isn't in the mood to be treated like a petulant teenager about to be embarrassed in front of her cool, new friend. "I met him on the plane." She could stop there—enough information, message received—but Caroline can never stop when it's *enough*. She has to continue her dedicated shock and awe campaign until nothing living survives.

"And I'm not upset over Kate's video anymore. People say weird shit when they're dying. It'll go like the rest of this family's plans...*nowhere*, but loudly."

I avert my eyes from Caroline's Cheshire grin and focus above me, on the rays of sun spread out in fiery points like blazing braids, then look down again, noticing Sean is still waiting for me to take his hand. I relent, impressed by his tenacity, his commitment to manners, and the slightly embarrassed look on his face, all of which tells me he finds this situation as uncomfortable as I do.

"Tell me you're at least not married," I say.

"I'm not," he says, with a slight hitch in his voice, piquing my curiosity. "I was supposed to be. But I'm not." His tone descends another octave. "This was supposed to be our honeymoon. I don't know why...but when she left me at the altar, I felt like I still needed to come here. That there had to be a lesson...likely an obscure one...in all the pain I was feeling."

"Sean," Caroline says, no doubt annoyed that his confession will only confirm my biases on her choices in men and in life, as well as her insistence on emotional aloofness—or as her psychiatrist says, "a state of self-willed unavailability."

"You really need to stop telling people that story," she continues. "It makes you sound like a loser. And it makes your trip sound a little...pathetic."

"I like to see things out," Sean says, remaining steadfast and honest in the face of Caroline's commitment to insincerity. "I don't close a chapter until it's done."

"I hate to break it you, but when she dumped you, that book closed."

"For her," Sean says, not moving an inch in his decision. "Not for me."

I find myself moved by Sean's mature relationship with grief, with his desire to plunge into finding an answer—one he might not even like—and come out on the other side of his tragedy a little wiser. I wish I could adopt some of his optimism about hurting and refuse to let all that suffering be for naught. In my experience, every time I've gone searching for what lurks behind the pain, for the first cut that initiated the wound, I've only found *more pain* waiting, tapping a Janus-faced watch, wondering what took me so long to get there.

Caroline leans in, close to my ear, and whispers, "We had a rendezvous in the plane bathroom." She pulls away. "You know what I mean?"

"Not for nothing," I say, ignoring Caroline and facing Sean, confused, trying to ascertain in a sober state just how he could contain such a profound contradiction in the center of his soul and not spontaneously combust, "but you don't seem like the kind of guy who wants to join the mile high club."

He's come to St. John on a vigil to mourn and excavate his past. But *on the way*, he decided to have sex with my sister in a plane bathroom. I'm not entirely sure how to make it all add up, but I'm pretty confident the end result would have to fall somewhere between Sean, in his grief, potentially helping Caroline realize the depth of her own. *Or* they end up forsaking that project, fucking for the next few days, and flaming out in a fiery mess before we step on the boat to spread Kate in the ocean.

"I'm not...not a very experienced single guy," he stammers, trying to dig himself out of the hole Caroline dropped him in. "I've never done it before." He laughs nervously, a staccato stutter denoting more fear than mirth. "I figured...*why not*." Suddenly he stops, removes his sunglasses, and studies my face. "I know you."

"I don't think so, Sean," I say, refusing to let him get away so easily. "I don't spend a lot of time in plane bathrooms."

"Madeleine," he says, snapping his fingers. "I stop there every morning on the way to the hospital. I see you behind the counter." He pauses, seeming almost hurt. "Do you not recognize me? I wave to you all the time. You wave back. Sometimes we even *chat*. You have kids. They drive you nuts. Your husband is a writer. He drives you nuts. You live in Foggy Bottom...." He stops again. "Nothing?"

"*Oh my god,*" I say, embarrassed that the familiar joviality Sean and I share almost daily—which has apparently *vanished* due to paranoia that Kate is going to open Pandora's box with barely a warning, the shock of meeting Oliver, not to mention Benjamin losing Kate's ashes to begin with—is the exact reason I opened Madeleine in the first place. I wanted my bakery to feel like your home away from home, *my home away from home*, a single nest, where I made the food people love when they need to feel loved the most. I wanted Madeleine to become the place everyone went for their firsts; the place you stopped in when you needed a home-made loaf of bread for the first big dinner you cooked for that date you were desperately trying to impress; the place you called to order your child's first birthday cake, which they would predictably smash; the place you bought your grandpa's favorite croissants or cupcakes before you met him in the park for a picnic.

I wanted Madeleine to be part of that memory.

As the saying goes: *food is love*. And my love is my food.

Even the store itself looks edible, like a slice of marzipan dropped onto the corner of Wisconsin Avenue, glazed by the cascading purple hyacinth vines dangling down the door, sprinkled with reflections from the magic lanterns hanging from hooks, and framed by the hand-painted *Madeleine* sign, crafted by Theo and Winnie seven years ago.

"You're a doctor," I say, wishing I was in the comfort of my bakery, flour in my hair, taking orders, running around wild, breathless, my feet aching. Madeleine is only a two-person operation run by me and my friend Camille, who I went to college with and needed something to do after a rather acrimonious divorce left her financially well-heeled but bereft of daytime activities. "A pediatric thoracic surgeon. You work at Children's National Hospital. Only like fifty people in the country do what you do."

Sean smiles, seeming glad my memory came back and I wasn't *another* unreciprocated relationship in his life. "You two are sisters?" He goes silent. "I'm so sorry. Then your stepmother passed away as well."

"Way to square that circle, Sean," Caroline says.

"Is *this*," he says, casually jerking his thumb toward my sister, "going to get me banned from the bakery? Because I don't think I can live without your frozen hot chocolate cupcakes."

I wish Sean hadn't mentioned Madeleine's signature cupcake, not today. That cupcake means more to me than chocolate and sugar. The desire for Madeleine to hold a special place in people's memories, the bearer of everyone's firsts, comes from wanting to enshrine a memory close to me. A memory involving the woman who became my stepmother—a shared memory embodied in Madeleine for both of us, a calling card for her to tell me it meant the same to her.

"Does she have my mother, Liz?" Paul says, awkwardly sprinting through the sand like he's fleeing an army of pharaoh's soldiers.

"Hi, Paul," Caroline says, waving, then turns to me. "He really shouldn't be sweating that much. Good thing we have a heart surgeon with us."

"I only operate on kids," Sean says. "I've told you that *every time* you make that joke."

Paul skids to a stop, spraying sand like rain. "Did you ask her?"

"No," I say, anticipating his reaction, which will be angry. "We didn't get to it yet."

"Caroline," Paul says, now breathing heavier from trying not to lose his temper at me too. "Do you have my mother's ashes?"

"Oh, yeah," she says casually, like it's no big thing. "I went back to Dad and Kate's apartment to get my Birkin bag for the trip, and I noticed Kate was just sitting there. Dad, Julian, and Tessa had already left. I figured the whole funeral thing might be tough without her." Her face freezes for a second in confusion. "Wait... did Dad just realize that?"

CHAPTER TEN

I FIND BENJAMIN NESTLED SNUGLY in the corner of his private infinity pool, arms stretched out, as if he was hugging his tropical kingdom sporadically laced in the fringy fingers of tamarind trees. He sips his gin and tonic and stares past me, toward a looming mountain with a blasted mossy face, taunting us with its enormity, each stone containing some memory inaccessible to any temporal path in our human possession. Above, the sky has turned metallic, swollen with cumulous clouds outstretched and bloated, pregnant with the possibility of rain, an event waiting to be born.

"Look at that sky, Elizabeth," my father says, pointing. "It's why my knee is killing me. If it would just rain, it would all be over. I wouldn't need to drive around in a golf cart to walk half a mile." He motions underwater to the controversial appendage under discussion. "It's bigger than it was two hours ago."

I make my way over to him in the deep end of the pool, ignoring his soliloquy on his old injury, the mystery box I know that will never open. "We found Kate's ashes."

"I figured you must have," Benjamin says, inscrutable. "You've been gone for two hours and ignored my texts, while I sat here panicking. Who the fuck had her?"

I kick off my sandals and sit down on the edge of the pool, sliding my feet into the water. "You might not believe it."

"I'm prone to believing whatever fantastical shit you have to share with me at this point," he says. "It's been that kind of week."

"Caroline," I say, repeating it again for emphasis, still shocked by that denouement. "*Caroline*."

Benjamin takes a long sip of his drink. "Of course. It would have to be her." Then he resumes his silence.

My father's words make me realize I shouldn't be surprised; in fact, Paul and I should have started our search with Caroline. I shouldn't have forgotten that when Benjamin makes a mistake, there is one person always there to point it out, to rub his face in the raw reality that he is not infallible. This person takes a certain glee in the fact that he left himself vulnerable to error, that his flank was exposed for an attack.

Caroline didn't bring Kate's ashes to be the savior, to ensure we have the most critical part of the whole reason we're all here. She brought Kate's ashes to make the point that Benjamin *didn't*. She doesn't care that her siblings would have been devastated, that all we want is to say goodbye to Kate. All she cares about is that in her imaginary game with our parents, she just put points on the scoreboard in her column.

She only cares that she won.

It's been like that as long as I can remember: from her childhood to her terrible teens, which were truly *terrible*; to getting kicked out of two Ivy League universities, saved only from a third expulsion by Benjamin and Kate's generous gift of a new library; and all the way up to and *beyond* Kate's surprise fifty-fifth birthday party, Caroline's high-water performance mark.

In typical Benjamin fashion, he spared no expense to mount the perfect evening at the Central Park Boathouse, a risky move from the start because Kate hated parties in general—let alone a surprise soiree. She hated to be the focus of attention, and was only comfortable with the spotlight turned on someone else while she controlled the beam.

As usual, I stood off to the side, joined by Nathan and Paul. We were each several drinks deep, not talking, but all meditating on the same subject: *Caroline was missing.* Each of us were silently imagining the inevitable fallout when Benjamin and Kate realized she wasn't there.

Except she was. We just hadn't recognized her.

I finally spotted her near a table, standing with Kate's clients, a tray of drinks in her hands, while she held court over a cohort of middle-aged men enjoying her company. My immediate thought was: *Kate's going to be thrilled. Caroline is finally taking initiative and networking.* Then my stomach sank when I connected the dots.

"I found Caroline," I said to Nathan and Paul, directing their eyeline across the room.

"The waitress?" Paul said. No doubt glimpsing how this night was going to end, and envisioning the emotional clean-up we were going to be in charge of handling, he snapped his fingers for more champagne to be delivered.

Nathan squinted, way behind Paul and me, absorbing the impact of Caroline's masquerade. "She's...she's wearing a tuxedo."

Suddenly, my father heard the roaring laughter coming from Kate's clients, tilted his neck in surprise that *anyone* could be having this much fun at one of their parties, and sought the source of the unwelcome levity.

The rest happened in slow motion.

He saw Caroline, sprinted over—Scotch in hand, the one big ice cube hitting up against the side of the glass like an errant boulder—and held my sister by the elbow.

She swatted his hand away and smiled at Kate's clients. "Don't make me drop drinks on Larry, Gene, and Luke." She took great pleasure in watching his blood pressure rise on the spot. "That would be embarrassing, Mr. Sunderland."

"I think we've sailed right passed embarrassing," Benjamin scowled.

Caroline let out a laugh, like a child caught. "Sailed. That's funny. Because we're right by the water."

His eyes were steely yet pleading. "Why would you do this to us?"

"Do *what?*" Caroline said innocently. "I'm working."

"*Working?*" He said, trying not to yell. "Here?"

"For two months," she said, enjoying the fruits of her epic plan. "The tips are fantastic."

"You've had a job here for two months?"

Then the intricacies of Caroline's plot struck him like a bolt. I watched his face as he struggled to process dedicating *eight weeks* to destroying his night. He'd always ignored her lack of ambition, tolerated her for remaining a teenager well beyond her actual age, while continuing to live off his largesse and offering nothing in return that would hint at a possible future. In Benjamin's calculations, Caroline was a write-off.

But this. This was a level of betrayal that outdid any of his wildest speculations of what Caroline was capable of.

"You mean, when I sent out the invitations to the party?"

Caroline didn't agree, but she also didn't disagree with his timeline.

"Why would you do this?" Benjamin asked again, still trying to make heads or tails of the surreal situation.

Caroline's face glowed. "I'm doing the same thing all the kids are tonight. Serving you. I'm just the only one being honest about it."

Except she wasn't being honest about any of our experiences outside of her own. Because Caroline inhabits a highly contentious universe of her own unique design that she willed into existence and is replete with her own pathologies.

"Fuck," Benjamin says, stretching his arm out of the pool to place his drink. "I'm never going to hear the end of this from her."

"Don't let her get to you," I say, trying to find some sympathy, some common ground with my new erstwhile ally, the only other signatory to Kate's grand plan. "It's not like you meant to leave them."

An unplanned shudder crosses Benjamin's face—then it hardens, reddens. "Of course...I mean, why the *hell* would I forget my wife's ashes, Elizabeth? Where did you even come up with an idea like that? That's fucking absurd."

"I never said you did." Although judging from his over-the-top reaction, maybe he did. Maybe he unconsciously left Kate's ashes behind in Manhattan to avoid facing the brute, unmovable fact of her death, that it is as certain and solid as the rocks he's staring at.

"Dad," I say, treading lightly and attempting to connect, to move beyond simple sympathy. It's a fraught activity at the best of times, like mixing up the red and green wires. "We all miss Kate. Everyone is handling her death differently. It's okay to let yourself just be *sad*. No one expects you to be okay. We need you not to be, in fact, so the rest of us feel a little more normal."

He wades through the pool to the stairs, languorously stirring the water, then walks out, grabbing a monogrammed towel resting on the lounge chair. "I'm fine, Elizabeth. I've had more time than any of you to imagine the inevitable." He wraps the towel around his waist. "And I don't need you to be my therapist. You run a fucking *bakery*."

I lift myself up from the edge of the pool and face him, not letting him bait me. I'm trying to be the bigger person, trying to remind myself I lost my stepmother, but he lost his wife. "Dad, denial is not going to help anyone. Least of all you. We can all get through this *together*." I'm desperate to make him understand that we need to break the curse of being atomized, isolated individuals, and risk falling together. "That was the whole point of Kate's video. It's the whole point of what I've been saying since you two got married. The only thing that can save us all is each other. And we can't save each other until we all *know* each other."

He waits for an eternity. A flock of birds soar above, migrating, while we stand like statues. "Do you think *knowing* more is what we need?" He removes the towel from his waist and drapes it on his shoulders, like a prize fighter entering the ring. He meets my eyes.

I'm saved from a *truly* unwanted glare-off with Benjamin—his preferred method of intimidation—by a notification on my phone. Assuming it's my husband, the interruption also makes me slightly annoyed that it's taken Nathan the better part of three hours to check in on my status. I plan on informing him that while he has been frolicking in the pool, or sunning on the beach—joined by the two loving children *I* gave him—that I have searched high and low for Kate's ashes and become an aunt again *unexpectedly*. I've also been assigned my stepmother's eulogy and am now currently waiting for Benjamin to burst a blood vessel, which is in the center of his forehead and throbbing like a control screen on the brink of nuclear disaster.

But I can't say any of these things. Because it is *not* Nathan. It *is*, however, a notification for our bank, politely alerting me that Kate Bernard has deposited five and a half *million* dollars into our account. There is, of course, no message attached. Just the money. A *lot* of money.

"What happened?" Benjamin says, noting the confused look on my face. Judging from his tone, he is *not* asking from genuine concern.

"Kate…" I say, hesitating, still trying to process both the size and the rationale of her unexpected gift. "Kate…deposited over five million dollars into my bank account."

He immediately grabs my phone from my hands and studies the screen. "That's impossible."

"I know it seems that way, Dad," I say. "She's dead, right? I mean, it's strange she can still be moving money around."

He begins waving my phone around in anger. "That's not how it fucking *seems*, Elizabeth. That's why you have wealth managers. To operate all your beyond-the-grave concerns."

His insult smacks me in the face. "I *do* know that. And give me back my phone."

He doesn't, and just continues haranguing. "This is not what Kate and I discussed. This is *not* the plan."

"It doesn't seem like much of anything is going to plan," I say innocently, trying to find common ground. "I *definitely* didn't get on the plane thinking Kate was going to make an attempt to save the family by airing all the problems that have kept us from being together. Life has a way of sneaking—"

He places my phone in the palm of my hand and clasps my fingers slowly around it. "Get the fuck out."

"Dad..."

"And you better not get used to that fucking money," he says, starting to walk inside and leaving me abandoned by the pool. "You turned it away *once* and you never get to have it again."

"Maybe," I say, starting to chase after him, "if you hadn't decided to enroll my kids at *Dalton*, I wouldn't have..."

He moves inside, and before he locks the glass door—another member of my family denying me access for the second time today, a cruel and undeniable metaphor for how they feel about me and what I want—says, in the same near growl:

"Dinner's at seven."

CHAPTER ELEVEN

"YOU'RE LATE," BENJAMIN SAYS, AS I wind around the tables of the waterfront restaurant, making my way to where he stands holding court over a table set for twelve, a lumbering leviathan with wooden legs. "For the second time today," he continues, rising from his chair, knee wobbling with effort. He sets down his Scotch and opens his arms again for his own idiosyncratic interpretation of a hug, not acknowledging our earlier argument, filing it away to be unearthed at the moment I least expect it, his usual modus operandi, the chaotic style of executive management he prefers. "Is there something I should know? You're always the first person at *everything*."

I hold off telling him that I'm late for dinner for the same reason I was late coming off the boat to the Eleusinian. I was throwing up. Violently. Almost near projectile. Starting from the moment I left his villa and walked into mine. Which is strange, because I haven't eaten all day except for a plastic-wrapped bagel and diminutive cream cheese on the plane ride over, and a single Aperol Spritz while out with Paul.

Once the nausea hit me, Nathan immediately came to my side, rubbed my head, and let my aching neck rest on his shoulder, while explaining to me how my throwing up had to be related to seeing my father, since it happened before I saw him and after spending a grand total of five minutes alone in his presence. He said it was probably anxiety and I was right to be feeling it. And on any other day, I'd agree with him. Many times my father has pushed the solidity of my stomach with a mere word, a mere shift in his vision, a mere shaking of his glass of Scotch in my direction. But this time I think it's Kate. In fact, I more than think—I know. I *know* when this feeling, this total existential unmooring happened, and why I haven't been able to hold anything down since.

It was two weeks before she passed away, the night before I had to go home to DC and attend the awards ceremony for Theo's senior class. He was slated to take home seven awards and sweep the board of possible honors, which he reminded me had been achieved without opening more than three of the assigned textbooks.

Kate and I were sitting in my old bedroom, now retrofitted with all the necessities for hospice care: machines that measured, beeped warnings, and fed out paper trails charting life signs, like stock market graphs that spiked or dipped with reckless abandon. IVs dripped, clogged, delivering medicine no longer attempting to keep Kate alive—merely comfortable until the inevitable. The night nurse would occasionally enter, check the machines, scribble a few notes on a clipboard, and then depart. It was a surreal feeling to be in the bedroom where you grew up now converted into the place where your stepmother was dying.

Kate was a translucent shell of the woman I had known. Gone was her powerful presence, the *looks* that could stop us kids in our tracks when she was angry, when she was disappointed, when she felt our potential risked being spoiled by lacking the adult foresight to see just *how* important it was that one of us played a particular sport, got a particular grade in a class, accepted an invitation to a dance with a classmate whose parent she was hoping to lure into a business relationship, or *declined* an invitation for a sleepover when the friend's parents just didn't measure up.

Gone were the reactions in her eyes, the coldness, or the occasional peek of warmth when she was pleased with you. Gone was her perfectly styled hair, the public *and* private face never without impeccable makeup, the designer clothes, the high heels she rarely removed before bed. In its place was a woman surviving by living through technology, a woman in a nightgown day in and day out, a stepmother barely able to complete a thought because the drugs were too strong, but the pain was too great to remain awake, which may have been the second most surreal part of sitting vigil by Kate's bedside. *Quiet.* She never treasured sleep. She barely even *slept*, viewing it as an imposition to all the herculean tasks before her that only she could execute. But now sleep was all she could do.

And in her endless rest, I found my thoughts affected by the quiet, found myself imagining how anything could possibly be the same once such a life force had been extinguished, snuffed out before her time—*she was barely sixty-five*. I felt almost mad at her for never stopping, and wondered if she had just toned things down *a little* maybe we could have had more time. In my heart I thought Kate was dying at sixty-five because she'd already lived two hundred years, and barely spent any of it with me.

And her endless rest was almost *cruel* at this point. It was the first time Kate had been forced by biology to pause, but we couldn't talk; we couldn't share memories; she couldn't impart words of wisdom that would carry me through when she was gone. She could barely form syllables.

To keep my mind from idling on another loss atop the *greatest* loss, I turned my eyes toward the digital picture frame on the table next to her bed, which cycled through a photo album my siblings and I had uploaded. Mason playing basketball; Meredith in a tutu at a ballet recital; Paul standing before the construction site of his new market; Julian in what appeared to be some kind of Central Asian bazaar; Caroline and her friends under the hot neon lights of a club opening; Tessa in a long black dress walking the steps to the Metropolitan Opera House; and Winnie and Theo fighting outside the Smithsonian. And I realized the true sadness of dying: there aren't any more *moments* to make outside the death itself. You are a true captive of time, and all you can obsess over are the things you haven't done, *can't do*, and will never do.

Then Kate squeezed my hand, as if she telepathically knew I was seconds from breaking down and wanted to bring me back to *this room*, this place, this time, the sole thing that mattered. "I'm going to make things right, Elizabeth." She struggled to keep her eyes open while she continued. "You'll *see*. I'm going to open your eyes." She tried to get out the next few words, switching to a whisper, a voice so soft it disappeared like leaves in the wind. But she couldn't find herself again. Her eyes shut, she returned to sleep, and she didn't speak to anyone again before she died, leaving me in a state of eternal mystery with an insoluble knot in my stomach.

"I couldn't find anything to wear, Dad," I say, realizing that *he* is joining me on this mystery, and ready to scream, before dinner even starts, an inauspicious sign.

"It's because you gained weight," he says triumphantly, like a comedian who started a joke ten minutes ago and finally dragged the audience to the punchline to massive applause. "I told you."

The second he lands his insult, I hear Winnie and Theo, *my* children, say, "Grandpa!" in unison, and rush over to embrace him. He takes them in his arms, holds them both close, and gives them the kind of hug I've waited over four decades to receive from him.

I walk over to the chair next to Benjamin, pull it out, sit down, and spot Paul across the table, who casually drops his menu and motions for me to take in the technicolor depression all around us.

I look around the table—a grim tableau. Tessa is micromanaging Mason and Meredith's dinner, reducing them to a binary choice between chicken fingers and grilled cheese; Julian, conspicuously *alone*, looking wan, waxen, and sweaty, scans and refreshes his phone nervously, likely wondering how long he can keep his Oliver-sized secret hidden; and Caroline is staring off at the bar, dreamy *and* annoyed, watching Sean sitting alone, reading a thick Russian novel with a very long title, sprinkled with words like "death," "despair," and "cancer."

"Hi, Auntie," Meredith says from down the table, her brown ringlets bouncing in the moonlight. She runs over, gives me a hug, and as I wrap my arms around her tiny frame, she attempts to whisper in my ear, but like with any eight-year-old, her words come out at full volume. "I miss Grandma."

Benjamin's attention is diverted from the menu to me. Meredith's raw, unprocessed sadness shakes him. "Everyone sit *down*," he barks out in response. "It's time to order."

Meredith runs back to her chair next to Tessa. The server arrives to take drink orders, and once my family has chosen their individual poisons, the chaos can resume. Benjamin doesn't care if the conversation devolves, but it must *devolve* after the boxes have been ticked and completed.

The waiter ricochets back and kneels next to my father. "Sir, is someone else joining you?"

"No," he says. "Why does it matter?"

"Then do you mind if I take the extra chair at the head?"

I look to the other end of the table, notice the empty chair that four months ago Kate would have been sitting in. *Twelve.* An oversight by Benjamin I'm sure, ingrained habit, but no less real for it. We are now a family of *eleven.* And being a family that prided itself on its size, on its every agglomeration, losing one person is antithetical to its very nature.

"If you don't mind," I say to the server, "would you leave it?"

"As you like," the server says, leaving Kate's chair in peace.

"Daddy..." Tessa uses that honey-tinged tone saved for when she wants something, interrupting the quiet moment I was sharing with Kate. "I just wanted you to know that Miles ready to serve as the new CEO of Kate's firm."

Hearing her personal dog whistle of Tessa's voice, Caroline retracts her attention from Sean and folds her hands into a cone to project her voice across the table. "That's so generous of Miles. I'm glad he can't make it to Kate's memorial on time, but he's ready to step up and run her business. And get a better title in the bargain."

"Daddy," Tessa implores again, transferring her anger over Caroline's unwelcome interruption into *more* saccharine. "Miles and I both want to try and take at least one thing off your plate. To give you just a little bit less to worry about."

"Just *stop*," Benjamin says, ignoring Tessa and looking around the table. He snaps his fingers for Caroline to pay attention. "I have an actual *serious* question to ask everyone." He pauses meaningfully, both to let the moment sink in and to make Tessa feel even *smaller*. "It's come to my attention that Elizabeth was the recipient of a large sum of money from Kate. Has anyone else at the table received any?"

Paul's face pops out from behind his menu. "Lizzie? You got money? Why didn't you tell me?"

"Dad," I say, turning my head to look at him. "I'm not sure this is an appropriate topic for a group discussion."

"I think it is," he says, thrilled with putting me on the spot, trying to turn my siblings further against me.

"I think it is *too*," Tessa says, following her pre-established pattern of behavior by immediately backing Benjamin.

"I agree," Julian says, and I throw a shocked glare in his direction. He's *seriously* going to gang up on me with everyone else when I know who he has stashed in his villa?

"What happened?" Caroline asks, not taking her eyes off Sean.

"How much money did you get?" Paul drops in, trying not to seem as outright aggressive as my other siblings but still trying to ferret out the information.

"It was nothing," I say, trying to shut this conversation down.

"Oh, it wasn't *nothing*," Benjamin says. "It was over five million dollars."

Everyone at the table looks ready to either spill their drink, fall off their chair, or turn me upside down to try and shake the five million out of my pockets.

"Can I have some?" Winnie says, shifting her attention for the first time this evening from my father to me.

"No," Benjamin says sternly to Winnie. "Your mother is giving that back."

"What about," Paul says, daring to get between Benjamin and his money, "if you give us *all* five million dollars, so Lizzie doesn't feel so alone. I mean...I'm sure my mother left something for all of us and Lizzie's just came through first."

"No," Benjamin says. "Lizzie won't feel alone when I have it back. Because *none* of you are getting any extra money. Everything that was Kate's is now mine. That's what we decided. And upon my death—which should be noted, won't be happening anytime soon—you will all receive the entire inheritance split into *five*."

"Wait," Paul says, clearly upset. "*Wait*. She's *our* mother. Mine. I'm her son. I mean, no offense to your kids Benjamin, but me... and Julian, we should get something now. Not have to wait until *you* die. You're not my father."

Paul's words visibly cut through Benjamin, like an unexpected knife in the back. Even I can't help but wince on his behalf—considering he's spent the last thirty-three years trying to convince Paul he's a reasonable, viable *father*. Meanwhile, he's made not one corresponding overture in my direction, relegating me to the status of just an afterthought that will always linger.

"Paul isn't wrong," Julian says, backing his older brother because he, *too*, needs the money. Or perhaps this is mutual fraternal backscratching so that Paul doesn't spill about the little visitor back at the villa. "It's not fair that our mother dies, and *we* have to wait. For Christ's sake, Benjamin, don't you think we've earned it? I mean, do you...does anyone here need to be reminded that she wasn't exactly a loving person? That maybe Paul and I deserve a little something for what we missed?"

Both Julian's and Paul's reactions fill me with dread, fulfilling Nathan's prophetic words on the boat when he said without Kate's velvet glove, the family would dissolve into an internecine civil war, and that Benjamin would attempt to hold it together with money.

"I'll just give the goddamn money back," I say, desperate, not wanting to watch everything fall apart or risk losing my brothers. "I don't want it."

"You *should* have it," Paul says. "You were the only one who was there with her when she was sick. But so should Julian and I."

"Paul," Benjamin says, folding his hands atop one another as if preparing to dive in. "You own several businesses. You're opening a multi-million-dollar market, the real estate of which is incredibly valuable itself. You have quite an ample trust fund." His eyes focus like lasers. "What more do you *need*?"

"You're a funny one to ask that question," Paul ricochets back. "What more do *you* need? You're insultingly rich. And you just added my mother's insult onto your *own*. What is wrong with you two? How much do you need to accumulate to forget she's dead? I mean...what the fuck are you going to even do with all of it?"

The answer is there will *never* be *enough*. Benjamin will continue to accumulate wealth, to break down barriers, to "progress" toward an invisible goal guaranteed to hurt the world until he dies. In the Bernard-Sunderland social circle, and in every article written by an economist looking toward better days of rampant *stimulation* to rescue a stalled country in so many ways, the great wealth transfer is a much-discussed and frequently bemoaned topic. *What is taking so long*? When are all the copies of Benjamin and Kate going to pass down their sacred fortunes to their carbon copies of children to carry on the torch of family legacy?

However, from my perspective, I don't believe it will ever happen. Benjamin and Kate, like the rest of their ilk, *have* to hold their money close to the chest. *First,* to continue to rule over their fracturing families with a green fist, and *second,* because of their innate—and real—fear about what their progeny will do with their money when they're not looking. My father knows. We won't continue to ruthlessly expand. At least not me. If the much-ballyhooed transfer is permanent, I will use the money to fix, to care for, the world they broke—to give Winnie and Theo and *their children* a fighting chance. I will try, with whatever means are at my disposal, to push for a greener planet, for a sky that still has visible stars, for streets that aren't paved with desperate people long forgotten by the state Benjamin and Kate stripped for tax purposes. I'd use the money for *food,* for everyone to have something as simple as a fucking *meal,* which is apparently impossible in the wealthiest country in the world.

But he'll never do it. Benjamin will *grip* that money harder with each passing year, will freeze it all into some untouchable trust, because granting us access to it would mean admitting they made mistakes that need to be *corrected,* that this is the world they granted us.

"What the fuck are *you* going to do with all of it?" Benjamin retorts back, proving my point.

Suddenly I hear Tessa, who has been curiously quiet for almost the entirety of the discussion, clear her throat, deciding to make her presence known. "I think I have an idea of what Paul plans to do with *all* of it."

I look over to Paul, whose eyes register bafflement, quickly followed by *fear.* Then I look to Tessa, who is looking down at her phone and begins reading from it in a practiced, studied tone, as if she'd spent the night trying to decide which emotion to lead with, settling on a highfalutin author reading from a terribly serious tome.

"This is from a Twitter account called Washingtonian Probs that got the scoop from an article about to appear tomorrow morning in the *Post*." She pauses again, working the drama, the crowd. "Paul Bernard, the famed local celebrity restauranteur, may have *overshot* in his latest project. It's rumored the trailblazing entrepreneur, who has dedicated his career to bringing the fineries of European cuisine to our city, culminating in his ambitious market currently being erected at the Wharf, is days away from being bankrupt, the dream plunged into insolvency...." She stops and hands the phone to my father, who is signaling for the waiter to bring him another Scotch.

"I don't need to read the rest," Benjamin says, swatting the phone away. "I've got a pretty good idea it doesn't get *better*." He turns his attention to Paul. "Does it?"

"It's just a rumor being spread by a competitor," Paul says, brushing it off and looking to me for help, but honestly, I'm as shocked as everyone else. It just doesn't seem *possible*. How could Paul have possibly made a mistake. He *never* makes mistakes. I do. That's the dialectic of our relationship. "I outbid him for the property, and he's trying to ruin me in the press to come in and get it at his price." He attempts to appeal to Benjamin, the *businessman*. "You know how these things go."

"I actually don't, Paul," he replies. "I've never had any articles in the paper about how I'm teetering on the edge of financial ruin. And none of my competitors would have the unmitigated fucking *gall* to write it. And I'm dealing with billions of fucking dollars. High stakes. And you're importing cheese into a brick treehouse." He runs his hand through his hair. "I never knew the restaurant business could be quite so brutal."

"It's not," Paul says. "And nothing's wrong. It's just to smear me."

"I don't know, Paul," Tessa says, looking around the table, gauging reactions, and rounding in for her triumph. "They've got *quotes* from people in your 'inner circle,' 'friends,' and 'vendors.'"

"Shut the fuck up, Tessa," I say, trying to help Paul by using the only avenue currently open—the habitual one, yelling at Tessa. That's an activity *everyone* gets behind. "Or at least try and hide how happy you are."

I turn to my father, who has now turned maudlin, the sarcastic rage being sucked from his face and replaced with a deep sadness. "I'm glad your mother isn't here to see this. I only wish someone had known this was going to be printed sooner. I could've had it squashed. But now…now it's *too late*. The Bernard-Sunderlands are just going to have to bear this failure like we've borne all the others."

"You want to talk about bearing failure," Paul says, rising to his feet and throwing his napkin on the table. "You're such a disaster of a parent, you don't know you have a grandchild."

On instinct, I get up with Paul, throwing my napkin on the table to match his. "*Paul.* Shut up. Do not fucking do this."

And while Paul and I glare at each other, we both notice Julian attempting to pull one of his patented sneak-offs while no one's looking.

"Julian has a kid," Paul says, looking straight into my father's eyes. "His name is Oliver. I have no idea how old he is, but he's here and you can meet him."

Then Benjamin rises from the table, joins Paul and I in throwing down his napkin, points at Julian, and bellows across the length of the restaurant: "Do you have a goddamn kid? Who is currently on the *island*?"

Julian looks back, meditates on answering, and instead of speaking, doubles down on running away.

CHAPTER TWELVE

BENJAMIN APPEARS STUNNED THAT JULIAN had the audacity to run away. No one leaves my father until they are summarily dismissed, and no one leaves dinner especially. He fixates on the nine faces in his immediate view, dismisses us as mere noise among the signal of Julian's betrayal, then looks down at his knee, which is obviously still hurting him, and begins going through a brisk pace of mental math, adding up the risk versus reward like he weighs every decision in his life. Apparently, the risk is worth it, and he takes off in an all-out near-seventy-year-old sprint, slightly hobbled, really working the arms, intent to persevere.

"Is he going to make it?" Caroline asks, watching our father blaze a trail from the restaurant into the resort. "I don't think I can bury both of them on one trip."

In my opinion, ignoring nearly everything Caroline says is just good protocol, so I turn my head in silent protest and realize the entire restaurant is staring at us. Our server is en route to inspect the unraveling situation. Seconds later, he arrives on scene bearing a solicitous smile. "Was everything not to your liking?"

"Oh no," Paul says, before I can answer. "Just put whatever we ordered on Benjamin Sunderland's room and tip yourself forty percent for the trauma that we all endure for *free*."

"That's very generous," the server says, leaving us almost as quickly as my father.

"Shouldn't we go after Dad?" Tessa asks no one in particular, still seated and sipping her wine.

"Shouldn't we go *after him*, Mom?" Winnie says, seizing on her aunt's dampened enthusiasm. "Because this is going to be *awesome*."

"Yeah," Theo says, chiming in. "I've never seen Grandpa that angry. I've never seen him *run*."

I feel Nathan's hands around my waist, his head leaning in close to mine, and a small hot whisper in my ear. "Yugoslavia, Liz. Yugoslavia."

Before I get a chance to end his gloating, I see the entire table—including Paul—has left and are following my children, who are leading the way to witness the impending blowout at Julian's villa... coincidentally located next to mine.

"What do you think?" Nathan says. "Should we go see the fireworks?"

"You know what," I say. "I'm going back to our room. Maybe I'll take a bath. Maybe I'll just go to bed. I don't know yet. But what I do know is I've had enough of *that* man and my siblings until morning."

Fifteen minutes later, I'm seated on the corner of the couch, flipping through the in-room dining menu—deciding whether I want to order *two* meals—when I hear Benjamin's voice piercing through the closed terrace door, echoing throughout the room and ricocheting off any inch of bare space.

"Everyone get the fuck out of here," he says, followed by a slight breathy pause, presumably from all the running. "Except *you*. You hear me, Julian."

I wait a minute before recommitting myself to choosing a dessert, and the world falls silent again, which it so rarely—*if ever*—does when my family is in the vicinity. I begin to allow my mind to empty, to decompress, to risk thinking of absolutely nothing for just a few spare seconds. I find my breath. I hear my elevated heartbeat. I risk inner peace, feeling the first waves of exhaustion wafting across my body. My eyes begin to close.

Until the door flies open and eight bodies storm through. They enter like the circus, barely even notice me sitting there, and stream out to the terrace so they can eavesdrop on the fight between Julian and my father being played out at maximum volume.

"Holy shit," I hear Winnie say, audibly excited. She's a loud teenager with a hot piece of gossip. "I can't believe Grandpa just said Uncle Julian killed Grandma *twice*."

"Ice cold," Nathan says, amplifying our daughter's sentiment.

I'm not getting up. I'm not participating in this. Outside of turning Benjamin's actually legitimate sorrow and Julian's actually legitimate misgivings of my father's parenting into a sideshow, I have a pretty good idea of how this is going to work out for all involved. My siblings seem to have forgotten the golden rule of growing up in the Bernard-Sunderland home. Benjamin hears *everything*.

I hear the side door from Julian's terrace ripped open. I hear heavy footsteps, followed by Benjamin's voice. This time, it's not directed at Julian.

"All of you get *inside!*" he shouts at the crowd on my terrace. "This is between Julian and me. If I wanted you to be a part of it, I wouldn't have kicked you all out."

After that, eight sets of footsteps stream in from the terrace. Their excitement is gone; the king has issued his decree to disperse, and everyone feels suitably chastised for indulging his finite patience.

Paul sits down next to me on the couch, and Caroline joins him, insisting we both shove over so she has more space. Tessa plops down in front of the television with Mason and Meredith, switching off my dining menu and flipping around until they find some suitable children's programming. And Nathan follows the kids off to their rooms, leaving me stranded, lacking a buffer, and alone with my siblings. *Again.*

"Don't talk to me," Paul says to the back of Tessa's head, ready to start the second round.

"I'm not talking to you," she says, refusing to turn and engage. She keeps her eyes glued to the television.

"Why do you always pull this kind of shit?" he asks. "I know you're unhappy. *Everyone* knows you're unhappy. But do you have to cause so much unhappiness to others?"

"But I thought it wasn't true," Tessa says, deciding to turn around. "If the article is nothing but malicious rumor and gossip, why would it be making you unhappy?"

"Because my fucking mother died," he says, looking at me in disbelief. "And I'm here…we're all here…to bury her. And even then, you can't stop trying to get one up on everyone. She's *dead*, Tessa. You can't make any of us look bad in front of her anymore."

"Whatever, Paul," Tessa says. "You can try and cover it all up however you want. But trust me. It will eventually come out."

"That's not entirely true," Caroline says, popping in. "Remember when I stole our neighbor's car and drove it to the Hamptons and spun out on someone's lawn? Dad and Kate kept that off *Page Six*, and they were fucking ready to print that." She puts her hand on Paul's knee, trying to comfort him—an emotion she is only able to access when someone has seemingly joined her in bringing shame to the family. "Benjamin's just upset. I'm sure when he finishes up with Julian, he'll be on the phone with his people at *WaPo*, and it'll never run."

"And even if it does run," I say, building off Caroline's unexpected interjection and affection, "no one will care. It's DC. Our media is nothing but gossip and failure on a grand scale. It won't even be a blip on the radar."

"Even if it doesn't run," Tessa says, refusing to listen to her sisters, "you're still bankrupt, Paul."

Paul grabs my arm, putting all his weight and rage on my shoulder.

"Cut the shit, Tess," I say, both to make her stop and for Paul to let go. "Paul's not bankrupt. It isn't even possible."

And it really isn't. All the rave reviews, the packed tables, and the breathless entreaties from the parents at Theo and Winnie's school to get them weekend reservations. That doesn't logically lead to someone being *bankrupt*.

If I'm honest about it, Paul's skyrocketing and perpetual success kind of makes me jealous. His first restaurant, La Maison de Francois, was such an overnight hit that it allowed him to open a second location in Adams Morgan, where he was hoping to attract a slightly younger, hipper audience: ultra-liberal couples looking for a date spot among their own kind. And it worked again, giving him the confidence and the bankroll to start his *third* business, a creperie in Dupont Circle. All of which were merely a warm-up, a testing ground for his titanic undertaking, the one that would make him DC restaurant royalty, turning empty space at the Wharf into a French market that would potentially outdo *Paris* in its variety and sophistication.

"Mother," I hear Theo say, as he bursts into the room and sees me on the couch. "Your phone keeps ringing." It takes a few seconds to register he's calling me, either from extreme hunger or from how scrolling through Paul's greatest business hits has made me and Madeleine seem positively miniscule in comparison. "*Your phone keeps ringing.*" He walks over to the couch and puts it in my hands. "Why do you not carry it with you at all times?"

"Because she isn't seventeen," Paul says. "Try and be nicer to your mother. Take the *risk.*"

"Because I was charging it, Theo," I say, to which he responds by walking away.

I look at the screen, see the seven missed calls from Camille, note that it's 8:00 p.m. in DC, and come to the rapid panicked conclusion that Madeleine burned down. Camille knows how rough

St. John was going to be for me and wouldn't randomly cluster communicate without an urgent reason.

Before I can call her back, Winnie runs down the stairs in a highly adrenalized state, jumping up and down, her pink iPhone with the shattered screen over her head.

"Mom. Mother. Momma." She fans herself in excitement. "*Elizabeth*. Put down the phone!"

"Winnie," I say, distracted. "Can this wait? I'm calling Camille."

"*Mother*," Winnie says again, getting more agitated. "I'm going to hurl this phone at you if you don't pay attention to me."

"*Winnifred…*"

"*Elizabeth*," she says, waving her phone in my face. "The fucking president came to Madeleine this afternoon. It's all over Instagram and TikTok."

She holds the phone steady so I can see the image. "Look at him," Winnie says. "He's holding a frozen hot chocolate cupcake and smiling. He never looks this happy."

"What?" I say, still in a fog. "*Who?* You mean, the president of the United States?"

"No, Lizzie," Caroline says, starting to scroll through her own social media. "The president of Nicaragua. He's in town for peace talks and got hungry."

Paul drops his phone, which is cued up to Instagram, on my lap. "She's not kidding, Liz."

I pick up his phone and stare at the post in disbelief.

The president, first lady, and their two granddaughters—Daphne and Natalie—are standing outside Madeleine, framed by the hand-painted sign, and holding up their sweets, smiling, ready to enjoy. Below the picture is a message from the president—or whoever handles his social media:

"My first taste of Daphne and Natalie's favorite DC bakery. I'm already in love with Madeleine. #EatLocal #ShopDC"

"Holy shit, Mom," Winnie says, her fingers furiously typing. "I'm going to be so popular."

"You live on social media," Paul says to Winnie. "How did you not see this before?"

Winnie rolls her eyes. "I don't follow Mom's account. My friends sent it to me."

Belatedly, Nathan, wearing pajamas and flip-flops, nearly tumbles down the steps holding his own phone, yelling out: "Oh my god!" He trips on the third step down, shocked, and almost tumbles the rest of the way down. "Holy shit, Liz. I'm glad I voted for him."

"Everyone *stop*," I say, reeling, floating. "I've got to call Camille."

I take my phone, get up, and walk out onto the terrace so I can be alone to call Camille, who answers on the first ring, breathless with excitement. She fills me in on the eventful day without stopping.

Madeleine had to stay open for an extra two hours to serve everyone in the line stretching down Wisconsin Avenue. The White House is holding an event to promote local DC businesses and wants us to make cupcakes and cookies for the day. We've sold out of everything—breads, muffins, cookies, croissants, cakes, brownies. Madeleine is empty. And by the time she finishes, I'm breathless as well.

"*Lizzie*," she says. "I didn't even get to the most incredible part. *Washingtonian* magazine wants to do a profile on you and Paul when you get back. The two foodie Washington power siblings. Madeleine's going to be famous. This is going to be..."

"This is a lot to process," I say, my anxiety rising. "I don't even know where to start."

"Let's start with...this is amazing."

"Alright," I say. I move into the corner, seeking shelter as if I'm trying to hide from a world to which I feel overexposed. "Do you need me to do anything?"

"No," she says. "Just enjoy it. I'm going to call the social secretaries at the White House and figure out the dates they need us. And then hire us a few extra hands…. We're going to be baking for over a thousand people."

One thousand people. My goal when I opened the bakery wasn't to have the head of the free world come in and turn my business into an overnight success. And I'm not *actually* jealous enough of Paul's multiple venues to make it come true.

Suddenly, Camille's voice drops out, leaving only silence. I stare down at my phone, registering the failed call on the screen.

I look across the water and see a lone sailboat anchored in the inlet, masts buffeted by wind and fate. I feel as alone as that vessel. Kate should be with me to share this news. She's the whole reason I opened Madeleine, and maybe the president lovingly holding up the cupcake I made for her would have finally forced her to take notice.

I emerge from the corner, cross through the door, enter back into the living room, and everyone except for my own family is gone. Nathan, Theo, and Winnie are waiting for me, still bouncing up and down and screaming, waiting to celebrate. This leads me to the undeniable conclusion that *no one* except for my husband and children are happy for me. My siblings are judging POTUS's surprise visit to Madeleine as ambiguous at best, and at worst, terrible for all of them. This is the typical response to any good news that comes my way in the Bernard-Sunderland family. When anyone else achieves anything, the most minimal achievement—a feat barely deserving of the term *success*—everyone must stop to celebrate it. But when I am singled out, when I am the focus, it's ignored. Or even worse…instantly belittled.

The president visiting Madeleine was never supposed to be in the cards. In fact, if you asked Benjamin and Kate, Madeleine shouldn't have survived long enough for the leader of the free world to pop in for a cupcake. My siblings' reaction to tonight's news reminds me of when I decided to tell my parents about my plans to go into business and open a bakery. I spent days crafting cupcakes, filling pies, baking bread, and decorating a towering wedding cake, all to give them a sample of the opening day menu at Madeleine.

Breaking any news to Benjamin and Kate—regardless of whether it trended good or bad—was always fraught with anxiety. So I recruited Paul for moral support and waited until several rounds of drinks were cycled through before Nathan and I carried out the plethora of desserts.

As I placed each item on the table, Winnie held up the sign she made with the store logo, tapped on her glass to get everyone's attention, and cued me to begin my speech.

"I have some exciting news to share," I started, shaky, still searching for my sea legs. "I'm opening a bakery. We have the spot picked out. And I wanted everyone at this table to be the first to know—"

"For what it's worth, having worked in hospitality, anything involving food is a tremendous financial risk," Paul said, sidelining me immediately, much to my shock and horror with his curious deployment of *moral support*. "And the reward—if any—is small."

"Elizabeth, you've got a good job with security," Benjamin said, building off Paul's unexpected lead. "Baking is a hobby. It doesn't pay the bills."

"Nathan pays the bills," Paul said, momentarily distracting me from Benjamin's dismissal of how hard I'd worked to put both a business plan and this announcement together. I wanted to break in, to remind him his own career wasn't worth bragging about—he was a "marketing director" at Marriott—and that all the vestiges of his much-vaunted success were paid for by our parents.

"Lizzie supported me with my dream when it seemed impossible," Nathan said, interceding on my behalf before I could engage with my stepbrother.

"I'm still not sure it is *possible*," Benjamin said, redirecting his ire toward Nathan. "You sold a few scripts. You're not exactly Steven Spielberg."

"He's not a writer," Nathan corrects, quietly fuming. "He's a director."

"They aren't wrong, Lizzie," Kate chimed in—*last*—her preferred position, giving her time to properly assess her route of attack. "It's not as if Nathan's in a secure enough industry for your family to take on that kind of risk."

"Do you have any idea what the competition is like for artisanal businesses in DC?" Paul said.

"And you *do*?" I said, finally having enough of his snark, which was usually directed at others. I was seeing a side of Paul I hadn't since we were kids and wondered why. Why would me opening a bakery upset him so much, to such a degree he would side with Benjamin and Kate?

"How do you plan to differentiate yourself from the competition?" Paul questions.

"You know what, Lizzie," Benjamin said, the designated peace-broker. "You should sit down with Paul and develop a business plan. This is what he does for a living."

"My business plan would be *don't do it*," Paul said, considering his nasty work finished.

A year later, Paul's inexplicable anger made *a lot* more sense when he set out on his own business venture, opening La Maison de Francois. And to no one's surprise, Benjamin and Kate were his biggest investors.

The memory of that night makes me even more exhausted than the entire day on St. John. I accept a flurry of hugs from Nathan and the kids, then tell them I'm exhausted and need to lay down, and that we can continue celebrating tomorrow.

CHAPTER THIRTEEN

Day Two

MY EYES OPEN WARILY, PROBING, and I'm unsure whether or not I'm still dreaming. I blink my lids until the contours of the bedroom come into focus. The island light streams through the windows, wrapped in gauzy white curtains that seem to be as sleepy and confused as me, letting themselves be dragged around by the breeze. My stomach is still queasy, unsettled, meaning I'm definitely not still asleep. If this were a fantasy, I'd feel better.

I reach for my phone on the nightstand, scrolling up on the photo of Theo and Winnie, and see that it's 10:00 a.m. I've slept close to thirteen hours, something I haven't done since before Theo was born and the days were still allowed to be lazy.

"Morning, sleepyhead," Nathan says. "I never thought the day would come when I'm awake before you and it's not because I have stayed up all night writing."

Maybe this is a dream after all.

But that illusion quickly fades when I look over and see Nathan's MacBook screen playing his latest movie, a Netflix sci-fi extravaganza that he was the sixth writer on and accepted significant compensation for instead of credit.

"They fucked it up," he says, sensing that since I'm awake it's time to start complaining. "I swear. I'd sacrifice all the money for *something* I write to turn out how I originally intended. The blood money I get in return for killing my work isn't cutting it anymore."

Clearly the news of my bakery has stirred up feelings about Nathan's own dreams. Not that Nathan needed any prompting to lament his career. Our status quo setting lately, and in increasing frequency, is Nathan complaining about his work. How he has been rendered a hack by his own talent for writing drama. He sees it as a double-edged sword, a curse laid upon his head, meaning I find myself in a sticky situation. If I don't answer him, he won't stop. And if I do answer him, it will open the door for *more*. I attempt a bold synthesis, a middle course, and just make an agreeable sound. "Hmmm."

"I'm going to quit," he says, more an existential mantra at this point than any kind of actual threat. If he did intend to *quit*, he would have made good on one of the six hundred other times he's mentioned it.

"You've hated everything you've written since the first screenplay you sold," I say. This is my role in the process, since everything related to Nathan is a *process*—from writing, to marriage, to raising Theo and Winnie, to dog owning, to operating technology—and much like with his art, there are no guarantees his life process will bear fruit.

"I didn't hate that one," Nathan says appalled. "I hated what *they* did to it. Once you cash that check, they own your soul. There's no going back once you take the easy way out and stop fighting for what you believe in. I think I was too tired, too scared to believe in myself and just say *no*."

I hear a sustained knock at the front door, usually an auspicious sign back home meaning a *friend* or one of the kid's *friends* have come to visit. But in St. John, that is not the case. And no matter how eager I am to escape Nathan's career crisis, I'm relatively sure I'd prefer it to whatever family member is anxious to come inside.

I turn to Nathan to see if he has any intention of going downstairs and answering the door, but he's popped his AirPods back in and has resumed angrily grumbling at his screen, presumably having restarted his movie. I get out of bed, wipe the sleep out of my eyes, tie my hair into a messy ponytail with a scrunchie on the nightstand, and valiantly attempt to put myself together, with success eluding me.

I walk slowly down the steps, dragging my feet, holding out hope that if I tarry long enough, whatever family member is on the other side of the door may assume we aren't home and take their crazy elsewhere.

I hear another knock—this time with a bit more force, begging to be heard—and can't shake the feeling it is Benjamin, the man who exists in a constant raging battle against "no."

I flip the lock, open the door, and feel all the blood fall from my face.

A woman who is the spitting image of Kate on her wedding day stands before me. The pale red hair, the near-translucent skin, the same freckles dotting the bridge of her nose, the same wispy frame… The only noticeable difference is the inside of her wrist, which is marked by a black Ankh tattoo. I suddenly fear I'm about to find out about a sibling who has remained a mystery, some further deviation from logic when it comes to our genealogy—aren't we already blended *enough*—that Kate's doppelganger may be one of the hidden secrets her video alluded to. Does this person hold the key to unlocking thirty-three years of Benjamin and Kate locking down their pasts under three tons of concrete? Because, except for the ink and the kind of earthy-crunching vibe she's giving off, this stranger is truly the spitting image of a younger Kate.

"You're Lizzie, right?"

I find it difficult to remember who I am, to not answer her question by calling her *Kate*, so I just nod a few times in the affirmative.

"I'm Persephone," she says, friendly, warm, and engaging, as if she's softening me up for the big blow. Maybe she's about to tell me she's our long-lost sister, and this trip is about to fully hit the side of the mountain. "I'm Julian's partner."

I nod again. Thankfully, my assumption is wrong. But I'm straining to get past one *small thing*. For whether one wants to wax overly Freudian about how we choose our mates, it can't be denied that parents seed the ground for a potential spouse. If you had a "happy childhood," you tend to search for your family's corresponding attributes in your partner; however, if your formative years were "unhappy," chances are you'll boomerang in the opposite direction, holding out hope that emotional fulfillment lies on distant shores. And if you avoid investigating the oedipal issue, you'll probably stay single forever, or turn to spirit-numbing bouts of meaningless sex, palliative narcotics, and liters of alcohol...which upon further reflection, may be the least painful and psychically taxing option.

Julian's solution to our childhood was to split the difference: to keep Kate's outer shell, but replace the cold, utilitarian, capitalist core with your average progressive. "I'm also Oliver's mom," she adds, interrupting my thoughts.

"Right," I say, adding actual words to my effusive gestures. "Oliver's adorable."

"Yes, he is," Persephone says evenly. "Would you mind if I come in?"

I don't explicitly invite her in—not out of rudeness but because I still can't get over her resemblance to Kate.

"Julian's told me a lot about you," Persephone says, once again, *evenly*, which is sort of disconcerting coming from a family where the only words said casually tend to be threats, while everything else is screamed. "He told me you're the only sane one in this group. The only one who cared when he was in trouble." She wanders around the living room, looking at objects and touching them, as if trying to decide if they need to be cleansed or blessed. "I figured I should come and talk to you since I think he's in trouble again."

My heart sinks. "Is he using again?"

She doesn't directly answer my question. "All this stress isn't good for him." She stretches her arms above her head. "It isn't good for me either." She works the tension out of her neck and shoulders. "I'm so stiff." Then she stops moving and meets my eyes. "Do you want to do yoga with me? There's an eleven o'clock class on the beach. I was hoping we could get to know each other a little better."

I want to decline, want to counteroffer that we sit by the pool on my terrace and sip iced coffee—while we get to know one another and she fills me in on Julian's troubles. But Persephone came to me asking for help, and if that requires me to have this conversation in downward dog, then so be it. My refusal would be entirely antithetical to the point of this trip, to Kate's final wishes. Sure, it seems strange that anyone would want to have an intimate conversation about their partner's troubles while sweating and stretching, until I remember *this* is the woman Julian chose. It's in keeping with my brother that she'd want to find our root chakra together as an opening bonding activity.

"Sure," I say, dreading this before the words finish passing through my lips. "I'll go to yoga."

"Have you done it before?" Persephone asks, which in all fairness she should have led with. But once again, considering she found true love with Julian, I'm just grateful she got there eventually.

"Yes," I say, starting to walk back upstairs to change into something more exercise appropriate. "But not for a while."

I *used* to be a runner. At first I ran to get out of the house, to lose my Winnie weight, to shepherd a few seconds away from a screaming baby, a meddling toddler, and an overwhelmed husband—who should have known what was in store after the *first* child, but desperately wanted the second.

Then I found out I really liked the activity behind my escape, realized that if I could flee the chaos of my life as a young, frazzled mom without breaking much of a sweat, maybe running had even *more* to offer and I hadn't quite exhausted its full scope of possibilities. Maybe I could both shed pounds and an identity through pure speed. Like reducing being a Bernard-Sunderland to a shadow I could leave behind me as a pavement smudge.

The more miles I logged, the more days imprinted on the bottom of my soles, the further away my deliverance from my family seemed. Like any poison or antidote, the effects are cumulative; one gains a tolerance. I hoped that if I increased the challenge, the demand, I could cure myself. There were days I started my sojourn on the Upper West Side and ended in another borough, so exhausted I would have to call Nathan to come pick me up because I didn't have enough energy left to make it home. Escaping the Bernard-Sunderlands through exercise was no small task. In fact, it was bordering on herculean.

I had hoped when we moved to DC that maybe I could let my routine slacken a little—*I had really started to despise running*—but relief proved elusive, even with three hundred miles between me and my family. It wasn't like I could add more distance—my kids had to go to school. I couldn't emulate Julian and move to a signal-less geographic void at the tip of Tibet. I was going to have to make do with my circumstances, which weren't optimal. Benjamin and Kate popped over on weekends, called constantly, texted tumultuously. I swear they were a bigger presence in my life than when I lived in the same city.

Searching for newfound peace—the nothingness at the heart of nirvana—I expanded my routine. I added in step sprints at the Lincoln Memorial, hoping that if I pushed hard enough and broke every natural barrier, that it wouldn't matter that decades had passed with words still unsaid, feelings unspoken, events unaddressed, and hearts broken. I understand now that I was asking far too much from running and from myself. The Bernard-Sunderlands would always be the Bernard-Sunderlands. There weren't enough miles in the world to make me forget.

But I couldn't give up. I'm a naturally stubborn person, but this went into areas where exercise ceased to be merely about getting your heart rate up. It was a matter of metaphysical survival, and you can't just shrug that off before it *still* hasn't reaped a reward. So, I kept running. And running. And running more. Until the day my body staged an emergency intervention and said—

No.

My body couldn't hold up as long as my family's collective omertà vow of emotional silence, and I tripped on the *Exorcist* steps in Georgetown, a historically haunted and demonically steep incline that had already claimed the lives of a fictional priest and film director, and now nearly included *me*. I fell upward, ironically, shattering my shoulder into a million little pieces. I landed face first and stained the pavement with a pint of my own blood. The fall was so *loud*, so disorienting, so awful that even the perpetually nonplussed university students carelessly circling by stopped to help me.

I walked myself home in a blissful state of shock, feeling nothing—*finally*. My arm hung limply by my side, a vestigial appendage. Nathan took one sideways glance at me when I walked through our front door, absorbed the extreme angle my arm now hung at, nearly passed out, then drank a deep draught of courage courtesy of an open IPA on the counter.

"Okay," he said, realizing I was in shock. "I'm going to take you to the hospital now. They'll know what to do."

Instead of heeding his words, I insisted that I needed a shower first. I would not make my appearance for the surgeon's knife in this condition. I didn't go *anywhere* defeated, sweaty, bloodied, or smelly. I was a Bernard-Sunderland.

Like the dutiful husband he is—and likely sensing I was going through way more than a physical injury—he acquiesced and helped me into the shower.

"Lizzie," he said, holding me up so I didn't pass out from the pain. "You're not going to your parents' house. No one expects you to look good with a broken shoulder. Kate won't be performing the surgery." He ran the water over my hair, rinsing out the dirt and leaves, then turned his attention to my shoulder. "*Fuck.* I think that's your bone."

It was most definitely my bone.

I was quickly processed in the emergency room, scheduled even *faster* for surgery—and we live in a city—then heavily sedated and introduced to my orthopedic surgeon, who assured me that he could likely retain most of my shoulder's mobility, but that I had some *serious* problems beyond a broken shoulder, that there was more at play here than a simple slip and fall from over-exertion.

My physical recovery took three surgeries, two titanium screws suturing my bones together, and months of physical therapy to regain three-quarters of my shoulder's original range of motion. And I still feel the pain on a cold day.

My mental recovery was equally as rocky as my physical recovery. Equally involved *pain*, deep pain, and epic unresolved feelings, the majority of which were unhealthily sublimated, and the expression of which are still embossed upon my psychiatrist's lumpy leather couch, like the fabric had turned sympathetic from holding onto the memories of countless contorted patients spilling secrets, and

I was the newest member. But I wasn't in the mood to be one of these patients, didn't want to join their group.

My therapist explained—in my opinion, *overexplained*—that my "version"—*he used quotes*—of running was an addiction, and that the only road to recovery was admitting it. With him as my guide, I had to examine the root cause of my commitment to flight that nearly killed me.

I didn't need him as my personal Virgil to figure that out. I fucking knew that the "root" of every Bernard-Sunderland's problem is being a Bernard-Sunderland. But I was still the most *together* sibling. I wasn't Julian, popping pills to annihilate a future that was never going to happen. I felt the pain. I luxuriated in the pain. What I *did* need from that psychiatrist was praise: mutual recognition that my method of handling my family was self-aware, coming from an enlightened place, a *healthy* place. That asshole didn't. He told me *none* of that was true.

I fired him on a voicemail message. A lot of help he was.

However, without external validation of my superiority over my siblings, I lost the urge to keep running. I suppose in a backhanded manner, the psychiatrist did kind of cure me, because I took a last look at my custom sneakers—my constant companions for the past decade and change—and said a solemn goodbye. I tossed them down the garbage chute in our hallway and never looked back.

CHAPTER FOURTEEN

PERSEPHONE AND I WALK INTO the full class on the sand, grabbing mats from the basket in the corner and rolling them out next to each other.

"*Namaste. My name is Kaia,*" *our spiritual guide for the morning says, sliding onto her mat.* "*Today we have an awesome practice that is going to balance the root chakra and ground you in gratitude.*" *She sits cross-legged, hands on her knees.* "*Let's begin in Sukhasana.*"

I gaze around at my fellow "yogis," which only heightens my annoyance that I'm skipping *another* meal. They're all a consortium of practitioners of conspicuous consumption, hoping to ease their guilty consciences, hoping to burn off the empty calories they drank while lying in the sun in the morning, gorging at dinner, and then drinking *again* until they passed out in a narcotic coma. People seem positively addicted to killing themselves on vacation, to traveling thousands of miles to court cancer. It's a uniquely American syndrome. Somehow prolonged suicide seems more inviting in better weather.

"*Head over the heart. Heart over the pelvis,*" *Kaia says on an exhale.* "*Take a moment to honor the line of the spine. Feel the stretch in the head, in the neck, and when you're ready, close your eyes.*"

I look over to Persephone, waiting for her to start this long-awaited conversation. She has her eyes closed and is perfectly mimicking Kaia's posture. I clear my throat audibly, disturbing the other "yogis" and earning a sharp rebuke from Kaia's profile.

"Persephone," I whisper, wondering how we are going to have this conversation with Kaia demanding inner peace. "It's not that

I'm not happy to meet you. And don't take this the wrong way...
but how the *hell* did you get here?"

She finally opens her eyes and whispers back, "Kate sent us."

"*Kate*," I repeat, realizing that Paul was right when we first saw
Oliver. He wasn't just indulging in the paranoia that comes with
being a Bernard-Sunderland—the constant unpeeling of family
conspiracies, the rumors whispered in room corners. *No.* We are
in Kate's game. And Persephone is living proof. "Kate knew about
you and Oliver all these years?"

"I knew about Kate all these years," Persephone says. "Kate
knew about Oliver and me for the past four months."

"Since she found out she was dying," I say softly.

"Regardless of what happened between her and Julian,"
Persephone says, "I couldn't let her die without knowing Oliver
existed. It wouldn't have been right."

"*With your eyes closed,*" Kaia says, "*I'd like you to journey inward, to
take on...when you're ready...the role of the observer of your own body.*"

"I knew Julian wouldn't want me to," she continues, moving
her fingertips to the edge of the mat and sliding meaningfully into
child's pose, which I valiantly try to mimic with a series of short
stretches, stretching my joints, and letting out a long, loud exhale.
"I knew he'd be furious. But I did it anyway. His anger toward
his mother was clouding his perception." She turns her head and
meets my gaze. I'm momentarily distracted by my curious interpretation of Kaia's direction. "I don't know. Maybe it's because I
lost my mother when I was young, and we didn't have the greatest
relationship...but I still regret every time we fought, even when
it wasn't my fault. Things change when people aren't with us any
longer. And I didn't want Julian to have that regret. I'd rather have
him hate me but have some peace with his mother."

I feel tears begin to fall, and fight them back. I don't like crying
period, let alone in front of a veritable stranger who has dragged

me to yoga. But right now, I think I may love Persephone more than any member of my family. Since I found out about Oliver, I've been haunted, gutted at the thought that Kate never knew she had a grandson, and how much she would have loved him. Because Oliver isn't *any* grandchild, he's hers—the sole *Bernard* grandchild—whereas Benjamin has managed to count four to his name. She never would have allowed herself to imagine Oliver, let alone meet him in the flesh. If Persephone hadn't been this brave, hadn't had the courage to do what Julian should've done years ago, Oliver would have remained a dashed dream, a fantasy to indulge while Julian ventured toward an ephemeral eightfold path and Paul remained a bachelor.

"Thank you," I say to Persephone simply, my voice strained. I offer her my hand across the mat, and she takes it, feeling my genuine warmth and gratitude. We're two mothers who know how a child changes your life, how family—no matter how dysfunctional—is important, and how a bond between women and children may be the strongest there is.

"How did Julian *ever* find someone like you?" I say, momentarily reflecting on the barrage of bad dates and drug-fueled liaisons—the women I had the pleasure of meeting before Julian left the country for clearly far greener pastures. "I've met his other 'girlfriends.'"

"Give your mind a rest," Kaia says, drawing her arms back toward her body. *"Press into the top of your feet. Move into a place of connection onto all fours. Bring the knees to the hip points. Walk your hands to the knees. And then pop up."*

"We met in Tibet. It wasn't that long after he got out of rehab," Persephone says.

The mere mention of Julian and the word rehab brings me back to some of our darkest days as a family.

After Julian was released from the hospital following his near-fatal accident, his condition prompted one of the few, rare times my father and Kate were forced to make a parental decision. Terrified and totally out of their element, they immediately sought professional help to take the burden off themselves and checked Julian into Promises Treatment Center in Malibu, California. As a bonus, their desperation came with a status upgrade. If they had to cope with the public embarrassment of their perfect family being fractured, they'd make it up on the back end by sending Julian where "Iron Man" went to get clean, joining many of their Upper West Side neighbors in choosing the elite citadel.

Kate, much to everyone's collective surprise, took an extended leave of absence from work—a cosmic event that wasn't repeated until the final days of her illness—and relocated across the country to be near Julian during his recovery. According to my brother, she attended every family therapy session, studiously and furiously taking notes, filing away every perceived slight, every thoughtless mistake, every repressed nook and cranny of Julian and the family's collective unconscious where she proved deficient, part of the larger problem sucking us into a vortex. Supposedly, she was actually listening, trying to fathom why he chose this lifestyle for the better part of a decade and counting.

To an outside observer, it appeared she was finally caring for Julian in the way he'd craved, loving him in the way he always needed. He finally felt safe, finally believed that if he fell someone would catch him. He was no longer walking a tightrope with nothing but shallow ground underneath. My brother, much as his behavior attested, was unable to handle life without knowing that it wasn't *all on him*, that he wouldn't be reduced to mere emotional scrounging and survival. As hard as Paul and I tried to convince him otherwise, to say he had us in his corner, Kate was the one he wanted, and he would accept no substitute.

But Kate's newfound devotion came with a steep price that dawned on Julian slowly, then all at once, reducing him to night sweats and dream demons. Kate could only love him unconditionally when his life was at stake. The writing flashed in bold neon before his eyes: unless he existed in a perpetual terminal state, Julian would have to let Kate be Kate—otherwise it would kill him, and he would head into an early grave chasing a phantom. And sadly, it might take her with him too. Kate couldn't be out of her element.

It wasn't worth it. He'd end up in the ground trying to gain access to her unfettered heart. No one, not even her *son*, got those moments out of Kate; they occurred behind several sets of closed doors, miles away from prying ears and eyes.

Kate could rule a small dynasty, could oversee five children, but she couldn't be *in* a family. Once Julian got a microscopic look at that dynamic, he quit searching for answers in cocaine *and* Kate, and embarked on his own *Eat, Pray, Love* journey to find himself, to find answers, to find a state of transcendental nirvana that was clean and clear, not inverted like everything else in our lives.

It turns out he did find peace on that journey. It was Persephone. The person who finally made him feel like he was safe in this world...which is likely why he hid her from us all.

"Take this moment to take stock," Kaia says, *"of living in these modern times that allow very little time for yourself."*

Persephone finishes telling me the story of her and Julian's love affair, including how Oliver was conceived atop a mountain—a fact I could have lived without knowing—and then says: "And now you know why I need your help."

"I do?" I say, wondering if there's some lesson in the story that I didn't register—like how a Zen master sends a student out with Koans to study, which aren't meant to be solved, but to test the pupil. "How do I know?"

"Julian is furious that I took Oliver to meet Kate behind his back," she says. "And even more furious that I followed Kate's last wishes and brought him here on a separate flight to meet all of you."

"I could see how that's a problem," I say, imagining that Benjamin's tantrum might have almost acted like a balm for Julian feeling betrayed by the woman he loves.

"Julian feels like he can't trust me anymore," she continues, "and to cope with Kate's death, he wants to go back to Central Asia alone, to try and 'rebalance'—to use his own words—so he doesn't start using again..."

"Because Kate's his trigger," I say, having been down this road myself with him.

"Except she can't be his trigger, Elizabeth," Persephone says, eyeing Kaia and following her into a standard downward dog pose. I attempt to execute the pose myself but start to feel the familiar ache in my shoulder. I spiral out of it and sit down on the mat.

"She's dead. Julian doesn't have any triggers left. He doesn't have excuses left...and that scares him the most," Persephone says. "When Kate was alive, it allowed him carte blanche to relapse if he ever wanted to. He *didn't*. But that door was always open. Now it's closed, and he's having a full epic freakout. Because everything, all his life decisions, are on *him*."

Persephone is raising a salient point—not just for Julian, but for all the Bernard-Sunderlands. Not only are we here because we've lost Kate, but we've also lost a person to blame for our life's mistakes—all of which she was guilty of, but *none of which* we can put at her feet in the future. We have officially graduated. The wrecking ball of adulthood can no longer be postponed, even for me. Julian, as is his wont, just happens to be the most self-aware that the ride is over, likely since he had the most at stake in keeping Kate around.

"Obviously, Julian doesn't like to be cornered," Persephone says.

"Obviously," I agree, also wondering who *likes* to be cornered, but not wanting to make Persephone realize maybe I'm not the one she should be talking to.

"Benjamin, your father, agrees with Julian about going back to Tibet—"

"There's a surprise," I say, realizing from the look on her face I wasn't supposed to respond.

"He's already booked a ticket to leave on the day after the funeral," Persephone says. "And it's *one-way.* Oliver and I are to be given an apartment, the funds for private school in Manhattan, and anything else we may find ourselves wanting for being *so* understanding of Julian in his time of need."

Benjamin's response to Julian's impending breakdown is my father to the point of fucking cliché. In his ideal world, there exists no problem, no mistake, no "incident," no rumor—true or false—that can't be canceled with a check, then quickly dropped down a hole, swept under the proverbial rug, and never spoken of again in polite company. Except for the past four months, the black hole of his life—the first incident in his existence on this mortal coil—made him face not only mortality but *impotency* in the face of something far stronger than him. Death. Time. The silent ticking away of *options.* Ironically, Julian's desire to flip the script back to wanton self-destruction allows Benjamin a return to his preferred bailiwick, and he's emboldened, salivating at the thought. Persephone and Oliver present a problem he can buy off. And Julian, someone who might remind him of Kate—of what's he lost, of the horrid potential of *feeling*—will be sent away to a far-away continent, the same one he would be inhabiting if he stopped moving and plotting for a second.

"If you're having difficulty for any reason," Kaia says, *"I can come over and show you how to modify the pose to fit your particular needs. No one should ever be in pain here."*

I'm—actually *everyone* is—aware Kaia is singling me out with this comment, shining a flashing light over my struggles. And I'm sorry she's not getting what she wants out of this class—I'm certainly not, and I'm not sure anyone *is*—but there are larger problems worrying me than my inability to line up my chakras.

"Except we both know Julian won't come back," Persephone says. "He'll run forever. Or until he finally kills himself. An ending that is apparently acceptable to him and to your father, but not *me*."

"Me neither," I say, nodding in agreement.

"So, you need to talk to your father…"

"Persephone," I say, "no one really *talks* to my father. You yell at my father. You throw something at him. You hang up on him. You ignore him for months. But you don't *talk*."

"Well, I need you to," she says, unmoved by my prior experiences. "And Julian needs you to. So does Oliver. You're the only one who seemingly has enough courage to talk to him." She smiles. "Kate knew it. She told me to go to you. Somehow, she knew this was how both the men in her life would take losing her."

"*Be kind and gentle to yourselves,*" Kaia says, while bringing her big toes together, sending her hips back into an extended child's pose.

"Okay," I say, breathing in, struggling to process both having to face my father without Kate as a buffer and stunned into silence by the fact she told Persephone to come to *me*. For years, I begged Kate and Benjamin to pay attention to Julian's addiction, to do *anything* to help him. Kate never trusted me to handle one of "her boys." She thought my approach was always lacking, or just plain wrong, and criticized my interventions to no end. But now, I'm somehow the one drafted to save Julian and his family?

CHAPTER FIFTEEN

I WALK OUT OF THE yoga class and want to head back to my villa, desperate to change out of my Lululemon yoga clothes—which barely fit—and into a swimsuit that will also likely not fit, but at least would be cooler and allow my skin to breathe. *But I can't.* The morning sun is scorching, an angry blood orange disc, eager to make up for lost time spent trapped under yesterday's clouds. And I'm stuck hunting down my father to stop him from making a huge mistake by enabling my brother's *even bigger* mistake.

I have no shortage of passive aggressive comments and petty judgments on hand for every Bernard-Sunderland occasion; in fact, there are so *many*, I've been able to abbreviate them down to shorthand to correspond with every act of poor parenting I've witnessed over thirty-three years. But when it comes to the next generation—the children of the Bernard-Sunderland *children*—I will fight on their behalf. I will go to war with Benjamin and Kate; I will draw a visible line that shall not be passed. They already messed up *their* kids, and I was relatively powerless to stop it, being a child myself. But they will not mess up our kids, including Oliver, who if Benjamin has his way will grow up in the lap of luxury without a father.

A mistake that I know—and Kate knows—I'm the only one who can correct. She knows it from experience; she saw it with her own eyes in real time. She must have remembered, clearly *remembers* the one time I broke script, the one time I didn't boil my complaints down to grumbled, yet pithy sound bites. The one time I yelled, screamed, and said and did things no other Bernard-Sunderland child has ever or *will ever* do.

This internecine struggle over the grandchildren started ten years ago, back when Winnie was five and about to enter kindergarten. We already had her school picked out.

Nathan, the kids, and I were living in Chelsea, and right across the street, a progressive charter school had opened. Theo was in his second year there and loved the alternative and immersive educational style. The teachers were dedicated, seeming as if they almost slept there with their unflagging energy to the kids. The campus had a rooftop garden that the students and teachers tended together, and every week they took the kids on field trips designed to enhance what they were learning in the classroom, opening their eyes to the city around them and showing them sights and places even Nathan and I didn't know. They had chickens, beehives, and sustainable cooking classes. It was everything I wanted for my children. A bold, unique path forward.

Too bold and unique, if you asked Benjamin and Kate, who had waited out Theo attending our Chelsea school in hopes we'd come to our senses. Their efforts went into overdrive when they realized Winnie would be following in the same "alternative" path. Behind our backs, they took our children to their preferred school's series of tests and interviews, and when they performed exceedingly well on both, enrolled them for the fall semester *and* paid the first year of tuition.

This was a school I knew intimately, because all the Bernard-Sunderland children had attended. A school, which if I was being generous, I'd call a well-oiled machine solely existing to mold the next generation of "elite" leaders—ironically, a title *none* of Benjamin and Kate's children could claim, considering that five current Fortune 500 CEOs were two grades ahead of me. And if I wanted to be *not* generous, I'd say that school was a soulless, heartless experience that stripped any essence of humanity and humility out of its students and incubated a complete amorality that valued money, status, and *power* most of all.

Obviously, I never had any intention of enrolling Winnie and Theo in such a place. I wanted *my* children to become conscious global citizens, to contribute to a better world—not run it. To strike out on their own path, maybe tear down an institution or two along the way instead of capturing them for people like their grandparents, who would extend their wasteful rule for another generation by wheeling out youthful proxies on their behalf.

It was quite a shock when I received a call from my old head-mistress, who was thrilled to be educating my children. I was livid. I was furious. I had never been that fucking mad at Benjamin and Kate in my life, and I've gotten pretty angry before. But *this*. This was an act of betrayal. And even worse, one directed against my children. Children who Nathan and I had painstakingly raised to not repeat my youth, so they didn't end up as traumatized and emotionally shattered as me.

I ran from Chelsea to the Upper West Side. Almost *sixty* blocks. And I didn't stop. I may have logged a personal record. When I arrived, the doorman enquired about my health, then waved me through to visit my parents. My body ached. I couldn't find my breath. I had sweated through every layer of clothing. But my deter-mination had not been dented by bodily exhaustion. I was *ready*.

I stormed into the penthouse, ignored the staff—many of whom had known me as a teenager and could tell this was *not the time*—and intruded upon Benjamin and Kate halfway through their salad course in the dining room. They looked up in horror, more I think from my physical appearance than my anger.

"How *dare* you," I said, picking up a carefully folded napkin from the table and wiping the sweat off my face, much to Kate's disgust. "Where in the fuck do you get off thinking you have the right to enroll Winnie and Theo in *that* school?"

Benjamin and Kate shared a surreptitious look and silently elected her to try and defuse the rapidly escalating situation.

"Lizzie," she said calmly, as if she were speaking to a screaming infant, not a thirty-three-year-old woman with two kids. "Your father and I didn't enter this decision lightly. We've waited for you to come to your senses. But we couldn't just stand idly by and watch you squander Winnie and Theo's futures, the family's *future*, and allow you to have them educated by some well-meaning hippies."

Benjamin, ignoring Kate's look not to intervene, added: "We can't keep telling our friends that Winnie and Theo go to a *charter* school. It's embarrassing." He shrugged. "Our grandkids shouldn't have to suffer while you still play-act rebellion. An endless rebellion that Kate and I *pay* for."

"*I* know what's best for Winnie and Theo," I said, then discreetly flagged the butler to bring me a glass of ice water. "If I wanted your input, I would have *asked*. But guess what—I fucking *didn't*. Because I'm well-versed in what both of your input looks like. The road to perpetual unhappiness, therapy, dysfunction…"

My father loudly scraped his knife on the side of the table, then took a bite of salad, employing his favored strategy to deal with me. Pretending I'm not there and just talking to Kate. "Is this a new dressing?"

"I think it's the raspberry vinaigrette," Kate replied, sniffing the tongs of her fork.

"I don't think I like it," Benjamin said.

At which point, I shocked them both and myself. I slammed both open palms down on the table, screaming out in pain from the impact and sending half the glasses tumbling to the floor. "Listen to me, *goddamn it!*" I screamed. "You are *not* to interfere with how I raise my children. And if you try again, you will never see me or them—"

"If you don't want Kate and I to have a voice in Winnie and Theo's lives, and to contribute to giving them the best future possible," my father said, pushing his salad to the side, done with diversions and ready to engage with the gauntlet I just tossed, "there's a very simple path to making that a reality. You can stop taking our money."

"I never *wanted* your money!" I screamed.

"Well, you don't spend it like you don't want it," my father said.

"Because that's all I have of *you*," I said, stranded between crying hysterically and breaking the table in half. "That's how much I want you to notice me. To love me. But instead of that, it's just another method of control. And now you're trying to use it against Winnie and Theo."

"No," Kate said, prepared to jump back into the conversation after Benjamin had done the dirty work. "We're not using the money to control Winnie and Theo. We're using it to fix your mistakes. As we've been trying to do all your life. You lead a life of exquisite privilege, Elizabeth. Nothing you do *matters*. You can make all the errors in the world and not suffer any consequences. But your children can."

"Well now you can suffer a *consequence*," I said, sick of the conversation, sick of them, sick of the money. I stormed halfway out of the dining room, then turned back, just in case the point hadn't been made crystal clear. "I'm done. I don't want your money. Winnie and Theo don't want your money. Nathan doesn't want your money." I watched the expression on their faces change ever so slightly, a realization that their bluff had been called, and by me. "You can both go to hell and take your money with you. Take it all."

I didn't wait for an answer. I didn't have to, because it came *quickly*. Before I had crossed into Times Square, I received a notification that my trust fund was frozen, and it remains encased in ice to this day.

Thirty-seven million dollars that I gave up unrestricted access to because I wanted Winnie and Theo to be spared from having to live up to Benjamin and Kate's expectations, to become my parents in miniature form and haunt the corridors of my home.

And if they were going to make good on their promise, I would make good on mine. Seemingly overnight, I accepted a promotion at work that I'd turned down three times because it necessitated a move to Washington, DC, and included a lot of travel—but came with an impressive pay raise, money we were desperately going to need given our new and shockingly diminished financial standing. Two and a half weeks after my blowout with Benjamin and Kate, Nathan, me, and the kids were on the road and relocating to our new home: a two-bedroom apartment in company housing until we had settled in.

Benjamin and Kate—being *Benjamin and Kate*—came over to see us off but didn't mention the trust. They wished us well in Washington, DC, where they came to visit us less than two weeks later, and then returned *two weeks later*, and never stopped returning, meaning my victory was almost entirely pyrrhic. I lost over $30 million and still kept Benjamin and Kate. But I didn't have the heart to cut them out completely. Sadly, tragically, *bizarrely*, I couldn't live without them either, even though we couldn't admit it. I suppose I am what Paul says: the worst sort of cliché, the only holdout left from Benjamin and Kate's wedding day, the sentimental fool still waiting for someone to make us a family. At least I did get to raise Winnie and Theo how I wanted, and Benjamin and Kate never interfered again.

"Mot-her..." Winnie's impatient tone intrudes my field of vision as I spot Benjamin sitting on the beach under a palm tree facing the direct sun, as if it can somehow scorch away all his current troubles.

"Yes, Winnie?" I say, watching her walk toward me, still waving her arms like I can't see her. "How may I help you?"

"I haven't seen you recently," she says, hands on her hips, assuming interrogation mode. "Does it make you feel good neglecting me? What? Now that the president is your customer, I cease to exist? After *all* the time I've committed to our relationship..."

I sigh, dig my flip-flops into the sand, and remove the option of running, which admittedly, I'm tempted to take. "Hasn't your father been with you?"

"He has," Winnie says, anger not abating. "And it's a sad day, Elizabeth. Sad. Day. When I'm reliant on *Dad*. Who, incidentally, is more reliant on *me*. I have had to listen for hours, *hours*, to his mistreatment, his dashed dreams, his crushed hopes...that aren't the fault of one person, but *all* of entertainment itself. *Mother*. I'm not a career counselor. I don't know what to tell him. And he must *really* need an answer because he doesn't stop."

"I don't know, Winnifred," I say, exhausted just hearing about Nathan's continued bemoaning even from a secondhand source, which is also just offensive on several levels. First, he's here to support *me*—to stalwartly stand by my side as I say goodbye to Kate. Also, the freaking president came into my bakery, and it only made a dent when it first happened, then we moved right back to focusing on his career. Is the president calling him to fix screenplays? Honestly, that's way cooler than anything he has on his plate currently, not to mention that I'm terrified about it. That doesn't cross his mind either. I was the sole income earner while he chased his dream—apparently now a nightmare. It's like the older Nathan gets, the more he carves out hours to engage in the kind of splenetic meandering favored by Benjamin. "Your father's going through something," I say, the eternal catch-all for all wives and mothers. "Maybe Grandma's death is making him reevaluate life."

Winnie squints. "Mother, they weren't even that close."

"Then maybe just death in general," I say. "Your father doesn't make a whole lot of sense even on his best days."

"Moving on," she says, reaching for my sunglasses because she obviously forgot hers. "Do you think you can possibly turn your attention to your child?"

"I'm sorry," I say. "What can I help you with? Do you want to go in the ocean together? Grab some lunch? Take a walk and chat?"

"No, *Mom*," Winnie says. "I need you to buy me tampons."

"Tampons?" I repeat, realizing my fifteen-year-old daughter has hit an awkward stage in her impending maturity. Winnie can't admit she still needs me and desperately tries to prove otherwise, usually ending up hoisted on her own petard.

I'm her part-time pharmacy, particularly when it comes to tampons, which she refuses to buy for herself primarily out of embarrassment—but also as an intractable political stance against the "pink tax." Regarding the latter, I have only myself to blame. I've taught her for years that period products should be free on basic principle.

Her act extends to behavior around her friends. She valiantly attempts to reduce me to my Amex card on Saturdays when she goes shopping in Georgetown with six other girls...until she hits a snag and needs to FaceTime me from the dressing room to get my opinion on how her leggings and crop tops fit.

I also function as an oft-abused dating guru as Winnie solicits my advice on the latest boy she's fallen for and will never date. She still hasn't gotten over the first boy she dated and callously discarded like a childish hobby, all because he had the audacity to *like* her. But I can't tell Winnie that, even though in her heart she knows I'm right. I can't know anything about Winnie unless she tells me. Yet at the same time, I'm also expected to know everything. It's a fucking emotional minefield rivaling Benjamin Sunderland in the land of mixed messages.

"God," Winnie says. "Do you have to be so *loud*? Do you have to tell everyone on this beach I'm on my period?"

A part of me wants to start laughing at how dramatic Winnie is being, inadvertently drawing *more attention* to herself by yelling at me. But another part of me wants to stop and rewind time, realizing that I'm still not ready for Winnie to be having her period, even though she first got it two years ago.

Time seemed ephemeral and endless when Winnie and Theo were babies. Each day was a carbon copy; the only question was which child would cry harder. Now, time has hit hyperdrive, turned relentless, and refuses to obey my commands to *slow down*. Nathan and I used to have sleepless nights because we had babies. Now the insomnia descends because our babies are growing up, and ironically, *they* have never slept more soundly.

They're ready to leave and run the world, just as Nathan and I have taught them. But I wonder if something got lost in translation along the way. They may be prepared to start living, but I'm utterly unprepared to let them go. This isn't how it was supposed to be. They're supposed to be unable to envisage a world without me.

I don't want to share them with the world. That means my world has ended.

"You got your period early?" I ask her.

"No, *Mother*," Winnie says. "I got my period on time. Like I do every month. Two weeks after you. It was on the calendar, remember? According to Dad, it supplanted his favorite poet."

I pick up my phone, show her my intricately detailed hourly calendar, and point out her mistake. "I'm not supposed to get my period until next week."

"Elizabeth," she says, sounding just like me at her age, "I know the entire basis of our relationship rests on you being right and me being wrong. But *you're* wrong." She points to my calendar. "You'd be right if it was three weeks ago."

I look again at my calendar, then back to Winnie, and realize she's *right*. The unthinkable has happened.

"Can you please go get me tampons now?"

"Winnie, stop talking," I say, still registering the gravity of the situation. "Just stop."

How can I be late?

"Telling me to stop talking isn't an answer," Winnie says.

I'm late. Somehow, I'm late.

I throw my bag over my shoulder, turn away from Winnie, and storm back toward the hotel. I haven't even made up my mind if I'm buying her tampons. I just know that I can't stand still, that perhaps there is a small modicum of mercy in relentless forward motion. Maybe Julian has a point.

"I'm going to assume you're leaving to buy me tampons!" Winnie calls. "Good talk."

I'm fucking late.

There must be an explanation. There always is. It could be emotional strain. When Kate's condition took a sustained and unyielding turn for the worst, toward the *very end*, I was devoured by my own anxiety, barely sleeping, and sporadically eating. I could also be hitting early menopause. Like *really* early. But I wouldn't know, because I had to skip my last OBGYN appointment since I was in Manhattan with Kate, and Dr. Marko doesn't make it easy to reschedule. I'm sure it's some combination of the two. Death and menopause.

Why not? I'm a woman, and we live in an untampered zone governed by daily extremes. Little things like: Do I pick up my sick child from school or sacrifice the big meeting I need to lead and recruit my half-as-talented male counterpart to go in my place so he can ultimately soak up all the glory, even though I'm the one who got the client in the first place? Do I finish the report due at eight in the morning that I haven't started or build Lincoln's cabin out of Popsicle sticks? Do I explore all of the unfathomable options POTUS waltzing into Madeleine opens up or do I keep it the place I always wanted it to be and not look back?

No wonder my period is late.

I'm gonna be *fine*.

CHAPTER SIXTEEN

I'M MOST DEFINITELY NOT GOING to be fucking fine. My mind races as I sprint to the resort store. I have been vomiting this entire trip. It marked my welcome to St. John. My clothes don't fit, and they did a few weeks ago. Food keeps turning my stomach.

Nothing is fine. Nothing has been fine. Nothing will ever be fine again.

"*Do you sell tampons?*" I ask the salesperson busy restocking the bulging shelves of the Eleusinian hotel market with branded polo shirts and floral flip-flops.

"Back of the store," he says, taken aback, almost concerned at how I entered his store in a flat-out run. "Bottom three shelves. Do you need me to show you?"

"No," I say, forcing a smile. If I just buy tampons then I don't have to discover just how *not fine* I'm going to be. "I've been doing this for a while."

I quickly exit the strained exchange, find the shelf stocked with feminine products, and commence a Pyrrhic search for Winnie's brand, Honey Pot—the natural, plastic-free option that saves the planet with each purchase—no chance *in hell* it'll be available in an island resort market, leaving me no option but to buy her Tampax and hear her lament until we touch back down in DC. And then for the next fifteen years.

And if the much-vaunted dry erase calendar in our kitchen is supposed to remind her when she's going to get her period, why didn't she pack herself tampons? Because I'm supposed to. I'm supposed to remember everything. Not Nathan though. I can't imagine he didn't see it on the fucking calendar. I can't imagine how anyone didn't see it on the calendar. It was probably a giant red circle devouring several weeks in its circumference. Apparently the only one who realized it was *Theo*, who would be the last person to mention it, because it locked Nathan into doing his homework for him. So once again, this is my fault.

I hold the Tampax box in my hand, weighing my future, and distract myself by trying to remember the last time Nathan and I conceivably could have had sex. It *had* to precede New Year's Eve. Nothing about Kate announcing the hopelessness of her illness and the truncation of her life would have put me in the mood for romance. Besides, I'm obviously not five months pregnant. I do vaguely recall having my period at some point when I was shuttling back and forth between Manhattan and DC. I'm *sure*. We have not had sex. It's got to be stress or menopause. Easy enough.

I commit to the Tampax, resigned, and begin to slowly trudge over to the register to complete my purchase and open Winnie's chance to begin aggressively opining.

"Fuck me," I suddenly say out loud. The salesperson looks at me, likely flashing back to my lively entrance, wondering what's wrong this time, and determining just how concerned he needs to be.

Nathan and I *did* have sex. It was after the School Without Walls auction. Nathan had decided it would be a capital idea to attend the yearly event—that it would help me relax. The night returns in flashes, like sharp blows to my solar plexus. I remember drinking too much. I remember telling a fully inebriated Nathan that it was asinine to spend $4,000 for a season of Capitals box seats, especially when none of us like hockey. Who is attending these games? I remember returning home. My memory is foggy. It moves in static lines off an old television. I remember shots of some vague alcohol in a clear bottle. I think the bastard told me it was George Clooney's tequila....

What did Nathan *do to me?*

Obviously, the auction and the drinking were all a part of his grand, intricately plotted plan to have sex with me. I should have suspected. The man is known for his limberness with narrative. And *limber* it was. God forbid he goes a few chaste months without rummaging under the sheets while Kate was clinging to her mortal existence. Sometimes life gets busy, *Nathan.* For Christ's sake, we are forty-three years old. Is it still necessary to have sex three times a week? I love sex. I have always been a fan. But at a certain point—work, two teenagers, an ornery goldendoodle, and the Bernard-Sunderlands—it's a *lot* of effort to get naked.

I start pacing in the aisles, and customers begin to share the salesperson's marked fear.

I would *never* mess up my birth control. It's been fifteen years of never fucking up, never having a close call. I do not make mistakes.

This can't be real. I'm out of sorts, befuddled, consumed by the stress of the trip. I wouldn't blink an eye if we were home.

Except I would. The last time I missed my period, had random bouts of vomiting on an empty stomach, and my clothes didn't fit, Winnie entered the world, and—to rub a handful of salt in the already festering wound—I'm now buying tampons for the same child.

I retreat, break my commitment to paying, run my eyes back up and down the shelves, regretting the Tampax, desperately searching for an acceptable substitute—*there aren't any*—and in the scope of my search, bang my hand into a pregnancy test.

I grab it—then drop it like it's on fire. I'm not pregnant. I don't need it.

And why the hell can I even buy a pregnancy test here?

I pick it up off the floor, read the back of the box, then return it to the shelf.

What person on vacation goes shopping for aloe, a tropical shirt, and a *pregnancy test*? I can't think of a bigger buzzkill than finding out you're pregnant at a resort. Who wants to know *that*? I'm sure the story traces its origins back to some snotty guest who didn't want to travel into town proper to get some pharmaceutical need met, then threw a fit, and ever since, the inside of this market stocks more tests and drugs than a Canadian border airport about to be besieged by Boomers on a fixed Medicare budget.

I make my way to the register, but when I think no one's looking, I run back, grab the test, elbow back into my former place in line, and pay with cash—so this purchase doesn't get charged back to the room, granting my father the chance to ask who bought a pregnancy test.

I hand over forty dollars, don't wait for change or a receipt, rush toward the door, barrel back to my villa at an absurd pace, hope Winnie isn't waiting for me, and prepare to swallow the test if anyone's there.

When I finally enter my villa, it's empty—all clear. I'm alone. But appearances can be deceiving. Living with Nathan, Theo, and Winnie readies one for sneak attacks, unexpected emotional sieges, and divisive battles over selected rooms. Like the bathroom.

I knock on the door softly, cognizant not to alarm anyone, burying my freak out for a few seconds. No response. I twist the handle. It's unlocked.

I storm inside, shred the box open, tear the plastic wrap, sit down on the toilet, and pee on the little white stick, the most punishing thirty seconds of my life thus far.

I put the cap back on, lay the test on the sink, and set a three-minute alarm on my phone.

Proust calls it the consolation of memory, but sometimes it isn't *consoling*, it's what you do to occupy your mind when you're terrified. I think nostalgia can be a vice, but that might be because

most of my memories have a grim aspect, a tinge of disappointment, a longing for love, and a burning question: *What did I do?*
And most of them revolve around me and Kate.

The intense island heat, the fear of the unexpected, and Kate's
conspicuous absence this time, bring me back seventeen years ago,
when I was pregnant with Theo during an unprecedented April
heat wave—which today wouldn't be considered unprecedented,
just the result of ceaseless crises where seasons are shuffled and
skipped. But in the early 2000s, it was an anomaly. Spring, the
typical time of rebirth—when the winter snows melt and perme-
ates the ground, allowing fresh seedlings to take root—had been
postponed for a baptism of fire.

Everything was late that year, including Theo.

Since it was as hot inside as outside, I decided to walk over to
the ice cream truck near our subway stop and indulge in a soft-
serve vanilla cone. I still had another week of eating for two and
wanted to take advantage of it. And I had *taken advantage of it*
during the previous nine months, gaining around forty-six pounds.

I resembled one of the clouds in the elastic sky, reverberating
with heat. I was puffy, swollen, about to burst with water and new
life, and subject to an unconscionable delay by forces bigger than
me. Above, the sun was also unable to exhaust itself enough to
allow another element to take center stage. Inside me, it was the
growing life who had plans of his own.

Once I arrived back at our apartment, I paused at the entrance,
psyching myself up to return to our small hot home, then flung
open the door and found Kate waiting for me in the hallway. She
was not as unprecedented as the heat, but equally uncomfortable.

"Your super let me in," she said, raising an eyebrow. "He didn't
ask me why I was here, or who I planned on seeing...just popped
open the door and that was that."

I noticed the Sarabeth bags in her hands. "You brought lunch. He probably figured there's nothing to fear from a woman in a Hugo Boss suit with sandwiches."

She laughed, but it was absent any humor. "Whatever you say, dear."

I smiled and gave her a kiss on the cheek, from which she quickly disconnected and said, "Wasn't that nice?"

Like everything else in our family, trading affection with Kate was always strained and awkward, but in a highly formalized manner. She expected the gesture but seemed to instantly regret the intimacy required to make it real. Love was better left as an aspect of pageantry.

Upon entering the apartment, Kate had the wind knocked out of her by the trapped heat. I told her to sit down at the kitchen table while I grabbed her a glass of water, which she had to make sure was bottled—as if when I married Nathan and moved into his apartment, I'd somehow surrendered to barbarous and base instincts.

Kate took a sip, followed by a long look around the room with a scowl on her face, pursing her lips tight to prevent herself from speaking.

I traced her glance, noting the way she scrutinized our home with eyes trained to pick out any flaw. This would eventually turn into a discussion point at dinner for years to come.

Her eyes came to a rest on the little nook that Nathan and I had turned into a nursery. The crib nestled into the walk-in bedroom closet; the clothes, many of which I'd already had monogrammed, stacked neatly on Nathan's now emptied bookshelves; and the basket overflowing with stuffed animals and children's books. Nathan and I had decorated the makeshift nursery with an almost prelapsarian enthusiasm, like somehow, we were papering over the flaws our own parents made.

Yet when filtered through Kate's ocular authoritarianism, the space became unsuitable, something that required defending, like all my decisions. When you spend your life focused through Benjamin and Kate's microscope, everything dies on the slide—poked, prodded, and drained of breath. That's why I treasured Nathan's unconditional love and infinite forgiveness, and why my father and Kate could never understand why I chose him.

"The baby's sleeping in a closet?" Kate said, in her typically unfiltered tone.

"No," I said, flashing back to a million other conversations that began with that same nudging disbelief, like when she met Nathan for the first time. Or when I declined coming to work for her right out of college. "He's right across from our bed without being near the radiator."

"But it's still a closet," she said, then eyed the stacks of books. "At least he'll be literate." She gave me a final, exasperated look. "Elizabeth, sometimes I wish your baffling rebellion didn't have to affect the quality of my grandson's life. To *subsume* him. I mean... throw away the penthouse we bought you, don't bring any of your furniture with you. Punish yourself and Nathan for whatever *we* did, which was to try and give you the best life possible. Even though it's become abundantly obvious you didn't consider it so. But please, for the good of the family, think of the baby."

What Kate didn't realize was that I *was* doing it for the baby. I wanted to raise our son outside of their purview, their influence, and their running commentary. I wanted to embrace their willingness to cloister themselves in the Upper West Side and live unscathed in their hinterlands. It was as close to hiding as one can get in a big city. All Theo needed to grow up differently was this apartment and me and Nathan's unconditional love. We had been so frustrated by our own families that we started one almost immediately after getting married.

But Nathan's apartment was more than a hedge against Benjamin and Kate's unannounced visits. It was one of the few times in my life I wasn't anxious. And while it lasted, it was bliss.

Until Theo got bigger, and *bigger*, seemingly to mock my intentions of raising him there, and he was abetted by Kate, who kept buying more and more lavish presents—toys, strollers, gear, stuffed animals—to the point that Nathan and I couldn't walk in the apartment. But that was Kate's mission all along, to force me out against my will under the cover of spoiling her first grandchild, who lapped it all up, and was inseparable from my father and Kate from the moment he emerged into the world. Six months later, I had to move back into my penthouse in Chelsea to accommodate Theo's haul, and Kate had won. I was back.

"What did you bring for lunch?" I asked, too hot, too tired, too pregnant to fight with Kate again. "I'm famished."

"Salads," Kate said. "I figured you might want something a little lighter in this heat." She looked me up and down. "Poor thing...you just look exhausted and uncomfortable."

I'd wondered if at any point in my pregnancy Kate would have revealed a maternal side, that when I found out I was pregnant, it might have awoken some dormant gene that would transform her into the mother I always needed.

"I can't believe how big you got. You look like you're having twins," she said. "Maybe you're having a girl?"

There was the Kate I knew. After nine months, the only hint of her showing any interest in my pregnancy had been to tell me I was fat.

"I only gained fifteen pounds with your stepbrothers," she said. "Believe it or not, I left the hospital weighing less than I did before I was pregnant."

I believed it. Her confession solved most of the mystery of why Paul and Julian are the people they are today. I suppose that

Kate, a woman who despised closeness, felt that she'd done enough by allowing them to grow inside her for nine months. Surely her sacrifices could stop there. She'd given them *life*—what more could her boys expect?

I pulled the salads out of the bags and sat down at the table, and Kate's phone rang.

"It's work," she said, her eternal refrain. "Go ahead and start eating. This will only take a second."

The alarm on my phone goes off, rocketing me back to the terror at hand.

I close my eyes, grab the stick off the sink, inhale and exhale, start panicking, realize *breathing* is actually my enemy right now, then open my eyes and hold the test up.

CHAPTER SEVENTEEN

I WALK ONTO THE BEACH and swivel my head right and left. *He's gone.* Benjamin has abandoned his palm-fringed post facing the sun. Did he spontaneously combust? I wasn't in my villa *that* long. I trudge through the hot sand barefoot, making my way toward his last place of occupancy, prepared to sift through the signs and see if he left anything behind to give a clue where he could have gone.

"Lizzie!" I hear someone shout from under a blue and white striped beach umbrella, and rotate my neck to find the source. *"Over here, Lizzie."* The voice continues following its initial overture and giving its identity away. It's Caroline, who must have been born with some psychic power that I'm unaware of, because she has this unerring ability to pick me out on a beach from quite a distance. *"We're all set up down here."*

I tread down the beach, snaking around reserved lounge chairs piled high with towels, avoiding the waitstaff scurrying from guest to guest taking orders. I finally reach Caroline, who is surrounded by a dozen chairs, one of which is occupied by Sean, her sole company, who is dead asleep, slicked down with Caroline's sunscreen and *glittering.*

I take a seat midway between them, unsure of what I've walked into. Things deteriorate and detonate on a dime when Caroline is left alone with a man, and I may have waded into either the prelude to a fight or the breathing room after the verbal battle.

"You're not going to sit next to me?" Caroline asks. "What are we...strangers?"

I don't get up. It's usually best to treat Caroline warily at first, then ease into proximity. "Where's Dad?"

"I don't fucking know," she says, pulling the brim of her navy Yankees cap further down her head. She wears that hat with such authority that it seems like an essential part of an enchantress's ensemble, a priceless tool to snag a bemused lover about to make landfall. "And I'm not looking to find him. You made a shrewd move skipping breakfast."

"I wasn't invited," I say.

"Oh yeah," Caroline says. "Everyone was mad POTUS came to your store. There was a group decision that none of us felt like blowing sunshine up your ass while we're here on such a solemn occasion." She smiles. "Everyone except me. I think it's rather awesome. You went and became a total girlboss, and all you had to do was leave the country."

"Caroline," I say, struggling to keep her on topic. "What happened at breakfast with Dad?"

"Oh, yeah," she says circling back to her original point. "He didn't know that Kate knew about Oliver. And that Kate *sent them* here. Apparently, he was blindsided. And he's decided…unilaterally of course, none of us were consulted…that *you* and "video" Kate can go fuck yourselves for deciding that what the family needed was to get real, for "secrets" to come out. He's going to make sure they *stop* coming out. How he plans on doing this with a dead woman I have no idea, but their marriage has always been pretty fucking weird." She reaches down, pulls up a Bloody Mary from the sand, and brings it to her lips. "Do you have any secrets you want to tell me about, Lizzie? Because frankly I've got so fucking many, I'm not sure which Kate is going to choose."

I *could* tell Caroline that I'm pregnant. That the test was positive. That it had to be positive. That I knew it the second Winnie opened her mouth. Before she spoke, my body knew it. It was a fait accompli. But most of all, I knew Kate wanted me to know; somehow from wherever she is now, I knew she wanted me to know.

"I don't have any secrets," I say, deciding against telling anyone about being pregnant before I've even had the chance to wrap my head around it. But even if I had, I still wouldn't start with Caroline.

"Aren't you fortunate," she says sarcastically. "But you've been boring all your life."

"I don't think I'm *boring*," I say, slightly offended.

"I mean...you've gotten slightly more interesting since the president walked into your rinky-dink operation with one oven and baked goods that sell out by noon. You realize that's just a license to print money now. That kind of endorsement over social media... POTUS is like the world's biggest influencer to half the country. The other half wouldn't be caught in your bakery anyway, so it doesn't matter." She sips her drink again and bites the celery. "And if Kate were here, she'd be proud of you. So is our father. They just can't say it. But they can't say *anything*. Like fucking hello is a stretch." She picks up her phone as a prop, like she's about to deliver a presentation. "Are you going to rename your famed hot chocolate cupcake after POTUS? That's a once-in-a-lifetime branding opportunity. It's a literal, pardon the pun...*baked-in* emotional tie-in."

"*No*," I say, with a level of harshness I hadn't intended. "That's personal."

"You could just say, '*Good idea Caroline*.'" She drains her drink to the bottom. "Look, I'm only going to tell you this once, and you can do with it what you like...which is probably nothing. Because that's how everyone treats my advice. But don't fuck this up, Lizzie. You have a golden path laid out for you. And they don't come around twice."

I run my eyes across the beach, looking for my father again. "Caroline, where is everyone?"

"Am I not good enough company for you?" she says haughtily, sitting up. "I invited you over. I could have just stayed here with sleepy Sean and sunbathed, but *no*, I thought that would be rude...."

"It's not a value judgment on you," I say, trying to calm her down. "I was just wondering. I haven't seen anyone all day, and I've walked most of this resort."

"Well," she says, counting down each person and their activities on her fingers. "Paul has been handling 'business' back home. Julian didn't show up for breakfast, so I'm going to assume that he's ditched his partner and child in search of cocaine. Dad, as you know already, is busy thwarting you and Kate. And Tessa said she had to have a Facetime with Miles before he gets here tonight."

"Don't you think it's weird Miles isn't here yet?"

"I *do*. Which is why I fucking said it yesterday at dinner, Lizzie." She blows a strand of hair off her face. "Why does no one listen to me?"

I ignore her frequent complaint, which is, because she's the baby of the family, that any point she bridges is immediately discarded. "Why do you think he's not here, then? If you have all these answers."

"Oh," she says. "*That* I have an answer for, courtesy of Darby."

Darby has been Caroline's best friend and professional partner-in-crime since preschool, making them an inseparable dynamic duo of chaos since they were both three years old. It started in kindergarten, when they would terrorize fellow classmates during nap time and story hour, earning their first logged hours of detention and phone calls home from the administration. Caroline and Darby entered middle school with a vengeance, with fully operational mean-girl streaks that, when they ran out of victims, they would turn on each other to stay entertained. Battles that my baby sister would generally emerge from triumphant. The *meanest* mean girl there was. In high school, they went to all the parties together, dated a different boy in every private school up and down Manhattan, and had a bit of a nasty shoplifting habit at Saks that Benjamin had to bribe their way out of, because Darby's father was a federal judge and couldn't be seen intervening on behalf of his errant daughter.

The only period when Caroline and Darby weren't together—and the city breathed a tremendous sigh of relief—was a brief stint after college when Paul finally paid attention to Darby's years-long crush on him, and they developed a friends-with-benefits arrangement that my stepbrother took for something more, and he has barely dated since. And in the end, Caroline won out again, getting her best friend back and leaving Paul broken, both of which emboldened her in equal measure.

The last time I saw Darby, she was hanging out with—and perhaps even semi-serious about—a man who could only be described as a Russian oligarch who owned a British soccer team and spent a tremendous amount of time clubbing. So, if somehow Darby is involved with Miles, no good can come from that pairing.

"Darby," Caroline says, practically panting with excitement, "saw Miles at a club last night. He was hooking up with a bottle-service girl and dropping thousands on VIP service and shots."

"*Miles?*" I say, screwing up my face in shock. "That can't be right. I mean...he's kind of a...a..."

"Fucking loser," Caroline says, mimicking my face. "Right? I know. I told Darby, no way it's him. Until she sent me this."

Caroline grabs her phone from her beach bag, taps the message from Darby, and enlarges the photo in question, which I have to enlarge further since I'm not wearing my glasses.

"Jesus, Lizzie," she says, noting how Miles's head is taking up a disproportionate amount of the screen. "How old are you?"

I ignore her, zoom in further, and *sure enough*, it is Miles. Undeniably. He is equally undeniably making out in a booth behind a velvet VIP rope with a very attractive young woman, who clearly isn't deterred by the wedding ring on his finger, nor the very fact she should *know better* in this day and age.

"That's Miles," I confirm, handing Caroline back the phone.

"I imagine it's going to be interesting when he gets here tonight," Caroline says. "I'm not sure how long I can keep this under wraps for. I mean…this is just too good."

Miles's existence in our family can be directly chalked up to the existence of Nathan, who—when I met him—was living in a rent-controlled, windowless studio apartment in Harlem, dutifully composing his first novel and temping as a customer support representative for an ill-fated internet travel start-up venture that folded quickly after investors realized they were printing stock vouchers like receipts.

He was drowning his recent unemployment sorrows at Gatsby's, a trendy SoHo bar back in the early 2000s populated by career people. He looked distinctly out of place, which is partly what drew me to him in the first place, and why I agreed to meet him for dinner a few days later.

He was *forty minutes late* to dinner but redeemed himself instantly by handing me a bouquet of peonies, pink blossoms exploding out of the twine, binding the stems together. He had no way of knowing these were my favorite flowers, yet somehow— after meeting me for a total of twenty minutes in Gatsby's—*he knew*. And those flowers sealed our fate.

But that fate was not a part of Benjamin and Kate's plan for me. To them, Nathan was an interloper, a vagabond, *seizing* on me to vampirize their accumulated wealth—of which he had no clue because I waited almost until our engagement to let him see my penthouse apartment in Chelsea or meet my parents—and to this day, they still act that way, even though he's a millionaire himself.

At around the same time I met Nathan, Tessa was madly in love with Dylan, a fellow junior at George Washington University, a school to quote Benjamin, "where all the rich kids who can't get into NYU go." Except Dylan wasn't rich. He was a DC native who hit the jackpot when the city decided to halt their brain-drain to the coasts by offering their brightest students lavish scholarship packages.

Dylan and Tessa were inseparable, and it was the one time in my life that I was proud of my sister. She had traded in her unyielding desire to be the "favorite," to live within the strict scriptures of our parents' proscribed lines, and embraced her own happiness, to whatever idiosyncratic extent Tessa was able to pinpoint what *happiness* resembled.

It was also the last time I felt close to my sister, the last time before Tessa morphed into the hellish Dorian Gray version of Benjamin and Kate's marriage, transforming into the rotting picture in the attic they face almost daily, a funhouse mirror of their own creation reflecting the cracks in their own peculiar arrangement.

After watching my own struggle with Benjamin and Kate over Nathan—which included endless hand-wringing over *my* ingratitude, accusations of dragging the family name into a bottomless gutter, threats of financial freezing, and Sunday "dinners" that turned out to be blind dates hosted with Nathan *present*—Tessa decided to take a flyer on not going through what I just did and unceremoniously broke up with Dylan. She destroyed his heart and *hers*, all to preserve the thing that meant the most to her: our parents' approval.

Tessa had a lot of first dates, and many of them might've become second dates, without Benjamin and Kate's intervention to avoid another Nathan calamity. Tessa liked everyone; they liked *no one*. She was so eager for a new partner, someone to heal her self-inflicted wound, that almost any applicant fit the bill. Our parents had slightly loftier standards. This wasn't merely Tessa's partner; it was *their* partner too.

Their selection was Miles, and they didn't travel very far to find him. They didn't even leave Kate's office, cementing the theory that busy executives tend to sleep with colleagues more out of convenience and proximity, as opposed to any deep-seated romantic stirrings.

Kate was preparing to leave Goldman Sachs and branch off into her own hedge fund, and Miles was her protégé. He was a Wharton grad, descended from a "good" family, bred for success since birth, and most importantly *single*.

Kate invited Miles over for family dinner in the hope that Tessa would be charmed by him, or if not *by* him—Miles did lack any discernible romantic refinement—then assuredly by the idea that they selected him for their daughter, as if he were a blessing bestowed, another verifiable action allowing her to believe she was the favorite. Yet I sometimes wonder if the family dinner invitation served a secondary purpose. They *could* have just had a cozy meal for four, swapping war stories about the perils of high finance while Tess merely stared, unable to relate, and refilled her wine glass—but they didn't. I think they wanted Nathan and me there, just to rub it in my face that this all could have been mine, had I just decided to follow their wishes, which always lead to happiness.

Except when it *doesn't*. But even then, I don't think it's Caroline's responsibility to shatter Tessa's life, even though it would be the best thing for my sister, for Mason and Meredith, and maybe the entire family.

"Caroline," I say, getting up to move closer to her, "you *cannot*..."

But before I can finish telling my sister to do the very thing I know would be best for Tess, Sean rises from his nap, quiets me with his hand, and points to the ocean. There's a man running at top speed with a child in his arms, with another man following, struggling to keep up and screaming at the top of his lungs for *help*.

"Something happened," Sean says, attuned to crisis through his career in trauma.

I follow his eyes and look to the water.

I recognize the people running. I'd recognize them anywhere.

CHAPTER EIGHTEEN

NATHAN AND BENJAMIN ARE CRADLING Theo across their arms. It's as if he's an infant again, only this time his long limbs spill across both their torsos, the father and grandfather unable to carry their grown son and grandson.

Blood pours from Theo's leg, dripping onto the sand and fizzing like a bad carbolic reaction. It coats Nathan's forearms, slicking them crimson. From the shoreline, I hear Winnie shouting my name.

Instinctively, I shoot up from the chair, knocking Caroline to the ground. I sprint to the water in my bare feet, desperate to reach him, feeling the pain in my heart first, my stomach second.

It's the moment I've dreaded since he was born and I nearly lost him, the moment I've spent all his life and *my* life avoiding, the moment where he was unprotected, left vulnerable to an outside force, and I wasn't there to save him like I'd always promised.

I made the promise the first night Theo was allowed to come home, after getting stuck in my birth canal. That had necessitated an emergency C-section, then Tessa had to donate blood because I'd hemorrhaged, all culminating with my new son *eventually* being born and immediately whisked away to the NICU, where his lung proceeded to collapse. His life nearly ended before Nathan and I had a chance to hold him.

That night, Nathan—begrudgingly, hemming and hawing, purposely leaving his keys, wallet, and phone behind to keep having an excuse to peek back in and make sure Theo was still breathing—left to get me sushi. It was the only food I'd been craving for nine months that I hadn't been allowed to indulge in. After he closed the door, Theo and I had our first moment alone, unmediated by neonatologists, nurses, crying sick babies, beeping machines, and intricate tubing.

I looked at my beautiful baby boy with a full head of brown hair and was seized by an almost primal sensation. I had to make up for, account for, the first fourteen days we didn't share together, the two weeks in which bonding was suspended and we were both were alone, isolated, and longing to assign an identity to the other. *Did he even know I was his mother?* I didn't get to hold him close to my bare skin, to let him hear my voice outside the womb. I didn't have the chance to nurse him, to put my finger in his tiny little hand.

I wasn't going to miss a second more. Neither was Nathan, and we collectively spent the last seventeen years compensating for those first two weeks, a fortnight that literally defined who we are, our inherent family dynamic, and spilled into how we raised Winnie.

And now our child is bleeding before me.

"I think he hit an artery," Nathan says to me, a minute after getting Theo settled on a lounge chair, and now frantically pacing around the perimeter of Caroline and my father, who are boxing in Theo. "He's going to need surgery."

"It's going to be okay," I hear a shadow behind me say, then turn around and see Sean running toward us. "I'm a doctor," he says, with a mixture of comfort and authority, the way I'm sure he speaks to parents daily before taking their children into the operating room.

"You already told Lizzie that," Caroline says, as if blowing a random strand of hair away from her face that was annoying her. "It was the first thing you told her. Like you do with everyone."

I hold a beach towel tight against the side of Theo's spurting leg and kiss the top of his head.

"My head is fine, Mother," he says petulantly, swatting me away. "It's my *leg*."

"I know you're hurt, pal," Nathan says, rushing to my side and blocking everyone else from seeing Theo, returning us to the days when we formed a protective triangle around our only child. "But you don't need to be angry."

"Elizabeth," Benjamin says, breaking apart our little world, "do you think you can move away long enough to let an actual doctor get a look?"

"*No*," I say, gathering up the fragments of our parental ecosystem that Benjamin threatens. "I'm not leaving him."

Sean tries to wedge his way in. "You don't have to leave. Just let me get a look at him."

"He just brushed up against come coral," Winnie says, leavening the situation with her curious version of empathy. "He didn't get blindsided by a shark."

"One person's shark is another person's coral," Sean says, trying to curry favor with Nathan and me so he can tend to the patient.

I finally allow him access, then convince a severely reluctant Nathan to move a few feet to the right, holding his heaving shoulders. We need to let the professional have access to Theo, but I know full well we're thinking the same thing: the worst feeling in the world is when you are the one unable to heal your own child.

"Hey, Theo," Sean says, taking a knee in the sand. He seems to immediately sense Theo is nervous, teetering on whether he thinks he's going to survive. "I'm a doctor."

"Hey, Sean, I heard," Theo says, sticking to the bare minimum of conversation. "I'm in pain." And communicating in slabs of epistemological fact. Which is predictable considering that Theo has never experienced much real pain, and the few times he faced any kind of discomfort, Nathan and I shielded him from it and made it disappear. We never let him play on the monkey bars at school after he made an offhand comment that it was too high off the ground; we never let him walk near the balcony railing; we didn't let him swim unsupervised until he was almost a teenager. These and *many* other activities Nathan and I believed were too dangerous have left Theo in a curious relationship with his own body. When he joined track and attempted to run the four-hundred relay, he believed he was experiencing cardiac arrest. When he had the hiccups for the first time, he thought his body was choking him to death, and when Nathan told him to hold his breath, Theo accused him of attempted murder. When he has a stuffy nose, he believes he has a brain tumor. Nathan and I—who have not only tacitly condoned, but *amplified* the behavior—bear the brunt of blame for what Sean is currently experiencing. But we don't care. He's safe.

"Okay," Sean says, defusing Theo's shortness. It's a trait he's likely noticed Caroline also possesses, but my sister can't trace the origin of her surliness to a near-death experience at birth, unless one considers emotional reciprocation to be near fatal. "You fit right in here."

Theo responds to Sean's attempt at levity by just getting mean, another trait his aunt has at the ready for anyone she's trying to brush off—which at any given moment in time, can encompass all of humanity. "You don't fit in. Why are you here?"

Sean tilts his neck to get a better angle on Theo's laceration. "I met your Aunt Caroline on the plane to St. John."

"You're friends with my aunt?" he says, scrunching his nose at the idea. "I think I want a second opinion."

"Theo," Sean says, remaining calm, "you need to stop squirming long enough for me to develop a first opinion." He grabs Caroline's water bottle, dumps the cold contents over the cut, cleaning it off to get a closer look at the extent of the damage. Blood runs all over the sand in rivulets, streaking the surrounding towels and Caroline's flip-flops, causing her to turn up her nose in disgust.

"What are you doing?" I shout. "You're *killing* him."

"I don't think we should let a thoracic surgeon look at a leg wound," Nathan says, putting his arm around me and looking for support in our shared hysteria.

"Right," Benjamin says, feeling his daughter and son-in-law's shared hysteria has been cranked up high enough to necessitate his presence. "A brush with coral is way beyond his pay grade. We're going to have to airlift him back to DC."

"He just needs a few stitches," Sean announces, tying a beach towel around Theo's wound. "Five or six tops. It's not serious."

"Not *serious*," I repeat, appalled at his flippancy, his borderline malpractice.

"I'm fine," I hear Theo say over my entreaties, and am rendered silent. I have *never* heard him say that before.

"Hear that, Elizabeth," Benjamin says, running his hand through his hair. He's clearly dissatisfied with how Nathan and I handled this incident, but has enough sensitivity—for once in his life—to not say it aloud while I'm upset. "He's going to be fine."

"I'll walk Theo over to the medical center," Sean says, rising from the sand and brushing himself off. Then he winks sweetly at Nathan and me. "I'll do them myself."

"Okay, sweetie, okay," I say to Theo while I grab my bag. "Dad and I are right behind you."

"No," Theo says, *sharp*, the wrong note in a symphony. "I want Grandpa. He's much calmer about these things."

I know Theo has always had a special place in his life for Benjamin, much to my utter disappointment, but his desire to have my father accompany him to get stitches is a bit much. It makes me wonder where Nathan and I went wrong, and how Benjamin snuck in—during our moment of parental weakness—and manipulated

Theo into thinking he was a fit guardian. Clearly, I need to watch Winnie much closer, now apprised of Benjamin's ability to creep in any crack in the door I've inadvertently left ajar.

"Dad!" I yell, annoyed he's Theo's choice, that he is taking my child away without lifting a finger, and pissed that I even have to live in a world where that's an option. But I can't quite cause a scene over that. I'll embarrass Theo; I'll embarrass Nathan; I'll embarrass poor Sean; I'll embarrass everyone except myself, because I don't really care. Instead, I select a work-around, a more palatable reason to force Benjamin back and conclude a piece of business I was tasked to perform in the first place. "You need to just let Nathan go with Theo and Sean. I need to talk to you."

"But I don't need to talk to you," he says, motioning for a bleeding Theo and a confused Sean to hold up while he dispatches his tiny problem. *Me.*

"Yes, you do," I say, annoyed. "I know what you're trying to do with Julian. How you're sending him away from his family. Persephone told me."

"Elizabeth...*no,*" he says, taking off his sunglasses to make me understand he means *this.* "We're not talking about this—"

"Well, I strongly disagree with that," I say, trying to hold my ground. "Kate..."

"*Look,*" he says, starting to turn away. "Kate, whatever her intentions, is not here to see the fallout from her dying wish to save us all. I *am.* It's not fucking saving anyone. And I'm putting an end to it."

"You can't—"

"No, *you* can't. And if you want to go against me, you're an army of one. You have fun with that."

"You're wrong, Dad," I say, while he's turning his back to me and ending the conversation. "I'm an army of two. I've got *Kate.*"

But he doesn't care; he's moved on to other topics.

"Sean," I hear him say as Theo disappears from my view, a skinny speck that used to be my beating heart, now seeking safety with Benjamin. "You need to come have dinner with us tonight. I chartered a private boat. Consider it a thank you from me to you."

"I'd love to," Sean says, also blind to the real Benjamin Sunderland lurking behind a seemingly gracious invitation. But soon he shall learn to rue the day.

"*I'd love to,*" Caroline repeats, mimicking Sean in a shrill whine while grabbing me by the elbow, distracting me from my longing for my lost son. "God, Lizzie. I'm so sick of him."

I turn my head slightly to watch Benjamin, Sean, and Theo fully disappear and notice the shadow of Nathan, clearly following them from afar, not trusting *anyone* with the care of our son but trying to allow the illusion that Theo has independence.

"Dad?" I say, turning around to face her. "I agree."

"No," she says. "Not Dad. *Sean.*"

"What the fuck happened?" Paul says, appearing a few feet away from us and walking over to our chairs. "Is that *blood*?" When he's closer, he looks down at the stained sand. "Yeah. That *is* blood." He turns to me, then to Caroline. "Liz? Do you have something you want to tell me? Are you striking our siblings now?"

I explain to him how Theo got hurt, how he took *Benjamin* with him to get stitches instead of me or Nathan, how Persephone took me to yoga, and how our father is tearing their family apart while simultaneously not allowing ours to heal the way Kate—and I—had hoped.

"I need a drink," he says once I'm finished.

"I know you need a drink," I say, furious that this was his go-to reaction. "We all *need* a drink. We all need a fucking intravenous of alcohol pouring into our veins. But what I really need is for you to be my brother and tell me things are going to be okay. That somehow this is going to be okay."

"Yeah," he says, concerned. "I want to tell you that too. Which is why I need the drink." He smiles, puts his hands on my shoulders, and draws me in for a hug. "Don't you want to come get a drink with me?"

"No," I say, pushing him away.

"Lizzie," Caroline says, interceding, "it's going to be okay." Then she turns to Paul. "You can fuck off and get your drink. I was talking to Lizzie. For once, you're not monopolizing her on vacation, and *I* get to have a big sister."

If there's one trait that defines Caroline—outside of burying her maturity way past its expiration date—it's an almost medieval jealous streak, like an exiled wicked sibling eyeing the royal children and waiting for revenge.

It took her a year after our marriage to warm up to Nathan. She felt my husband was monopolizing my time, and our relationship had stripped me of my independence—specifically, my independence to hang out with her. She continued this love-hate relationship with my children. When Theo was born, she described her fresh-from-the-hospital nephew as "needy" and "codependent." But it was with Winnie that Caroline finally met her match. My daughter was actually more possessive than her aunt when it came to me and refused to negotiate, screaming her head off when Caroline challenged her. To this day, Winnie is still the only person in the family Caroline begrudgingly respects for beating her at her own game.

Paul, still looking for company, eyes Winnie on her phone and snaps his fingers to snare her attention. "You. You're coming with me."

"I don't want a drink," she says, not lifting up her head.

"No. We'll find you froyo," he says, as if negotiating a hostile merger between rivaling businesses. "And you can have it while I drink."

"Okay," Winnie says, seeming to consider the deal equitable. She wanders off with her uncle, leaving me alone with Caroline—who wants to talk about *men*.

"I was saying," Caroline continues tartly, "before we were interrupted by our alcoholic brother, that I'm done with Sean."

"It's been less than thirty-six hours," I say, not surprised Caroline has cooled on Sean in that short of a timeframe. She's done that before. She's tossed men aside in less time. The noteworthy piece of news is that Caroline, who never attends a family function without a date in tow, is about to kick aside the guy filling that designated role in a totally atypical *family* situation. Which means on some level, Sean isn't fulfilling his basic role, which is distraction without any feelings attached, arm candy to be ditched once an event Caroline wants to distance herself from has ended. I can't ask Caroline what the problem is without risking her immature wrath, but judging from my prior experience with my sister, Sean must be trying to share his feelings with her, or she must actually have feelings for him. Either way, he is on the way out. "What did he do?"

"He's...clingy," Caroline says, ticking off each flaw on the fingers of her right hand. "He's so depressed. He reads Russian novels and philosophy books with a highlighter, nodding and scribbling whenever someone rhapsodizes on their suicidal thoughts. Then he asks me if *I've* ever felt that way. No, Sean. Not until I fucked you." She moves on to the left hand. "And he keeps telling everyone he's a doctor. I mean, Lizzie, I'm not a person who defines themselves by what they do."

"Thankfully you don't," I say, trying to subtly insinuate Caroline does very little except capturing her life in Instagram stories with pithy narration, interspersed with dropping Benjamin and Kate's names to get into restaurants.

"I'm just saying," Caroline continues, getting huffier with each complaint, "he's not my kind of guy."

"Do you mean sensitive? Available?" I ask, opening the dreaded annals of Caroline Sunderland's dating history, almost exclusively composed of married men with immovable wives canceling out any hope of commitment, and thus posing no danger to her true unbending commitment: self-destruction.

Her toxicity really shined the time we went to Benjamin and Kate's Hamptons house, when she dragged me out at eleven at night under furious protest on my end, saying I wasn't her sister anymore, that having children had changed me, that our closeness—*Caroline is close to people?*—had slackened, bruising her tender feelings and ego. Much as I expected, she drank too much, hooked up with every man who even looked in her general direction, and then made me leave in a Volkswagen Passat, where she dry humped her date in the backseat, and I rode in the front with his best friend and my "date"—lucky woman that I was—who was coincidentally an actual Uber driver whose phone kept exploding with ride requests, all of which I was afraid he might stop and pick up.

On the ride back to Benjamin and Kate's—Caroline had invited them there to keep the party going—she started to look unwell. Turning to look at them in the backseat, I appealed to the man's better nature and suggested my sister wasn't in any shape to consummate the relationship. There was always tomorrow. Caroline didn't agree, threw a fit, then tried to hit me with a Louboutin heel—all actions that made the man in the backseat realize I was right, and this wasn't the night.

Caroline's anger at my presumed act of sabotage didn't end after we left the car. She marched into the house, flipped on all the lights, and continued screeching that I betrayed her, that I took away her fun out of jealousy that it wasn't me, and that I would pay for ruining her good time. Finally, I grew tired of listening to her and decided to take a shower to wash the Passat off my body. In the interim, Caroline crept into my bedroom, took off all her clothes, and snuck into bed with Nathan, who had passed out hours earlier due to his feet swelling up from sunburn. She woke him up—always a mistake—explained that I wasn't around and no one had to know, but this had been on her mind for a very long time. Then she attempted to kiss him.

Nathan bounded out of bed in the dark, fell over two pieces of furniture, and began throwing articles of clothing at Caroline, telling her to get dressed before I came back.

I did come back.

And I personally glimpsed a part of Caroline that I never thought would be directed toward me—her demonic spitefulness.

"I don't care that he's available," Caroline says, as if I've missed the entire point. "I don't want him."

"Caroline," I say, straining not to bring up any of her past and keep this a positive talk. "What's the worst that could happen if you give him a chance?"

"The worst," she says, "is what I'm looking to avoid."

"Maybe don't," I say, understanding that talking to Caroline about emotional risk is like talking to Theo about physical risk— except one of them is kind of my fault, and the other is Benjamin and Kate's. But ultimately, their issues stem from the same root: a desperate desire to shield our vulnerability. "Maybe embrace the worst. Maybe your worst could be somebody else's best. And maybe one day you could be that someone who has the best."

"Oh Jesus, Lizzie," she says, mimicking vomiting. "The worst part is we both know you believe that."

"I'm just saying. Maybe he's not the one to throw away after thirty-six hours. Maybe he deserves at least *one dinner*." I smile. "Can you try that? Just for me?"

Caroline sighs, resigned. "I can't promise you that."

"I will stop talking...something we both want...if you just *promise*."

"I will try my best," Caroline says. "That's all I can give you."

CHAPTER NINETEEN

AS I STEP ABOARD THE smaller boat—a sea-faring vessel dotted with my family's sad, unforgiving faces—that has been tasked with taking us to the *bigger* boat Benjamin chartered for tonight's dinner, I can't help but think that not only is no one trying, but we all appear to be passengers on the same craft that dragged Dante across the River Styx into the mouth of hell. Fourteen silent pilgrims, all equally afraid in their own way and realizing there is no turning back. There is only the future and the implicit promise of chaos. And much to my own chagrin, I'm a part of it, equally guilty of not trying, of ignoring my own advice, of removing myself from my family and spending all afternoon with Nathan and the kids and never mentioning—in fact, willfully ignoring—that I'm pregnant.

Once Theo returned from a snappy six stitches, a suturing maneuver I'm sure Sean could perform in his sleep, we had lunch, then spent the rest of the day by the pool. I was even uncharacteristically willing to "play" several fraught rounds of table tennis with Theo, throwing a few games to spare myself his erratic sportsmanship and let him luxuriate in his inability to lose without mass recriminations about the unfitness of the resort's equipment, about how he'd forfeited the game before he even stepped up to play on account of not being set up for success. How could he work with such *weak tools*? With shoddy paddles and half-deflated balls?

I also patiently allowed Nathan and Winnie to marinate in their half-invented personal crises, which gained in fury the more they spoke. Like Winnie's apocalyptic rage over needing an SAT tutor when it wasn't required of Theo. I wanted to answer it was because he got a 1590 on his first try, and Winnie came in around five hundred points lower on her PSATs. Nonetheless, I let her fulminate—logic be damned. I nodded; I agreed; I took her hand in mine and let her cry at the injustice of it all.

Then, while I watched Theo and Winnie play volleyball, I listened to Nathan continue his raging soliloquy on the writer's life, unsure if he'd finally succumbed to writer's block or if he just hates being pigeonholed as a particular type of a writer: one with very expensive and very successful projects that stir up great controversy on film Twitter, which only gooses their grosses. Once again, I nodded and agreed; I took his hand in mine and let him cry at his caged creative spirit yearning to break free and soar.

On a normal day, any other day, I would have stopped them cold, cut them short, pointed out the patent absurdities, the maudlin turn toward personal melodrama that runs through my husband and children like an emotional isthmus. But I didn't.

Getting pregnant again never even crossed my mind. Nathan and I never thought about, never seriously discussed, having a third child—and for the brief moments we did after Winnie turned two, we laughed it off, never wanting to be outnumbered by the kids. It was simple defensive math. Our family is defined by that math.

Now Nathan and I are raising teenagers, and our life is centered around being the parents of high school students. We host sleepovers for Winnie's six closest friends, who rotate in importance on a weekly basis. We carpool with parents of other teenagers when Theo has Model UN conferences or homecoming dances. We never eat dinner before eight thirty, the time at night when everyone finally has a second to breathe. Our family vacations revolve around going to Rome, Athens, or the South of France—not riding *Dumbo* or the teacup ride. Our television schedule alone is incredibly irresponsible and unproductive for an infant. What are they going to think of *Succession* and *White Lotus*?

And just as our family has evolved, Nathan and I have evolved with it. And although I have my depressive moments, my incurable sadness about my time with Theo and Winnie ebbing away, you can't go back. My plan to cure my empty-nest syndrome over the house I had painstakingly created for Theo and Winnie was to take some cooking classes with Nathan, maybe start a book club, perhaps take an impromptu trip to Paris for a weekend. But never was having another baby considered, not even at my lowest moments. Nathan and I can't start over from the beginning. We've seen too much; we *know* too much. We've eaten from the tree of parenting and have been exiled from the garden of ignorant bliss.

All of which is why I didn't tell Nathan, because I'm not sure it's what I want. Honestly, I have no idea what I want in any aspect of life, let alone having this randomly dropped on me. And until I make up my mind, I plan on keeping the news to myself.

I take another look at my family's grim visages and deduce that, when it comes to the events that took place in the intervening hours since I've last seen them—events I'm currently not privy to, and that will likely come to the fore once the first cork is popped, the first cap twisted, the first cubes of ice tinkling at the bottom of a glass make their presence—all will be revealed in a torrent of alcohol-laced recrimination.

After a brisk five minutes of staring at my assorted siblings, it becomes obnoxiously clear that Caroline has violated our agreement and isn't trying in the least with Sean. She isn't even sitting with him. Instead, she's placed herself next to Julian, and they both sport a weary expression backed by a slouching posture that fills me with fear that they're trying to assume liquid form and escape through the cracks in the floorboards.

Persephone and Oliver sit across from Julian, and I have to admire her tenacity, her brazen bravery to stick with this absolute *shitshow*, even after I told her that my first attempt to change

Benjamin's mind about talking Julian out of his imminent flight hadn't exactly moved the needle as much as either of us had hoped. But I would try again. She told me I was strong, that she saw in my eyes that I could handle Benjamin's pressure, and that I could hold her family intact just the way Kate had promised, then hugged me—none of which made me feel any better.

Sean, the designated outsider, is sitting next to them, listening to Persephone read to Oliver, who seems distracted and confused, unable to be comforted by his mother's dulcet tones, likely because he's on a boat of hostile strangers, who aren't going out of their way to make him feel welcome, least of all his father. Sean, on the other hand, seems captivated by the struggle of the small woodland protagonist of Oliver's book, as if he sees himself in the uphill challenges facing the sprightly squirrel. Caroline, also struggling, has taken to texting me, berating me, blaming Sean for not making this any easier on her and threatening to throw him overboard.

I slide into a newly emptied seat, and Paul joins me, asking a few speculative questions about Madeleine and trying to give some of his own shopworn advice, having received an initial bounce after the Obamas dined at his first restaurant. He recommends I seize the moment because in this viral age the window is even smaller, and my president isn't as popular. Unfortunately, Paul is sidetracked from schooling me in the signal-to-noise ratio of social media by Winnie rushing over to subject him to a fuselage of TikTok videos, to which Paul politely nods, reminds her she might be getting spied on by the Chinese government, and reaches for the flask in his pocket.

I turn away from Winnie and Paul and am immediately besieged by Mason and Meredith, who have roped me into adjudicating the rightful owner of a portable battery pack for their iPhones. I try to broker a compromise and notice Tessa looming on the periphery, sipping a High Noon that she wrapped in a paper towel and carried on board, while staring at me slack-jawed and occasionally elbowing Nathan—who is absorbed in quiet contemplation by the side of the boat, as if some answer to his crises lies at the bottom of the ocean—to point out how good I am with her children, who seem to have dedicated themselves to punishing her for some mistake she is unable to pinpoint. Nathan nods sagely, perhaps finding an equally depressed ally, and listens intently to Tessa enlarge her central thesis. Both Mason and Meredith refuse to eat anything unless the nanny cooks it, refuse to read unless the nanny picked the book out, refuse to give their father the slightest bit of *shit* because they're afraid if they say anything he'll be gone even more, which means that Tessa, who is never gone, has to defend Miles's decision to be a totally absent parent so her own children—*who hate her parenting*—don't hate her.

In an unaccustomed move, Nathan silently absorbs the information and replies, "Yeah. You're in a world of shit." Then he helps himself to a gulp of Tessa's drink. "Maybe you should spend less time wondering what they think of you as a mother, and just be their mother. Because they're never going to be happy with you." He notably doesn't hand Tessa back her drink. "I thought Lizzie and I did everything right, then we ended up getting stabbed in the back." He finishes his exegesis on the eternal ambiguities of parenting and points at Theo and Benjamin, who are standing at the helm of our small craft, as if they are Ahab and Starbuck pondering the abyssal vastness of the sea and the bruised purple in the sky above, presaging a stubborn storm that refuses to appear.

It's quite a fitting posture as Benjamin's chartered yacht for this evening comes into view, another sterling example of his unrivaled commitment to terrorizing the natural world—because who could be expected to reserve a boat that's able to dock in the ample space provided by the resort and wouldn't run ashore and destroy the already vulnerable beach? But I think there's more in tonight's theatrical choice for a meal, a selection that dovetails with his decision to take command of the next few days and *unseat* Kate, which means Benjamin needs to block all access points, coming or going, and leave us all marooned with no outsides, no escape, no hope, a literal captive audience to whatever villainous mind games he has in store for us.

Fifteen minutes and a varied assortment of cocktails to imbibe later, the family is still in its atomized state, flitting around the vast yacht singularly, munching a panoply of imported hors d'oeuvres and not any closer to speaking. Except one of us.

Benjamin clinks his fork to the side of a champagne flute and calls the family to attention. "First, I want to welcome our guest of honor. The doctor who is never off duty, even on vacation. The man who single-handedly saved my grandson from the hands of subpar resort physicians. My new friend, a friend of the family now, *Doctor*—"

Caroline grabs my wrist and leans into my ear. "Like he needs another person to tell him he's a doctor."

"Sean," Benjamin continues. "Sean, what is your last name? It seems wrong to toast a guest on my yacht and not know his last name. It's bad form."

I turn my head and see Sean, who is clearly uncomfortable being feted in baroque splendor for the bare minimum of his skills. "Pierce. My last name is Pierce."

"Sean *Pierce*," Benjamin says, raising his glass and then falling silent, pausing. "I think I know your father."

Benjamin does. Sean's father is named Arthur, and they sit on the board of the Public Theater together, a seat that costs a minimum of a million dollars for the pleasure of not missing the rehearsals for the next *Hamilton* and the status bragging rights attached to having seen it before everyone else. *I* know the Pierces as well. Sean's older sister, Chloe, was in my class at Dalton, and we distinctly did not get along. I found her old-monied, tradition-bound evaluation of one's worth being tied to the precise date of your family's appearance in the New World to be quite tiring, a feeling I vented to her at homecoming. There was also her consistent nose upturning at the fact my parents were divorced and my family was blended, a rarity back in the late '80s, and further proof of my family's "mutt" status, having arrived in this country two hundred years late and contributing to the moral decline upheld by families like hers.

The Pierces had another thorn sticking in Benjamin and Kate's craw. They had more money. Money that went back centuries. Money that preceded the Civil War.

Someone like Sean is my father's equivalent to bagging the white whale, the Vanderbilt, the Rockefeller, the Astor. It's a family name he has always wanted one of his children to marry into, and which we have all staunchly refused, to such an extent that they had to build Miles into the closest approximation they could find. But Sean is the real thing; I can tell by the glint in my father's eye. It's as if he'd spent years walking a beach with a metal detector, searching for buried treasure, and finally unearthed it.

And now that Caroline knows that Benjamin *knows* who Sean is—and is impressed with him, and would *more* than approve their budding relationship—my sister is going to cut him off possibly before this dinner is over. He has no chance. Which is a shame because—and *maybe* I'm reading too much into this—he seems to have followed my path. He started out ensconced in all the trappings of Manhattan privilege, then rejected its underpinnings, picking a career outside finance and moving to a different city to start over, to forge a life beyond his last name.

"Well Sean *Pierce,*" Benjamin continues, in a flushed afterglow, having found an avatar of historical wealth on his yacht, "you're no longer a stranger to me, or my grandson, or the rest of my family. All of whom are very, *very* happy to have met you."

Caroline expectedly grabs my wrist harder and speaks through gritted teeth. "Speak for yourself, Dad."

After waiting an appropriate amount of time to pass following Sean's coronation, Benjamin clinks the side of the glass *again*, apparently full of celebratory news this evening. "And without Sean," he says, winking, offering a little in-joke between him and the imagined son-in-law he wants most in the world, "this second piece of good news wouldn't be able to be celebrated. *Theo*, do you want to tell everyone...or should I?"

Theo, on the spot, instinctively demurs, immediately arousing my suspicion. "You can go ahead, Grandpa."

He laughs. "I'd hoped so." Benjamin raises his glass. "Theo has come to his good senses and decided to attend Harvard in the fall."

"What are you talking about, Dad?" I say, switching my gaze back and forth between Theo and my father, completely blindsided. Weeks ago, we sent in the deposit to secure Theo's spot in the freshman class at Sarah Lawrence, a school—up until thirty seconds ago—I assumed was his dream. He seemed to spark to the self-guided curriculum they offer, which appealed to Nathan and me as well. It would allow Theo a wide base of exploration—both educationally and internally—and enough exposure to find his passion, before ultimately sending him off to a career of his choosing, or at the very least, graduate school. We visited the school three times since his acceptance to make sure it was the perfect place—the model home away from home—and also to beta test every conceivable traffic route from DC to Bronxville, in case Theo ever needed us in an emergency. Theo didn't even express a passing interest in applying to any Ivys.

"How are you going to Harvard?" I ask Theo, the information getting blurrier the longer I think about it. "You didn't even apply."

"That's in Cambridge, pal," Nathan jumps in. "I don't think you can go that far away. And I haven't explored any of the routes."

"I did apply," Theo says, instinctively inching closer to Benjamin. "I just didn't tell you. Grandpa helped me fill out the application and paid the fee for me."

I disengage from Theo and whirl toward my father. "*You* did this."

Benjamin puts his hands up, feigning innocence. "I didn't, Elizabeth. He came to me and asked."

"Don't you think *you* should have told me?" I say to my father, then turn to Theo. "Don't *you* think you should have told me?"

"No," Theo says, obviously hiding his own secrets from me this afternoon, as I did to him. Both rather epochal pieces of information to keep folded in our corner pockets. "I felt like you were more convinced than me about Sarah Lawrence, but you'd moved things so far along, I didn't think I could turn back. I told Grandpa. He asked me what I wanted to do, and I told him. I wanted to go to Harvard and study comparative literature."

"But you *were* convinced," I say, straining to not scream, to spell out the ingredients to Benjamin's spell that he cast. "Until you got your grandfather involved." This is what my father does. He takes what is concrete, what is fixed, and tortures it into bizarre geometric patterns of unexplored possibilities that leave you in a brain fog until you just agree with him to make it stop. Only this time, I can't move to another city to get my children further away from him. It's a little harder to relocate Winnie at fifteen than it was at *five*. "It's how he controls everything. Including *you* right now."

"I'm not controlling him," Benjamin says, seeming almost hurt I leveled the accusation against him.

"Oh, for fuck's sake, Dad," I say, losing any semblance that there are children or Sean present. "You don't know how to have any relationship based upon anything else. Just look at *us*. Any single one of us will tell you that's what you do."

As I should have expected, Benjamin takes me up on my dare, moving his eyes off me and facing his children. He scans Tessa, Paul, Caroline, and Julian to decide where to start, choosing which of my siblings will become the sacrificial scapegoat, the Bernard-Sunderland sin-eater to remove the sting from my accusation.

My eyes follow his, performing my own equation to decide which brother or sister will be called to account. It's *got* to be Tessa. She will always take Benjamin's side because she is the biggest victim of his control, the Stockholm syndrome sister, and to disagree with my father's methods would be to indict the core of her being. He's certainly not going to ask Caroline, who will deliver a tongue-lashing dissertation on Benjamin's crimes and misdemeanors that would make mine appear milquetoast and cautious in comparison. Paul, who feels he has little to gain or lose by defending Benjamin—because he's not Luc, his biological father who can do no wrong—is also a risky ally. He's less volatile than Caroline, but also has less longing for Benjamin's attention, which makes him dangerous.

Then I see Benjamin's eyes stop and widen when he reaches Julian.

I should have known. As evidenced by the current Persephone and Oliver situation, Benjamin wields a titanic amount of power over my little brother. He always has. He and Julian never went through that awkward stepfather-stepchild situation that can sometimes take years to overcome, to build trust, to make it safe to love. From day one, Benjamin was Julian's father and Julian was his son. It was almost surreal how instantaneous their bond was formed, the ease around each other they had, which was an enormous contributing factor in alienating Paul from both of them.

Paul could never get over Luc leaving them behind. He could never accept or forgive Julian for seamlessly turning the page on a man his older brother held so dear, as if he were simply a chapter he had skimmed And most especially, Paul could never accept Benjamin as a viable surrogate when his real father was still out there and—in his mind—just waiting for a sign it was safe to love him under these new circumstances.

"*Jules*," Benjamin says to my brother in a welcoming baritone, as if he just fell off a bike and suffered a scraped knee, and he wants to encourage him to get back on the road. "Do you think I'm controlling?"

Julian points to his chest, as surprised as everyone else that he was chosen. Like most of us, he probably assumed it was going to be Tessa. "Me?"

"Yes," Benjamin says, looking at me. He's flaunting his ace in the hole, taunting me with the knowledge that my brother is going to betray me because he *has* to. Benjamin's control is the only thing that may save him from Persephone's will to save Julian from himself, an option he still hasn't reconciled in his own mind. "Am I controlling, Julian? You can be honest." He tries to give his best approximation of safety to speak freely. "That's what this trip is all about. Honesty."

Julian begins to stutter out a series of meaningless monosyllables interspersed with jerky, apologetic hand gestures.

"There's no *wrong* answer," Benjamin says, impatiently waiting for the right answer, the one he longs to hear, but unable to rush Julian, who will break down from the stress before validating my father. "Take your time. Chew on it. Masticate thoroughly."

I watch poor Julian suffer, trying to drown in Persephone's and Oliver's eyes, then look back to my father, imploring, pleading.

"I mean...I don't necessarily see things the way you do. Right? Like we see the world very differently sometimes." Julian rubs the side of his face, scratching the stubble on his chin. It's the same awkward two-step of anxious tics he exhibited when I first asked if he was doing drugs. "I could...kind of *see* where Lizzie could get that impression. There are times when I may ask myself, *why* would Lizzie think that way.... Why would her impression trend in that direction...."

Benjamin, fitfully fucking furious that he didn't simply get a "*yes,*" holds his hand up. "Stop. Please." He opens and closes his palms, about to get volcanic. "The only one. Julian is the only child I know, *besides my beloved Elizabeth,* who I know will answer me truthfully. Whose love or censure never comes with strings attached. So, this must be what I am." He looks to the heavens, as if he's summoning the ghost of King Lear to inhabit his body so his dramatic monologue will climax with the proper poetic sting.

"What saddens me—what *shatters* me—is that what all of you have interpreted as control is what it takes to keep all of you sane and sound enough to tie your fucking shoes in the morning. You think this is easy? You think any one of *you* could do it? Do you seriously think any one of you could *afford it*? Emotionally. Financially. Spiritually. Do you?"

"Yes," I say, tired of doing things my father's way, tired of the diminishing returns, tired of having to fight for Julian, now Theo, soon Caroline, never Tessa, and to my surprise Paul, who never wavered from my side before, and has already disagreed with me three times on this trip. Paul is consumed with confusion over losing Kate, his world drunk and spinning, leaving him unexpectedly vulnerable to Benjamin's artful ploys. Which is why I can't hold it in any longer and shout. "*Yes!* I think I can. I think there's a better way forward beyond your control. And so did *Kate.*"

Even Benjamin seems thrown aback, silenced, glaring like a lion suddenly realizing he's been in a hunter's scope the entire time. We've been dancing around this denouement since we all watched

Kate's video and these wheels were set in motion, although if I'm honest, my father and I have been on this collision course for three decades. And I'm sick of it. Sick of him. I can't bear another hour of it, and I don't think anyone else present can either.

"Fine, Elizabeth," he says, mimicking the act of washing his hands clean. "It's all yours. You win." He looks away from me, throws up his arms to the rest of the family, and proudly announces. "Guess what. That means you're all fucking disinherited. Have fun with your lives. Best of luck."

After performing his Pontius Pilate routine, Benjamin waves goodbye and begins strolling to the stairs at the back of the boat. He nearly capsizes halfway down, curses his knee, then boards the smaller boat *alone*, leaving his family behind.

For a second, none of us actually believe he'll do it—that he'll come to his senses and realize we'll all be stranded if he goes through with this. Then we hear the growl of the motor, the harsh cadence of the whipped water, and yes, *it's actually happening.*

"How the fuck are we going to get off this yacht?" Caroline screams, running toward the stairs and trying to flag Benjamin down before he disappears. "This is fucking ridiculous, Dad. Even by your already disappointing standards."

Paul whisks a cocktail from the circular tray of a passing server and stares at his reflection in the bubbles. "I guess we could call the Coast Guard. I mean...what else do they do?"

CHAPTER TWENTY

MY BROTHER WAS WRONG. THAT is *not* what the Coast Guard does. I was informed of Paul's mistake when I called them and the man who answered the phone made light of our situation and explained in heavy-handed sarcasm that the Coast Guard does not rescue millionaire families stranded on a yacht in the Caribbean after their father threw a fit and left them all marooned. He noted his offense that anyone could possibly imagine that rescuing rich people is the function of a Homeland Security department, and wrapped up by mentioning that if I truly believed that, I should reevaluate my life. I told him I didn't need the judgment, and from my purview, if they weren't going to save my family, Homeland Security should spend the time investigating the brewing Civil War in our country and not make a forty-three-year-old woman in the midst of a crisis question her choices in life.

I recovered and made my walk over to the captain, who had witnessed the events, and joked he was happy he got paid in advance. I applied my famed charm. That didn't work. I quickly begged. That didn't work. Then I offered him a generous bribe to get the smaller boat, or even a fucking rowboat, to come back and get us. That worked. He left that conversation $1,000 richer for getting on the radio.

Thirty minutes later, we are finally on the seven-minute boat ride back to land. I never imagined *seven minutes* could feel this long. Theo is mounting an open rebellion against me for being surprised in the first place that he went to my father about his college decision, when all I did was apparently push Sarah Lawrence on him, never asking if it was what he wanted and insisting it would be the proper place to help him ease into a life absent of his loving parents, who he would never be able to be away from for more than five minutes. I attempt to answer, to defend my cause, to stop him from making a huge mistake—but he shuts me down and refuses to listen, rendering mute all my entreaties.

After he finishes fulminating, Tessa takes over and treats us to an extended digression on how we all need to thank *her*. She says if she hadn't been the loving, dutiful, respectful daughter who prized both the lifestyle Benjamin and Kate provided us with, and appreciated their loving—albeit unique—approach to parenting that we *choose* to remain ignorant to, my father might have been serious about disinheriting us. But he would never disinherit Tessa, thus we will all be saved by the very things we mock her for. And much like Theo, Tessa doesn't allow any commentary or challenges against her narrative.

As the boat approaches the dock, I have never been happier to see land, *any land*. The skipper ties down the boat, mooring it, and we begin walking back to the Eleusinian in blessed silence. For approximately thirty seconds.

That's when I see a man running across the beach in a branded Eleusinian polo shirt, calling out my name into the night breeze. I consider running back to the boat, desperate to avoid another confrontation tonight, but he's definitely spotted me, and there is no tactical retreat.

"Ms. Sunderland," he says, stopping short and kicking up a spray of sand that dusts my sandals and dress. "My name is George. I'm the manager of the resort."

"Hi, George," I say, but he's quickly distracted by the sight of Sean among our party.

"Mr. Pierce," George asks, dripping with customer service, as if he's turned into a human comment card. "How are you enjoying the honeymoon suite?"

Before Sean can declaim the indigenous beauty of the resort and the superb accommodations, I cut it short. "George. What can I do for you?"

"Well," he says, looking at the children in the group and leading with discretion. "Perhaps we can discuss this in a more private location."

"You don't have to, George," I say, appreciating his tact but seeing no need to go down this road. "My father just abandoned us all in the ocean."

"*Yes*," he says, the consummate salesman, completely glossing over my father's betrayal, knowing full well where his bread is buttered. He's relieved I handed him the inroad to introduce a potentially combustive topic. "Your father is what I needed to talk to you about." He leans in a little closer and speaks to me in sotto voce. "He's canceled the credit cards of everyone in the family. I'm going to have to ask for an alternate form of payment for all of you to be able to stay here." He opens his hands in supplication, as if the enormity of this task is beyond him. "I hope you can see this from my side. What else am I to do?"

As George guides us to the front desk, we begin to shrink in numbers. The great bailout beginning. Nathan, who is still reeling from the sideshow of Theo choosing my father over us, volunteers to take all the kids to dinner, since for the *second* night in a row no one has gotten to eat before Benjamin explodes. This leads me to speculate that the next company my father brings to market should have a personal touch, his own diet plan, where instead of eliminating carbohydrates, processed sugar, and corn syrup, he just takes you to dinner and *screams at you*, ending the meal before you take a bite. His unfettered anger would remove any chance of backsliding and cheating because you never eat. It would allow the whole world to experience what it's like to dine with him, a luxury I've known all my life.

As Nathan and the children seek sustenance and safety, Paul and I are left leaning against the cherrywood front desk of the Eleusinian—my hair rustling from a breeze sneaking through the white shutters—while we wait for George to tally up the room fees and incidentals. I watch my siblings anxiously pace the length of the lobby; try to stifle a laugh from watching Tessa nearly crash into a patch of streaming succulents rising from terracotta pots, as she frantically texts Miles; note Caroline examining the vines and fragrant petals trailing the wall, trying to determine if they're real or not without touching them; and see Julian crash down on a pristine leather club chair, ask someone who is clearly a guest for a Diet Coke, and then stare at the slowly rotating ceiling fan above.

George looks up from the computer, runs his fingers up and down the screen, hits a few final keys, and then smiles. "The total for the rest of your stay with us, which we are so thrilled to be able to provide in the manner in which your very loyal family deserves, is one hundred and forty-five thousand dollars." He extends his hand, waiting for it to be filled with a credit card. "Will I be splitting this over five cards?"

"No," Paul says, laughing and pointing to me. "It's a good thing Kate left you an inheritance, because the rest of us are suddenly financially embarrassed."

"I would have gotten it anyway," I say, knowing I'm the one who put my siblings in this position. Taking care of them right now will absolve me of my guilt. I know my father cutting them off is the right thing—even if they don't know it yet—especially as they process Kate's death. They will have the chance to look at themselves, to take stock of their decisions without the distorted mirror my family's wealth provides. I did it and am a better person for it, now freed from the control mechanism that comes attached to the blood money. The more you try and run from the fortune, the more they throw at you. Kate was right, in theory, in her video. We do need to heal; we do need to let the sins and secrets out; we do need to mourn her; but even with her heart on her sleeve, she discounted my father and *his* needs, which run counter to her plan. My siblings and their children, the next generation, are now my broken fortune. But they also need a minute to adjust, to keep the gaping wound taped shut. I can give them that.

I hand George my Black Amex, already hearing Nathan in my mind—like a drumroll announcing the finale—complaining that my family is a loss leader and that they break the bank emotionally and in reality.

"You're amazing, Lizzie. Thank you so much," Julian says, likely relieved since $20,000 at minimum is a pretty big reach on an NGO salary. He slaps the armrest in a eureka moment and rises from his chair. There's a light in his eyes I haven't seen since the day they let him out of rehab, when he was filled with dreams to find his inner "ohm," to scale the peaks of Tibet and glimpse the eternal equilibrium behind the setting sun. "You've just inspired me. It's so fucking clear. It's been there the whole time and you parted the curtain for me. You let the light seep in."

"It's no problem, Jules," I say, a little floored by the sudden onrush of hidden meaning in just paying for his room. "I'm here for you."

"No," he says, frustrated I can't see it. "You made me see I can live without Benjamin's money. You do." He looks me in the eyes, waiting for me to meet him where he is. "I've got a *job*. Persephone has a job. Fuck it. Fuck Benjamin. We're better off."

Caroline turns away from the vines, her oceanic eyes filled with furious waves. "It's what I've been saying for years, Jules. *Fuck him*. You all saw him as some lesser of two evils because he was around less than Kate. But he's a fucking asshole."

"I *know*," Julian says, bowled over that someone is inhabiting his dimension, which I must admit seems a pretty wonderful place to be right now—a place filled with an obscure form of hope.

"Getting us disinherited may have been the greatest thing you've ever done," Caroline says. "It gives me the chance—the opportunity—I've always wanted. I can hurt him the most if I make it on my own." Caroline puckers her lips and slightly flares her nostrils, both telltale signs she is formulating an intricate plan that will force our father to stand up and pay attention, much like the infamous Boathouse incident. When Caroline devotes her full resources to her passions, nothing will get in her way. Anyone who attempts to come between my sister and victory will have hell to pay.

She reminds me of Kate when she gets like this, which makes sense considering she had the most time with our stepmother. The only caveat is Kate faced a far most hostile terrain. She had to open the door in a field—and in a time—where women weren't allowed in, and especially not one exhibiting those traits. And they don't just factor in at work. An ambitious woman also had to contend with losing friends, losing boyfriends, losing husbands, losing life outside of work because she had to do everything—*everything*—better to get ahead.

"I mean...*I've* got three degrees." Caroline continues, reminding us of her achievements. "I've got an MBA from Wharton. I speak French, German, and fucking Mandarin. There has to be a job I'm qualified for."

Tessa stands in the corner, a shade of flushed shame and a naughty smile dancing across her face. "It pains me to say this, but neither of you are wrong."

"Tess..." I say slowly, feeling borderline fearful for my sister's mental health. The disinheritance may have been the final blow that shattered her carefully appointed life. "Are you okay?"

"Oh, I'm fine Elizabeth," she says, tapping her foot. "Your little faux pas has given me a chance to prove to Daddy how invaluable

I really am. He might have been able to take me for granted before, to simply *overlook* that I am the public face of this family...." She pauses for effect, to let her indispensability, her epic awesomeness hit us like the ton of bricks she expected. Leave it to Tessa to take our father's financial temper tantrum and flip it around into an opportunity to prove how superior she is to all of us.

My sister has never been able to process that she is not the favorite child, that no matter how much she may try to nauseatingly flatter Benjamin and Kate by copying their life down to carpet fibers, she doesn't get to wear that crown. The problem is that her quest is purely quixotic because Benjamin and Kate already had a favorite child, and she couldn't measure up: *money*.

"I am the only one who has lived up to what Manhattan expects from a Bernard-Sunderland. This *glaring* truth has been able to escape him because I have never asked for the proper acknowledgment or my true worth," Tessa says proudly. "My absence will force him to see it. And we will survive, until Daddy comes crawling back to me and *begs*."

"Tess, not for nothing," Caroline says, "but wasn't Miles supposed to be here tonight?"

"He's *coming*, okay Caroline," she responds indignantly. "He just got fucking held up because he's working and important."

I shoot Caroline a harsh glance, silently ordering her to shut this down—that everyone is in the midst of a profound breakthrough that I will not allow her to destroy. If I'm honest, I may not *love*, appreciate, or even fathom the quasi-self-serving and spiteful manner in which my siblings are approaching this unforeseen chance to embrace change, discover love, uncover hidden happiness, achieve psychic symmetries, find their true selves, or intend *anything* approaching altruism. But I'm going to make the concerted effort to view this particular glass as half full. I must steel myself for the growing pains, and hope that at the end, better intentions bloom. But in the meantime, I will take this small win. A rather expensive win for a very ambiguous outcome.

"Who's hungry?" I ask. My voice ricochets off the walls far louder than I intended, as if trying to glue the potential fractures inherent in this situation with *sound*. I repeat the question, a little softer, and work up a smile. "I'll buy dinner." I realize after uttering those words, that was already understood. Then I turn to Paul, our resident gourmand, ready to solicit an opinion on a good restaurant. "What are you in the mood for?"

He doesn't answer me; instead, he does a slight two-step of confusion against the hardwood floor. "You go. I don't think I'm hungry. But when you're done, we need to talk."

CHAPTER TWENTY-ONE

WHAT'S WRONG?" I ASK PAUL, sitting next to him on a hammock on the Eleusinian terrace. The ocean behind us is aglow from the bone white moon, the gentle waves spangled with astral light. The thick woven ropes rock back and forth, and Paul and I sway with them, the languorous motion quelling my residual anxiety from my father's one-man yacht show. It didn't help that dinner with my siblings—an impromptu meal at the resort's buffet-style restaurant—involved chastising me for expressing my obvious concern over Paul instead of hanging on to every word of their plan to overthrow my father and burn down the proverbial bastille.

What my blissfully unaware siblings misread is that I wasn't concerned about what Paul might want to talk about; I was concerned he wanted to talk in the first place. The cornerstone of our relationship is that I talk and Paul listens, and after I've finished downloading my crisis du jour, he attempts to either render a decision favorable to his sister, or simply gives me a hug when there is no solution and all I needed was to vent and be supported. But he's barely—maybe two or three times over thirty-three years—requested a conversation. When Paul is in his preferred emotional climate, he will talk your ear off and be the life of the party. But when the topic of our family's trauma is raised, he strategically retreats, pretends, or, most likely, *prefers* to maintain that he's untouched, that he's managed to float above the damage for all his life and sublimate whatever may have lingered into a thriving career.

He digs into his pants pocket, pulls out a pack of yellow American Spirit cigarettes, takes one out, and lets it rest in the corner of his mouth.

"We quit," I say, horrified, yet strangely nostalgic. I think back to all the times we would lounge around Columbia between classes, chain-smoking and comparing hangovers.

"*You* quit," he says, searching his other pocket for his lighter.

"When did you start again?"

He finds the lighter, brings it to the cigarette, waits for the amber glow at the tip, then takes his first drag. "Liz, I never stopped."

"You've been hiding a smoking habit from me for twenty years," I say, appalled and betrayed, seeing Paul through a different prism. I'm sad that he wouldn't tell me, and sad that he thought he needed to keep something so insignificant a secret from me. "Anything else you aren't telling me?"

"That's what I'm *fucking* trying to do," he says, his voice echoing across the empty landscape. "But all you do is worry that I didn't agree with you about staying, worry about my relationship with our siblings, worry that I'm smoking. Worry about things that affect your world and not mine. Or more precisely, my role in *your* life as you see it. The life in which I apparently don't have any agency if I disagree with you."

I'm floored by his anger. It's not as if I've never seen Paul upset; he is, after all, an angry person. I've witnessed him verbally eviscerate every person in our family on a rotating basis. He just never does it to me. The Paul talking to me right now is the Paul reserved for the rest of the world. I just never thought I'd join their ranks.

I put my arm around him, trying to calm him down and get my brother back. "What is it? You can tell me. Is it about Kate?"

He rips my arm off him, practically jumping off the hammock. "You fucked up, Lizzie!" he shouts, terrifying the young couple clearly out on a romantic honeymoon walk, forcing them to turn back. "You fucked up big time. And most of the time I'm safe from your stupidity, but this time you got me trapped in it. And I want to *scream*."

"What did I do to *you*?" I yell back, confused and legitimately wounded by my brother's words. Paul may be my closest sibling, but that doesn't give him license to scream at me like some kitchen staff minion who burnt the special on a night the *WaPo* food critic came to review his newest restaurant.

"You just had to keep pushing Benjamin," he says, exhaling a pissed off plume of smoke through his nose like a restless mythic dragon caught in his cave. "You pushed him, and you pushed him, until he snapped. For what?"

"For the family. For *you*," I say, furious he could misinterpret my intentions and paint my worrying about him in such a negative, destructive light. "You have been a mess this entire trip. And have been siding half the time with Benjamin."

"Because I *need* him," Paul says, and I nearly tip off the hammock. Those words have never crossed his lips before. He has never sought out my father. In fact, he has adamantly *refused* him.

"But we don't need him," I say, trying to find any logic to hang onto just as I feel it slipping away, as if we're entering a twilight, upside-down universe. "The family is better off without him."

"Lizzie, *news-fucking-flash*," he says, throwing his arms out for emphasis, "the ship on our family sailed years ago. It hit a fucking iceberg. It crashed. The violins came out. Women and children amassed in lifeboats. And I have been happy to indulge in your fantasies of some possible future, as long as no one got hurt. But now I'm getting hurt." He stops pacing, stops smoking, stops moving period. "I need my trust fund." He runs his hand through his hair, sending his dirty-blond locks up in thick spikes. "I'm fucking bankrupt. Just like the article says. It's all true. I'm way overleveraged and construction has stopped."

After letting the words linger in the air for a minute—"I'm fucking bankrupt"—Paul seems almost relieved, as if the secret was weighing him down. Except it's not shared between both our shoulders. It's shared between him and *Benjamin's*. A situation I'd only ever glimpsed once before.

It was the opening night of La Maison de Francois, a prickly affair for Paul—both businesswise and emotionally—that was fraught with frayed nerves and the potential for a broken heart. As the days ticked closer to sharing his restaurant with DC, he sent out intricate, thickly embossed personal invitations to the family, plus Luc and his wife. Our siblings being *our siblings* declined, one by one, citing reasons such as a hot new club opening, tickets for the second part of Wagner's Ring Cycle—*it's a commitment, Tessa reminded him*—and a trip to a friend's private island. Even Kate had to see her biggest client, which couldn't be moved—an excuse that I never totally believed, as it seemed to be an overdesigned story to either avoid the chance of seeing Luc again or to miss the fallout when he inevitably didn't come. That left only Benjamin and me to represent the Bernard-Sunderlands, an outcome I didn't relish. I avoid one-on-one meals with my father, who can barely keep his composure when there's twelve of us present, let alone the child who's given him the most grief.

But much to my surprise, Benjamin was in a banner mood, soaking up the haute clientele out to fete Paul's triumphant opening. My father glided around the restaurant, a de facto maître d', hobnobbing with critics, senators, and congresswomen. He sung Paul's praises and jokingly promised campaign donations if everyone told a friend to visit La Maison de Francois. At first, I assumed Benjamin had gone full-court press so another Bernard-Sunderland would be lauded as a success in the media—but it became clear my father was sincere in his pride, basking in the only child to achieve such a level of public success. Caroline didn't have a job; Tessa didn't have a job after her art therapy debacle; Julian worked with an NGO devoted to Tibet; and I was the proud proprietor of what my father saw as an "underachieving" bakery. It was a side of

Benjamin I'd never seen before, a night we've never shared before or since, a night in which he still pointed out all my flaws, but we almost had *fun* together.

But the more vocal Benjamin became about Paul's achievement, the more sour and depressed my brother turned. I knew why. The answer lay on small table in the window with a "RESERVED" place card resting atop a handmade blue floral tablecloth, with the name *Luc Bernard* written below. A small table that stayed empty all night.

"I'm bankrupt," Paul repeats. "I put up the other restaurants, the creperie, my house...all of it...to put together the Wharf market. And everything possible has gone wrong. We're months behind, over budget, there's a fucking rat problem, and I think we found a dead body. Point is, I'm hemorrhaging money, and it won't stop...." He pauses, out of words, his problem seeming even worse when spoken aloud. Then he comes back to the hammock and sits next to me. "I need the trust to just get by."

My stomach sinks; my heart skips several beats and aches. I love Paul so much it feels like I'm bankrupt too. I wish he had told me sooner. I wish he wasn't puffed up with so much false bravado that he had to wait until the bitter end to even broach the topic. If I had even an inkling that Paul was in this kind of trouble, I never would have tangled with Benjamin in such a public manner that was guaranteed to knock him back on his heels and do something drastic. My whole goal since I was ten fucking years old was to make Paul's life easier in our family, to show him it was possible we could blend, and to let his guard down and accept it. That we wouldn't disappoint him. And I just did. I open my mouth, ready to say the magic words and pour the elixir that will erase all of Paul's problems. I feel the syllables coating my tongue like a bitter pill: *I'll talk to my father. I'll apologize. I'll admit defeat. I'll give him whatever he wants if it will make you stop hurting.*

"The most fucked-up part," Paul says, piercing the silence, "is Benjamin may be the only one I can trust right now. Did you happen to notice who wrote the article for *WaPo*?"

I shake my head, still unable to speak, to find the words to undo getting everyone disinherited.

"I'll tell you," he says. "You know how Kate set up a scholarship a few years back at 'American University'? Well, the author of the piece about me just happens to be the recipient of the second year's award. Her name is Mia Pearson. And clearly Kate instructed her to ruin my life. The only question I have is…after ruining it throughout my life, why did she have to finish destroying it from beyond the grave?"

Suddenly, the words *I'll admit defeat* seize, refusing to pass my lips. It's not out of stubbornness to capitulate to Benjamin for the good of my stepbrother—I've got the farm on that particular indignity—but because Kate knew how destructive Paul's life was to himself. She knew that it was nothing but an elaborate camouflage to bury his hurt over his biological father, and he was using it as a cudgel to never accept Benjamin and never forgive her for—in his mind—ending her first marriage. If I go to Benjamin and plead out Paul's case now, it would be *wrong*, like undoing what his mother was trying to. It would be nothing but palliative, like the care the doctors gave Kate on the last days of her life. The agony may subside, but it's still an illusion. The dream is still going down; the end is fucking nigh.

When you've been abandoned by a parent, it's not hard to spot a fellow traveler; at least my mother had cut the cord, whereas Luc let it linger as a cruel tease. For Paul's syndrome to be cured, he'd have to see what I see, what I've seen since the beginning—that La Maison de Francois was just one brick in an eventual skyscraper of denial that walled him off to keep him from shattering.

Except the tab has come to be paid. He should have quit a restaurant ago, when after receiving his third invitation, Luc asked

Paul to stop communicating with him, likely freaked out that at the age of thirty-five, his son's need for him hadn't dimmed but grown stronger. That was when Paul really flew off his axis, abandoned a shared galaxy, and nearly stripped away the last vestiges of hope. Clearly a truly titanic undertaking would make Luc see the error of his ways. In his mind, the problem was solely one of magnitude; my brother had merely been thinking too small for his father. *But this*. The Wharf market was the one, and his future hinged on it.

He just didn't see how right he was.

But I'm not going to be a party to continuing the lie, to allow him the methadone drip of additional money.

"Benjamin will give you the money," I say, trying to put him at ease while implying that I have no intention of helping him pursue this path. "You just need to ask him. In fact, he's *dying* to give it you."

"Just talk to him, Liz," he says, drained, trying to avoid taking the simplest way out, as if to postpone the suffering, to remind him that going to Benjamin means *giving up*. "You owe it to me. I've backed you. I've been there for you. I've never asked for anything except this."

"What I owe you," I say softly, almost in a whisper, hoping my calm delivery will accentuate the sincerity of my message, "is to tell you to sell the business. You've had restaurant groups begging you to let them expand what you built, to franchise it around the country. You're holding on to them, even if it costs you everything, to not have to say goodbye to your father. They don't make you happy anymore, and neither does a life waiting for him to notice. Kate knew it.... And now we all know it."

"And what?" he says, the rage returning. His mouth is a rictus of buried passion, his eyes brimming with tears. "You're *seriously* going to judge me for holding on to a hopeless, thankless, soul crushingly disappointing relationship because it hasn't worked yet? What the fuck do you think we're doing on this island? You've got a lot of nerve."

"There is *no* comparison," I say, getting off the hammock this time and talking down to my brother. "You refuse to go all in with me because you're afraid we're going to not catch you if you fall. *Try me*. I'll fucking catch you. Christ, even Benjamin—for all his faults—will catch you. But you won't let go. You'd rather sink yourself than extend a hand to me when all I've been trying to do is grab yours. Admit it. Admit you need us, and you're too scared we're a bunch of fuck-ups who will let you crash. Well, *you* crashed, Paul. You crashed because you tried to go it alone. You expanded past the breaking point, and now you're choking."

"At least I fucking tried, Lizzie," he says, also getting off the hammock and facing me. "You won't even get in the game. It's like when I tried to teach you how to play soccer and you kicked the ball and hit a butterfly, so you quit. Something *innocent* got hurt because you tried to step outside your box. A box that apparently keeps you limited to making three dozen of the most popular cupcake in the fucking District a day. Like every one of them is that fucking butterfly. And for what? Who opens a business to play footsie with profit and then pull back when it's imminent? You're the only person who looks at the president patronizing their business as a *curse*. You can barely talk about it. You can barely mention it. When it's still *all* that's been on social media for close to thirty-six hours. Did you even *look*? Don't answer. I already know. You can accuse me of a lot of things, Lizzie, and I'm guilty of them. But the one thing I did was try and fail. You won't even try. Because what— Benjamin might be proud of you? You'd have to admit maybe his and my mother's business acumen wasn't all wrong?"

"Fuck you," I say, turning my back on him. I'm ready to storm off and make a scene on the way, but then I reconsider, delivering the final coup de grâce. "There isn't enough mint chocolate chip ice cream *anywhere* for me to like you again. You're not who I thought you were."

CHAPTER TWENTY-TWO

Day Three

I SIT ON THE TERRACE of our villa, the sun mummified in cumulous clouds making its sleepy appearance over the mountains; rays strain to shine through all that heavenly gauze, and the clouds are holding back a raging storm that will not be denied much longer. I had a horrible night's sleep preceded by a horrible fight with my brother. But the universe seems to be taking mercy on me, granting me my typical morning routine, as if to say: *You've earned this, Elizabeth. Here are a few minutes to yourself for the first time since you left DC.*

The cup of freshly brewed coffee with a sprinkling of sugar and oat milk reminds me I'm still alive, reminds me of the person I was before we stepped on to the plane to St John. That person is *not* a person who can wake up and go. I need a full, uninterrupted ninety minutes to gird myself for what the day has in store, and no one can be with me. Not Nathan, not the kids, not even Barry. Before lunches can be packed, before clothing disasters can be faced, before I head out the door to the bakery, I need me, my coffee, my phone, and *silence*. In that order.

I pick up my phone as if it's the conductor baton that begins my personal symphony. I start by checking the Amex app, prepared to ferret out any unauthorized Winnie charges, followed by the Citibank app, wherein I look at our family's balance and Madeleine's balance and shake my head at the disparity between the two. Long gone are the days when I made more money than Nathan, even *with* Kate's recent out-of-the-blue infusion.

I move onto my horoscope, hoping it will tell me I *will* make more one day, that Madeleine will inch and crawl into the black—or if not black, possibly purple, or pretty much any color except red. Then I inspect Threads with one eye closed in fear, making sure the world didn't end while I slept, that there are still seven continents and eight billion people walking the earth. Finally, I tap Instagram, my ambient social media app that gives me the same feeling some people get from visiting a spa or listening to New Age music. The recipes, the interior design suggestions, the houses I want to buy, the vacations I want to take. I lose myself in relaxing aspiration.

But this morning I can't bring myself to pull up the app. All I want to do is dive into my happy place, but I don't want to visit Madeleine's page. I also don't want Paul to know anything I don't. I'm in the mood to prove him wrong but fear he might be right. I hold my breath, tap the icon, go straight to Madeleine...

And Paul is right.

I am instantly swept in by the narrative social media has built around my little shop over the past twenty-four hours: the new smiling faces surrounded by the familiar pastries dusted with sugar and filled with fresh fruit, the breads straight from the oven, and the pièce de résistance—my hot chocolate cupcake.

Camille has also been active, filming the crowd lining up outside the bakery starting at six this morning, everyone desperate to be the first in line when she opens our doors at nine—all so they can acquire one of the run of limited daily cupcakes that will be available today. I'm torn, squirming in my seat, not finding solace in my coffee. Each and every one of the people in line seem exactly like the people who shopped at Madeleine before the president visited: a mass of like-minded customers all looking to make memories surrounded by the people they love, which I suppose POTUS was trying to do as well with his own grandchildren. And even though they have the best intentions, each one of them is pulling a piece from me.

My advanced mourning for the lost intimacy of my store is rudely interrupted by my phone with an incoming text:

Meet me at the dock in half an hour.

Followed by the three elliptical dots…

Dad

As if I didn't know it was him. It's entered into my contact list with the exact same sobriquet, although occasionally replaced by the vomit emoji depending on my mood. But the mystery isn't who sent the text—it's why the hell are we meeting at a dock? Have I wandered into a Scorsese movie? Are we Teamsters? Or does he want to finish the job he started last night by luring me back out into the water and leaving me behind to face the elements?

"Elizabeth," my father says as I approach him forty-five minutes later on the sun-drenched dock. His normal greeting of "sweetheart" remains unspoken, which means he has decided not to forgive me yet for challenging him. But he's also forced me to meet him without any notice, transferring his control to a different task. I refuse to let it go unnoticed.

"No hug?" I ask, an act of deliberate provocation.

"Thanks for meeting me," he says, still not leaning in for a hug.

"Did I have a choice?" I ask, wondering if not showing up suddenly became an option.

"Everyone has choices, Elizabeth," he says, vaguely threatening. "You have them. I have them. And everyone around us now dances to what *we* choose. A lot of responsibility, isn't it?"

"Dad," I say flatly, already stressed and wondering how to return to my terrace. "Why are we here?"

He begins leading me down the dock, pointing at boats dotting the turquoise water and surrounding us on both sides. "We need to decide on the right boat."

"I'm not getting on a boat alone with you," I say, folding my arms. I'm still scarred by last night.

"The right boat to spread Kate's ashes tomorrow at sunset."

"Oh," I say, the reason I'm here finally becoming transparent. My father is still in deep denial about Kate's death, and even though I'm the last person he wants to see right now, he knows he can't face it alone.

He strolls the length of the dock, eyeballing boats, doing quick mental math to make sure they can accommodate the size of our family plus two new members. "How are your brothers and sisters handling being cut off?"

He's not wasting any time diving in. Maybe I'm wrong. Maybe he didn't request my presence to help him plan Kate's funeral. Maybe he just wanted gossip. "They're actually taking it surprisingly well. You underestimated them, like you always do," I say, hiding the truth for my own entertainment. I'm not going to deny myself the pleasure of watching his face when he discovers the majority of my siblings are all bent on destroying him, nor give him the chance to outmaneuver me and ground the project to a screeching halt.

"That *is* surprising," he says, playing along and not showing his hand either.

"My eulogy is going well," I say, twisting my own blade while lying through my teeth. I haven't written a single word, but two can play at this game, Benjamin. "I'm excited to tell everyone about a Kate they didn't know as well as they thought they did. I wondered at the beginning why she picked me, but it's clear now. We were very similar. I knew a Kate no one else did, even if she never verbalized her emotions explicitly."

"What exactly do you think you know that has eluded both her husband and four other children, that only *you* have managed to discover?" Benjamin asks, seeming more curious about my interpretation of the events since we've been at St. John than angry at my needling.

"That she and I were on the same page the whole time," I say, basking. "That *you* were the one holding her back. That you've never wanted us to blend and be a family this whole time. I mean, she didn't tell you about Oliver for a reason."

"Well," he says, "then neither of us knew her all that well, because she didn't tell you either. And you're supposed to be her secret sharer all of a sudden. It seems like she had a few misgivings about both of us, didn't she?" He slows down. "Did it ever occur to you, Elizabeth—and I don't mean this to sound as belittling as it likely will—"

"I'm sure it will," I interrupt, fully stopping and folding my arms.

"Losing Kate is a different experience for all of us. I think we all lost something imperceptible, something we can't put our finger on, and maybe won't for years. I think she could be her own person—sometimes to a fault, and sometimes to wonderful results. But she was *always* Kate." He nods, waiting for me to accept his basic supposition before insulting me. "But I think you're further behind than *all* of us. I think you can't see anyone or anything else except your own grief. And I think it's making you say and do some things you don't fully understand. I think it might even make you slightly dangerous."

"Dangerous?" I repeat, not feeling belittled but insulted. "Because I broke your control over the family—"

"No," he says. "Because you don't know why you did it. You don't know what you don't know. We've been doing this dance for years...but now you're flailing, you're angry, you're grieving. And you're too busy instructing everyone else, including *me*, on how to grieve to admit that you're not doing any of your own. But it's going to hit when you leave here, and you'll never be the same. Stop trying to solve everyone else and worry about you."

He stops and points to a multihull sailboat. It has three masts currently being hosed down. "What do you think about that one? I think that'll fit all of us."

I don't answer, amazed at his ability to just unload all of *that* on me, and—without missing a beat—move on to the vessel that will shuttle Kate to her final resting place.

"I'm going to book it," he says, approaching the captain overseeing the maintenance and talking with him for a few minutes. It leaves me alone to contemplate his emptiness, which is deeper than the ocean that will be Kate's new home. Even *that* has a bottom.

He returns to me, his right leg dragging behind the left, his knee threatening to buckle. "We're set. Tomorrow at sundown."

"Dad," I say, "did you seriously just invite me here to watch you book the boat that I know you've obviously been looking at since we got here? You never make any decision this fast." I sigh. He's exhausting, frustrating, and playing one of his patented games to send the world spinning again. But it's going to be hard to top disinheriting my siblings and leaving us stranded at sea.

"You know me too well, Elizabeth," he says, cracking a smile. "I always tell people: As much as it drives her insane, we're the same. She is, without a doubt, out of *all* my children, my daughter."

I let out a sound trapped somewhere between a groan and a muffled scream. "*Out* with it. What is your plan for today?"

"It struck me this morning..." he begins, voice drifting, as if experiencing some kind of sense memory. "I bet Elizabeth thinks she really got one over on me. It was bold getting everyone disinherited. But I wonder if she knows that *she's* been disinherited as well."

"What the *fuck* are you talking about?" I say, ready to storm off or have him checked for a stroke. "Are you delusional? You froze my trust fund ten years ago. *I* haven't taken any money from you since."

"And I didn't say *you* took it. But someone has."

I panic, manic thoughts swirling in my mind. "Who? What are you *talking* about?"

"As in all of life, Lizzie," he says, purposely infantilizing me, lording his power, "all problems emanate from inside your own house."

CHAPTER TWENTY-THREE

WHAT MY FATHER WAS TALKING about is the absolute nadir of our relationship, the echoless rock bottom from which there is no conceivable return. This is his worst manipulation, his worst deceit; it's the deployment of his nuclear arsenal. He has done to me what the rest of his kind have done to society—shaped it in his own image and drove a stake through it unceremoniously, right when people were at their most vulnerable and paying the least attention to his generation's malevolent backstage machinations. He did it to toy with me, to make sure I'm never really living in the world I think I am: A world diametrically opposed to his own. A world he is *still* running.

"Nathan!" I scream, marching into our villa and starting my search. "*Nathan*," I call out, throwing open doors—*even closets*—in furious confusion. "We need to talk, *Nathan*."

I walk upstairs to our bedroom, check the bed, the shower, then the kids' room, where both Theo and Winnie—in a matter of forty-eight hours—have rendered the floor nearly invisible. Wet towels, bathing suits, inside-out shorts, stained t-shirts, Winnie's dresses, Theo's plaid pajama bottoms, unopened books to be absorbed through osmosis, and a random AirPod resting atop a Squishmallow like a decorative cherry, all *mock* me. I resist the urge to dive in, to lend order to my children's chaos, to make this formerly pristine room feel just a little better about itself. But I hold it in. I have far bigger business to attend to.

I return downstairs, shaking my head in despair, and spot Nathan through the terrace doors off the living room. I pull open the glass separating us, and he doesn't stir, marinating in his own creative mind, outlining a fictional creation, a fantastical world—*just like mine* apparently—and I am immediately struck by two things.

One, I fervently wish I had never answered my father's text. I wish I was still back in my morning Zen spot, pouring myself another coffee and blissfully scrolling Instagram. Second, I wonder—is *this* what my husband does when I leave the house for Madeleine and he tells me he's overwhelmed with writing, that he can't even see an end in sight? Does he just spend an hour writing dialogue to absolve his conscience and then brew a fresh pot of coffee and go online shopping until I come home?

"Nathan," I say, shoving him on the shoulder to get his attention, "do you know what my fucking father did?"

Before I can begin, tears run down my cheeks in even rivulets. The sobs start, and as Nathan waits with bated breath, I share the depth of my father's deceit, hoping that at some point a magical alchemical conversion occurs, and that the old adage that every event occurs twice—first as tragedy, then as farce—is actually true.

I break it to Nathan that he never had his *big break*, which sows confusion in his eyes and mouth, both of which crinkle in the corners. It's as if he's trying to find the joke, but there isn't one.

When I decided to take the position in DC and relocate us to our nation's capital—coinciding with my refusal of Benjamin and Kate's trust fund—apparently my father didn't take it well. He didn't warm to the idea that I would be on my own and insulated against his influence.

But I wouldn't be for long.

I imagine a little demonic lightbulb went off in Benjamin's mind. He saw a chance to fuse the personal and the business, a barrier that was always flimsy in father's case, but that he obliterated when faced with trying to control me from afar. At the time, my father was expanding his portfolio into the newly bourgeoning streaming services, which were picking up steam. He invited swathes of the tech sector, producers, directors, agents, and actors to his offices to assess the viability of the market—*was this just going to be a fad?*— and the size of his risk. And wouldn't he just be the dutiful father-in-law, the favor bearer casting coins to the peons, if he happened to mention his son-in-law was a major undiscovered talent, toiling away in the wretched bowels of obscurity? Although it might seem like *they* were doing Benjamin a favor, in reality, Nathan was the safest investment they could make. *Of course,* there wasn't any pressure attached. All the Hollywood folks could say no, could say the talent pool was topped off, hang a "no vacancy" sign over LAX. But they didn't. They took Benjamin's money. Nathan's career was born. And whether I knew it or not, I was back taking Benjamin and Kate's money, just through a silent investor this time.

"Well, this just became a whole lot fucking *easier*," Nathan says, relieved. He presses down a button on his keyboard. "I've been sitting here all morning trying to figure out how to tell my agent I quit. I don't need to decide anymore. Your father did it for me."

"Aren't you *angry?*" I ask, frustrated that he's taking this well. Why can't he see what I do? That our whole life—*his* life, in particular—is a lie built upon a lie. "My father used you to keep me under his thumb."

"In a sense," he says. "But in a weird way, he ultimately must have thought I was pretty good to begin with. He's never said that to me before."

"Are you defending my father to backhandedly validate your own talent?"

"No," he says, trying to diffuse my encroaching apoplexy. "*Maybe.* Look. He's never liked me and never supported me. He offered me money not to marry you. But for him to build his entire plan to keep you close around my success, he must have thought I had it all along. Everyone gets into Hollywood through a favor, through knowing *someone*. But you stay on your own merits. And my own merits have kept me close to the top for over a decade. Benjamin didn't do that. *I* did. And sharing his little revelation because you're pissing him off doesn't make my own achievements go away."

I let Nathan's logic swirl around in my mind for a minute. I try on another perspective, performing my own Schrödinger's cat experiment with my husband's career—*if I'm not looking will it still exist?*—and from a certain vantage point he might be correct. My father may have provided the "in," but the success that followed is entirely Nathan's own. I feel my anger diminishing, settling—yet paradoxically, I have no desire *not* to be mad at someone right now. So I quickly shuffle antagonists from Benjamin to Nathan and rip into him.

"Wait. *Wait.* You just emailed Simon that you quit?" I say, his theatrical keyboard stroke suddenly adding up now. "You can't just quit. When did you even *decide* this?"

"It's been brewing for a while," he says reflectively. "But I decided when the president walked into your bakery. It's your time to shine, Lizzie. And I want to be there when you do—not on a plane to LA, or whatever foreign country a studio chooses to shoot in for tax credits, trying to fill plot holes so men in tights can travel to another galaxy and the audience will *suspend* disbelief. I want you to expand your business. I want you to build it, so it matches your dream. And I want to be a part of it."

"Nathan," I say, moved by his decision, by the love I know is always there even if we have fewer and fewer chances to show each other these days. "Madeleine isn't going to grow. It's not going to expand."

"That's ridiculous, Lizzie," he says, annoyed by my constant refrain of how if the bakery gets too big it loses its meaning. "It *always* should have expanded. All POTUS showing up did was lift the lid of the most undiscovered secret in the country. Madeleine. That's why social media is going nuts. No one knew about it. And once they got a taste, people started coming from all over. You can't just let that sit idle. You owe it to yourself; you owe it to people to share yourself and your cupcake with them."

"That's not *it*," I say, even though that's definitely part of it. In my stumbling denial, I find myself painted into a corner and blurt out the only piece of news that can give me some air. "How can I expand Madeleine when I'm pregnant?"

Nathan leaps out of the chair, then rushes over and grabs me in his arms, nearly toppling me over the railing as he wraps me tight in his burly arms. "When did you find out?"

"Yesterday," I say softly in his ear.

"Why didn't you tell me *then*?"

"There's just been so much going on...and we haven't had a moment alone," I say, but honestly, I didn't tell him because I'm unprepared—unprepared to admit the reality of our life in this moment, unprepared to change, unprepared for a different future when the present is so unsettled. The great irony is that Nathan was the one person who could have helped me prepare, but I knew once I told him, I'd have to make a decision about the pregnancy. There's also the reminder that the person I told first, both times I was pregnant before, is no longer here with us. "Tell me, how am I supposed to build a thriving business *and* have a baby? Those are not analogous to each other."

"It's easy," he says, ending the hug and looking me in the eyes. "We'll be partners."

"But we *are* partners," I say, half pleading with him to end the improbable optimism. Are we—*how can we?*—having another baby? And this time at forty-three. It was hard enough in our twenties, so why is he pretending otherwise?

"Somewhere along the way," he says, searching for the right words, a rarity for Nathan, "we became partners in making money. But less and less in life. I want to switch that."

I hear Nathan's melody, but I'm not loving the lyrics. Partners *in money* equates our relationship to my father and Kate, which is something I've done everything in my power to avoid. Nathan symbolized my choice, my rebellion, my search for the person who would work for me and not my parents. But if he distills the current shape of our marriage into two parallel train lines crisscrossing only to add another set of zeros to a bank account, then we've joined not only the ranks of my parents, but my friends, the parents at Theo and Winnie's school, Tessa, and even Camille.

Most marriages start out with the best of intentions, then—when no one's looking—they morph into a different arrangement, one in which both partners avert their eyes as ambition and success take the wheel. Certain lifestyles replace a life together, until the perpetuation of that lifestyle becomes the sole reason you're still together. And inevitably, when the ride slows down—once all the money has been made, once the vacation spots have been exhausted, once the second house has birthed a third house that stays empty—you realize *that* is the center, and the center cannot hold. You've outgrown each other, because no one *grew* except the status and acquisitions, and the only thing left is to divide the spoils as you go your separate ways. Is Nathan saying we're *those* people? Am I really as much like Benjamin as he just told me?

"Are you telling me you want a divorce?" I say, with such force it should be accompanied by a sharp lapel grabbing. It's an admittedly irrational response, but he should get used to it. I feel my hormones surging, overturning logic.

"Liz," he says, trying to take down the temperature. "I'm trying to tell you I want to spend more time together."

"How do you plan on doing that?"

"By becoming your *partner*," he says again, emphasizing the term. "A role I've only been able to occasionally inhabit for over a decade."

"Being partners is great and all," I say, "but I'm not even sure I want to have another baby. My life is up in the air. There's no *ground*. And we're old. We aren't twenty-five anymore...."

"Maybe that's not a bad thing," he says. "Maybe we were genuinely fucking insane for having Theo at twenty-five. Everyone told us we were too young. They might have had a point."

I pause and try to remember back all those years. What we were possibly thinking—or at least, what I was thinking—when I decided having a baby in my mid-twenties was a banner idea? Maybe that's why I had to learn I was pregnant on this trip, why the news had to cosmically coincide courtesy of Kate, who was half the reason I likely *started* a family just a few years out of college.

Because I had so much love to give, yet so much of it had been squandered, unreturned, laying fallow, begging to go *somewhere*. Because it was always about creating the family I wanted and had always been denied access to in life. It was always about correcting the mistakes of Benjamin and Kate for another generation, who I was determined to have grow up differently. And most importantly—although I definitely didn't know it back then—it was about *redeeming* myself, about being surrounded by people who would love me for who I was, who needed me in their lives simply for being *me*. As opposed to Benjamin and Kate, who always acted obligated to see me and willfully denied me love when I went my own way—or to be fair, willfully denied me love almost as a matter of principle.

"I'll support any decision you make," Nathan says, coming back to me and wrapping his arms around me again. "I'm just saying, we have a chance to do things differently this time, Liz. Half the parents in Winnie and Theo's school are *still* going to be older than us. It's not unheard of."

"Yeah," I say, pulling away. "But what about Madeleine? What about Winnie and Theo?"

"You're not alone," Nathan says, taking my hand in his. He knows when I'm not sure about a decision, I pull away from affection. "I want to be with this baby in a way I wasn't able to be when Theo and Winnie were little. I want to be able to visit Theo at..." He visibly and audibly almost chokes on the word. "*Harvard*. I want to meet Winnie for lunch. I want to put on an apron and make some cupcakes. I like Camille. It'll be fun."

"That sounds great for you," I say. "That sounds like what you want. But I don't know what *I* want."

"Liz," he says, starting to sound frustrated. "You don't have to know. You could build Madeleine out and hire more people to pass off some of the responsibility. Fuck, you could sell all the recipes, peace out, and move to the South of France. Your choices are unlimited right now. All you have to do is just make *one*. The first one. After that, the rest can fall into place."

Nathan is right—the only choice I need to make is about the pregnancy. I know that part of me oscillating, and feeling unsure, stems from Kate not being here anymore. I don't know if I can bring a baby into this world without her, without telling her, without seeing her reaction, without seeing her dawning disappointment when she realizes I'm going to do whatever I want to. But the brutal truth is that *everything* in my life forward is going to be a decision made without her, an event passing made conspicuous by her absence, and this baby will be the first marker. But maybe starting over, with a new life coming into our world, is the right place to start.

Unfortunately, I can't find that same kind of clarity when it comes to Madeleine. My bakery isn't just a business—something to be worked around and slotted in between sleepless nights, feedings, and the usual challenges that comes with a baby.

"So, we're really going to do this?" I say, still half in disbelief. "Have *another* baby? Another little human to love who is going to leave us, but this time at *sixty*? Nathan, we have half our lives left, and I still can't handle Winnie and Theo leaving."

"Well," Nathan says charitably, "by the time we're *sixty*, we may want this one to go."

"I'm setting some ground rules up front for this one," I say, getting more excited at the prospect of Nathan actually partnering for this child. "You are getting up in the middle of the night. You are going to exist on four hours of sleep. *You* are going to the park, exhausted, unable to look into the sun because you're so tired. You're going to cry a lot. It is very fucking hard work that you missed."

"Still excited," he says, smiling wide.

"No matter what, I'm not helping," I say. "You know me. I can't not sleep for at least seven or eight hours now. I get cranky. I get sick."

"I know that well," he says, seemingly even *happier*. "But now that you've made that decision…what are you going to do about Madeleine? Are you ready for another change?"

"Not feeling that one yet," I say. "I need to still think about that."

"Okay," he says, resigned to the fact that most decisions aren't easy for me. It takes me several days to select a television show to watch in bed, because I just can't bear to be disappointed as I fall asleep. "Do you need to think about going to the pool? Or is that a decision you can make on the spot?"

I roll my eyes. "Let me just change."

CHAPTER TWENTY-FOUR

NATHAN AND I FIND THE perfect creamy white double-chaise sofa lounge chair by the packed pool. It's a mix of direct sun for him—apparently only one of us is worried about wrinkles—and shade for me. I place my towel on the plush cushion, order a sparkling water and a Bloody Mary for Nathan, and open *The Corrections*, which Paul recommended to me a few months back.

I commence unwinding poolside, finding comfort in learning from Jonathan Franzen that family dysfunction extends across all fifty states and socioeconomic brackets. Franzen's fictional family, The Lamberts, merely have less money to indulge their problems, but *problems* they do have, and their version of a funeral in St. John laced with the choice between rebirth or death is roughly commensurate with Enid's last Christmas dinner. And as I open the eighth chapter and realize the depths of Chip's financial penury—in which he's being supported by his sister Denise—I wonder if Paul was trying to send me a message all along. Maybe I should have opened the book sooner and saved ourselves a great deal of trouble.

"I fucking hate you!" I hear someone scream at the end of the pool, and since I'm unable to *not* people watch, especially when the situation is heated, I find my eyes drifting to the source of the commotion. *"You ruined my fucking life you spoiled bitch."*

This is serious, and although the heat shimmering off the parodically blue water partially obscures my vision, I can make out certain disconnected features of the woman yelling. But before they get a chance to coalesce into a frontal figure, she's in action, pushing—almost *throwing*—her nemesis into the pool, creating a cannonball-sized splash. As the wave subsides, I realize I know both the person floating and the *pusher*.

"Is that your sister?" Nathan asks, pointing to Caroline swimming by us and shaking water out of her ear.

"Which one?" I answer, moving his finger slightly to the right until it lands on Tessa, who is waiting for Caroline to make her way out of the pool so she can continue screaming. "Do you think I need to get involved?" I ask, looking for Nathan to assume his usual role of benignly agreeing with even my more outlandish ideas and sentiments.

"I think you have to," he says. "Or we might get kicked out of the hotel."

"Is that the worst thing possible?"

Unfortunately, Tessa seems to have the worst thing possible already planned. Since Caroline hasn't returned to the deep end where my sister lies in wait, it appears she's going to *jump in* after her, refusing to be ignored.

"Okay," I say, rising off the chaise, defeated. "I'm going."

After resigning myself to publicly owning up to the fact that I not only know but am related to the unhinged women making a rockstar-style scene, I convince Tessa and Caroline to finish whatever high-pitched argument—that is rapidly threatening to devolve into personal violence—in a more secluded, private location. And as I drag them, kicking and screaming, to a series of volcanic gray rocks creating a barrier between the beach and the sand, I take great care to keep my head down, attempting to give the impression that I'm merely a good Samaritan who intervened in this fracas and am not related to the perpetrators.

"Tess," I say, holding my hands up, trying to instill a little calm. "What the fuck are you doing? And why are you doing it in front of people?"

"*Lizzie,*" Caroline says, trying to win me over to her side before the story unfolds. "She's trying to kill me."

"I got that impression," I say. "The entire Eleusinian did."

"I'm doing this *publicly,*" Tessa says, strangling the English language with her forked tongue, "because that is the level of my humiliation. My humiliation that will follow me back to Manhattan, where I will be humiliated again."

I look to Caroline, wondering if she showed her Darby's message. Maybe Tessa has seen Miles's unexpected extracurricular activities.

"Miles isn't fucking coming!" Tessa shouts.

"To St. John?" I ask, surprised that *she's* so surprised, considering we're spreading Kate's ashes tomorrow at sunset. That doesn't leave Miles much time to grab the next flight.

"No, Elizabeth," she says, turning her rage upon me. Caroline takes this as a chance to escape, but I grab her wrist, refusing to be left alone to face Tessa. "He's not *coming* because he's leaving me. I'm getting divorced." She laughs bitterly. "And I bet all of you couldn't be happier. You can't wait for the chance to make fun of the only person who cares about this family's image."

I don't want to smile or revel in her discomfort, but I can't help and feel the slightest pang of schadenfreude—because the more everyone could see her marriage was circling the drain, the more I bore the brunt of Tessa's anger.

My sister and I inhabit opposite poles. We each have—or had—a husband. We each have two kids. I married an artist and moved away. Tessa married Kate's protégé and moved next door. The way Benjamin and Kate flattered her decisions and openly rebuked mine was her pride and glory, her personal hammer against me, and she loved every time she got to use it; in fact, the more and more Miles slipped away, the more she ruthlessly whacked me with it.

The confirmation that her life just exploded in a total auto-da-fé can't help but bring a smile to my face. I know it doesn't make me a good person, but sometimes it's impossible to be a *good* person to your sister. Sometimes it's easier to love a stranger.

"Like I thought," Tessa snaps. "Look at you. You're overjoyed."

"Don't be happy, Lizzie," Caroline says, still trying to run away no matter how hard I grip her wrist. "Save yourself."

"You shut up," Tessa says to Caroline. "You're the reason all this happened."

"Can someone please start from the beginning?" I say, feeling more like a referee or high school principal than a sibling. "You know. The reason you threw Caroline into the pool."

Tessa blows a strand of stray hair from above her lip. "Miles thought Kate was going to leave him in charge of the company after she died. Someone had to run it, and since he was family, he figured he had it in the bag. *That* was why he was staying married to me."

I feel like that does go a long way toward explaining why Miles stuck around, despite having checked out of the marriage. But it doesn't explain why Caroline was nearly drowned. While I'm mentally catching up, Tessa takes another lunge at Caroline.

"Is it because you're so wrapped up in yourself you can never see the harm you cause me? Or are you so harmful because you're so wrapped up in yourself?"

"It wouldn't fucking matter if your life wasn't so easily *harmed*," Caroline says, taking a big risk and shooting off her mouth.

Tessa turns back to me. "But I haven't gotten to the biggest betrayal yet. Kate, the woman I spent my life trying to impress... to convince that I was the only one who could carry on what she built...went and fucked me in the end. She tore down the life I built *for her*, Elizabeth."

"But *how?*" I demand, trying to focus Tessa, who—with each word—is returning to the same frenzied state as back at the pool.

"She left the company to Caroline," Tessa says, and nearly collapses.

"Is that true?" I ask Caroline, almost ready to join Tessa in falling to the ground in shock.

Caroline aggressively nods, a combination of confirming Tessa's point and projecting blind fear. "She did."

"Did you *know?*" I ask, trying to fill one of the hundred gaps in the story so far.

"Of course I didn't," Caroline says. "I would have told her she was fucking crazy."

After absorbing the blunt force trauma of that news, I remind myself that Kate was the most methodical, cautious, Machiavellian person I've ever encountered. She wouldn't leave her business to just anyone, regardless of familial ties. That line of thought continues like an unspooling thread, returning me to last night in the lobby where I watched Caroline react to Benjamin removing her financial stability. She didn't cower; she didn't hesitate; she didn't recriminate me or run back to him begging for money. She plotted, took stock of what she could offer the world, and rebirthed herself in under a minute. She rolled with the punches, never doubting that she would not only survive, but thrive.

I realize now it was her first baby step toward maturity, toward a self-realization through the fulcrum in which she felt most comfortable—taking revenge on my father. But that doesn't mean the attempt wasn't real, doesn't mean she hasn't felt stifled for years; it meant that Benjamin's actions gave Caroline the room to reflect without him, and that was her analysis.

I must give my sister credit where credit is due. She is graduating, and has moved past torpedoing Kate's birthday party to make a point. She's realizing that a person with her kind of wiles has a lot more options in life. She can't glimpse the option yet, but that's where Kate came in. She saw what Caroline was capable of long before any of us, and she also knew that Caroline would only become who she really is if my stepmother forced her into it. The only person with the sheer will to force my sister into anything was Kate. My stepmother didn't get to her position without being able to spot her own kind, and Caroline—more than anyone else on this planet—is Kate's kind, the only plausible substitute, the only Bernard-Sunderland as committed to relentless growth and acquisition as the woman who raised her. Caroline *likes* money, likes power, and takes the upper hand in relationships within sixty seconds flat. None of the other siblings are capable of that; we're too wounded, too busy trying to love or save one another that other people rarely enter the mix.

"She was fucking crazy," Tessa says, seconding Caroline's thought. "She was at the end of her life. She didn't know what she was doing." She points to Caroline, her finger shaking in rage. "You don't possess even the rudimentary skills to run Kate's company." She picks up her phone. "I'll text Miles and tell him you want him to take over. That you'd be *grateful* for him to rescue you. Even if Kate wasn't."

"Put down the fucking phone, Tess," I say, not matching my sisters' volume but coming close. "You know that's wrong."

She laughs, quivering with spite. "Do I?"

While she's distracted, fixing me with her grin, I rip her phone out of her hands and hold it behind my back. "Tess, I think we seriously need to consider Kate did this for a reason."

"Oh, I am considering it," Tessa says. "I *begged* her to give Miles the company when she was sick. I practically got down on my knees and cried for her to save my life. And she said she'd *think* about it."

"She thought about it," Caroline says, then cowers behind me.

"Now you know," Tessa says, seeming to run out of rage. She sputters like a machine low on oil, ready to start devouring itself. "Now you know my secret. Isn't that lovely? My whole life was a sham, and the woman who birthed it took it away."

"But that's the whole point, Tessa," I say, trying to make her see the larger plan. "Kate didn't want you to stay married to someone who only wants you for her company. She's trying to fix her mistake. She's telling you to fly free and leave him behind."

"Okay," Tessa says, not buying my rationale. "Two fucking *problems*, Lizzie. One, I don't think my life is a mistake. Two, you got me disinherited. So what am I supposed to do without Miles's salary?"

"You were probably going to have to make do without his salary either way, if you look at it rationally," I say. "I imagine somewhere in Kate's instructions to Caroline, he was the first one to get fired."

"This is my *life*, Elizabeth," she says. "It's not some wind-up toy for Kate to assuage her guilt. There are real consequences."

"But are there?" I say. "Maybe what you're looking at as consequences are opportunities to stop living a lie."

"I love my lie!" she yells. "My lie is everything I wanted. I love it so much, it's true."

"Just because you want it be true," I reply, stunned by the depth of her delusion, "doesn't mean it is."

"Please, Elizabeth," Tessa says. "Don't talk to me that way. I'm a grown woman with two children."

"So am I," I say.

"No," she says. "You're cruel. After Miles didn't show up for Meredith's birth, you left me too. I tried to reach out to you afterward. I called you. I texted you. I made a dozen visits to DC by myself, schlepping two kids alone just to see you. For *years* I did that. And you never thawed. You'd made up your mind. You judged me for staying."

She isn't wrong. As she continues screaming at me, I'm forced to remember, to reconnect with a memory I pushed aside because it was easier than continuing to care, to try and intervene in something hopeless. How was I supposed to find a silver lining in Miles not showing up the day my niece was born, nearly stranding Tessa and leaving her alone and terrified?

Tessa, who is perpetually prepared—controlling to the point authoritarians would tell her to take it down a notch—had been refining her birth plan since she found out she was pregnant. From the hospital she would deliver in, to the labor and delivery suite she had booked, to rigidly scheduling who could visit and when each person was allowed to arrive, no detail was left undecided.

Admittedly, I, too, had my own birth plan with Theo. It was slightly less controlling but equally planned out down to the millisecond, and look how *that* turned out. So I advised Tessa to embrace the chaos of childbirth. I just didn't imagine the chaos would turn out to be Miles.

As her delivery date loomed closer, Tessa would check in with Miles's assistant daily—sometimes hourly—to ensure he was never far from home and his calendar left uncluttered. But on that fateful Tuesday morning in October, Tessa's water wasn't the only thing that broke.

Tessa called Miles. He sounded full of joy and surprise, and promised to meet her at the hospital. He might even get there *first*. That's why Tessa couldn't suppress her shock to find herself alone when she arrived.

She checked in, demanded a speedy epidural, and resumed calling Miles. He didn't answer. She sent off a litany of increasingly hysterical text messages. No answer. She was starting to worry something horrible had happened and regretted the hectoring tone of her texts. She imagined Miles at the bottom of the Hudson

River, checking his messages with his last breaths, only to find himself called *a fucking prick*.

Tessa backtracked and called Miles's assistant, who informed her that he was in a last-minute and unavoidable meeting and would be there soon. Tessa continued to *wait*, too stubborn—or frankly, too embarrassed—to call anyone else. Those defensive actions to protect Miles and their marriage evaporated when she was nine centimeters dilated. She texted me, knowing I was in New York for meetings, and Nathan joined me to take meetings with publishers about the novel he wanted to write. One of our few trips without our kids, and of course it was for work. Madeleine.

I left Nathan behind at the lunch spot by the Hachette building and met a distressed Tessa at the hospital, who seemed to be having more pain understanding Miles's absence than the fact that she was in labor. And she was six hours *out* of labor when Miles finally made his appearance. Tessa, to her credit, tried to put on an understanding face of the dutiful, long-suffering wife, but the cracks were visible to our family who descended upon the hospital room when the baby was born, and they were most visible to Kate.

Six months later, Miles was unceremoniously fired from Goldman Sachs, and a seemingly stunned Kate graciously offered him a position at her firm. And since then, Miles has been more and more noticeably absent from family holidays, dinners, vacations, and now Kate's *funeral*, all of which corresponded to him having less and less authority and autonomy at work. Kate had been bleeding him to the last drop since that day.

And to be fair to my sister, her words are *hurting*, stinging me with their honesty. I want to tell her I didn't make an instant judgment, that I wasn't callous or cruel like she sees me. I tried to tell her to leave Miles on every one of those trips to DC, those texts, those calls, and she just ignored me. I pushed through her veil, told her that she and the kids could stay with Nathan and me until they got on their feet. I assured her, promised her, that our father and Kate would get over it, that they weren't that attached to anyone except each other—let alone *Miles*. I attempted to drum it into her head that she took the wrong message from Benjamin and Kate's marriage, that they did in fact love each other tremendously and had an unbreakable bond that went way beyond sharing a lifestyle. They did share their *lives*. It just couldn't be replicated outside of them, and my sister was proving it daily with her own marriage, proving it in such a fiery failure that even Benjamin and Kate were beginning to doubt the utility of their own union.

When she wouldn't listen to me on those subjects, I started advocating for Mason and Meredith. The children deserved better, and sometimes an unhappy home is more damaging than a broken home. She was raising my niece and nephew in an immaculately appointed lair of falsity and treachery, just short of the Borgias. She didn't budge. She had made up her mind. Tessa was going to add an extra layer to a mask already threatening to weigh down her face; she was going to stay with Miles because admitting defeat was tantamount to confessing her whole life was wrong, that things started going astray when she abandoned Dylan in college, and every step after was a lonely consolation for the moment she turned her back on the truth.

I did take it too far one time. I did tell her she "deserved it," that the world of ice she inhabited was the logical result of turning your heart off, and she would be stuck in her own purgatory until she realized she had the keys the whole time to get herself out. I did tell her to "fuck off back to Manhattan" because she wasn't serving herself up as the lone savior of the Bernard-Sunderland name, she was humiliating it, denigrating it. Everyone in Manhattan knew her fucking marriage was a joke except *her*.

"You're all wrong, Elizabeth," Tessa says. "I didn't stay for Miles. I didn't stay for the money. I didn't even stay for Mason and

Meredith. I stayed for me. I'd sacrificed too much, years ago…I *still* sacrifice too much. I can't just pull up stakes and let it go."

Listening to the delusion with which Tessa clings to her fairy tale against all odds makes me realize it was never meant to be a fairy tale in the first place. It was never about disappointing our father and Kate. It goes all the way back to Dylan, but even deeper than I imagined when she first left him. Tessa didn't want to avoid the headache of marrying someone like Nathan; she wanted to avoid the headache of finding out why Dylan loved her that much. And now I'm beginning to see why.

No one had ever made Tessa the favorite before him, and once she got what she always wanted, it opened a very dark and very deep door. Then she ran as fast as she could. If Dylan could love her and see how special she was, why couldn't our parents—the people she tried the hardest to please, the people she placed atop an unshakeable pedestal? That was a question she couldn't face, a question that would have thrown her whole happy childhood into tumult. So she preferred to go to sleep, and my father and Kate helped her. They gave her Miles, who would never make her the favorite—never convince her there was something to love about her in the first place—and blissful unconsciousness could return.

But with Miles gone, she has to *wake up*. She has to face exactly what Kate said in the video. Something has been wrong all along in the life she sacrificed Dylan for.

"You're worth it, Tess," I say. "I know it. *Dylan* knew it. Kate knew it too. That's why she didn't leave the company to Miles. And somewhere you know it too; you're just afraid to admit it."

Tessa breathes in deeply, letting my words sink over her in a way she hasn't since the laboring at the hospital. She leaves me in silent suspense for what feels like—and may actually be—five minutes, before saying, "Maybe."

"Maybe" is more than I have gotten from Tessa in the entirety of our relationship, so I will consider it a small win. Then I turn to Caroline, who is clearly annoyed the conversation moved away from her and expects reciprocity from me for the oversight. "You're worth it too. Kate knew it. That's why she left you her company."

Caroline, to her credit, doesn't tease me like Tessa, doesn't make me think she will return with a treasured insight after deeply considering my interpretation.

"I still can't believe Kate left me her company. Is she fucking crazy? This is all my fault. If I hadn't been so brazen about all my mistakes, I'd have had a secret for her to spill. Instead, I got the fucking company." She looks to me, her eyes all pupil and retreating lid. "What am I supposed to do, Lizzie?"

"Wait," Tessa says. "What am *I* supposed to do?"

"You know what's weird," Caroline says suddenly, moving on to a new topic as she normally does when she's run her course, even if no one else has caught up to her. "Your secret's the only one that hasn't come out yet, Lizzie. What are you hiding? It must be good if Kate's saving it for last."

CHAPTER TWENTY-FIVE

AFTER SENDING MY SISTERS TO the beach so I could return to the pool without being seen with them, I settled in with Nathan and ended up falling asleep for three hours, shrouded in my white towel, sunglasses still on reflecting swaying palm trees in the black lenses. I was depleted, so exhausted, that I started dreaming the second I closed my eyes.

The precise content of the unconscious movie splashed across the back of my eyelids—my lashes like curtains—comes back to me in strobing flashes, jarring spurts, the cataclysmic events of the past three days interspliced with the kind of Jungian, esoteric, archetypal imagery pulled straight from a universal nocturnal language that accompanies deep anxiety. Like random goats—maybe even a satyr or two—a psychic with a bad cold working two separate wild decks, all of which portending doom; my teeth falling out in handfuls while I stand before a mirror trying to jam them back in the empty sockets; being stranded in a depthless ocean, a boat with no driver passing me by; and sitting across a dinner table from Kate and having her tell me that I'm letting her down, that I need to be better, that the family rests on me, and I only have twenty-four hours before we spread her ashes.

Although I can't remember falling asleep, what wakes me up is vivid.

Around four thirty, my phone explodes. There are forty texts from the sibling group chat in just as many seconds. This must be an exchange so scintillating, so wild and wooly, that they can't be contained, and a feverish dialogue has ensued. I grab my phone expecting a breakthrough: expecting Paul to admit my advice was heartfelt and honest—*although hard to hear*—and he was making calls to let the businesses go; expecting Tessa to have been so moved by my words, so ecstatic about mutual recognition, that someone else realized what Dylan meant to her, that she was ready to move on without Miles; expecting Caroline to accept Kate's testament to her, at times, almost subliminal talents—inconspicuous to everyone except my stepmother—and accept the inherent impossible risk in taking over Kate's company; expecting Julian to have had a breakthrough and save himself from drugs and wanderlust, and finally understand that family is the most important thing, that if you lean into the people closest to you they can get you through the hard times...not *hard* narcotics.

But I know all of that. I know what my siblings are supposed to get out of Kate's plan. I've been seeing it. Caroline's question—the source of my anxiety-drenched dream—haunts me now on another level. What am I supposed to get out of all this? I don't have any secrets. Well, I'm pregnant, but Kate can't know that. She's not Hamlet; she's not lurking on my terrace telling me to rise and avenge her death. I'm left with the fact that, as the days in St. John dwindle, I think her "surprise" is the $5 million. She told me she loved me the only way she knew how to express it. A *bonus*. My siblings were given an otherworldly reckoning to put their lives on a different path, and I got paid.

I pick up my phone to investigate what could have sent it buzzing into overdrive and am greeted with now over *fifty* texts, all with the same message loud and clear: What did I plan on doing for family dinner?

Dinner. They're hungry. We've had soul-bearing, gut-wrenching confessions and wall-to-wall conversations for the past twenty-four hours, where regrets, failures, and hopes for the future were discussed. And now I'm reading *sixty* texts discussing dinner.

There's only two or three restaurants in the fucking resort—how can eating be the catalyst for such an in-depth exchange? I look again to be certain dinner is the only topic.

It is. I breathe deeply, grip the lounge chair cushion in frustration—but then gently remind myself they are all a work in progress. I need to look at this dinner as another chance to impress upon them the necessity to move forward, to not backslide into comfortable old habits, to not turn away from the unknown. Just because something is new doesn't mean it can't be done.

And it needs to be done quickly.

I think back to my dream, to Kate telling me we're running out of time. She's right. I'm down to draining hours, to sped-up seconds before we leave St. John. I have one day left to usher my siblings onto the right track, the one both my stepmother and I know is their sole salvation, before we get on a plane and lose this chance forever. If they return to their anti-fragile existences and start gluing the pieces back the same way they looked before, I will have failed—failed them and failed Kate.

I text back: *Looking forward to seeing everybody at 6:30!*

Which is followed by a series of equally enthusiastic responses from my siblings, minus Paul, and studded with glittering emojis and GIFs.

I turn over to Nathan to tell him the news. "They want to have dinner."

"That's...not surprising," he says, rubbing my knee sympathetically but not sharing in my confusion. "One thing you can count on your family for is—even at the height of dysfunction—they stick to ritual. They can spend a week fighting and *still* show up for dinner." His face lights up with a charming smile, a smile that almost takes me back to the early days of our relationship, when we couldn't imagine an hour without the other's company. "Do you mind if I don't come? I think I need a break."

"Of course," I say, remembering this is day three with my family. Nathan is an only child, who—after a predictable immersion time—begins to look at spending time with the Bernard-Sunderlands as being trapped in a very small elevator with a traveling circus hurtling down to the basement at top speed. "If you're not going to come, then I'm going to suggest a siblings-only dinner," I continue, struck by the opportunity that Nathan's absence just dropped in my lap. Maybe if it's just the five of us—I know eventually Paul will relent; I'm not entirely sure he can even pay for a meal—I can pick up where we left off with our life-altering conversations while getting to the short-term root underneath all of them: we're spreading Kate's ashes in twenty-four hours, and we have barely even talked about it.

I grab my phone and text the group chat my master plan, tossing it off casually. The idea is met with unalloyed enthusiasm. Tessa is thrilled the nanny can take over for the night—she hasn't had much time away from the kids on this trip—Julian is thrilled he has a plausible excuse to evade Persephone and Oliver, who he did spend all day with. Caroline is potentially the most enthusiastic, sending skull emojis next to Sean's name. Unsurprisingly, we receive stony silence from Paul.

"This is awkward," I whisper under my breath to no one in particular, as I walk into the restaurant, take a seat at our table, and spot my father dining alone at a table set for two. He's eating his traditional Caesar salad—likely before some kind of red meat—and deep into his usual transition from daytime gin and tonics to a bottle of pinot noir with dinner.

"I think it was supposed to be," Julian says, also whispering as he sits down on my right side.

"Do you think he sees us?" Tessa asks softly, leaning in on my left.

"Can we not focus on Dad," I say, knowing that if we do things will escalate quickly, and I won't get what I need out of this dinner. "Let's just try and have a nice time." I unfold my napkin, drape it across my lap, and turn to Julian. "I was so happy to hear you spent the day with Persephone and Oliver." I continue before he has a chance to answer. "I just remembered...I've got to give Persephone the name of the fabulous Montessori Theo and Winnie went to before we moved. Oliver would love it. I can't wait to have you all in Manhattan. It's a quick train ride and you *know* how much I love being an aunt."

Julian chokes on his water, coughs spasmodically into his hand, and starts flushing deep red. "We're not entirely there yet, Lizzie."

That was not the reaction I had hoped for. After Julian's financial breakthrough in the lobby last night, followed by a day with his family, I had assumed—*always a mistake in this family*—things had settled down. I had thought Benjamin's rash financial severing had changed my stepbrother and that he was going to embrace domesticity realizing the true *cost* of my father's largesse.

An awkward pause comes on the heels of Julian's ominous ambiguity, followed by a seismic crack of thunder, which punctuates the moment, ruptures across the restaurant, upsets the unprepared diners, and prompts an eerie evocation of my own childhood, the memory of when my father and Kate would be on a trip to some far-flung locale and the five of us would build an enormous—and always structurally deficient—pillow fort under the dining room table on stormy Manhattan nights, a distant time when we used to lean into each other when we were scared instead of pushing everyone away.

"There's no instruction book on family," I say to Julian, trying to make us both feel better. "You'll find the way that works for you."

"That's what I'm doing, Lizzie," Julian says, gripping his glass so tight I fear it might pop under the pressure and spray the table with projectile shards.

Thankfully, the server appears from out of nowhere, as if a trap door opened and he materialized like a magic trick. I turn, expecting to be handed a menu—but he's holding a bottle of pinot noir, the same vintage Benjamin is in the process of finishing off.

"This is from the gentleman over there," he says, pointing to my father. Benjamin doesn't turn around to see how the gift is received; he feigns disinterest, focused on chewing his steak.

"You can send that back to the gentleman," I say, also refusing to look in my father's direction. Ninety-nine percent of me hates, despises, when he meddles, and I don't have time right now for him to start adding wrinkles to my already ramshackle plan—especially when one percent of me can't help but feel my heart break when I notice he hasn't asked the server to remove the second place setting. We both know what that means.

"Are you crazy?" Tessa says, mortally offended. She grabs the bottle like it's perched on the precipice of a high cliff. "We're keeping this."

"It is a *gift*, right?" Julian says. "We can disagree with Benjamin. We don't have to see eye to eye. But we don't have to be rude."

"You can do whatever you want," I say. The server makes his way around the table, filling the glasses, but when he reaches me, I place my hand over the oval lip and decline.

"Jesus, Lizzie," Tessa says, with an uncharitable sneer. "You're being ridiculous. Turning down Dad's wine won't prove anything. Everyone around this table knows you're *so* much better already, so you might as well just have a drink. It's free."

"It's not about Dad," I say, avoiding the real reason I declined. Nathan and I haven't had a chance to tell our own children about the baby yet, and they definitely deserve to be told before the rest of my family.

"Look," Tessa says to me, "you might as well know I've decided to ask Dad if I can move in with him."

Julian looks to Tessa, baffled, his neck slightly craned in confusion. "Tess, I know you miss my mom and you're worried about your dad, but that seems a little extreme."

I shouldn't have expected more from Tessa. I spent days, months, years trying to convince her to leave Miles, and now that she is face to face with her impending divorce, my sister has decided to go in the exact *opposite* direction of what I'd suggested. Instead of taking the chance to find someone who values her in the way Dylan did, she's returning to the source of why she feels this way in the first place.

Before I get a chance to say something to Tessa—which appears to be a continued and increasingly confounding exercise in futility, but which I *also* can't give up on—Caroline passes behind my chair, doggedly followed by Sean, who is trying to continue a fight that my sister clearly considers finished.

"Your stepmother left you her company for a reason," Sean says, as Caroline holds up a hand to emphasize that he needs to *stop talking*. "You can't just toss away her dying wish because it's inconvenient to you."

Caroline sits down, slouches, and puts her elbows on the table. It's frustrating to me that she's already regressing, already indulging in her preferred way to handle adversity: retreat to her teen years and yell at our father until he cleans it up because he owes it to her for some reason known only to my sister. Except he isn't here, and she's going to need to find another outlet.

"Hey, Tess," Caroline begins, ignoring Sean completely. "Don't worry. You don't have to get divorced. I'm not taking Kate's company. Go ahead and call Miles."

Tessa exhales, as if the scales of her destiny tipped in a direction that stopped crushing her. "Thank god."

I think this may somehow be worse than Tessa choosing to move in with our father, which, in the annals of awful ideas dreamed up by my sister, had a pretty good chance of shooting straight to the top. Tessa's awful decision is amplified by Caroline also leaning into her worst instincts, which I *also* should have counted on.

"You can't do this," Sean says, ripping the words from my mouth. Even though he's virtually a stranger, he sees my sister in all her multi-faceted problematic dimensions—usually my self-imposed curse.

"No. *You* can't," Caroline says, her eyes flaring, her lips flaring, her nostrils flaring, her ears pinned back in anger. "Where the fuck do you get off thinking you know me enough to begin telling me what's good for me? You're presuming a hell of a lot for a guy who was my way to kill time on a plane. And who I admittedly *like* to fuck...which is why we keep doing it. But I have no interest in hearing what you have to say. Shut up and do what you're here for."

"You're lying again. You saw in me *exactly* what I saw in you. We're two people trying to grieve losing something they thought was special. In my case, because I grieved, I was able to realize I was *wrong*. You won't even fucking start. And you won't take your stepmother's company, 'cause if you do, you've got to admit she's gone and loved you."

Caroline ignores him and looks to me. "Hey, Lizzie. Am I correct that this is a siblings' dinner *exclusively*?" She fixes her rabid gaze back on Sean. "That means you can go."

Sean, astutely realizing he's crossed into the land of diminishing returns, pushes in his chair. But before leaving, he exposes the elephant in the room *again*, and this time it seems even bigger. "You can tell me to go. You can hide. You can burn your future. But the pain will come, Caroline. It's inevitable. Hurt is like gravity... it always lands."

Sean's words tear through me. He saw deeper into Caroline than even I did. Kate leaving her the business did two things my sister can't recover from. It made her realize just how much Kate loved, trusted, and ultimately admired her. And it meant Caroline could never forget our stepmother, no matter how hard she tried. Every day she would go to work and be reminded of how much she was loved and how much she had lost. And Sean just politely shoved it in her face as his parting remark.

A second crack of thunder births a bolt of jagged white-heat lightning, dividing the four corners of the sky into a chessboard that punctuates Sean's words. This is a sign all of us should probably interpret as some kind of unmistakable omen.

As I'm trying to find a way to help Caroline feel her way through what Sean accurately diagnosed, Paul—*I guess he decided to come*—storms over to the table. Not acknowledging anyone else's presence, he approaches Julian and shoves him so hard that it almost knocks him out of his chair. And while thoughts of how to shield this dinner from further public embarrassment cross my mind, I can't help but feel like I'm fourteen again, and the walls of our home are shaking with my stepbrothers' raucous inability to process *any* emotion without throwing each other into inanimate objects.

"Give me the fucking coke," Paul says, a demand I haven't heard in over a decade. I'm immediately thinking about what it's going to be like having a brother who is an addict again.

"What the fuck are you doing?" Julian says, straightening the shirt that Paul nearly knocked him out of. "I don't have any coke. Where the hell do you think I'd even get it?"

"This resort is filled with rich white people like us," Caroline points out, evoking a glare from Tessa, who hates any references to *privilege* in her company. "And they all have coke."

"They might," Julian says defensively, "but that doesn't mean I have any. For fuck's sake, I was with Persephone and Oliver all day. How would I even get it?"

"I saw you get it in the lobby before you came to dinner," Paul says, ready to pounce again. "I followed you here after I calmed down." He notices he's short of breath. "Which I seem unable to do."

I realize—by the redness in Paul's face and the heave in his chest from lack of breath—we have gotten *much* older since the last time we had to face Julian about this. None of us are the same people anymore, and we all deluded ourselves, thinking that when enough time passes with a sober stepbrother that the worry can subside. It doesn't.

We were kidding ourselves.

Paul's reaction fills me with fear, with anger that was always waiting to bubble back up. I feel it myself, feel wholly unprepared to even entertain going back to this version of Julian—the vampire simulacrum of my brother. I'm not ready for the outright panic that occurs when you don't hear from him for a few days, the frantic calling of hospitals and fellow junky friends, and counting down the hours until you can file a missing person's report. And that's forgetting the constant lying, the endless stream of assurances that *this time* the message has permeated the soft matter of his skull, only to discover he went out and got high the second he finished talking to you. It's a feeling of utter despair, of total nullity.

Paul doesn't allow Julian another chance to lie, to evade. He simply sticks his fingers into the front pocket of Julian's shirt, extracts the freshly sealed baggie of cocaine, and hides it in his enclosed fist before anyone else in the restaurant can see. I breathe again, relieved that—for the time being—the drugs are out of his reach.

"Stop telling yourself you need Benjamin to save you, to indulge your wanderlust to *stay off* drugs," I say, coming clean myself. If Julian intends to go back down this road, I'm going to unburden myself and tell him why. I know it won't stop him, but I won't give him the absolution I did last time. I know now it was wrong, and I still can't forgive myself for it even when he was staying sober.

"The wandering is an excuse. You'd stay put except you don't want to deal with Persephone and Oliver watching you destroy yourself. Being coked out never made Kate the mother you wanted, and being coked out isn't going to bring her back either. You're going to have to live with the relationship you had. And you're going to have to forgive her."

"Maybe I will, Lizzie," he says. "But you're going to have to live with who she was too." He points to the cocaine in Paul's hand. "And I will show you fear in a handful of dust." Then he looks back to me. "You're the most scared person at this table. And you should be." He starts walking away while tapping rhythmically on the face of the Patek Philippe my father got him for his thirtieth birthday. "Tick-tock. Tick-tock. Lizzie's running out of time to save us all. But ask yourself *this*—how do you save people who don't want it? What do you do with an ungrateful survivor? Because that's what you're working with here. And with your fucking self, Elizabeth."

I burst into tears. I had forgotten just how cutting Julian can be when he's separated from what he wants. It's a trait both he and Paul share, a trait they both inherited from Kate—the undisputed queen of slicing your soul from stem to sternum with one single word.

CHAPTER TWENTY-SIX

AS I WALK PAST THE torches alighting the pool area, my tears won't cease. Julian's warning plays on repeat in my head: *I will show you fear in a handful of dust.* A fitting choice of words to contemplate under an unsettled sky.

But I don't need Julian's veiled threats about time running out; I know it is. It's been running out since 1988, since my father and Kate were married and presided over the most botched family blending in recorded history. I've watched the failures, the sins, the betrayals, the self-annihilation, and the lies pile up into a bonfire of our own vanities.

And then, at one minute to midnight, Kate left us her video. I had hope once again, the same hope from when I was ten years old and wanted someone to make us a family, a *hope* that was never carried through so I picked it up in the interim, waiting for someone to relieve me. And they never did.

But when Kate spoke, when she laid down the truth verbally and then followed it with *actions*, it felt like she finally had left us the tools to go back in time and set it right, to save us. I took her plan to heart, following it no matter where it took us, no matter how dark it looked, no matter who was mad at me, and no matter how exhausted and hopeless it looked. I never wavered; I stayed lit for the six of us regardless of the time of day.

But my efforts aren't working. As much as it kills me, as much as I wish it otherwise, as much as I love all of my siblings and even my father, not only do I have no idea how we're going to say goodbye to Kate...I also don't know how we can make it after. It's hard enough to say goodbye to the only mother I have known, but the whole family is going with her. It's a long goodbye to the last thirty-three years. How am I supposed to leave the past when there is no future?

I approach our villa hoping someone is up. I need to talk to Nathan, but if he's not up, I'll accept the kids as a substitute. Theo and Winnie may not engage with any of my darkest fears, or the questions gnawing at my soul, but at least the time will be filled and I'll get a brief respite from my apocalyptic musings of my family dissipating, dissolving, and going their separate ways.

I swipe the key across the sensor, walk inside, and am immediately accosted by darkness. I turn on the living room light, begin to walk upstairs, and am assaulted by a familiar sound—the guttural blocked sinus baritone of Nathan snoring. Even with the door shut, I'm amazed that anyone can sleep through Nathan *sleeping*.

I enter the bedroom, warily approach Nathan's side of the bed, and begin gently rubbing his shoulder, hoping he couldn't have entered *that* deep of a sleep by ten thirty. He doesn't move. I lean down to kiss his lips and he kisses me back, the way he always does when I try to wake him up that way. His reciprocation always makes me fall in love with him a little bit more, because even in full REM, he instinctively knows it's me and wouldn't lose the chance to show affection. But he still doesn't fully stir. I try another kiss, and when our lips disconnect, he starts smacking his together, mimicking chewing, then wakes up for a moment to tell me he loves the muffins I've made, puts his head back on the pillow, and goes back to sleep.

Slightly confused about why Nathan is eating my muffins in his dream and what his resting mind is trying to sort out, I take that as my cue to check on the children and hope for a more conscious audience.

I gingerly knock on their door, having been lectured on my propensity to barge in unannounced on their "personal space" and my inability to respect boundaries. No one answers. I take that as an unspoken cue to proceed. Winnie is in her bed, cocooned in several blankets like a molting moth with her feet peeking out from each layer. She can dream through Nathan's commanding pharyngeal performance since she has an AirPod tucked into her left ear, like she passed out taking a customer service call. I approach her bed and—hoping to save her hearing—slowly pull the AirPod out as if it's the pin to a hand grenade. I give her a kiss on the forehead.

I look over to Theo's bed, hoping his anger has tempered and he has more than two words to say to me—but he's also asleep, his face illuminated by the glow from the laptop laid across his stomach. I watch him initiate a turn to his other side and reflexively spring into action to save the computer before it meets the floor.

This is why he's needed four laptops throughout his high school career. He falls asleep "working"—definitely never *gaming*—forgets to take the computer off his bed, and without fail, at some point during the night sends it rocketing across the room with his skinny body, leaving behind a smashed screen, a popped keyboard, or a dented hard drive.

Of course, he predictably shuns responsibility for destroying his computers, blaming it on the spirit-crushing amount of work the school has assigned, work that *requires* him to toil late into the evening so he can attend a prestigious university. Then he laments the curse laid solely on his head by the shoddy manufacturing of technology in this penny-pinching world, where every cent saved means another row of profit in a quarterly report. He finishes by folding his arms, huffing, and claiming his smashed laptop was an entirely unavoidable consequence of twenty-first-century living.

I'm balancing the computer in my hands, walking it over to the table by the sliding doors overlooking the water, when I notice

Theo has actually been working. I blink twice, convinced I'm hallucinating, only to realize I'm cradling undeniable proof Theo finished his assignment that he had given to Nathan. I sit down, stare at the pulsing cursor, and read:

"T.S. Eliot's "The Waste Land": An impassioned analysis by Theodore Charles Daly"

A bold and highfalutin title, but I'd expect nothing less from my firstborn. It also bears noting that Theo's given himself top billing alongside T.S. Eliot, as if he's the first person to undertake a close reading of possibly the most pored-over modernist work outside of James Joyce's bibliography. Thankfully, Theo is ready to chime in and end a century-long debate:

> "The Waste Land" is a very, at times painfully, symbolic, fractured, confusing, apparently esoteric, at least according to the introduction, multi-lingual poem. T.S. Eliot goes across many centuries without the help of transitions, while alluding to other works I have never read and don't understand, but are supposedly Pagan, Arthurian, Christian, and Buddhist.

> Or so my father told me. Frankly, I didn't see any of that in Mr. Eliot's poem. In fact, as I reached the third part, I began wondering if he was just a mean person committed to confusing teenagers in the current century. What does a line like this even possibly mean?

> "He does the police in different voices."

My instinctive urge to either slam the screen shut and be thankful Theo has already been accepted into college—Harvard included—or begin editing the document, paring down the personal attacks on Eliot, is overpowered when I spot the next paragraph and realize my son is merely clearing his throat, warming up for his epic start:

> *However, after nearly dying yesterday at sea, when my femoral artery was sliced open by a patch of coral, causing me to lose two pints of blood, and require immediate emergency care to save my life...*

I don't think he's hyperbolizing; Theo *does* likely feel that way. And Nathan and I are the reason why. I'll give Theo a pass on that paragraph and admit that in one of our valiant and misguided attempts to parent, Nathan and I overshot the mark.

> *And upon having my leg repaired, torturously, for what seemed like days, "The Waste Land" suddenly started to make a great deal of sense to me. It is one of those poems that isn't for everyone. In fact, if pushed to answer, I'd say it's not really intended for anyone. That's not why T.S. Eliot wrote it. He wrote it for people who are ready for it. And when you are ready for it, it finds you; it's waiting for you. It's there to help.*

If I had to imagine a poet who would be the presiding spirit over the past few days, it wouldn't be T.S. Eliot; it would be Lewis Carroll. I feel like I've been led about by a white rabbit, introduced to citizens who speak in nonsense jabberwocky, and am in constant danger of decapitation. But I also can't brush aside the fact that Theo is engaging with a literary work—not only engaging, he's making it his own and finding his own path to the inside of the mystery. I couldn't do that at his age. I don't think Nathan could have either. And the fact that I'm this surprised shows me I don't know everything about him, and I should keep reading on if I'd like to meet another side of my child:

"The Waste Land" talks about a world trapped between stages. About an old world passing away and a new world waiting to be born, but unable to do so, because there is a drought. The "drought" isn't only based in rain, but also spirit and culture. Everyone and everything in "The Waste Land" is dead. And we've been here before. Modern England is no different than Arthurian England than ancient crop festivals to Demeter in Greece. Civilizations and their cultures have died before and all from the same cause. They get exhausted. And civilization, in T.S. Eliot's poem, is cyclical, and about to complete another rotation. But only the rain can bring it. And the rain will not come.

I know how T.S. Eliot feels because I feel that way sometimes too. That we, as people, as a planet, are back in the same place he was talking about in 1922. We can't commit to living. And we can't commit to passing on and letting the rain fall. The signs are all there. From the moment I was born we have been at war. War with other countries. War over money. War over guns. War over the earth. War with disease. And finally, war with each other. The rain must come.

I know it wasn't always like this. My grandparents tell me what it was like when they were seventeen and I don't recognize it. It isn't the same world or the same country. Even when my parents talk about being my age it seemed better. Although they will tell you the cracks were starting. That is fair. It takes more than seventeen years to need rain festivals. But at least they had the world before it cracked.

In "The Waste Land," the Fisher King, the keeper of the grail, needed to heal his wound to make it rain again, to kickstart a new era that would be followed by the Buddhist thunder of time signaling the Fisher King's success. The thunder will speak a new world.

I wonder if the Fisher King will ever come out of hiding. I wonder when the thunder will break its silence. I wonder why they've left us all alone. I wonder why no one wants to save us.

As I close the laptop screen, I have heard the thunder as well. I have to let Theo go. I have to let him go to Harvard. I have to admit my father was right to help him do it. I've always tried to insulate our son from the hermetic trappings of the world in which I was raised, a private world inaccessible to most, and—in my opinion—sterile and deadly to those who inhabit it. But it is only *my* opinion, and even though it isn't my first choice for Theo, it is the right choice for *him*. I can't deny him that chance. He has a mind like Nathan and me, a mind that will thrive at Harvard, a mind that will grow ever more glorious nurtured by what they can teach him about literature.

I also know he will survive the world I rejected and return unscathed—because they can teach him about literature, but I've taught him about character, about how to be a good person in a world that allows few opportunities for goodness. His interpretation of T.S. Eliot is laced with our life together, a life in which I've always tried to teach him to look outward, to pay attention, to never sleep, to never put your head in the sand and compensate with privilege, because it is illusory. To be aware is to be *alive*, and when things are at their worst—when war, when violence, when the daily threat of guns are in their school, when the planet is depleting, when the rights I was born with are stripped from my daughter, *his sister*, when the potential collapse of democracy is playing out on the streets in the very city in which he lives—that is the time in which you do not *stop*. In which you find the hope, find the meaning in the struggle.

And that's when I understand why my family's own struggle—and it *is* a struggle—is failing. Everyone should technically feel delivered. We should be finding the relief Kate promised on her video. The problems we consigned to their own burials have never been spoken out loud, not even to ourselves.

But as I just learned from T.S. Eliot, the problems we face today go back to 1922, and even though they are cyclical, they have a beginning. That's the thing Kate forgot. The thing I forgot. The thing that keeps our shared dream fluttering away every time it's within reach. None of us knows why things went so wrong in this family in the first place, we just know with every fiber of our being that they did, and the turns have been inexorable and unstoppable.

What good does it do if you bring everything into the open, if the reasons why we all hit rock bottom remain shrouded in mystery? My siblings and I have ripped off the veils, only to find the same gaping crater of grief staring back at us. We can't go any further until we go back to Benjamin and Kate, to the people seemingly without pasts, the people who hit pause in 1988 and never turned the tape back on.

A plan coalesces. One fraught with swallowing a lot of pride, more than I may be able to bear. I tell myself it's to save the family, and it'll be my last attempt to set things right before we take a final trip with Kate. But even then—it *sucks*.

I have to capitulate to my father. I have to tell him he was right about Theo. I instantly begin to seize in agony at the thought. I have to tell him that, although I've spent my whole life lecturing him that he's doing everything wrong, rebuking any offer that wasn't exactly on my terms, and rebuffing his attempts to love me because it wasn't how I wanted to be loved—that in the case of Theo and Harvard, he's ultimately right and I was wrong.

Is this really worth it?

I force myself to stop thinking. It will only make it worse. I need him to know I love him—*and I actually do*—so he can help me show my siblings how much I love them. Then I pull my phone from the pocket of my dress, tap on Benjamin's name, and text:

Dad, I'm sorry. Can we have breakfast tomorrow?

Then I enter into a showdown with the three bubbles, indicating that my father is really mulling this over, likely feeling the same way I do and oscillating between the curiosity of why I'm apologizing versus what strings this heartfelt mea culpa has attached.

The three bubbles pause, followed by:

Meet me at 9:00 a.m.

CHAPTER TWENTY-SEVEN

Day Four

AFTER TURNING BACK TOWARD MY villa a minimum of six times—apologizing to Benjamin is never freeing, never elevates nor vanquishes the emotional load; it usually involves you groveling to his stone-face, followed by years of "I told you so" at family dinners—I finally walk into my father's villa, and seemingly on command, my stomach is more uneasy than me. It might be morning sickness rearing its ugly, unwanted head. Or it might be the predictable result of swallowing the bitter pill of capitulation, turning it sour. I look around the window-wrapped living room, spot my father on the terrace through the glass, and make out the butler setting up coffee at the table. The pool looms behind them, the still water moving in freeze-frames.

"Hi, Dad," I say, walking over to give him a hug. "Thanks for seeing me."

My father puts down the morning newspaper he likes to thumb through over breakfast, the only area in his life where he remains an analog man in a digital world.

"Hi, sweetheart," he says, upgrading my status to where we first started this trip and putting his arms around me for an unusually long time for him, as if he's sizing up the situation and trying to read the plan in the hug. "Sit down. There's coffee and orange juice already, and the eggs Benedict and bacon are coming out."

"Sounds delicious," I say, hiding my feelings behind my first sip of orange juice while the thought of runny poached eggs dripping with creamy hollandaise sauce causes my stomach to flip.

"Not to start things off controversially," he says, meaning to start things off controversially in what promises to be the longest breakfast of my life, "but it didn't look like your dinner went as smoothly as you would have liked." He brings the coffee to his lips, awaiting my reaction before drinking and savoring the seconds in between. A thin smile is pressed against his cup. "It's not as easy as it looks, is it, Elizabeth?"

"No," I say loudly, followed by a little laugh, trying to drown my desire to run with inappropriate volume. "It is not at all."

"You're welcome for the wine, by the way," he says, never missing a chance to highlight a perceived absence of manners or to be flattered for his unfailing generosity. "Do you want to tell me about it?"

There he goes. He wants to gloat, to rub my face in failure. And all I want to say is—you've had thirty-three years of dinners ending in tears and recriminations, and you want to give me shit over *one*? I remember a string of summer dinners where the check would come, my father would whisper something to Kate, they would exchange angry whispers, and she would abandon him at the restaurant, which meant I had to drive him home. But it's my fault. Everything runs like clockwork when Benjamin Sunderland sits at the head of the table. *He is insufferable.* Could he at least fake the slightest recognition that he may have played some small part in how we all turned out?

"Everyone's struggling with tonight, Dad," I say, hoping that if I appeal to him with the wellbeing of all his children, maybe he'll finally entertain a question. "That's why I'm here." I watch him pour hot coffee from the carafe into his cup and stir. "Why do you think we never totally blended as a family? Why are we like this?"

"Elizabeth," he says, remaining a solid slab in the face of my earnestness, "I don't think that. *You* think that."

"We all think that," I say, losing my first layer of attempted calm. "Even Kate thought so. Jesus, Dad. Didn't you watch the video? It was the entire point. We never became a family. And I'm asking...I'm *begging* you, that before we spread Kate's ashes, you do your part and try to help us heal before it's too late. Just answer the question. *Why?*"

He drops his coffee cup down on the table like a weight, letting me know I've gone too far. "Elizabeth, I'm going to give you a piece of advice that will help you with your own parenting. When you get to be my age, you resign yourself to the fact that your kids are *your kids*. You're never going to understand them. You learn to expect it." He pauses, breathing deeply. "But I certainly never expected that from my wife. And even after being with Kate for thirty-three years, I am still struck dumb with whatever she was trying to get at by exposing everyone's mistakes and hoping that it would make everyone heal in three days."

"Dad," I begin, determined to keep going even though my stomach is telling me to cut and run. I feel so nauseous that it's difficult to sit upright, and I'm fighting with my whole being not to throw up. "I think you're full of shit. I think you're scared. I think you're selfish. And I think you know *exactly* why—"

Before I can finish, the butler returns with breakfast and places two plates in front of my father and me, warning us they may be hot. I take one glance at the bubbling sauce, the yolk-stained china, and the grease from the Canadian bacon intermingling in a puddle at the center, and I can't hold anything down.

I excuse myself, run back into his villa, rush past the downstairs bathroom—desperate to make sure my father doesn't hear me getting sick, which will open an entirely different round of intense questioning—then run into his bedroom, slam the door, and barely make it in time to throw up.

Five intense, sweating, hugging-the-bowl-as-if-it's-a-close-confidant minutes later, I pull myself up off the floor. I use the sink to hold me up and try to wash my face with shaking hands. Then I look into the mirror and realize there's only so much I can do. Benjamin's questions are inevitable, and for a brief second, I entertain running out the front door and not telling him.

But I can't. I have to know. I have to go back in. I throw some cold water on my face, then some more, and pull my hair back into a ponytail. I try my hardest to approximate looking and feeling semi-human again. I exhale. It will have to do.

I walk into the bedroom to leave, and from the corner of my eye, see an envelope on the table. Not an abnormal thing in itself. That's what surfaces are for, to house things. But I'd recognize the handwriting on this envelope anywhere. The obsessive E, the looping L, the barely existent I except for the dot, the Z like a personal statement, the A, as if it's battling the Z and upcoming B for supremacy, the second E even straighter than the first, the T with a stalwart cross atop, and the H resting at the end, like two intertwined fingers pointing to look inside.

Kate.

I pick up the envelope, weighing it in my hands. It's thicker than one would expect from her, an avowed woman of few words. From the age of ten, I waited for Kate to become the arm I hid under when events shook my life. I wanted her to fill our relationship with emotional security, with shared sentiment. It never happened. And it's not as if she didn't have a chance; we shared graduations, a marriage, grandchildren being born. Time blessed her with multiple openings to summon her feelings, to commemorate the import of the momentous event in words.

On my sweet sixteen, she gave me a bracelet from Cartier; at my high school graduation, she gave me the keys to a Mercedes; when I finished college, there was a Burberry coat waiting for me; on my wedding day, she affixed a pair of diamond earrings to my lobes; when Theo was born, she placed him in a two-thousand-dollar stroller; and when Winnie came into the world, I received a sapphire necklace, her birthstone.

What I didn't get on any of these storied occasions was a letter, a scribbled note, or even a fucking card. I lack a single, solitary milestone accompanied by Kate's words performing all the heavy lifting. I suppose she wanted me to convert the number on the price tag to emotion, like exchanging dollars for euros. But there is no equivalency.

Words require the heart and the heart only. There is nowhere to hide.

Suddenly the door flies open, and my father rushes into the room, seemingly panicked. "You've been gone forever. Are you okay?"

I stare at my father, speechless, holding the letter tight and not interested in answering *his* question. I want to know why he has a letter from Kate for me. Was he planning on giving it to me tonight? Can I have it now? Can I have her final thoughts, so I know exactly who I'm saying goodbye to tonight? Is there one for everyone? Is this the final link to close the loop she opened with her video?

"That's not for you," Benjamin says, pointing at the envelope, his finger waving. "Give it back."

"Not for *me*?" I say, confused by his tone. I hold the letter up to the light. "I think that's my name, Dad."

"Just give it to me, Elizabeth," he says, voice booming, seemingly to cancel out any resistance or questions with sheer vocal force. "Now."

"But it's not for *you*," I say, not entirely sure why we're fighting, but sure my father is fighting. "Why do you want it so badly?"

"Just forget you saw it," he says, inching closer, trying to bring down the tension—and failing with his strained body language. "It doesn't matter. If you give it back, all this goes away."

"All *what?*" I say, now certain he is never getting this note. "What goes away, Dad?"

"Elizabeth," he says, standing almost toe-to-toe with me, "I can't explain it to you. But if you have any love for me or this family, you will give me that note."

"Get out of my way," I say, frustrated and ready to leave. I'm dying to see what Kate has committed to paper that has made my father panic for the first time in my life. He isn't collected; he isn't negotiating. There's no poker face where you know he has an ace in the hole that he's waiting to spring. He's just scared. And his fear is actually freaking me out.

I just want to get out of this room. I feel trapped, like the walls are closing in. I feel as if the roof might rip off any second and suck my father and me into a parallel universe where our fight will continue until the end of time.

But I'm out of time. This family is out of time.

"I'm leaving," I say, storming past him. I run down the stairs to the front door with my father matching my every step in perfect sync, shadowing me, muttering random expletives that I'm not entirely sure are even directed at me.

I reach the front door and put my hand on the handle, imagining the fresh air suffusing my face. But before I open it, my father says, "If you walk out that door with *that* letter, don't plan on coming tonight."

"That's pretty desperate, Dad," I say, waving the letter in front of his face. "You're just making me want to open it more."

"Elizabeth," he says, voice warbling, "if you take that letter… if open that letter…you will destroy this family. You will destroy everything Kate and I built. And most probably, destroy yourself in the process."

"Well then maybe you shouldn't have left it on a table. You could've shredded it. You could've fucking burned it, like anything else put down on paper you don't like," I say, pointing to his own unexamined subconscious. "Examine yourself on this one, Dad."

His eyes become so hyper-focused, I fear they may never close again. "I'm not lying to you about this. We can never come back from what's in there."

"This family isn't coming back from this trip," I say, ripping open the door with such anger that the hinges squeak for mercy. "I highly doubt whatever is in this letter is going to take us over the edge. We live there already."

CHAPTER TWENTY-EIGHT

UNDER A HOT COPPER SKY, I walk the length of the beach. I let my shadow lead, watching it cast exaggerated limbs across the sand and stop at the lip of the ocean, which is pulsing a burnt, glossy green. Kate's letter is in my hand, still unopened—not because I've decided to heed my father's advice and refrain from reading it, but because I'm trying to find an isolated enough location where Benjamin can't find me and try one last time to convince me not to read the only letter Kate has ever given me.

I spot a break ahead, a trail that turns away from the open topography of the beach. It's an elevational shift that promises too much toil for Benjamin's bad knee.

I begin to trudge up the hill and realize I am not wearing the right shoes for this, nor do I possess the cardiovascular health for this to promise the ease I had hoped for. My flip-flops sink into the red and black mud, the color of a smeared shade, like the face of a mirror when a lamp in the next room moves. Then fruit starts to fall—hard ossified hides plummeting from tall trees and being fought over by hungry birds. Kind of like how my siblings handle their own *emotional* hunger.

The further I go, the darker it gets, and the more I need to be certain someone can rescue me. I pull out my cell phone, check for reception, and a single full bar mocks me to turn back, all but assuring me that if I keep climbing much higher it, too, will disappear.

It gets darker. I keep my cell phone out and turn on the flashlight. The sky disappears behind a canopy of labeled overgrown trees informing tourists of their rarity. West Indian Locust. Kapok. Genip. All interesting facts. Facts that will never help me in life. And neither will the sleeping bats peacefully dangling from their branches, upside down, their tiny wings crossed. I try to tiptoe through the sludge to make sure they don't wake up and see me.

I stop and hunch over slightly, hands on my knees, straining to breathe. I wish that—in my escape from Benjamin—I'd had the forethought to buy a bottle of water. I see some stray clusters of boulders slightly up ahead and rush toward them, desperate to sit.

But when I approach the rusted mineral slabs—sunlight streaming through their broken columns—I realize they aren't *innocent*, they are architectural remains of a time out of joint. A wooden placard announces they are called "America Hill," and there is a short history inscribed below for visitors, of which there are *none* except me. They must have happier families and less demanding things to do in St. John.

The sign informs me that this once mighty landed estate was built at a high note of conquest during the empire's drive for sugar, which is described in unsettling—and almost erotic—terms. However, once the sugar demand dried up, the structure was shuffled into a safe house for exiled cold war Caribbean dictators on the run from their own people. But they're all gone too. And now the stones have assumed their final incarnation as a fucking disturbing tourist attraction seeped in centuries of blood, which strikes me as what always happens when America—or my family—gets its hands on something. We take the tragic and turn it into luxury. With that discovery, I decide this is the right place to open Kate's letter.

I trace my fingers over Kate's handwriting, the closest I can come to ever having her hand in mine again; with each letter, the memory I have tried to keep bottled up the entire trip comes flooding back. It's the whole reason Madeleine exists.

Almost three years before Kate became Benjamin's wife, before she met Tessa and Caroline, she met *me*. A moment in time never spoken of again. Sometimes I think I dreamt it, invented it to keep hope alive. But I didn't. It happened on a snowy day in Manhattan not long after my mother left us.

Benjamin and I were out one afternoon shopping for *him*, and to even the score I demanded a trip to Serendipity 3. The minute we walked in, my father saw the lunch rush, spotted the line to get a table, and wanted to leave; that is, until he heard a woman call his name and walk over to us.

"Benjamin," she said. "How are things going?"

"Outstanding. I've got a big IPO coming up. When it gets closer, I'll call you with a tip. You'll thank me...."

The woman seemed simultaneously indulgent and annoyed that my father couldn't stop talking about his success. "Aren't you going to introduce me?"

"Right," Benjamin said, excusing himself and addressing me. "This is Kate Bernard. She was my colleague at the old firm."

Kate lowered herself eye-level with me. "And this must be Elizabeth."

"In the flesh," Benjamin said. "Say hi to Kate. She knows *all* about you."

I extended my hand, which was wrapped in a unicorn mitten that changed color in the rain or snow. "Hello."

Instead of accepting my gloved fingers, Kate took me in her arms. She kept me there for an eternity, nestled against her chest, so close I could discern her heartbeat. After ending the hug, she rose back to standing height, smiled, and said, "I hear you love the frozen hot chocolate."

"I do!" I said enthusiastically, unable on any occasion to tamper down my love for sweets.

"I love it too," Kate said, smiling. "The next time I see you, we'll have one together. I hope it's sooner than later."

Kate never wrapped her arms around me like she wanted to stop time, never held me close, never *held* me again. And we never did have that long-promised frozen hot chocolate once she married Benjamin. I suppose I figured if I opened a store that *served* them it would unblock whatever barrier kept her from sharing one with me. Finally, I gave up, and just started sharing them with everyone else instead.

CHAPTER TWENTY-NINE

Dear Elizabeth,

Diagnosis is a tricky thing. We've all been led to believe, either by reality or our own hopes and desires, that if a problem can be diagnosed it surely can be cured. The undoing of that assumption was the hardest part for me. You can receive a diagnosis that is merely that. A diagnosis. It can lead nowhere. The doctors couldn't have been clearer about the nature of my illness, but with that knowledge came only certainty of the end. That paradox, wisdom without profit, has left me four months with nothing to do but reflect on another broken instrument that is an intimate part of me...but the one that can be saved.

Our family is also a sick patient that can be diagnosed, but one that—unlike me—can ultimately be healed. Yet to do that, I must accept the grim conclusion that I have been an integral part of our current state. To the point that there are times I'm tempted to believe I have internalized all of our illnesses, and as my own metastasized, you all followed. The sicker I became, the family followed in sync.

At times I even wonder if I'm the right one to do it, even though I know it falls on me. I am under no illusion as to how I am seen. And although my death will leave a hole in everyone, the rationale will differ with each person. Some will remember me fondly, like my grandchildren, with whom I was finally able to parent, absent the pressure that they would judge me as they would judge their own parents. They have all been pure pleasure.

Others will remember me as a distant deity, a specter haunting the house even while living. A mother who judged in the same manner, wantonly, cruelly, distinctly unmotherly, while atop the lofty heights of my own achievements, which I hoped to leave to all of you, but from which you turned away as if it was all diseased itself.

Of course, I am speaking of my own children.

The chasm will be largest there because I put it there and left it gaping, unfixed. Reparation would have required admitting the original wound, the first hurt, and I lacked the courage to do it. But I could bring you all back to St. John. I could record a video when I first realized how everyone, including Benjamin, reacted to my illness, and I knew I needed to stop the fallout. I could even engineer from front to back the exposure of a lifetime of sins and omissions in the hope that bringing them into the light would cause them to fade. I could even sit down and dictate this letter to my nurse, as I'm too weak to hold a pen in my own hand. The ultimate insult.

You have just left me tonight to go home to Theo. And I failed again. I started, but I couldn't finish. Why can I tell a complete stranger the truth, but not my own chil-

dren? That's the hardest part, Elizabeth. Realizing that all the bravery I translated into my career was a poor sublimation for the cowardice I carried in my personal life. This is what possesses my final thoughts. I passed my own weaknesses down to everyone else. Except you. I left that video for you. And I leave this for you because I know you will do with it what I couldn't.

At one of our many infamous dinners, you stood up and claimed Benjamin and I had erased everyone's pasts prior to us getting married. You said we willed a collective amnesia on all of you to obtain the lives that we wanted, and that the only way our marriage worked was to live in a perpetual present without past or future. You said we prematurely forced Julian and Paul to bury the trauma of Luc leaving. You said that made my oldest son unable to forgive me and left my youngest son without anyone to love him. You said you and Tessa were also prematurely forced to forget the trauma of your mother moving to Colorado, so I would feel more comfortable. You said Caroline was the only one with a shot, and we managed to screw that up too. That we had a blank slate and even that turned to shit. You said the refusal to admit we were all damaged, including Benjamin and I, was what made it impossible to blend our family. Because how can you blend people when they can't even exist as people in the first place?

In that you were right and wrong. The poison had been planted far earlier. Benjamin and I made you all mimic us. We poisoned all of you to hide our own truth. But you are right. We were never a blended family. We never even tried to be a blended family. Because your father and I couldn't even blend. How could we show all of you?

But the most tragic part may be that your siblings did blend. They just blended the entirely wrong way. It was you who never did. You seem to have sensed a mystery underneath, that there was something bigger afoot than just our aloof parenting. You have hunted for reasons. Why does your father not have a past? Why do I not have a past? And you have made both our lives frequently miserable because you couldn't just blend in misery and be like your brothers and sisters. But you glimpsed something better for them, and you can't get it without this.

You have waited long enough. And I have nothing left to wait for.

You believed I couldn't give you the love you craved because I placed my career and our family's name before you. This is the correct interpretation based on the available data. But it is clouded. Your vision is constricted, your perception choked off. You are missing a piece.

You are missing you.

When I was twenty-one years old, I met the man who turned my life upside down. I fell in love instantly. His name was Benjamin Sunderland.

Your father and I were inseparable. He had just graduated from the MBA program at Wharton and joined a prestigious firm as a financial analyst, already eyeing the corner office before he got his first suit. I had just finished my undergraduate degree at American and joined the same firm in a different department. I wasn't there more than a few days before he asked me out, but me being me, I made him wait a few more before I accepted, even though I knew in my heart the answer was "yes" before he finished asking.

We were terribly serious on all fronts. When it came to one another and when it came to what we wanted out of life. We wanted money, success, luxury, status—sometimes me even more than him. The great irony being that I created a monster. He ended up outpacing me in the game, earning even more than me in the long run. And he loved to hold it over my head.

It was a few months into our love affair when we found out I was pregnant.

I was pregnant with you.

We were going to be parents. We were going to build a life. We were terrified. We both knew what a baby meant, the sacrifices it entailed, the balances it would bulldoze. Neither of us quite knew how we were going to pull this off. We just knew life was never going to be the same. And it wasn't.

A month before I was due with you, our firm offered me a life-changing chance, one they never offered women. The gilded key, the glass ceiling was mine for the taking, mine for the crashing. I was going to be promoted and transferred to the London office after you were born. With one simple move, one simple change of locale, I would be on the track to the C-Suite. My dream.

Your father was on his own path forward at our firm and already growing restless, looking for the next big move, the next notch on his resume, the next position that would bring him closer to being his own boss. He knew what moving to London with me would cost him, and he wasn't willing to do it. He wasn't willing to conjoin our futures, wasn't willing to bet on anyone else except himself.

After endless nights of debate, fighting, soul-searching, in which I begged and pleaded with him to come, he made the hard decision easy. There was no way he was coming. He would stay behind with you, because there was no way I could start a new job and give it the commitment I deserved while being a new mother. He would get a bigger place, hire help during the day, and after you were born, we would alternate monthly visits. I'd come to Manhattan to see you. And he'd come to London the next time. And the two years I was supposed to be away would just fly by.

But they didn't. They got harder and harder. The trips became more and more infrequent on both sides. Work got in the way. I would go two or three months without seeing you.

A year into my stay in London, your father called me to tell me had a confession. He had started seeing someone, and he wanted to get married. He was lonely. He didn't want to raise a baby alone.

I was furious with him for betraying me and got on the next flight back to Manhattan to confront him and take you back with me. When I arrived at the apart-

ment, Benjamin's new girlfriend, Roxanne, the mother
you knew before me, answered the door. I introduced
myself, and she seemed vaguely aware of my existence.
But what wasn't vague was how inseparable you were
from her. I don't even think you knew who I was. I tried
to hold you and you screamed, only finding solace again
in the arms furthest away from me. I couldn't take you.
Something in me snapped. I was too young, too weak to
fight, too confused, too scared to work out a solution. All
I knew was that it seemed like Roxanne would give you
a better life, and be the mother I wouldn't be.

I was held hostage by my own plans, my own wants
from life. I was making strides in my career unheard of
among women at the time. My brass ring of becoming
an executive wasn't a fuzzy dream; it seemed attainable.
I had worked too hard to pass it up. And as strange as
it may seem today—although it really shouldn't—there
weren't options in 1978 for someone like me. There
weren't many female bosses; there weren't sympathetic
workplaces; there simply wasn't any compromise. A
woman had a career or a woman had a family. There
wasn't a gray zone. Or if there was, I wasn't the right
woman to see it. And I knew after spending a few hours
with Roxanne that I had to let you go. For you. For me.
For your happiness. It was the hardest thing I ever did,
but I believed at the time it was all I could do to ensure
you were loved.

Not long after that day, I looked for anyone and met
Luc. Luc was the first one to make his presence known.
I needed the polar opposite of Benjamin, someone with
family money who almost looked at success as an

annoyance, like a horrible flu with no solution except to bear it and occasionally medicate with binges. He had his uses. He was handsome. He was fun. He was spontaneous. He was easily bored like me. But most of all he allowed me to forget, to bury the past so I could find a way to go on.

My company brought me back to the US when you were three. Luc and I were married by then, and Paul was a baby. Two years later, Julian joined him.

Everything seemed ideal. The fact that Luc didn't have much of a career—outside of traveling to the South of France occasionally to make sure his family's cheese was imported correctly on the US end of business—meant he was able to stay home with your brothers while I kept climbing the corporate ladder. A climb that continued without a hitch until Paul turned five and Luc decided he was finished. He couldn't take the domesticity and didn't want to be a stay-at-home Dad—both self-imposed but clearly unsatisfying. He moved on to live his best life with the nanny he had hired to help him with the boys. She was also French. I should have seen the warning signs immediately.

Right around the same time, Roxanne couldn't live with Benjamin anymore. Even she lacked the requisite patience and love to handle him. Your father was such a walking crisis that she needed a full detoxification and moved to a commune in response.

Not long after both Luc and Roxanne departed us for greener pastures, I saw you and your father in Serendipity 3, and immediately knew I couldn't let either of you go again. I called him the same night, said we should meet up, and six months later we decided to make our plans from years ago a reality. I can't lie and tell you it was smothered in romance. It had an air of pragmatism around it. We both knew neither of us had fared well outside of the other, and we would probably be alone if we didn't finally commit. The fact that both our families had grown exponentially in our separation was a cause of celebration. The fact that they both ended in rancorous divorces and situations unfit for children made our marriage a necessity.

There was only one problem. You.

We couldn't tell you who you were. That would have to be kept a secret. I didn't agree at first, but I begrudgingly came around once your father explained that you would hate us both, and that we had to admit you would have every right. Neither one of us had the requisite spine to let you hate us, even though as parents it was our job. We decided it would be best for the sake of the new blended family that everyone started off on an even keel. We decided it would be best for you as well.

The irony is that, even though we kept our history a secret from you, you made our lives a living hell anyway. But it was a rebellion, at times an outright hate, that your father and I could accept because it was abstract. You hated us because we were your parents, not because we hid who I was and who you were. I couldn't let you hate me for the right reason.

I imagine—if I know you, and I must confess I do—that you are filled with righteous anger, indignation, and may have stopped reading this letter in the middle. You're probably already packing your bags and searching for the fastest flight out of St. John. You aren't wrong to feel these ways. But you don't have to forgive me right now to love your siblings, or to love your father.

What you do need to do is tell your brothers and sisters what's in this letter, no matter how hard your father tries to prevent it—and he will try. I can't guarantee how your siblings will react in the present, but I do know in the future they will be relieved to know who you are, because only through truth, only through knowing we made all of you this way, can the five of you move forward and be the people we strangled through our own selfishness.

From when I tried to hire you at my firm the minute you graduated from college, to every friend and colleague you spurned an introduction to, then moving into a one-bedroom apartment with Nathan when I offered to buy you a penthouse, to throwing your trust back at us, to putting my grandchildren in a progressive public high school, to opening a bakery and having no plans to open another one—which I still maintain is an enormous error—you are truly your own person. One I admire for frustrating me more than any other person on earth.

It's why I deposited $5 million in your account. Benjamin and I should have given it to you in the first place. It was what we invested in Paul's restaurant. Not that it would have mattered, though; you wouldn't have taken it. Take it now. Take it and introduce everyone to the memory we shared. A memory I hid in both your *life and your business. That's why I sent the president to Madeleine. I've known him for over twenty-five years, since he was a senator and one of the first clients at my firm. I knew you wouldn't take the money and follow through on my instructions to expand and share. So, I didn't give you a choice. And he will keep coming back until you have done what I've instructed. He promised. Your other siblings need to find their destiny; you need to stop putting it off.*

I didn't love you the way I wanted in life, my beautiful daughter, but I want to give you the only thing I can in death.

You.

Live life, Lizzie. Live it without pain. Stop suffering. It doesn't help. It can't save you. Only honesty can. Lies weigh down every second, minute, day, year. I lived sixty-five years. Some consider that short. I felt every second of it. It was exhausting to live in denial.

Tell everyone who you are and let yourself soar. Let the years pass you by unnoticed without the lead weight of falsity.

And please, find it in your heart to carry this love of mine with you always.

Goodbye, my darling.

You were the best of me.

I love you,
Mom

CHAPTER THIRTY

I PLACE THE LETTER IN my lap, wipe away the hot mixture of sweat and tears stinging my face, then glance again at the ruins of sugarcane fortunes. I realize that I did make the correct choice reading *my mother's* note in this teetering testament to the rise and fall of empires.

My mother and father have done to me what time has done to the direct ambience around me. I feel these stone, historical orphans deep in my soul, their stoic method of being blasted by time, aware it's not worth fighting the purgation of progress that will tear you apart. I nearly contemplate kicking a small piece of one off and taking it home with me, the same way people who lived in East Berlin kept the souvenirs of their exile—not only to remember what kept them chained, but to remember it can't keep you chained *forever*. And I have to assume on some level I have been freed; I have been granted the hidden key to my own sundered self. But if that's true, why does it feel so horrible?

I stand up, dust off my clothes, and decide if I don't start walking now, I may not make it home by dark—*I'm not moving that quickly these days*—or I may lose my sanity. Neither of them are desirable options, and I think I've sacrificed enough for Benjamin and Kate.

I start to retrace my steps, sliding on mud and leaves. It feels like an elemental return to nature after swimming in over seven pages of the most *unnatural* way to treat your child. But after nearly falling on a clump of rotting fruit, I just want Nathan. I want the one person in my life who can make this go away, the one person who isn't hiding a monumental secret from me, the one person who actually wants *me* to be me.

As I continue my way back down the hill—which I don't really think is a *hill*, more like a miniature mountain—Kate's words echo in my ears and bounce off the corners of my brain. It's almost enough to distract me from the combination of hard-backed bugs I have never seen before and screaming pain my legs haven't felt in years.

I'm glad Kate had her say—got it *all* off her chest and left me alone with her truth. I cup my hand above my eyes to block out the sun, but all I want to do is scream into the center of it, to end the world in a solar inferno so I won't have to suffer alone, so I can drag billions with me and make them hurt like I do. It's one thing to be destroyed; it's a far different thing to be destroyed by a note from beyond the grave.

I don't even know who I'm mad at, but I think it's Kate. I really do. I waited all my life for her to accept me, love me, give me more than she ever could or would. And in death, she finally found her voice but took mine away, stealing my identity and putting something hollow and unknown where *I* used to be.

Who am I?

Who am I now—to my siblings, to Nathan, to my own children? The person I was for forty-three years just vanished, evaporated. It's almost like *that* Lizzie was possessing my body, then moved out and trashed the place. I'm a stranger. A pretender.

For a woman who didn't like words, Kate sure found a hell of a lot of them to deconstruct me from my own existence. But I shouldn't be surprised *my mother* went ahead and dumped the smoldering shambles of her lies on me, pulled the pin, ducked, and demanded to be committed to the sea—likely to avoid getting scorched from the fallout—all to avoid seeing how I'd react. She knew. That's why she waited until she was dead.

I suppose that even with all this new information, one part of me gets to stay the same. My mother did abandon me, just not the mother I thought. It wasn't Roxanne running to the hippie compound. It was Kate. And Kate, being Kate, managed to abandon me without actually *leaving*. That's a coup de grâce of manipulation and duplicity, one she could seamlessly juggle for over four decades. In her last days, I was holding out hope to hear she adored me and was proud of me. That I was the daughter she never had.

Not that I was the fucking daughter she *did* have.

That may not even be the worst part. The worst part is, she finally told me everything so I could go and salvage the family she destroyed by not telling them about me in the first place. I'm half-convinced—*maybe three-quarters*—that if the family wasn't in such dire straits, wasn't composed of six people all about to go their disastrous own ways, that Kate never would have told me. I don't think it's out of the question, especially if history is my guide. It's *Kate*.

Her confession was as manipulative as the original lie itself. Before telling me to go out and save the family, she could've given me a few motherly morsels of advice on how to save *myself*, on how to process her confession, how to retain who I am while ripping the veil off her real identity. It feels like her revelation was as self-serving as her initial leaving. She left me twice: once so she could lead her life, and again when it ended.

But Benjamin's life hasn't ended. Our relationship doesn't share the same grim turning of time. I can confront him. I can know that enemy. He shares her guilt and has the added benefit of still being here. Unfortunately, I can't deal with him yet; I can't confront him in this mood. He'll find some way to turn Kate's letter against me, or to use my entirely justified rage to further some plot of his own. He will try and co-opt my feelings so he can move forward with this family in a way most amenable to what *he* prefers, not what they need.

I can hear him already: "Great. You know the truth now, Lizzie. Don't tell anyone. It'll just be between you and me. Maybe this can even bring us closer." I picture him closing his mouth with a thin half smile. "I told you the family would never survive this."

He won't even say he's sorry, because being Benjamin means you never have to apologize.

"Nathan," I say, as I finally walk into our villa, fresh from trudging down the hill and across the sand, which in the interim turned to gelatinous concrete, instead of the soft grains from when I started. I look down and realize I have half the mountain floor sticking to my legs, then scratch my head to make sure I don't have any hard-backed bugs in my hair.

As if he was somehow empathically aware that the nuclear payload had dropped, that the bottom of this epic trip had been found, I find Nathan awake, not showering, and within spying distance in the living room. He's wearing a pink bathing suit and waiting for the kids to finish an argument upstairs so they can all go to the beach.

"I've got *new* news," I say in a rush. "You don't know who I am. The kids don't know who I am. None of Washington, DC, or Manhattan know who I am. Even *I* don't know who I am."

He looks at me in confusion. "I'm sorry. Can you repeat that? It sounded like you don't know who you are anymore." After saying the words, he sits down. "Like existentially?" He raises his eyebrows, sympathetic and curious. "I mean...I agree our world, and more specifically our place in the world, has never been hazier. Maybe it's even right to question whether in these times we actually *exist*...." Now he seems almost excited that the problem could be existential. He's really rolling, traveling down a rabbit hole of his own fears and anxieties. Except mine isn't a *fear*. Mine just came tangibly true. "Is the whole world a simulation? I think about these things too, Lizzie."

Normally I would indulge Nathan's flights of rhetorical fancy, even when all I want to know is what he wants to eat for dinner, but the mention of a certain *food* sparks a questioning lecture about how *said food* is being taken advantage of politically and will be seized upon by the Republican Party to drive a wedge between certain Americans who eat it and some who do not eat it, which then takes us down a blind alley back into the late 1800s, where he begins quoting supposed wise men and pulling out German and Russian words that sound like severe sinus infections, and I'm still standing there, frustration rising, and no closer to finding out whether we're eating salmon or tuna. Eventually I cut him off and ask if any of these wise men were married, and if so, do you think they did this to their wives?

"*Stop*," I say, cutting short the sludge of his thought process and realizing I need to get right to the heart of the issue. "Kate is my mother."

Nathan crosses his legs and leans back, looking concerned. "Liz, Kate *is* your mother."

"No. Like Kate is *my mother*," I repeat, punching the last two words to really drive the point home.

"We agree on that," Nathan says, satisfied he's found the mutually agreed upon starting point for a debate over whether or not I've gone crazy. "Everyone here knows Kate is your mother."

Frustrated and not in the mood to even entertain the idea of starting at the beginning and taking him through the lie that is my life, I hand him Kate's letter. "Just read it."

Nathan takes the letter from my hand, shakes it a bit—almost marveling at its density—and begins reading. I watch him closely as he absorbs the years of betrayal, the years of deliberate misinformation, the carefully choreographed performance that I called

Lizzie Sunderland coming unglued, and his reaction could only be called *intriguing*.

He looks like he's reading a book. He runs his fingers under the words to keep pace; he stops and chews seemingly forever on certain sentences; he laughs once or twice; he has to pause to wipe a tear; his eyes keep getting bigger as he reaches the last pages, almost riveted; he stops again, possibly to contemplate grammar; and finally, he exhales, seemingly spent, and places the letter down in his lap.

"Well?" I say, waiting for him to speak and filling the silent gulf. "*Well?*"

"I mean…it's…I mean…" Nathan can't find the words, which for a writer is a pretty rare experience. His loss of speech validates my anger, my confusion, and every single emotion I've felt since reading Kate's letter. "Benjamin and Kate have done a lot since I've known them. Plus, all the things they've done before we met that you told me about. But this…is pretty beyond the pale, even by their already low standards." He puts the letter down on the couch, walks over, and wraps me in his arms. He's so close I can feel his heart beating against mine. "What the actual fuck?" His voice rises, as if he's going through it with me, and I suppose he is. We've always gone through everything together. My pain is his, and his pain is mine. "How could they hide that Kate was your biological mother for forty-three fucking years?"

From the corner of my eye, I see Theo and Winnie running down the stairs in their bare feet and bathing suits. The cosmically confused look on their faces makes me realize Nathan said that last part too loudly, a nasty habit he's developed over the last decade that he blames on "hearing loss" from his "sinus issues," but that I think is really his temper becoming shorter with age. Normally I'm wary of his affliction and counsel him to keep his voice down, but in the heat of the moment, good sense had abandoned me.

"What did Dad just say?" Theo asks, letting the words roll around and finding they don't add up, because they *don't*. "Grandma was your real mother? How did that even..." Then he gives up and reaches the same place I currently inhabit. "*Why?*"

Winnie looks to me, to Nathan, to Theo, a dawning realization working its way across her face. "Wait." She begins running back upstairs, and before I can catch up to her—before I can try and comfort her now that the truth is out and perceptions are changing by the second—she is already on her way down, waving her iPhone in her hand. "Everything makes sense now."

I run my eyes across all the members of my little family, and no one seems to think it makes sense. Nathan has picked up the letter again and is seemingly performing a close read of the text to search for more clues; Theo is staring at the rotating ceiling fan, counting how many times it turns in a minute; and I'm the worst off, because even though they're struggling to process it, I don't even know where to start.

"I worked on a project with Grandma when she was sick," Winnie says, eyes lighting up as she embraces the satisfaction of a plan unfolding perfectly. Her reaction makes me instantly realize why Kate would come to her with a secret project. Just like her grandmother, and her Aunt Caroline, Winnie *loves* to be included in a grand design. "She told me it would all make sense the night of her funeral. That's when she told me to show it to you."

I walk over to Winnie, curious to see what could possibly be on her phone that would make anything add up—especially if my mother was in charge of it. "Baby...what project did you work on with Grandma?"

Winnie opens the photo album app on her phone, takes my hand, and leads me over to the couch to sit down and look at pictures with her. I see Nathan and Theo share a silent exchange, seemingly deciding they also need to be a part of the answers Winnie can provide.

"Grandma had me take pictures of her old photos and create a digital album. It wasn't hard, but you know...grandparents with technology." She laughs, obviously remembering the overflowing praise from Kate that she received during this process.

Winnie turns on the television, then taps on her iPhone to mirror her phone on the screen. We watch her open an album labeled *Elizabeth 1978*, and see the pictures come to life in sixty-five inches, slightly fading along the edges with age.

The first one is a young Kate, all of twenty-two, holding a newborn, *me*, in a tightly wrapped, standard-issue pink and blue hospital blanket. The sheer exhaustion on her face mixed with joy reminds me of my own when Theo and Winnie were born. Winnie waits for me to fully absorb the picture, looks to my eyes for a signal to continue, and I nod that it's okay to keep going.

She begins to scroll through the photos. I see me on my first plane ride; me in London in a stroller, wearing a pink crocheted hat before Big Ben; then me wearing the same hat, but being wheeled around Central Park by Kate. The pictures, flipping one after another, fill in the blank spaces, connecting the collage of missing pieces of my life. The only photographs I've ever seen of my infant years were either with my father, or with Roxanne *and* my father, all of which followed my first birthday. But my first year exists again. The year with Kate. And the photos testifying to it wash over me, threatening to drag me out to an emotional sea I fear I can't return from.

I start to cry, tears speckling my cheeks like morning dew on plants after a nighttime storm, the lingering signs of fresh life after creative destruction. I take Winnie's phone. I go back to Kate holding me in the hospital, which not only substantiates my real birth—grounding me in this new history I'm trying to fit into—but reminds me again that she won't be in the hospital when I have my third child.

"Mom," Winnie says, tears rimming her eyes, moved by the photos, moved by her grandmother's confession. But I can tell she's also crying for me, crying for her own mother, who is crying for *her* mother. "Grandma wanted you to know she loved you more than anything."

As I listen to Winnie, it becomes clear that Kate picked the perfect messenger. It would have been easier for her to ask her assistant or one of the myriad interns she used to fire with wanton abandon to help her construct the album. There would be no risk. Kate wouldn't have to worry about the secret coming out or being spilled before the precise moment she wanted. But she didn't do that. She chose Winnie. She wanted to share *our* secret with my daughter and to give Winnie the biggest piece of herself before she was gone, a tribute to the closeness of their relationship and the bond between generations of women. She trusted Winnie would do the right thing and wait to tell me, that Winnie understood the importance of the task she had been given.

And just as finding out about my father and Theo applying for Harvard together behind my back changed my perceptions of my son, Kate has now taught me something about Winnie. My daughter is far more mature, far more able to swim in the murky waters of adult problems, than I'd ever given her credit for.

Winnie has been the baby in our family for fifteen years, and Nathan and I have never stopped treating her that way. When she was born and didn't come out with a life-threatening condition at birth, we almost didn't know how to react—but *not* worrying didn't seem to be the right option. We didn't want there to be any gap between the attention we devoted to Theo's physical condition and how Winnie was being raised. Except Winnie didn't have any problems to attend to.

So Nathan and I became slightly overattentive to how she felt. We worried if she was unhappy. We worried that she had everything she needed to ensure she never had to want a day in her life. And we have done that for all her life.

I know I need to let Winnie grow up and become an independent teenager, but I can't accept that she's ready, that I could still be a good parent and let her go. I still walk her to school every morning, even though Theo could. Then I take her to Starbucks, and we sit down together on the bench that faces the school's front doors and make sure she's prepared to handle whatever her day has in store before I say goodbye. Before she leaves, I make sure she's remembered her lunch, which I still make every day and pack with carefully curated charcuterie and organic snacks instead of just letting her get Chipotle with her friends. Inside that lunch I've also left her a message on a sticky note, just to let her know how much I care. I even still encourage her to have sleepovers at our house instead of her friends' houses, so I know she is safe and sound when I say good night.

It's almost as if Kate wanted to give me one last final revelation: to see Winnie in a different light, to see someone strong enough to carry a secret for months and never waver in her promise.

"Thank you," I say to Winnie, holding her tight. My anger starts to be replaced by love and admiration for the daughter that I raised, and the daughter that my mother just helped me see. "Thank you for giving me these."

"Mom," Theo says, trying to hide his tears by rubbing his eyes and sniffing, "it's been hard for me to say goodbye to Grandma. Like harder than I expected. Because she's just *gone*. But if you're her daughter, then she's not gone. There's still a part of her with us." He gives me his hand, and I'm struck by how it covers mine. I remember when it could fit in the center of my palm. And with that memory made flesh, I know I can't go on holding another truth from Winnie and Theo. If they can accept Kate being *my* mother, maybe they can accept me being a mother again.

"I know you two have had a lot to process these past few days," I say to Theo and Winnie, gauging their reaction, "but I was kind of hoping Dad and I could share some happy news with you." I hold my breath in anticipation, hoping they can handle one more thing.

"Yeah," Winnie says. "We could use some."

"You're getting us a car," Theo says, offering his own interpretation of what my good news might bring.

I take both their hands in mine, then look at Theo. "Okay, first off, your sister isn't old enough to even have a permit." Then I squeeze down on their fingers. "We're going to have a baby."

I watch Nathan's reaction as intently as I watch to see how the children respond. He's silently estimating how they will take the news and likely wondering why I chose *now* to tell them. But he's rolling with my decision. Hopefully Theo and Winnie will do the same, although their silent, almost subliminal shared communication is still trending ambiguous.

"I know this will be a big change—"

"Mom, please," Theo says, looking to his sister. "We're *thrilled* for you to have a new person for you to pay attention to." He laughs so sweetly, purely, and genuinely that I know everything will be fine.

"You two can be a little *much* sometimes," Winnie says, pointing to Nathan and me. "Honestly, it's time for both of you to start from the beginning again."

And as my youngest finishes her thought, it prompts a chain reaction, a eureka moment in me. The *origin*. The beginning. We have to go back to the beginning.

I've been so caught up in my own anger, so misled and distracted by Kate's letter, that I lost sight of why I went to see my father this morning. I went to break the dam, budge the ice, and find out what went wrong at the start so I could fix our family in the present. I went to uncover why they never let us blend.

But I didn't need my father. I needed my mother. I needed the secret, the gift only she was prepared to give me.

I stand up, ready to round up my siblings, sit them down, and introduce them to the sister they've had all along—but under quite different circumstances. I'm going to save the family I have always needed. I just need to know where they are.

I take out my phone and furiously text Paul. And then I wait. And I *wait*. It's the longest minute of my life, which joins the collection of longest minutes of my life, most of which happened during this time in St. John. Finally, he texts back:

> *"We're leaving, Liz. We've all had enough and decided we're going home."*

I pound the letters with such force I nearly drop my phone:

> *"You can't leave. I need to talk to you."*

To which Paul responds:

> *"I think we've all done enough talking for the time being."*

I crack, realizing I can't tell them over text. I have to see them one more time.

> *"Just tell me where the fuck you are."*

CHAPTER THIRTY-ONE

AFTER A SEEMINGLY ENDLESS AND progressively crankier chain of text messages, Paul finally tells me that the family is already on their way to the boat that will take them to St. Thomas, where they will board their flights back home. Flights that will forever change all our lives because they don't even know why they're leaving. They think it's a stance. They think it's an act of volition, of rebellion, a final *screw you* to my father and Kate. But really, they're all still acting out the roles they were programmed to play. So thoroughly have they internalized our parents' definition of who they are that they now interpret their own sabotage as obeying their free will. And if they leave now, they'll never understand why they keep doing it. Leaving Kate's funeral *before* the funeral even starts is just another symptom, not the actual syndrome.

Whether they realize it or not, they will never forgive themselves. They are cutting off their noses to spite their faces, because one of the people who made them this way has also given them the key to unlock themselves.

I check my Apple watch and realize I only have ten minutes to reach them before the boat leaves the resort. Ten minutes to travel half the Eleusinian property.

I sprint out of our villa, already exhausted and still shedding remnants of nature from my hair and legs. I make my way to the pool, where I will likely scare *normal* families—who are not escaping their mother's funeral and are instead enjoying the sun, or maybe even a cocktail by the poolside bar—with my frantic speed. As I reach the sign listing all the restrictions to frolic in an

Eleusinian pool, I realize my running technique has really deteriorated. I need to start putting my arms into it, or maybe try kicking a little higher with each step.

Because if I'm late, Kate's plan will have been for nothing—the plan she spent the last months of her life working out and putting into motion, the plan she staked the survival of the family she had a hand in ruining on. She brought us all back to St. John after seeing the way we reacted to her illness that fateful New Year's Eve. She realized that once she was gone, everything risked falling apart without her iron hand to bind the unnatural together. But first, it all had to become unglued.

She knew what my siblings would do; she knew what my father would do; but most of all, she knew what I would do, because it was what I wanted all along. She knew I had waited thirty-three years to spring into action, to have carte blanche to try and make our family work, and I would resolutely not stop until things were better. I would drag my siblings kicking and screaming into *feeling*, talking, opening up, and baring themselves, until we were all broken down and ready to be created anew in truth.

Except that wasn't the end. We couldn't become one until we knew why we were always *five*. And that was the special gift, the magic elixir that she had to share with me first before I was sent out to tell them.

I race onto the beach and throw my flip-flops off before accidentally stepping on a shell, nearly knocking over a child's sandcastle, and kicking sand onto some honeymooners trying to make the most of their remaining time before having to start being married. I want to stop and tell them to treasure this time, that it's never coming back, and a wrecking ball—called mortgages, kids, careers, and dogs—is going to put an end to whatever dreams they shared on a paradisal beach. But I can't. I barely have six minutes left to get to my siblings, and I'm not exactly sharing news that's going to fare well with severe compression. In my opinion, finding out that Kate was my mother requires a larger berth to let it really sink in.

I nearly miss the right turn onto the dock, and I'm breathing so hard that directions have ceased to have meaning. I seem only able to go *forward*. Then I take my first steps onto the wooden dock and hear the captain yell out that the boat is leaving in five minutes, which only throws additional anxiety on a mission already fraught with more pitfalls than I can successfully maneuver. It's getting to the point that I may need to fake a heart attack to get them to stay.

I face the boat, waving my hands back and forth like I'm trying to help land an airplane, while shouting to my siblings, "Don't leave! You can't leave. Get off the boat."

Paul is the first one to register my wild gesticulations. He looks at me curiously, half amazed I made it in time and half disappointed that I did. "Lizzie," he says, making his displeasure manifest verbally. "I told you we were leaving."

"You have to get off the boat," I say, fighting through his icy stare. The remainder of my siblings appear behind him, as if to lend moral support against my onslaught and make sure that the sibling most likely to succumb to my wishes doesn't give in and back down. "I *need* to talk to you. Get off the boat."

"You can talk," Paul says, granting me an audience, "but we're not getting off the boat."

"Are you fucking kidding me?" I say, annoyed that I raced here and cut my foot on a shell, all to try and help them. It's easier to negotiate with Winnie and Theo, and that's saying something.

"Elizabeth," Tessa says, who is no doubt glimpsing a missed flight, a delayed return to Miles and her fake life in Manhattan, which I already tried to mess up by urging her to admit she deserves more. "I don't want to stay on this island for another second."

"I agree, Lizzie," Julian says, holding Oliver's hand. Their clasped hands make me wonder whether this is a temporary reunion or the real thing, but there's no time to find out right now. "This place is seriously bad for my health."

"What the fuck is it now?" Caroline says, her blue eyes burning a hole through me with their focused anger. "Every time I see you, something else goes wrong in my life. Is this your parting gift?"

Caroline isn't wrong. It is my parting gift. But it's also my parting gift to make them not *part*. They deserve to know who I am. They deserve to know who they are. And they deserve to have more time to process it, but that isn't always a benefit. The hardest lesson I learned from Kate's final days was that it isn't any less painful to die slowly or quickly; either way, it just *hurts*. So I'm going to make this quick.

"Kate was my birth mother," I share boldly, bluntly, not easing into the fact but just putting it out there. I wait, letting it sink in, watching it translate onto four faces each experiencing a different emotion at different times—but all trending toward the same place. I see some pensiveness; I see some confusion; I see what I hope is a trace of happiness, but it quickly turns to anger. Finally, the expressions settle in, and the words begin.

"What?" Caroline says, her reliable self always getting in the first word. "What the fuck, Lizzie? When did that even happen? Like logistically? Did Dad fuck Kate in a time machine?" Her caustic comments get harsher the more she looks to hide from an honest reaction.

"*Elizabeth*," Tessa says, picking up where Caroline left off and throwing some unprocessed rage on top. "Why would you lie? Why would you say such a horrible thing? Are you *that* desperate for attention?"

I don't answer right away. I have my own initial feelings to sort—like how I didn't expect my sisters to be the first to answer, and if they *were*, I didn't expect their reactions to be to hate me. I try to move past the visceral nature of their responses and realize it couldn't have been any other way. My sisters were the two who had the most of me to lose. We have spent our entire lives intertwined, conjoined, *sisters*, and there is no deeper bond. But our bond was even deeper than most because it had a shared history, our own origin story—a mother who abandoned us. But with what I just told them, I am no longer abandoned. I can't avert my eyes, can't take away from them that they are right to feel like I'm abandoning them too.

Caroline looks at me like a stranger, then turns to Paul and Julian. "You two are awfully quiet. Why?" She turns her ocean blue eyes with long lashes on them. "She's *all* of our sister now. You gained half and we lost half. Isn't that about right, Lizzie?"

"I'm sorry," I say to Caroline. "I didn't tell you this so you would hate me—"

"I can't deal with this shit right now," Julian says, cutting me off. He's clearly exhausted and worn out. "This...trip has just been way too fucking much for me." He starts to turn his back on me, reject me, not giving me another second of his time. "For real, Lizzie. Do you honestly think this is what I needed to hear?"

"I *do* think it's what you need to hear," I say, well aware of where Julian is living right now. But I have to pop his bubble of self-protection, because this and only *this* may be able to prevent him from going back to drugs again and again. "I think it might help you understand why Kate loved you in the way she did. It was never you. It was that she was living a lie. She couldn't be herself around you because she was *never* herself."

"I gotta be honest," Julian says, turning his back fully, totally unmoved by my pleas, "it's too little, too late. The damage was done years ago. And just because you can tell me *why*, it doesn't mean it didn't happen." He takes a seat by himself, and Persephone and Oliver move across from him. Persephone contemplates Julian's scowl, which is threatening to turn into tears. She dips into

Oliver's bag and pulls out his book, then goes over to my brother and puts her arm around him.

In the background, I see the skipper start to untie the boat from the dock, reminding me of the precious dwindling seconds I have left to make my siblings see what I can, what Kate's message meant. The captain yells, "Two minutes…"

I turn to Paul, my last potential ally, hoping the closeness we've shared will allow him to see that this revelation will finally set us on the path I've always envisioned for our family, the one I've tried to make him see for over three decades. "Paul, please say something."

Paul looks at me, then back to my siblings, torn between change and stasis. He runs his fingers through his hair in frustration, trying to figure out what side to come down on. "What do you want me to say, Liz?"

I feel tears bubbling in my eyes when I realize how far we've started moving away from each other these past few days. The more I try and show him our family is possible, the more he hates me. "I want you to say that you'll stay."

"I can't give you that," he says, putting his hands on the railing as if relying on the metal to hold him up. "Who are we even burying?" He looks to our four siblings. "I mean…who *was* my mother? Sorry…*our* mother. She's a stranger I'm supposed to say goodbye to." He shrugs, trying to drown all that he's feeling into a mere nuisance. "And all this stranger has done is make my life harder. But I'm supposed to just give her what she wants in death? What did I get? She drove away my father. She lied to me that I had a sister. Then she did what she always does and dumped it in all our laps and told us to solve it. I'm sick of it." He swats his arm away, as if banishing everything I've said, forcing it to stay on St. John and not follow him home. "And you should be sick of it too. Because, not for nothing—and I'm saying this because I do love you—*you* paid the steepest price. Fuck it. Learn to say 'fuck it,' and let it go."

Caroline steps into the vacuum of speech ripped open by Paul and decides to close it. "Lizzie," she says, drawing out my name until it sounds like it may explode in separate letters. "I didn't exactly hear everything Paul just said because I honestly wasn't listening. But I think I speak for all of us when I say, we really need a fucking break from you."

"Don't *go*. Please!" I shout, but the boat engine drowns out my words—my final cry for them to stay. I go back to waving my arms again, as if they can't see me. But I know they can. I watch the boat drift away from the dock, and with it my hope for bringing us together. I have hopelessly overestimated the power of the truth. I expected it to shield me, when it just broke my heart instead.

I sit down on the dock, let my aching legs hang off the edge and dangle right above the porcelain water. All I can think of as I watch the boat inch further and further away is—maybe my father was right. Maybe I did just destroy the family. Maybe the foundational lie that he and Kate told everyone was too embedded, too tied into everyone's role in the family. It went beyond the three of us and dragged all of them down with it.

I let my bare feet fall in the water, the calm enveloping my skin. I'm hoping for some sympathetic transmission, hoping the gentleness of the water will allow me to forgive my optimism, and Kate's optimism, when we both thought that this was the time. It had finally arrived. But I never looked at it from my siblings' perspectives. Their reality was constructed upon the deliberate obscuring of my identity. It was the rock upon which they built themselves; it was who they knew when they looked in the mirror for the past thirty-three years. It's hard to let a dream die, even when someone you love shows you that it is a dream. I should know better than anyone. People will do almost anything to have their dream be true.

Paul—my other half, the speaker of dark truths I choose to overlook—was right. I should be the angriest of them all. I should have reacted how any rational human being would by having an epic fight with my father and ostracizing him for the rest of his life. I should have booked the next flight out. I should have pulled up my stakes, run back to DC, and tried to bury what I know.

But I couldn't. And they're the reason why. If my siblings hadn't decided to leave me behind, I would have explained it all, explained why—although *yes*, our parents lied to me, hid me from myself and all of them, it's not just the root of their identities. It's why we even fucking exist in the first place. If Benjamin and Kate had made their relationship work from the beginning, everything and everyone I know and love today wouldn't be here. I wouldn't have my brothers. I wouldn't have my sisters. I might not even have Nathan, which also means no Theo or Winnie.

I might not have made most of the decisions that make me who I am today, but I don't have the slightest doubts or regrets about any of them. Oddly enough, the universe I call home is courtesy of Benjamin and Kate bungling and backing themselves into having a family—*this* family that drives me to derision daily, but who I can't imagine a life without. Our parents' lie created my truth. And no matter how many detours our lives took, things are how they were meant to be.

At least I thought they were.

"Hi, sweetheart," I hear from behind me, and immediately get goosebumps. I guess my father has been watching this the whole time—probably luxuriating in my failure, enjoying my defeat, and waiting until I was at my lowest, fully beaten, before approaching me. "I told you. I told you it would destroy them. There was a reason Kate and I kept it a secret all these years. And that just proved how right we really were."

I keep my back turned to him, not interested in hearing him justify himself.

"The problem you've always had, Elizabeth, is that you expect too much from people. Especially your siblings. I don't. I know who they are, and who they are is not the sort of people who can handle a whole lot of truth. Your brothers and sisters can't handle anything. You can't take a ton of dynamite, let it off in front of them, and expect them not to run. I hope you're happy. I hope you got what you wanted."

I rise off the dock, shake off a few splinters, and walk right past my father, pretending not to see him. "I didn't get what I wanted *yet*," I say. And when I make it back onto the sand, starting the walk back to my own family, I think I know what to do. I know how to make them come back. My father's words only made crystalline what I felt when I watched them all disappear into the blue: that I will *never* give up, that this family is worth saving, and that I will run myself ragged until they can see it too, until they realize what each of them is worth and how we can't blend, we can't come together, until they come to *themselves*.

It's my mother's message. It's my message. And just like when this all started three days ago, I have to lean on her once again.

I pull out my phone, open our family's group chat—*named by Caroline and attesting to her own amazingness*—and will the universe to grant me this one last chance. Their last chance. Our last chance.

I have Winnie send me the photo album she put together, then send all my siblings the pictures of my first year with Kate. Finally, I write:

> *You're not wrong. Kate was a stranger in a lot of ways. But she was the biggest stranger of all to herself and wanted to change that. She didn't want us to spread her ashes without knowing her. She wanted the people she loved to have the whole her, for good and for bad, and*

to say goodbye to who she really was. And whether we agree with all of her decisions or not, that was brave, and we need to be brave too and forgive her. You all need to come back so we can say goodbye to who our mother wanted us all to know. She gave us herself finally, and we can't reject that. You've got to understand that there are precious minutes left to all of us, even in death, and Kate took her final ones to save us. And if you don't come back, you're not only missing Kate's funeral, but you're missing meeting someone new in nine months. I'm pregnant. You can't let me bring a baby into this world without any of their aunts and uncles. You can't cut this family apart when we finally have a chance for something new....

CHAPTER THIRTY-TWO

"ONE DAY ALL OF THIS *will be gone, Lizzie.*"

Kate had said that to me four months ago, in a conversation—a near monologue that was so out of character for my mother that it has haunted me ever since. We were on this same beach, where I'm sitting now on my towel-lined lounge chair, sipping a mineral water and compulsively checking my phone. I'm waiting for my siblings—*I'll take one sibling at this point*—to respond to my message.

"All it will take is one or two more storms," she continued, pointing to the shrinking shoreline. The sea was going its own way and carving its own territory in opposition to the Eleusinian's imposed boundaries, which the staff had demarcated by a row of empty lounge chairs, almost challenging nature to step an inch over the line. "Your father and I talk about how we might need to rethink our investment here," she said, weighing who would win in this battle between corporate *want* and natural *need*, and like any good businessperson looking to the terrain for answers. "Well, your father talks about it more. You know how he hates to lose. You know he only gambles when he's certain he's got a sure thing." She smiles, almost bemused by my father's attempts to extend his control into weather patterns. "I keep telling him the resort is prepared. That they'll rebuild. That a storm doesn't always mean the end. They have had them before, and they will have them again."

She lowered her sunglasses, motioned for me to look at the sand with her. "You can see it—right, Elizabeth? Look at the ocean pushing up against it...eroding the shoreline. And the shoreline is pushing back further and further into the sand."

I followed her eyes, then watched the top of a tiny wave capped with foam. It breaks, spills, reconstitutes, and curls itself around the foot of my chair.

"It's deceptive, isn't it?" Kate said, waiting for me to see what she was seeing. But all I could find in my field of vision was *her*, my mother, the woman who only had a few months left on this planet and who I wanted to make every second count with, but who was apparently set on delivering a lecture on the potential dangers of investing in island property. "Something that travels in inches, so subtle you can barely see it, but the entire time it's reshaping nature."

Then she laughed—a genuine oddity—and painted this talk with an even more abstract coat, as if I was looking at a figurative drawing and she had sprayed it with strange shapes. I can count on one hand how many times I'd heard Kate emit *her* idiosyncratic version of a laugh. If you were to hear it randomly, experience it without knowing her, you might mistake her laugh for a deep cough or a throat-clearing she was trying to keep under wraps—some obscure biological process that was able to explode, bubble over, and burn her mouth on its way to becoming.

"We should probably go into the water," she said, rising and motioning for me to follow. "While it's still willing to have us."

I look up from my phone and stare across at the same clear ocean that is still reshaping sand, still moving boundaries, still forcing the lounge chairs to move further back from its shoreline. And I think I finally see what Kate wanted me to—the poetic wisdom that only comes from facing your own boundary that also won't stay fixed. Even back then, four months ago, she was preparing me for this trip. Her plan was probably already being subdivided into cost-benefit columns in her mighty utilitarian mind. Kate never left anything to chance; in fact, she had a detailed, color-coded spreadsheet for all occasions, both business and family. Our vacations were legendary for how many different colors and drafts they went through. She certainly wasn't going to take any chances once she knew she wouldn't be around to put her plan fully into motion. And she wasn't going to take any chances when it came to being understood. It just took me until today to root out the meaning. Her death would be the storm, would leave devastation and wreckage in its wake, would root out anything too weak to survive another day. But at the end of all the chaos, there would be the people to rebuild it. *All of us.* Destruction may be the end of something, but it is also the germ of new life.

I have been given the opportunity for new life, literally with our growing baby. But also professionally, with Madeleine, my other baby that—just like Theo—is ready to go out and introduce himself to the world, and—just like Winnie—is ready to grow up and broaden her horizons. Madeleine was never about building a business; our profits prove that. But profiting off something built to house the most precious memory of my mother would have destroyed the point, a *point* that, just like Kate's soliloquy about the gentle ebb and flow of growth, I also missed.

I've never been intrinsically against Benjamin and Kate's business strategy of restless growth and windfall paydays. I'm not exactly poor myself—that would be rank hypocrisy. But what I wasn't ready for was to let my relationship with Kate—that one hug—out of my grasp. Not until she could see it for what it was. And she did. Now there isn't any reason to keep the secret between us anymore, no reason to house our unspoken love in a single storefront like a living museum to a slice of time I want to preserve, whatever the cost. Everything about Madeleine is awash with my desire to hold onto that memory, to not share it and only let it out in fleeting moments. This is why I purposefully make barely a handful of frozen hot chocolate cupcakes every morning and haven't shared my recipe with Camille. I'm the only person who can bake them, and I feared if I made too many, my memory might run out.

At this point, it also might be the only part of my family left for me. Even my eternal optimism is having a hard time putting a positive spin on their silence, which—two hours later—is deafening. They genuinely do not want to talk to me. But even if they're not ready now to make this journey with me, at least I can share Madeleine, share my own origin story with the world—or at the very least, our nation's capital. I can stop hiding, stop squirreling memories, and introduce them to the real Elizabeth Sunderland, daughter of Kate Bernard, the woman who inspired my most popular sweet treat. The woman who made me understand that in every loss there is still new life.

Just as I'm starting to text Camille a litany of *things to do* when I get back—get in touch with POTUS's event planning staff; take every order they have; hire four more people; and start looking for a new space to expand into—I see the shadow of a man holding a Russian novel that appears to be weighing him down, physically and spiritually.

"It seems like we have more in common than your cupcakes," Sean says, taking a seat in the lounge chair next to mine. He pushes his sunglasses over his eyes, dropping his tome in the sand where it sinks on impact. "I got left at the altar. You got left at a funeral."

For the first time in days, I laugh. I laugh so hard it takes me by surprise. "I vote that we don't take the blame."

"I might have to for mine," Sean says, motioning a request to pour some of my water into his empty bottle. "I use my status, my family, and my job as a veil—as an excuse to ignore what I really am, what the *Sean* hiding underneath really wants. I scare myself. But at the same time, even though I know I'm hiding, I'm too weak to admit what I want. So, I surround myself with anyone willing to believe the lie I show the world. Then I push them away when they've outlived their usefulness, when they try to get to know what's *beyond* the presentation. That's what I'm mourning here. The loss of my latest golden excuse, who publicly abandoned me when she realized I'm a man without qualities because I'm afraid to admit those qualities." Sean starts detailing his discoveries to me, clearly relieved and unburdened, making me wonder if his fiancée left him his own letter that he just found. "I must admit that I am impulsive. I am passionate. I am romantic. I like sex. I like a lot of things people who come from our background try and keep hidden."

I'm a bit thrown by Sean's boldness. I'm all for reckless honesty, but even I'm not pulling up a chair next to virtual strangers and presenting them with a buffet of all my darkest and most personal problems. But even though he can make things distinctly uncomfortable, there is something I do like about Sean. I appreciate a fellow traveler, a spelunker of souls, when I see one, and although Sean may prefer to dig with a hammer while I prefer a spoon, it doesn't take away the earnest validity of his approach. I also feel badly that he went searching for an answer in Caroline and she abandoned him too. These are tough times for those of us who feel.

"You really learned a lot about yourself these past few days," I say. "Was it the novel?"

"Actually, it was Caroline," he says, and Sean's seemingly disconnected mention of "liking sex" suddenly seems obvious. "She called me last night after dinner. It was the strangest thing...." So far, Sean's story already checks out. "She didn't apologize for telling me to leave. In fact, she didn't even mention it. Nor did she mention her stepmother's company again. She just said everything I just told you with a great deal more cursing. Then, when I thought she was going to hang up and never talk to me again, she said she would be in DC next weekend and I should take her out to dinner." He pushes his sunglasses down so I can see his eyes—the window of his soul. "It was all very confusing. But I'm going to go with it."

"When it comes to Caroline, that's all you can do," I say, still assessing the psychological profile Sean dropped in my lap. I'm trapped between feeling bad that he's been living his own lie for so long, and feeling proud of my sister for taking her first step. Caroline may have hastily exited dinner and may have left St. John madder at me than ever before—and honestly, may never speak to me again—but at least I know she has the capacity for change, to glimpse a grown-up future that may drag Sean along with it. I can't convince myself that one dinner with Sean means that she'll take over Kate's company and carry on her legacy, but I can find some small solace knowing she's ready to move on, even if it's without me—*for the time being*. I think back to Kate, think back to the storm, think back to the builders, and realize I can't count on her plan to work exactly how I had hoped. I can only believe that it will *work*.

Before I can tell Sean to tell my sister how much I love her, that I *need* her, I feel a tap on my shoulder. I turn to my right and see my father in his favorite Hickey Freeman suit, the one Kate bought for him a few years ago for his photo shoot where he was named "a person to know" in whatever industry he was currently capsizing. He's holding what appears to be an oversized vase close to his chest.

"Come on," he says, short and curt. "We're going."

"Where are we going, Dad?"

He points to the sky, where a series of storm clouds mummify a hidden sun. "It's almost sunset. We're going to spread Kate's ashes together."

CHAPTER THIRTY-THREE

MY FATHER APPEARS TO BE on a vision quest, one that barely includes me. I try to keep pace with him, to match his stride, but he's walking so quickly I feel like we're back on Fifth Avenue at rush hour, and the ability to bob and weave is a survival tool—not an option. But we're all alone. There's no one around us; there's no one ahead or behind us.

There is literally just us.

"Dad," I say, getting close enough to risk speech. I'm aware that he's at his breaking point, so I try to work within very specific parameters when it comes to my father. "I don't understand. There isn't anyone here except us. This feels a little…wrong."

"This is what your mother wanted," he says, not turning around and talking into the wind. "And we owe it to her. Kate wanted this to be her final resting place, and I'm going to give her exactly that. A promise is a promise."

I allow myself to lag behind a little, trying to figure out what to do. I think about texting Nathan to bring the kids over, so they don't lose the chance to say goodbye to their grandmother. Then I think about texting my siblings and letting them know this is happening, but they're probably all in the air by now, and even if— by some aviational miracle—they have reception, they'll think it's another ploy to get them to come back. *Except it isn't.* This is happening right before my eyes. I even consider turning back myself, seeking refuge. These are not the circumstances under which I want to say goodbye to my mother. But I'm stuck. My father has officially lost the script, and if I don't stick around to stop him, he *will* do this.

In record time, we reach the sailboat he reserved for Kate's funeral—a sailboat that was supposed to hold fourteen people, and we're just two, something the confused captain realizes immediately as we approach.

"Dad," I say, reaching to hold him back as he climbs aboard. I try to grab him and talk some sense into him, but he escapes my grasp. "We can't do this. We just *can't.*"

He sits down on one of the seats and places Kate's urn next to him. "We're doing this."

I follow him onboard, but I don't sit. I *can't* sit. If I sit, I'm quietly condoning his absurd mistake and letting Kate's incredibly strenuous plan be for nothing. The problem is that we are outside the realm of my mother's original intentions. Benjamin has gone rogue, a common tactic he likes to employ when negotiations start going south. According to Benjamin, you have to take the opponent off guard, and invert the situation, if you still want to come out on top. My mother knew this; after all, she warned me that he would be the final barrier, the last one to come around. I just wish somewhere she had left me another video, another note, on how to handle him if it came to this. But she couldn't know. Kate was the one person my father didn't debate, didn't negotiate with. They were always in sync. They were always partners.

Benjamin has been my fight all along.

"Dad," I say calmly. I consider appealing to some surviving—but dormant—logic still swimming in his head, but my plan is immediately belied by the expression on his face. He looks like a trenchant toddler having a public fit. I try and come up with a new idea. In my total desperation, and sinking to Benjamin's level, I lunge to grab Kate's urn, hoping to take my mother back to safety until the whole family can be reunited, *whenever* that may be.

"*Don't do that,*" he says, swatting away my hand. He's talking to me, *treating me,* like I'm the tiniest dog in the park looking to pick a fight with a mastiff or a husky in an act of desperate compensation.

I groan, frustrated that I tried my last-ditch effort *first* and failed. "Why am I even here? Why did you ask me to watch this?"

"Because this is *it,*" Benjamin says. "This is the new family. Me and you."

I want to interrupt him, to tell him that this isn't a *family.* We can't go from a house of people to just me and him—that's not the beginning we're supposed to return to. We're supposed to go back thirty-three years. Not *forty-three.* He's taking our time travel experiment back too far to when no one exists but the two of us.

"You wanted to go back to the beginning," he says. "You got it. It's you. It's me." He points to Kate's urn. "And it's your mother."

"Dad," I say, becoming as belligerent as he is. I refuse to go down his train of thought; I know it's a dead end. "They're going to come back. Maybe not this week. But they will come back."

"Elizabeth," he says, dumbfounded. "They're *not* coming back."

"How can you be so sure?" I ask, never having seen my father doubt the validity, the possibility, of this family. We may have disagreed on how it should be run. We may have disagreed stridently on how to do it. But I've never heard him doubt the fundamental fact that we *are* still a family. Even when he told me at the dock that I had ruined it, I didn't believe that meant he was going to give up, to resign himself to our dissolution. I thought he was like me— just the opposite side of the coin. I thought we both knew that, no matter what, you never stop fighting for what you believe in.

"Because we *fucked up,*" he says, his voice rising yet spread out evenly between us. He's not just yelling at me. He's yelling at himself. He's yelling at Kate. "They're not coming back because of what we did. I disinherited them and they left. You told them the secret Kate and I kept for forty-three years to make them stay, and they *still* left. I think we need to face the reality that you and I aren't offering them anything they're interested in. Money or truth just aren't in their bandwidth."

"But at least we gave them the room to make a decision," I protest, while feeling a horrible drop from head to toe. It's as if a fever just overtook my body and I'm about to pass out, because I know there is a kernel of truth in what my father is saying. But that can't be. If it's true, then this is more identity shattering, more of an end to my world than finding out they lied to me. It's that *I* lied to me by sharing the same fantasy Benjamin and Kate did. It's admitting Paul was right all along and there never was a family to fight for in the first place.

"But at least we gave them the room to make a decision," I repeat, trying to hold on, to not be dragged down by his nihilism. "Without the money and without the secrets, they finally know who they are. And when they come back, it will be for the right reasons. Because we gave them a chance to find out who we are as a family. Honestly. With no tricks."

"Make a *decision?*" he says, even more appalled than when I tried to reclaim Kate from his clutches. "Your brothers and sisters can't make a fucking decision. You've seen what that looks like. You're kidding yourself. Get in the game, Elizabeth. It's *over.* We killed it. At least I'm big enough to take responsibility. You should join me."

But I do take responsibility. I take responsibility for what I believe is right. Because if it isn't right, then *I'm wrong,* and Kate's wrong—not just in terms of what we wanted, but in the larger schema of every single thing. He's telling me that I don't even know the people I thought I was closest to. He's trying to drag me down into the same dark place where he's residing, to cancel out the light, but I won't go. "I refuse to believe that. If you and I killed it, then it wasn't anything in the first place. And even you know that's not true."

"But it *is*," he says, standing up and inching closer to me, leaving Kate on the seat. "I thought they loved me for *me*, but they just wanted money. You thought they would love you for telling them the truth, but they didn't. The whole thing was so goddamned fragile...being pasted together with money and lies...and we were the bulls in the china shop. We broke everything. We did the wrong thing for them." He sighs and crosses his arms, exhaling his own truth. It feels like he's burying the family along with Kate. "We only thought about ourselves."

I never did anything for myself. All I thought about was them. If all I wanted to do was save them and this family, how could that be wrong? How can you break people apart by caring too much?

The captain, who has been trying not to eavesdrop on our steadily escalating debate by distracting himself with music on the radio, finally turns around. "Can we go? Do we have everyone?"

Benjamin looks to me, then nods. He considers this issue solved; he thinks he's convinced me. "This is everyone. You can go."

"No!" I shout. *The issue is not solved.* We didn't take this too far— if anything, we haven't taken it far enough. We can't quit now. We can't give up. Kate thought her plan would fix it. "You can't go—"

"Elizabeth, I'm paying," my father says, cutting me off before turning to the captain. "You can go. It's the spot we talked about."

"*No*," I say again, seizing the opportunity my father left open. I grab Kate off the seat—where she had been left unguarded—raise the urn over my head, and hold it over the rail of the boat. "If you move one more foot, I will spill these ashes myself."

"Elizabeth," my father says, and I imagine he's moving from negotiation with an adversary, to the daughter holding his wife hostage. "I'm not blaming you. I'm not blaming me. I'm blaming *us*.

So, let's do this together. Just the two of us. Like it's always been. All I need you to do is hand over your mother. Gently."

"Tell me it's not over," I say, starting to break, straining at anything, at the island air itself, as his words become more and more clear, more undeniable. The blame has been reasonably assigned; the evolving opinion is one that I cannot bear. I did help kill what I loved the most. "Tell me you're not right. Tell me they're coming back. Tell me we can bury Mom in a few months when they're... when they're *back*."

"I can't do it, sweetheart," he says. "They may be your siblings, but they're my kids. And I know them in a different way than you ever will. You see their best faces. And I see them for who they are. I love them. I don't want them to be gone. But the bare fact is, they don't want us anymore. We told ourselves the same lie—that if we gave them everything, if we told them everything, then that would be enough. But it wasn't. At the end of the day, they rejected us." He tries to stay resolute, but even his chin starts to tremble. I wonder if this bothers him as much as it's destroying me. "You said you wanted to live in truth. I'll live in it with you. But *this* is the truth."

I start sobbing. My chest heaves, and I want my father to stop the pain. I want him to prevent my own grief—the grief I've held in for the past three days, the grief I've tried to hold in abeyance for the past four months—from erupting.

I have become what I accused everyone else of being. I'm as guilty as they are—actually, I'm *more* guilty. I chastised them for not facing their own grief, when all I did was sublimate my own pain by making them face their own. And the more it hurt, the more I made them all hurt. I made them hurt *for me*. I pretended I needed to save them from their own flaws, when I needed them to *save me*. I have always needed them to save me. I am the one who has kept that from happening because I couldn't need them. I am my father's child. I am Kate's child.

We have always been a family. We have all blended except me. While I was trying to force it, my siblings went around and blended behind my back. It's true. They all made the decision to leave together. It was the first decision I've ever seen them make unanimously, and it was to abandon me. I can't help but cry through the irony. I was the one who wasn't ready. I was the one who pushed us to the brink. I am the one who deserves their silence.

I turn to my father, who seems torn between asking me if I'm okay and trying to take Kate's ashes back. "I need you to bring Mom back."

"I can't," he says, moving closer to me. He reaches over, taking my mother's urn out of my hands and returning her to the seat. "That's all we have left."

"It's not all that's left," I say, unable to keep any secrets from him anymore. Everything has come out, has been dangled before the light. Everything is bleached, baked, and stripped down. Including me. "I'm pregnant. I'm having a baby. And there's no family left."

My father falls quiet. He sits down in the vast ocean of unoccupied seats, lowers his head, takes his glasses off, and rubs his eyes, waiting an eternity, as if squaring what he wants to say with his own body.

"Then there is a family left," he finally says. "There's a new life. A new baby. A piece of Kate to carry on." He smiles, sweet and sad, like he's found a reason for optimism but almost feels guilty to show it in the face of everyone else's desertion. "Jesus, Elizabeth. I don't think I've ever needed to hear something that *badly*." He turns to the captain and yells, "Don't go! Don't leave the dock."

The captain stops the engine one more time, and judging by his expression, seems ready to pitch both Benjamin and me overboard.

"You're right," my father continues. "We can't do this. We have to wait for the baby to say goodbye. We have to complete the cycle.

We have to complete the rotation. We have to say goodbye to Kate, with her newest grandchild present."

And with those words, the father I have been waiting for all my life appears. But it took losing Kate and my siblings to finally find him. It feels like a wave has poured over me, and I can't break the surface of the water. My heart is whole and broken at the same time. And I think it will be that way forever. I will walk around as one-sixth of a person. I have lost four siblings and a mother I never knew as my *mother*—but I have Benjamin, although I don't know for how long. It's biology. It's nature. One day he will be gone too, just as Kate is gone. And once that happens, there will be nothing left to remember this family by, except the way it ended.

But in that haze of grief, I see my father's point: there will be nothing left, *except* the next generation. There will be Winnie, Theo, and our newest addition. And inside each of my children is a part of me, and a part of *them*.

"Okay," I say, nodding to my father and feeling relieved. "We'll try again in nine months."

"You know," my father says, rising from his seat, "not to praise my powers of observation...but I told you that you'd gained weight."

I grit my teeth and try to hold back my natural inclination. He's *trying*. I have to as well. "And you were right. It's just—maybe, in the future, you don't have to *lead* with that. Maybe you say that after the hug, after telling me you love me, after asking how the flight was."

"I'll take it under advisement," he says, moving toward the front the boat, an exit that seems overdue.

I follow behind him, holding Kate's urn. "Do you want to hold Mom? Or should I?"

"That's okay," he says, slowing up so I can reach him. "You should probably bring her home with you. I've got bad form on that issue recently."

As we step across the dock and back onto the Eleusinian out-skirts, the storm arrives. Benjamin and I see it pummeling across the night, ripping stars from the sky and replacing them with clouds blown up like balloons, ready to drop and cover us with a fine rain.

My father stops to take off his suit jacket—one of his prized possessions—and wraps it around my shoulders so neither me nor Kate's urn will get soaked.

The rain rapidly becomes a warm storm, pelting us with huge drops, followed by thunder and lightning, which instead of presag-ing the incoming—yet eternally delayed—disturbance, are actively participating.

Shanti Shanti.

"Dad," I say, through the drops falling from my lips and eyes. "How the hell are you moving this fast? I can't keep up."

"Strangest thing," he says, not looking back, just pressing for-ward, "my knee stopped hurting the minute it rained."

I nearly stop in my tracks, thinking back to Theo's paper, to the document that showed me not only my son, but my father from an entirely different angle I'd never contemplated.

"The Fisher King," I say, under my breath, realizing my father, much like Eliot's royal monarch, had been wounded, and that wound had poisoned everything around him, including the land and everyone in it, until he realized he was the problem, and once again—it rained. I wonder if Theo was writing about his grand-father the whole time—what he hoped he might become in the future, once he was able to set aside his grief, and see that *he* needed to make room, to let the next generation be born and show him the way. And he finally did. He saw it in my baby.

As we approach the Eleusinian, where seemingly hundreds of workers have popped up out of nowhere and are dragging furniture inside and boarding windows shut, I can't help but think about the message of Theo's paper:

"The Waste Land" finds you when you're ready.

Maybe it was waiting for me. And Theo was the one who saw it.

Was T.S. Eliot doing more than contemplating his own reality back in 1922? Or was he somewhat in touch with the inner workings of the Bernard-Sunderland family? Or possibly, just *possibly*, families have always been like this, and we're just the following millennium's baroque evolution.

And I have to remind myself that Kate's letter may have forever altered our family, that my siblings may never come to terms with my truth, my history, that there may not and perhaps may never be a family left...

CHAPTER THIRTY-FOUR

One Year Later

AND THERE WASN'T A FAMILY left when Benjamin and I got back to the hotel. And there wasn't a family left when I finally pulled into the garage of the Watergate—one goldendoodle richer—safely at home in DC. There wasn't a family left when Winnie and Theo returned to school, when I walked back into a bustling Madeleine still abuzz from the president's visit, or when Nathan celebrated his unemployment for weeks. There wasn't a family left when my father made the first of many visits to DC to see Winnie and Theo, to gently *nudge* me not to look back when I started looking at new spaces for Madeleine, to castigate Nathan for his laziness and his need to find a hobby, which Benjamin decided would be golf. There wasn't a family when he taught my husband how to play, or when he purchased Nathan his own clubs and monogrammed bag, or when he helped build the crib for his newest grandchild. There wasn't a family when we moved Theo into Harvard and Benjamin bought thousands of dollars of merchandise, attempting to wear *all of it* in one single weekend, becoming a living advertisement for the Crimson way of life. And there still wasn't a family left when I went to my monthly OBGYN visits and shared pictures of that month's sonogram in the sibling group chat—always left unanswered.

There wasn't a family for days, weeks, months, after our fateful trip to St. John.

Until 1:00 a.m. on August 27, when I was woken up by a commotion coming from the courtyard. I got out of bed, looked out the window, and saw several of my neighbors standing outside their apartments wearing pajamas and yelling at a staggering man dressed in a suit. I slid up the glass, stuck my head out, and quickly realized it was Paul.

I raced down the stairs and out the front door, awakening both kids and the dog—but not Nathan—and made my presence known on the scene, profusely apologizing to the other residents. I told Paul to "shut up" until I got him back to our place, a command he was having difficulty processing, adamantly accusing my neighbors of not being "neighborly," and saying they could have just pointed him in the right direction instead of trying to turn a hose on him. In my brother's inebriated opinion, this entire city had developed a real mean streak in the past few years.

Upon getting him onto our deck, forcing him to drink some water, and stopping him from lighting the wrong end of a cigarette, he finally spoke.

"I'm not sure if you've noticed," he said archly, raising an eyebrow, "but all my restaurants have closed. I also lost all the Wharf properties. All painful. Spirit-crushing, even. But I tried to endure. Until I just got evicted."

"But Benjamin gave you your trust back when we got back from St. John," I said, knowing that my father gave my siblings back their money in the hopes that they would forgive him, that they would come back, that we could be a family again. So I was a bit confused about how he didn't have enough money to pay his mortgage.

"He did do that," Paul said. "But I was trying an ambitious experiment to see if I could pull myself out from under without it." He took a drag from his cigarette. "That has failed. And I feel like I'd be failing again if I used it." He gave me a half smile.

"Someone told me I should stop chasing my father and just give in to Benjamin's attempts to try to be one." He begrudgingly, *very begrudgingly*, put his hand on my foot to get my attention. "But I started thinking...what if I didn't need a father? What if I was past that and had been past that for a long time? What I *really* needed was a sister. *That* I could accomplish."

"Paul," I say, "how long did it take you to come to that conclusion?"

"It's been brewing," he says. "The eviction kind of sealed it." Then he gulped down the entire glass of water. "Are you, by any chance, interested in hiring a business manager who has a great deal of experience in expansion, that in your case, *isn't* driven by deep personal longing? Cause I really need a job. And a place to stay."

And it was as simple as that. Paul was back in my life, sleeping on our couch, and apparently never leaving, even once he returned to semi-financial solvency.

In October, Sean Pierce appeared in Madeleine, interested in more than his usual morning order. He pulled me aside and requested, on Caroline's orders, an urgent *business* meeting that she would fly to DC to attend personally. Sean said this was a rarity these days, as my sister had been clocking regular transcontinental hours as the "new" Kate, and had grown—in Sean's unbiased opinion—even more difficult. But he'd never been prouder of her.

At the much-vaunted meeting, Caroline, wearing a power suit, offered to buy out Madeleine, which Paul loudly disagreed with. Caroline was not pleased that Paul came back into my life, and that I had the audacity to simply *forgive* him and turn him into a business partner overnight. From there, the meeting devolved into a struggle session over who I loved more. Once it was settled—in Caroline's mind, at least—that she still held a special place in my heart never to be challenged, she handed Paul and me each a thick white envelope with our respective names embossed on the front.

When I opened it, I found an invitation to her and Sean's engagement party at the Boathouse inside.

"I expect to see you there," Caroline said, walking to the door. "This time I'm not working there. I'll just be celebrating."

Around December, Tessa returned to my life, but through an extremely wayward back channel. I received a follow request from Dylan on Instagram, and after accepting, a DM immediately followed. He said he'd noticed recently, while skulking around Tessa's account—apparently part of his regular routine—that Miles had been noticeably absent, and wondered if this meant she was single? He didn't want to get in touch with her to ask on the off chance that she wasn't actually available—or even worse, that Miles had possibly perished in some horrible way and he'd just be making things worse. I assured him that Miles was very much alive, very much an asshole, and Tessa was very much single—a fact I knew from Benjamin, who kept me up to date on Tessa's life. Then he asked me if I would broach things with my sister and see if she might be interested in meeting up for coffee, since—considering how things ended up last time—he was a bit gun-shy. But he'd never stopped missing her, even after his two failed marriages, which I took to mean that he'd be even more able to stand Tessa at forty than at twenty, when he was full of love. Now he was full of *reality*.

I waited a week. Then another week. And after three or four messages from Dylan—in which I assured him that I was just waiting for the right moment since Tessa was a mercurial creature—I finally did it. I called my sister, who unlike Paul or Caroline, wasn't all that surprised or happy to hear from me.

"Hello, Elizabeth," she said sourly. "I assume you know the children and I are living with Dad. That Miles and I are officially divorced. That he tried to get me back and I refused. And that you were right, I deserve better. Although there hasn't been anyone who's agreed just yet." She was Tessa still, not bothering to ask anything about me and diving into her own predicament. "Have you ever tried online dating? Likely not, since you married when you were twelve. But these men are not interested in getting to know *me*. And Dad won't set me up with anyone from his office this time. He keeps telling me *I* need to find the right person for me. That he won't make that mistake twice...."

"*Tess*," I finally interrupt, "shut the fuck up." Now there's a statement I've missed saying the past eight months. "I heard from Dylan."

"Oh," she said, shocked. "And *that's* why you called. Not that you missed me. Not that your life is incomplete. Not that you can't imagine Winnie and Theo growing up without me. You called me because of Dylan."

"Pretty much," I said, refusing to give in to Tessa's prolonged guilt trip.

"Well, thank you," she said. "And I love you. And please give me his contact information."

And I did. And they talked. And they talked. And he is coming to Caroline's wedding with Tessa next summer.

On New Year's Eve, the one-year anniversary of Kate announcing her illness and turning our world upside down was to be created anew when none of us were looking. Nathan, Winnie, Theo—home on break—and me were quietly celebrating the holiday with our traditional four courses of appetizers, byzantine board games about the birth of railroads, and binge-watching movies. We had just passed the opening credits when I went into labor, and Nathan drove ninety miles an hour for the two-mile trip to Sibley Hospital, where at 11:59 p.m., Kate Sunderland Daly, weighing seven pounds, five ounces, was born in a bizarre synthesis of my two other births. She came out quietly *and* with a full head of hair. And within twenty-four hours of being home, Paul, Caroline and

Sean, Tessa and Dylan, Mason, Meredith, and Benjamin descended upon our apartment, bearing more gifts and life advice than this baby could ever need. It was particularly moving, heartbreaking *and* heartwarming simultaneously, to watch my father with Kate. He took her on a full apartment tour, explained she would be the chief inheritor of his empire, and stipulated the moments when I should and should *not* be listened to.

When baby Kate arrived and breathed new life into the Bernard-Sunderland family, completing the circle Kate set in motion, it was bittersweet. Not only was her grandmother not there to welcome her into the world and into our family, but neither was Julian.

After a thirty-day post-St. John return to rehab, Julian had found his footing again—the ground upon which he could fall and be safe. Persephone and Oliver. This time he *knew* it. And once he was released from the program, he and his not-so-secret family moved to Oregon, where he actually bought a house, set down permanent roots, and enrolled Oliver in kindergarten. Julian, who *did* take the trust back, used it to set up a transcendental meditation foundation in Kate's name, and made Persephone the executive director. Julian has been thriving, healthy and clearheaded, and to stay that way, he decided he needed to remain absent from us for the foreseeable future. In the name of his mental health, he needed a vacation from our family's *vacation*. As much as that hurt, I knew it was for the best—not only for him, but for keeping his own family intact. I would rather have Julian alive and with Persephone and Oliver than with us and *dead*.

And now it's one year later, one year to the day of boarding the plane to St. John, that I begin my walk to the podium, standing in the middle of the living room in my father's penthouse. A room packed with the people who made Kate's life. Her friends, colleagues, business associates, and family. All the very people I knew my mother would want to be present to say goodbye to her in the way she *deserved*, whether she knew it or not.

As I weave my way through the crowd to deliver the eulogy that I have had a year to compose, and finally finished last night, I brush up against Julian standing in the crowd with Persephone and Oliver by his side. Almost instinctually, without thought, he grabs me and hugs me, and doesn't let go, nearly crumbling my speech and smearing my makeup from tears.

"Hey, sis," he whispers. "It was always you." Then he lets me go, gives me one of those obnoxious hair ruffles that he used to deliver with delight when we were kids, and sends me on my way. I don't ask when I'll see him next because I know it will be soon. He is back. And now I can begin again.

I stand behind the podium and look at the photo of Kate next to me, her ashes standing before it. I scan the crowd, where I spot Nathan, Winnie, Theo, and baby Kate in the front, waiting. I swallow hard, unfold my notes, and feel my mouth open. The words emerge before I even know what is happening, as if Kate intervened one last time to steady my hand:

"Kate Bernard was my mother...."

The End.
Washington, DC
June 2023

ACKNOWLEDGMENTS

GROWING UP IN A BLENDED family is loud. It is a constant commotion filled with unexpected visits, festering fights, awkward vacations, strained screams, and resentment threatening to break out at every moment. I have lived that way for thirty-five years.

Until three years ago, when the world fell silent, and my family—all inhabiting different geographical locations—managed to not go silent with it.

But I did. Absent their physical presence for the first time since I was ten years old, I wasn't anxiously dreading the next family vacation, the next birthday party, the next visit to DC from my father and stepmother to see my children. I was finally at peace. Except I wasn't.

I joined the rest of the world in having a collective nervous breakdown brought about by a combination of a raging virus, political and social unrest in my own city, my children faced with adult problems far before they needed to be exposed, and a climate catastrophe being kicked down the road again.

It was only then that I understood the often repeated saying: the personal is the political.

I realized that everyone felt like a broken child from a blended family that was falling apart around them, and perhaps if I dug deep enough in myself, if I laid out all the truth I knew, that although I couldn't save the world, I could make people feel like they weren't alone, and that within the tragedy there are bouts of humor, actual love, genuine forgiveness, and mutual understanding. Much like the world itself.

The future is unwritten. None of us, including my family both real and fictional, will never truly be at peace. But maybe, just possibly, we can understand why we never will be, and not take it as an excuse, but a call to be better.

And I couldn't have done it without my husband, Nick. His relentless persistence in finding me the time to write this novel, then rewrite it, then write it a third time is the only reason you are reading this book today. He is the love of my life, my biggest fan, the person who believes in me when I don't believe in myself. I am lucky to have him, today, yesterday, and for always.

I also need to endlessly thank my children, Charlie and Lilly, for not only being the inspiration for Theo and Winnie but for being the best kids a mom could ask for. For lending an endless hand with dinner or dishes or walking Barry. For making me laugh when I wanted to cry. For allowing me the privilege of watching them grow up and being an eyewitness to their pursuit to change the world, to make their voices heard, and to genuinely being the two best humans.

Which means I also need to thank Barry, my eccentric goldendoodle, who sat next to me for hours on end while I put words on the page, but did manage to run upstairs and hide when I got frustrated.

I would also like to thank my agent, Simon Trewin, who saw the possibility of this novel from the moment I sent him the first chapter and never gave up on it. And honestly, for never giving up on me. In this business, you need someone who believes in you, to stand by you when everyone says "no". And he is that for me, always.

And of course, I need to thank my editor, Adriana Senior, who championed this book to its end product. Who gave me a chance, who gave me the notes I needed to unlock the story for me. This book is the best version of itself because of her. And I hope this is the beginning of a long journey together.

Lastly, I need to thank my family. For being big and loud, and messy. For helping me find my way in this world. For making me laugh. For loving me. I hope you still love me after this. But seriously, you are everything to me, you are my origin, my own broken fortune.

ABOUT THE AUTHOR

ALY MENNUTI HAS ALWAYS HAD two passions: philanthropy and literature. She satisfies one of those by being an executive at an international nonprofit consulting firm and has helped a diverse range of high-profile clients reach their philanthropic goals. However, she's always had a desire to express herself creatively and carve out her own role as a writer in a writing family. Finally, in her forties (and with two children hitting their teens and deciding Mom is really uncool and not needed to hang out with anymore) she has the time and headspace to tell her own stories. She lives in Washington, DC, with her husband, Nicholas Mennuti, a novelist and screenwriter, their two children, Charlie and Lilly, and their eccentric goldendoodle, Barry.